D1091938

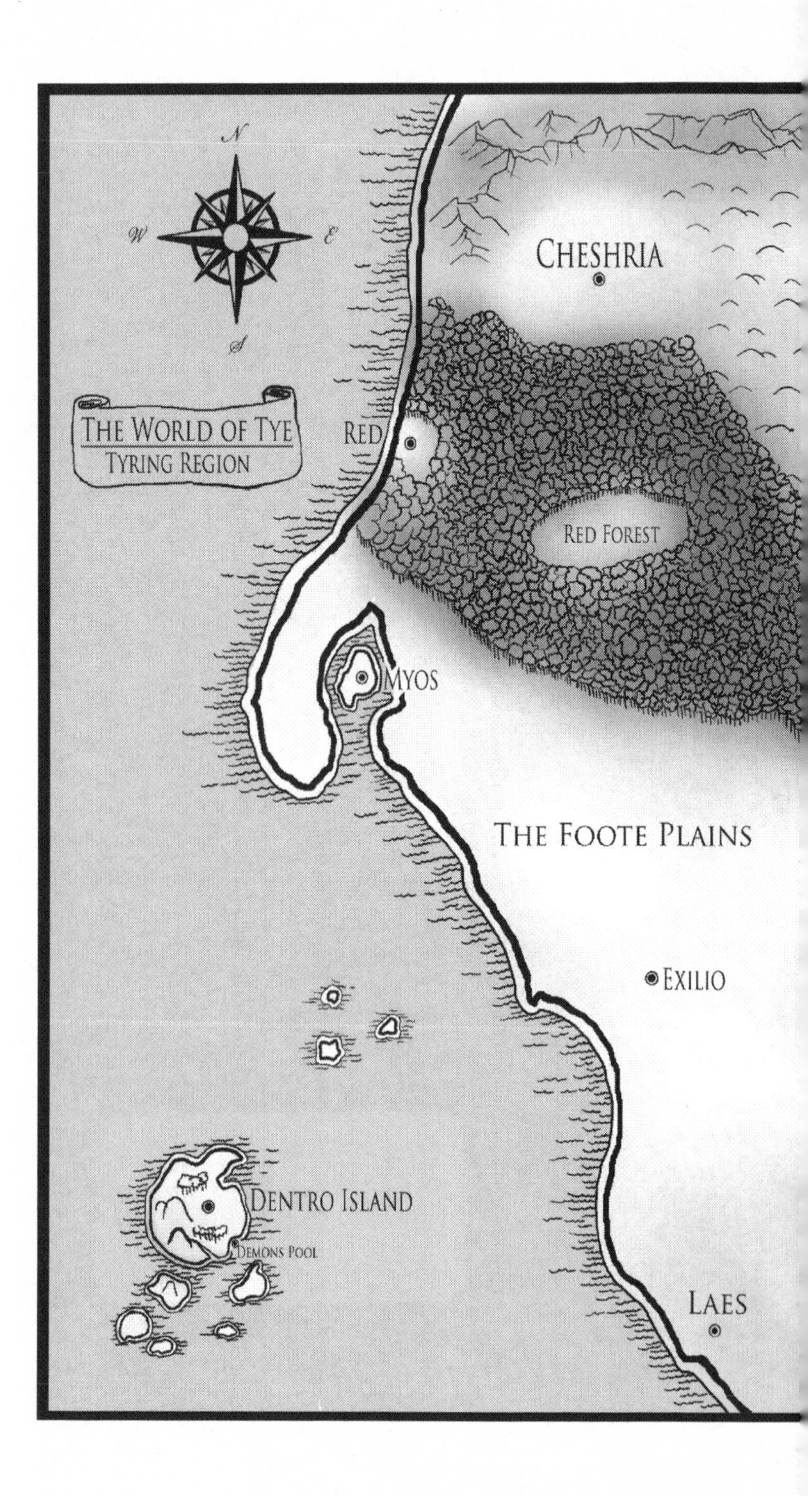
N
W
E
S
The World of Tye
Tyring Region
Cheshria
Red
Red Forest
Myos
The Foote Plains
Exilio
Dentro Island
Demons Pool
Laes

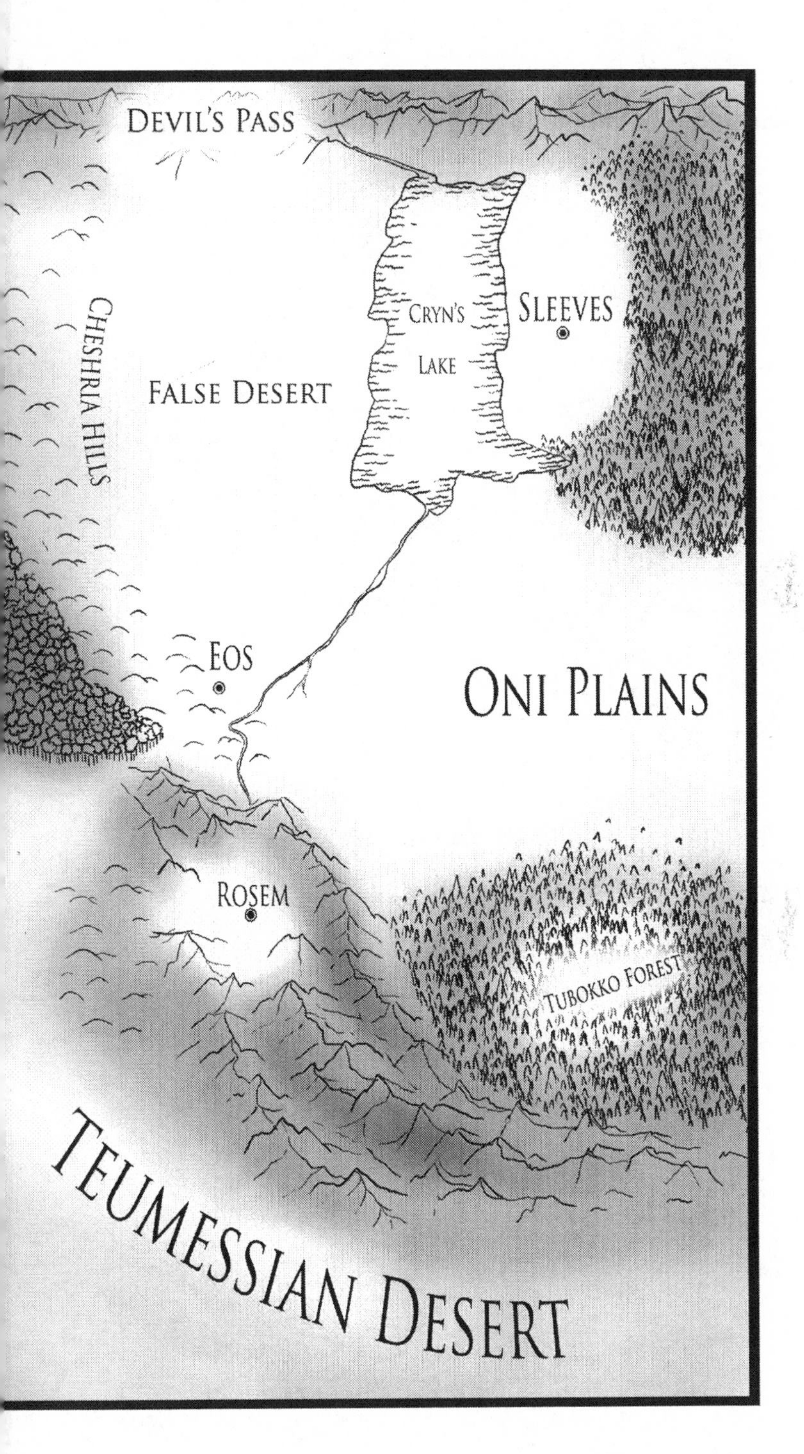
Devil's Pass
Sleeves
Cryn's
Lake
Cheshria Hills
False Desert
Eos
Oni Plains
Rosem
Tubokko Forest
Teumessian Desert

The R.J. Tolson Page-Turners
&
Upcoming Works

The Chaos Chronicles Series

Book 1:
Zephyr the West Wind, Final Edition

Book 2:
Hugh the Southern Flame

The Project: Limitless Series

Volume 1:
The Success Initiative

Other Releases:

Blood Red Love

Sage Endeavors: A Collection of Short Stories

Deep Truths

Lost Chronicles of Rave

Zephyr the West Wind, Original Book Soundtrack:
Electronically produced instrumental pieces directly inspired by the book

For previews of upcoming books by R.J. Tolson and more information about the author, visit www.rjtolson.com

Chaos Chronicles Book 1: Zephyr the West Wind

Final Edition

R.J. Tolson

Universal Kingdom Print of RJTIO

Universal Kingdom Print
United States of America (USA)
Visit our website at www.universalkingdominternational.com

Affiliates:

RJTINC at www.rjtinc.net
Forever Trust Charity at www.forevertrustworld.com
BurstOut: www.burstout.net
RL Infinity International at www.rlinfinityinternational.com

Universal Kingdom Print, Forever Trust Charity, RL Infinity International, BurstOut and RJTINC are all divisions of RJTIO LLC.

First Edition: September 2011

Tyring Map Design by: Nolan Kabrich

ISBN: 0615686435
ISBN-13: 978-0615686431
Universal Kingdom Print

Words From the Author

I believe in will power.... Not the will of just those deemed strong, but of the fire burning within us all. Just like there is a light inside all of us, there is also darkness. It is a part of what makes us human, what drives us and what allows us to love and understand one another.

Sometimes we are so busy being afraid of that darkness, the darkness in all of our hearts, that we try to shun or destroy it. But it is not until the point where we realize that because one cannot live without the other, accepting and understanding both the light and dark only makes us stronger. Never stop believing in yourself, whether or not others choose to. Discover your will of fire and live your life to the fullest.

I owe my knowledge, compassion, skills, success and belief to my mother, father, grandfather, grandmother, my whole family and the friends that have always been there for me through both the good and bad times. Thank you.

NEVER. GIVE. UP.

Veritas

-R.J. Tolson

CONTENTS

Prologue	Chaos Chronicles	13
1	Dentro Village	17
2	The First Trial	25
3	The Second Trial	33
4	The White World	38
5	Leon	48
6	The Unmei Collection	59
7	Exilio	70
8	My Will	80
9	Sky Pushuu	91
10	Delphi the Wise	100
11	Autumn's Breath	112
12	Tyring	122

13	Vanishing	134
14	Flash Change	149
15	Deadly Beauty	163
16	Bad Tourists	174
17	True Fear	184
18	Cryns Lake	194
19	Punishment of Sleeves	207
20	Three Month Discipline	217
21	Friendly Rivals	228
22	Devil's Pass	239
23	Bloody Past	255
24	Demonic Misconceptions	264
25	That Hated Smile	277
26	Growth	291

27	A New Chapter	304
28	Red Snow	318
29	Hate Among Brothers	333
30	Homecoming	345
31	Farewell	363
32	Explosion! King of Cheshria	375
33	The Chaos Demon	387
34	A Predicted Future	398
35	A Brother's Final Gift	410
36	The Day That Came Too Slow	426
37	Over and Out	440

Chaos Chronicles

Prologue

Long ago, in a time long forgotten by history, the rulers of the universe known as gods lived among humans, even choosing to mate with some throughout the many worlds.

Their children, humans with paranormal abilities, lived peacefully until a select group of them referred to as "chaos" decided that they were too high above the humans to live with them. In a war that affected all of the worlds throughout the universe, chaos erupted.

Forced to kill over half of their children in order to save humankind from enslavement and extinction, the gods disappeared from human eyes, after scattering the destructive weapons of their children, known as crystals, across the universe.

Before all of the gods returned to the heavens, four of them entrusted their unborn children with the fate of the universe. Their hope—that after saving their own threatened lands, they would come together and erase chaos forever.

This is the story of one of those children.

Book 1:

Seventeen years ago, in the island village of Dentro, lived a large and powerful demon. With just a howl, mountains were obliterated. With the help of an outsider, the chief of Dentro destroyed the demon and sealed its dark power within three powerful ancient weapons: a spear, a shield, and a sword. After leaving the unwelcoming village, the man who had helped destroy the demon took the sword in an effort to keep the village and its people safe.

Months later, a villager bore the son of the outsider. Carrying the child of a stranger was in violation of a sacred village law, and everyone knew whose child the boy was. Born into a village filled with hateful people, Zephyr grew up not knowing why he was so hated. With no friends, and eventually no family after the passing of his mother, Zephyr was forced to survive by himself as an outcast.

Zephyr's only wish was to make his mother proud and force the village to recognize him—while surviving in a world filled with demons, paranormal abilities, love, hate, and undiscovered lands.

*It's **always** felt as though I was **missing** something.*

Love

Truth

***All** I've ever wanted was to **be** like **everyone** else.*

Friendship

Understanding

*Maybe, this was all just a bad **dream** I could **wake** up from somehow.*

Reality

*I'm just **so** tired of being **alone**.*

Pain

-Zephyr

Chapter 1: Dentro Village

I'd heard people say that being able to understand other people's emotions is a gift beyond comprehension. Of course, I myself did not see the significance in that statement. Whether it was because I was seventeen, came from a small village on a small tropical island, or simply hadn't had enough time to broaden my horizons, I just could not fathom the gift that I had been given by whomever may have created this world that I called home.

Life is something that I think we all take for granted at first, and some do their whole lives until they can't anymore. What is the purpose of life? And even more to the point, why am I here? I had asked myself this over and over, unable to figure out a reason. I didn't even stand out from others my age, aside from my name, Zephyr.

Life was simple in Dentro, on this island surrounded by what seemed to be endless amounts of water. I'd asked myself time and time again why we all ended up here, on this island. And if there are any other lands out there, why did we, and even more so I, end up on this one? And if there are other lands...then we really are just a small piece of something a whole lot greater and bigger.

Lately, this was all I had been thinking about. Of course, someone like myself who was low on the food chain compared to all of the other people in my village had time to drift off and think about such things. Now, I know what you're thinking. This kid Zephyr is crazy to be dreaming up such foolish thoughts—why isn't he getting ready for a mission or something?

By the way, missions are quests assigned by the chief of Dentro Village that potentially allow a person or team to leave the island for some given reason. Also, missions are only assigned to those who are deemed worthy by what is known as the Council of Elders—really five grumpy old villagers who have nothing better to do with their lives. I couldn't even try to ask for a mission, as I had not completed what is known as the Trial of Adulthood. But all of that would come into play soon enough.

Anyway, I always wasted my free time imagining myself leaving this village and exploring the world beyond it. But like always, I had to come back to reality. Sitting up from my bed, I shook my head to move the stray pieces of my hair from in front of my face. Standing up, I felt the regular unpleasant sensation in my muscles that comes after lying on my rock-hard bed made of straw and held together by Sea stone.

Sea stones, unlike other rocks, are rocks that formed in the deep sea over thousands of years and gained some of the magical properties of the sea; these range from creating invisible rays that kept land creatures away to healing and other undiscovered properties. When used to create beds, they offer quicker physical recovery and keep demons from coming within a certain vicinity, although I don't really understand how it works myself.

After stretching my muscles a bit by doing jumping jacks, I looked around my room. Living in a very small one-room house just ten paces long and wide, I always liked to keep it clean. On the left, I had a small desk that rose up from the Sea stone foundation of my house, and next to my bed was a small box filled with a large number of different weapons that I used for different tasks. Of course, now you're definitely thinking, *What, a box full of weapons?* But don't worry about that for now, that explanation also comes later.

Walking towards the door, I opened it to look upon a small pathway that branched in two directions; left towards the village square, and right towards the south dock, also known as Demon's Pool. Directly beyond this path, in front of my house, were hundreds of sky trees that went as high as the human eye could see.

Each tree was bright green with a trunk that was large enough to enclose three or four regular-sized people. They would make excellent climbing trees, except that if you climbed too high, sky beetles would swarm and attack you with their deadly poison.

Closing the door behind me, I stepped onto the left side of the path. Next to my house on each side were tons of other small one-room houses where all of the other villagers lived, stretching all the way to the beginning of the village square.

It was a long walk down the dirt path towards the village square, and as I finally arrived, the path and sky trees came to an end and the hard ground surface became soft, warm sand. Looking towards the square, it seemed as busy as usual. Every afternoon, every village resident not away on a mission was in the village square—either buying food or weapons, or just hanging out.

Each of the shops was made of Sea stone; some had actual indoor buildings, such as the weapon shop, while others, like the strawberry shop, had small stands. All of the buildings were next to each other and formed a circle around an area that was known as the village center. In this area, all important village events occurred: quarrels, death fights, the announcement of new laws, mission assignments, etc. Beyond the square, at the opposite side from the path to my house, was the north dock, or Heaven's Dock.

As I continued walking towards the village center, I ignored the glances and displeased looks that people around me gave and smiled back at them. In response, they all looked away and tried to act like they hadn't notice anything. Reaching my destination a couple of feet before the village center, I looked up towards the village chief's two-story office and residence.

The office's Sea stone had been painted red using crushed fruits, and the doors were made out of sky tree bark. I put my hand on the cold doorknob and pulled. As I entered, I recognized the familiar sweet scent of cinnamon.

In front of me was a large desk covered in papers. Behind the desk was a slim, elderly man with a round face and a long white beard that stopped slightly short of the floor, wearing scruffy but nice-looking shorts and a t-shirt. As I walked up to the desk, he looked up and smiled.

"Good afternoon, Zephyr boy."

I laughed. He always called me boy, no matter how old I became.

"Good morning, Chief." I tried to sound excited. I mean, the Chief, as everyone called him, had invited me yesterday to come to his office this afternoon and chat before the ceremony. In a few hours, there was to be a ceremony that would decide whether the people I had passed when I entered the village would continue to ridicule and look down on me or start to respect me.

"Zephyr boy, I hope you are ready. This is your fifth ceremony. Even though you have failed four ceremonies in the past, I have believed and will always believe in you and your potential," he said, looking back down at his desk.

"I know. I know," I muttered.

The Chief looked worried. "Have you studied properly this time?"

"Yes," I promised. "It's just that—" But before I could finish my sentence, the Chief dropped his head and started snoring. "Chief!" I yelled.

"Oh, oh! Ha! Sorry, Zephyr boy. You know me and my little difficulty," he said, laughing.

I did. The Chief's narcolepsy didn't make him any less powerful a figure in my eyes, and the villagers were all used to it. Somehow, his condition didn't seem to undermine his authority with any of us.

"But I do hope you complete the ceremony this time. As you know, I cannot send you on any missions outside of the village or even to hunt or train in Demon's Pool until you do. I have a good feeling this time, though. Don't let me down. It's almost time, so head over to the ceremony grounds by Demon's

Pool."

"Yes, Chief," I murmured. Turning around, I grabbed the doorknob and started to push the door open, when the Chief spoke again.

"Remember this, Zephyr boy," he said in the deepest voice I had ever heard him use. "This ceremony is a life or death situation. I've saved you all of the past times, but I cannot do so this time. If you fail, you will die."

"I plan on succeeding, Chief," I stated. "I won't let you down." I walked out of the office feeling mostly confident, but slightly scared. Death was not a joke. And for all I knew, mine could be rapidly approaching. Stepping off the steps that led back into the Chief's office, I stepped onto the soft sand. As my feet slowly sank into the welcome heat, I calmed down. The sand always seemed to have that effect on me. Forcing myself to move from that spot, I quickly increased my pace as I walked back towards my house.

After lying on my bed and thinking for a while, I thought to myself, *if I ever want to discover the rest of the worlds and the other pieces to the puzzle of life, I have to move past this test.*

I quickly changed into my combat clothes: tight white shorts that wrapped around my tan skin, a white t-shirt, sandals, and a small white headband to keep my long, gray-and-black spiky hair from getting in my eyes.

Grabbing my white combat gloves from my weapons box next to my bed, I pulled them over my hands so that only the parts of my fingers beyond the knuckles were visible and rubbed my hands together to make sure the gloves were on tightly. Opening the door, I took a step and walked onto the path, closing the door behind me. Turning right, I began to walk towards Demon's Pool.

Chapter 2:
The First Trial

Ever since I could remember, the people of Dentro, aside from the Chief, had looked down on me. My father was not from the village and had left before I was born, and my mother had died when I was six years old. After her death, the Chief had taken care of me until I was old enough to live by myself. The Chief was my father in all respects but blood.

When the villagers had found out that my mother had gotten pregnant by an outsider whom they knew nothing about, she was ridiculed and lost all of the villagers' respect. Eventually, she became too weak and sick to handle the pain of being alone and passed away. The Chief gave everything to me. He was my father, and my hero. And so, as I walked down the path towards Demon's Pool, I made a promised to myself; I would not let the Chief down.

Unlike the path leading towards the village square, the route to Demon's Pool, Demon's Path, slowly passed into a cold and darker climate. The sun and heat became shielded by clouds, and the sky trees to my left began to look less healthy and alive. The bark, normally bright green, slowly became darker as I walked, until it almost looked brown. After minutes of walking, I finally came to the end of the path, only to be blocked by a large number of people filling up the entrance to Demon's Beach—exactly where I was supposed to be for the ceremony. Trying to find a space between the people to get to the end of the beach, I accidentally bumped into the back of a person wearing a red rain jacket and a hood.

"Watch it!" said the woman in an angry voice. Turning around, she noticed that I had been the one to hit her. "Oh," she said as she scowled and made way for me.

"Thanks," I replied with as much enthusiasm as I could muster. Taking the opportunity the woman gave me, I stepped in front of her and made my way through what seemed as an endless crowd of people of all ages wearing different-colored rain coats. As I began to reach the end of the mass of people, I came to a large platform.

The platform, seemingly almost as large as the beach itself, which spread far enough to fit five hundred people, was filled with different items. On one side stood a bunch of cages containing some of the many demons that had recently been caught on the cove, a few hundred feet away from where the platform stood. On the other side was empty space. The space meant to be used for the upcoming test.

In the center of the platform stood the Chief and a tall figure with long gray hair. Refocusing to try to see who it was, I realized it was the Chief's second in command, Hovan. Hovan was known as a cruel and greedy man who wanted the Chief to retire or find death so he could become the village head. Looking up and smiling with his pale, round face, beady black eyes, and mustache, you could tell he was enjoying the attention.

"Men and women of Dentro," he began in his mocking tone. "You came here today, just like every past year, to witness the Trial of Adulthood, the test that has been given since the founding of Dentro. To begin the test, I give you our honorable and yet elderly chief, warrior of the past and current head of the ancient house of Deka that helped found Dentro!"

As the citizens' applause died down, the Chief began to speak.

"We begin life by copying everything that we see. Crawling, walking, talking, and everything else that we do as a child has been copied from past generations. Speaking as a member of one of those generations, I thank you all for coming to see the next generation as they begin to take on the responsibilities of adults and show us the strength of their wills!" said the Chief as he pointed towards a row of four teenagers.

"The Trial of Adulthood is a test given to those deemed worthy at the age of thirteen by the head of the village. These children will be chosen by one of the five ancient stones of the universe: the Sea stone, Ouranos stone, Void stone, Balance stone, or Dream stone. As stated by our ancestors, only when the time is right shall the stone shine and choose its partner. After being chosen, the child must prove himself to his new life partner; after he does so, the stone will reshape itself into the item best suited to that person, essentially joining two entities to become one—" Interrupted by his own cough, the Chief concluded his speech. "Let us begin the ceremony as I call each child up to the table beside me," he said, waving his hands over a table covered by a white cloth. "Let us begin!"

Taking this as my chance to get in place, I slowly walked up the platform and joined my four fellow participants, standing last in the line beside Hovan. The first person took his place facing the Chief in front of the table. The kid stood amazingly tall, over six feet, with short black hair, tan skin, and a lanky figure. Looking up at the boy, the Chief spoke.

"Are you ready, Nicholas?" asked the Chief.

"Yes, Chief," he stated.

As Nicholas replied, the Chief pulled the white cloth from over the table. Now uncovered, the table revealed five crystals, each the size of a hand and shaped like an egg, sitting on the table a few inches apart from each other. Being too far away to tell each of the egg-shaped stone's colors, I tried to use my memory from the past tests: the Sea stone was a shade of blue, almost dark enough to be thought of as black; the Ouranos stone was clear surrounded by a blue aura; the Void stone was a mixture of yellow and black entwined; the Balance stone was all black; and finally the Dream stone, a simple gray. They had been etched into my mind as beautiful.

"Reach out your hand," said the Chief.

Nicholas slowly put his right hand directly above each of the stones until he reached one that slowly began to shine brighter and brighter. As the stone began to reach what almost seemed to be the brightness of the sun itself, Nicholas picked up the Dream stone and smiled. As he did so, the crowd began to cheer to the point where Nicholas turned around and yelled:

"I did it!"

As the cheers died down, the Chief spoke.

"I suggest you silently wait so we can continue the ceremony, Nicholas," the Chief said in a low voice, his smile showing that he was pleased.

"Yes, Chief," Nicholas said as he walked back over to us and sat down next to me.

After what seemed like years, the three other participants were chosen and received their stones, until I was the only one left. I walked over to the table where the Chief was and stood upright to face him. All of the rocks that the others had taken had been replaced with new ones.

"Are you ready, Zephyr boy?" asked the Chief.

"Yes, Chief," I replied.

"Place your hand over the stones," he stated in a serious tone.

I slowly put the palm of my hand inches above each stone, starting over the dark blue Sea stone, which began to shine a little, but not enough, then moving to the black-and-yellow Void stone, which also began to shine. I looked up in surprise and confusion towards the Chief, but he just smiled and shook his head no. Continuing my process of moving my hand, I placed it over the all-black Balance stone, which slowly began to shine, as did the gray Dream stone.

"I do not understand," the Chief stated. "Only one should shine brightly, and yet each so far has shone, but not enough to have chosen you. In the past, you could not even pass this part of the test, as they would not shine at all. This is truly unbelievable."

I couldn't help but think that I was going to fail again. Not knowing what to do, I forced myself to stop thinking about failure and willed my hand to move over the final stone. As I placed my hand over the clear stone, nothing occurred. *This will not happen again,* I thought. *I will not fail the Chief…or myself!* Seemingly as those thoughts filled my mind, the Ouranos stone abruptly began to shine as brightly as Nicholas's stone had.

I picked up the stone and felt a huge rush of energy flow through my body. Happiness seemed to fill me and all of my thoughts to the point where I could ignore the fact that, even though the crowd had clapped for all the other participants, they weren't for me. The thing was though, in this moment, I did not care. I had finally been chosen by a stone. I walked back over to sit next to Nicholas and the three others, one boy and two girls, and couldn't help but smile as I looked at them. Turning around, the Chief began to speak.

"We will now begin the second and most dangerous part of the Trial of Adulthood. Each participant will take a turn fighting for their life against a B-class demon voted on by the village. As you know, a B-class demon is two levels away from the toughest demons in existence, the S-class, and so they are not something to be taken lightly. The risk of death is high, and we cannot save you from it. But from this risk comes great reward: the awakening of your true spirit, and the tool to create your path towards the future."

With this reminder, everyone in the group began to look

uncomfortable, but we all knew ahead of time, and the fact that everyone else in the village older than us had completed this task seemed to keep them from being deterred.

"Are you ready?" Hovan screamed, turning from the crowd to face us.

We all looked around at each other's faces; Nicholas, the two girls with almost identical faces, the pale skin and large, round eyes that were common in the village, and the other boy, with black hair and brown eyes, who looked older then he actually was. Our new stones in hand, we faced the master.

"We are ready," we all stated, and the crowd erupted in cheers.

Chapter 3:
The Second Trial

"Who wishes to go first?" asked the Chief while offering a smile that did not extend to his eyes.

"I will," stated Nicholas.

Turning around, the Chief looked towards the crowd of people beyond the platform.

"Nicholas shall be the first to take the Second Trial of Adulthood," said the Chief sternly. "Let us wish him luck, as he fights for his life against the great demon, the Karkinos!"

As he finished, the Chief walked over and patted Nicholas on his shoulders. "Come with me," he said softly to Nicholas as they walked over to the large, empty space on the side opposite the monster-filled cages. After placing Nicholas on the side closest to the steps leading down towards the crowd, the Chief and his assistant Hovan walked over to a large cage. Standing on opposite sides of the cage, Hovan and the Chief unlocked the bars keeping the monster within the cage and moved aside to let it move about freely.

As the Karkinos pushed its head and slowly its whole body out of the cage, we all had a clear view of the demon. The Karkinos was a crab. Not just any crab, but a colossal red crab. The space allotted for the fight between Nicholas and the

Karkinos could barely contain the full reach of the monster and its pincers.

Each pincer was twice as large and long as Nicholas himself, while the body of the crab gleamed bright red. Its eyes, blacker then the night sky, stared straight at Nicholas as though it did not notice the hundreds of people beyond him watching. As it moved farther outside of the cage and closer to Nicholas, the Karkinos stamped its four pairs of feet which seemed to create a loud crackle sound as each pair hit the platform floor.

Standing only a few feet away from Nicholas, the Karkinos opened its large pincers as it readied to attack. Nicholas, defenseless with no weapon or sword and only his crystal in hand, stood firm. In the few seconds after, the Karkinos lifted one of its pincers and jabbed at the point where Nicholas was standing. Nicholas quickly dropped to the ground on all fours and disappeared from the Karkinos's view. Moving its black, beady eyes, attached to branch-like eye stalks, the crab searched slowly and silently for its prey.

Finally, it moved its eyes around to look at its back and under the shell covering its belly. But as the colossal demon crab brought its eyes under its belly to search, Nicholas jumped from beneath the Karkinos's pincer to the audience side of the monster.

As he did so, the crab seemed to become alert, as it brought its eyes up to look at its pincer. Recognizing that the Karkinos had to see everything before acting, Nicholas jumped straight through the eye stalks of the demon and onto its upper shell, landing with a ***thud***. Turning around so he had the same view as the monster, Nicholas clenched his fist tightly, drew back his right arm, and launched it at a lightning-fast pace towards a small crack in the Karkinos's shell.

As he did so, holding his Dream stone in his left hand, dark, wispy clouds began to encircle and cover Nicholas's whole body. As Nicholas became less and less visible, the Karkinos fell to the ground, and a crackling sound rose once again.

All around Nicholas and the Karkinos, the air seemed to become harder to breathe. It felt as if something was pushing down on me and seemingly everyone else in the area, as many people were brought to their knees. It took everything I had not to sit down, so I forced myself to breathe and keep calm as the clouds around Nicholas subsided.

Nicholas looked almost exactly the same, over six feet, with short black hair, tan skin, and a lanky figure, but this time his less prominent features seemed to glow more. His eyes were completely gray, and he held a large gray axe with black swirls running along the lines of the two blades at the top of the weapon. The axe was almost half his size and seemed heavy enough for him to need to hold with both hands.

After a few seconds of breathing, I realized that the air around us seemed to be back to normal. Apparently the Karkinos realized this too, and it started to use its legs to lift itself up after its abrupt fall. Without wasting a moment, Nicholas lifted up his axe, which seemed to shine, standing out from the background of the dark blue sky, and brought it down on the crack right between the eye stalks of the monster's shell where he had punched earlier with his bare fist.

As his axe collided with the crack, a bright light flowed out of the Karkinos as its soul left its current body to be reborn as another. The great Karkinos's eyes dropped towards the platform, and the rest of its body soon fell with them.

Staggering at first, most likely from the fall and the amount of energy it must have taken to awaken his Dream stone, Nicholas rose to his feet and turned toward the crowd. His axe slowly began to dissipate into a cloudy substance that encircled his neck, gradually taking form as a necklace with a small, gray, crescent-shaped moon that sat on top of his white t-shirt on the middle of his chest. Sighing in relief, Nicholas walked over towards the group of students while clearly forcing himself to smile at the crowd. As he did so, the crowd erupted in applause and shouts of joy. He had completed the Trial of Adulthood and was now looked upon as a true adult. *Good for him,* I thought to myself.

"Please quiet down!" screamed Hovan over the applause. "We will begin the next trial immediately!"

The crowd's noise quickly died out while Nicholas sat down beside me. As I was about to congratulate him, I heard my name called, much to my dismay.

"Zephyr, it is your turn. You will now face the Barghest! Good luck to you, my boy," the Chief said to me as he looked me in the eyes. "Good luck to you."

I smiled and laughed. I had never gotten this far within the Trial. Because I had not passed the First Trial, I was not able to witness the Second, and so this was my first time seeing and participating in it. And the worse thing about it was that I was being forced to fight the Barghest...a demon dog as large as the Karkinos, but smarter and more powerful. Within the village, the general order if you came in contact with one was to run—for every time it took a bite from you, it took a piece of your soul with it.

Chapter 4:
The White World

I was ready to face the Second Trial, of that I was sure. But the fact is, when the Barghest walked out of its cage and glared at me with its shining yellow eyes, I felt as if every bone in my body was going to melt in fear.

The Barghest was an oversized black dog with gray hairs that covered its whole body. If it had been just that, maybe I wouldn't have been so scared. The demon's face was shaped like a monkey's, while its pointed ears stuck straight up into the sky. Its mouth, which was so large that it had to keep its head below the rest of its body so it would not tire out, was filled with teeth five times larger and sharper than a human's. The yellow eyes, combined with the completely blood-red face and gray hairs, just seemed to paralyze me.

Of course, that was one of the natural effects the Barghest had; it shocked its prey into paralysis and ripped them apart before the shock wore off. I guess you could call me lucky, but the demon seemed to want to take its time with its new food. It slowly walked on all fours towards me as it wagged its scruffy tail, until it was only a few feet from me. The Barghest itself only stood five feet tall, but the intense glare of hate it gave and the fear I felt made it seem bigger.

The Barghest whipped its head up as it stared at the dark blue sky and opened its grotesque mouth, letting out a loud, ear-piercing sound. As it howled, the sound seemed to strike fear into the surrounding area, as it was so quiet after the demon closed its mouth that the only sound I could hear was the growl from its muzzle. *Oh great,* I thought to myself. Everyone else was just as scared as I am, but they were all just spectators. Lucky them.

Before I could continue my thoughts, the Barghest opened its mouth, crouched down, and lunged straight for my head. With my Ouranos crystal in my right hand, I evaded the demon's first attack by quickly jumping a few feet to the left, towards the edge of the platform. The Barghest quickly turned its head so it could focus its vision on me and began to slowly move towards me again.

Unlike when Nicholas faced the Karkinos, I had no idea of how to defeat the Barghest. *This is crazy,* I thought. The Barghest opened its mouth again and again tried to bite my head off by lunging at me. As it did so, I continued to weave to either side of the beast, until it eventually seemed to decide that its strategy wasn't working.

As the demon began to crouch down on its four legs again, I myself prepared to evade by turning my feet to my left side, facing the audience. Before I could react, the demon quickly pushed of its legs in an attempt to charge with its mouth wide open; its speed far exceeded my own, and time seemed to slow down as the beast was within a foot of me in milliseconds.

My feet stuck in place, I had no choice but to try and jump to the side as I had originally planned. At the last second, in an attempt to reach me before I could evade, the Barghest lunged, lifting its claws into the air. Dropping to the side I had jumped to with a loud ***thud***, I felt an intense pain. But before I could register where it was on my body, the Barghest had apparently decided to attack in succession this time and had quickly turned around and lunged on top of me.

The sheer force of the Barghest landing on top of me was enough not only to force the air out from inside my stomach but for me to cough up blood. With the demon planted directly on top of my body, I could not feel my lower half. The Barghest's head lay so close to my face that I could feel its horrid breath, which reeked of death. I tried to will my arms to move, but they were locked in place by the beast's front claws; it took all my energy to force myself not to let the crystal fall out of my right hand.

What can I do? I thought to myself. I had never been very good at fighting, but in this situation I could not think of any way to escape with my arms locked while unable to move the lower half of my body. I waited for the monster to open its mouth and to bite into my flesh, killing me, but instead it lifted its head so that its eyes were clearly staring straight into mine. As it released my arms, lifting its two front legs, a sharp pain that felt like hundreds of needles stabbing me simultaneously on both my biceps rocketed through my body.

"**AHHH**!" I yelled. I know maybe you're thinking, *what a wuss*. Actually, if you are, then I am sorry to say I'm not a god-like creature who can endure pain easily.

As the Barghest lifted its front legs and moved them inches from my face, I realized how truly ignorant I had been during the battle. As children, we were all taught certain essential rules about fighting, one of them being to truly take in all of your surroundings to use as defense or offense if needed. This included details about your enemy; the monster dog didn't have four legs as I had originally thought, like a dog, but instead he had two hind legs and two human-like arms.

On the end of his arms were long, skinny fingers, and on the tip of its fingers were the large claws that had just caused me so much pain. Not allowing me any time to think about my realization any longer, the beast pulled back its two arms so that both claws faced me. As it did so, for the first time during the fight, I gazed back into the creatures eyes as it stared at me.

At a young age, we were taught that the demons and nonhuman creatures of this world had only three emotions and thoughts: pain, anger, and killing. But as I gazed into the yellow, sun-like eyes of the Barghest, I felt like the creature was more intelligent than we were taught.

The Barghest seemed to realize that I was staring back into its eyes. It stopped preparing to swipe its claws at me, and its crazed attitude seemed to calm down a bit.

But that moment seemed only to last for a second. The monster clenched its teeth together and began to bring down its claws once again. Less by my own thought and really more instinctively, I ignored the pain in my biceps and forced my hands up over my face, closing my eyes as the creature's claws made contact with the skin on my hands.

I expected to feel pain, but instead I felt warmth. The feeling was so familiar, like sticking my feet in the soft, warm sand—but this time it surrounded my whole body, while the warm sensation also seemed to travel through my insides. Momentarily forgetting about the life or death battle I was currently involved in, I opened my eyes.

I seemed to have entered a completely different world. All around me the ground, the sky, and the rest of the space was completely white. There seemed to be a warm breeze that continually blew and stopped, blew and stopped. There was no sound, no one else, and no Barghest in sight.

I laughed out loud. I couldn't help it. Was this heaven? Had I failed the test a final time and let down the Chief? I quickly did a three-hundred-and-sixty-degree turn as I realized that, wherever I was, it was completely empty. As I realized this, I dropped to my knees and started to punch the white ground.

"NOOOOO!" I screamed. If I had died, there was no way I could explore the world and prove the villagers' idea of my mother and me wrong. They thought of me as a failure. And if I had been killed, then I truly had let down my mother and the Chief. "Why?" I screamed again. "Why must I always lose everything?" As I brought my fist up, preparing to punch the ground again, I felt a soft tap on my shoulder.

"Why do you call yourself a failure?" asked a warm and comforting voice that seemed to flow like a river as it spoke. Turning toward the source of the voice, I came face-to-face with a boy I had never seen before. The boy had light tan skin, wide blue eyes, and long, flowing brown hair with strands covering both of his eyes. He slowly backed away to stand a few feet from me as I still knelt on the ground, and he smiled one of those smiles that people give when they think everything is going to be all right.

"Who are you?" I asked.

"I am a reflection of you," he replied.

I laughed. "A reflection of me? What does that mean?"

"It means I am the manifestation of all your hopes, dreams, desires, and as such, I guess you could say I represent what is known as your heart of hearts."

"My heart of hearts," I mimicked in a frustrated tone. My knees were beginning to burn, so I rocked back and sat down to talk to the boy. "That really doesn't help me much."

The boy sighed as he also sat down. "I am sorry, but now is not the time to answer all of your questions, for we are running out of time, even while in this world."

I moved my head to look around. "Where exactly are we again, my friend?" I asked.

"You can call this your inner world," he said, also turning his gaze to observe the white space. "Time moves more slowly here than in the real world. Your inner world is a space created from the connection you have with the Ouranos stone. For your understanding right now, you can also say that I am an image of the Ouranos stone's will."

"Oh," was all I could muster up to say.

"'Oh' is correct, Zephyr. Earlier, when your

consciousness first arrived in this world, you though that you were dead. That is not the case, as I hope you have gathered."

"Yeah, I figured that," I stated. "What do I do now? The Barghest is about to kill me."

"Using our power, the power of the crystal and the dormant power inside you, I have forcefully pushed the Barghest off from on top of you," he said. "He will not kill you, yet. But we are now out of time. In your current state you cannot keep your mind within your inner self while you have such wounds to hinder you."

As he finished speaking, I looked at my hands to see and realized that I could almost see straight through them. "What's happening?" I asked, waving my hands from side to side.

"Your conscious mind is going back into the real world. You must defeat the Barghest if you ever want to fulfill your goals," he indicated, while his image began to slowly move further away from my vision.

"What is your name?" I asked quickly, before it was too late to do so.

"I thought you would never ask," he replied. "I am your awakened Ouranos crystal and partner, Sora. When you wish, call for me. I will help you find the path to what you truly seek."

"Truly seek—" I began to ask, but before I could finish,

Sora disappeared, along with the rest of the white world. Opening my eyes, I gazed upon the platform of the Trial.

Instead of the scene I had expected—the Barghest laying on top of me while bringing his claws down on my face—I found that I was standing up, bleeding still but with much less pain than before.

Standing just beyond the end of the platform and facing the opposite side where the cages of monsters were located, I tilted my head to the right to get a view of the crowd. I saw that everyone had momentarily taken off their rain coats because of a warm breeze that seemed to be riding through Demon's Pool.

As the warmness that had covered and filled my body while I had been in my "inner world," as Sora had called it, seemed to lessen, so did the warm breeze. The crowd began to put on their jackets with a rustling sound, amplified by all the people doing it at once. Noticing that the stone had disappeared from my hand, I looked directly in front of me towards the Karkinos monster cage where the four other participants waited with Hovan and the Chief, all gazing directly at me. Before I could ask about the Barghest, I heard a loud shuffling noise and turned my head to the left.

The Barghest had apparently been thrown off me fiercely enough that it had to stand back up. As it stood, turning its red nose and face to the sky and opening its mouth, it let out the death-screeching howl like it had done at the beginning of the battle. As it finished, it brought its yellow eyes down so that it could stare into mine.

This time, as I gazed back into its eyes, I felt different. Less scared, I guess you could say, though I have no idea why. Picking itself up off all fours and standing only on two feet, the Barghest began to growl, bringing its claws up to its sides as it slowly closed the space between us. *Here goes round two,* I thought to myself.

Chapter 5:
Leon

No one seemed to move for seconds. Not even the Barghest. I expected it to lunge, like before, but instead it seemed to just stare at me intently. Originally the beast was only around five feet tall as it walked around on all fours, but as it stood up to its full height, with its large, human-like arms in front of it, it seemed to tower over me while still a few feet away. I had a brief thought that maybe I should back away a little, but it quickly fleeted as I decided that this had to end at some point. I moved my left foot in front of the rest of my body and pushed my left arm farther outward then my right. Both hands balled into fists, I stood in a ready stance as I waited for the Barghest to attack.

The Barghest covered the few feet between us in seconds. As it reached me, it raised its arms, opened its claws, and slashed down on where I was standing. Its left arm came first as I jumped backwards fast enough to avoid the claws. As it came, I was also ready for the second attack; I ducked as its right claws made a horizontal slash that seem to cut the air above me. It was the Barghest's third attack I wasn't ready for. It spun around with the force it had created from its horizontal slash and hit me with its large tail. ***Oof***! It hurt as it knocked me off my feet, but I was okay and quickly recovered.

Standing back up, I quickly began to jump backwards as fast as I could while the monster created an onslaught of slashes aimed for my face and chest. Without realizing I was doing it, I stepped back with my left foot to begin to jump backwards, but instead I almost fell off the platform—a short, five-foot fall that would have disqualified me from completing the Trial of Adulthood. The monster, seeing that it had me corned, lunged.

As I saw the Barghest leap through the air towards me, I felt trapped. *I'm gonna die,* I thought. For some reason, Sora's last words resonated in my mind.

Call for me. I will help you find the path to what you truly seek.

In those quick milliseconds, I decided that if I wanted to find what I truly sought, even if I currently didn't know the real meaning of those words, I had to survive. The claws of the Barghest were centimeters from my face when I thought: *Help..me...fight!*

It happened instantly. It even took me a second to comprehend what was going on. I was floating. Looking down, it was apparent that it was just high enough for the Barghest to completely miss me and fall off the platform. Before I could react, I suddenly stopped floating and dropped to the ground with a ***thud***. *Ouch!* I thought. My legs and arms felt weak, while the rest of my body ached. As I tried to get up, I felt a firm hand on my shoulder.

"Let me help you," said a low voice with a confident tone. I didn't resist, surprised, but thankful, as Nicholas helped me up. As I stood, the Chief appeared in front of me and smiled.

"Isn't it illegal to help me during my Trial?" I asked in confusion.

"Yes, but your Trial is over," said the Chief with a chuckle.

"How?" I asked. "I haven't killed the Barghest."

"No, but you have fulfilled the requirements of the Trial," he replied. "You have been chosen by a crystal, faced a demon while awakening your connection with the crystal, and either forced the beast off the platform or released its soul from this world."

"Oh. Great," was all I could muster.

"Your Trial is over," the Chief repeated. "Go home and rest, as you do not need to stay. In two days' time, come to the village square, and we will finish the last part of the ceremony." It had taken everything I had to finish listening to what the Chief had to say, and I still wanted to ask him about the "awakening." Instead, everything went black, and I passed out.

The first thing I saw was a black-haired boy. I had barely opened my eyes before they felt so heavy I had to close them.

...I looked around to see that I was in the village square. The whole village seemed to have gathered around a small, black platform spreading about ten feet long and wide that had been erected in the middle of the square. In the center of the platform were two figures that I couldn't see clearly enough to identify.

Slipping my way through some of the villagers surrounding the platform, I moved closer until I was a few feet away from the platform. Looking up, I saw Hovan, but unlike earlier at the Trial, he had light brown hair and no mustache, and he looked much younger. Next to him stood a woman with long black hair, tan skin, a thin figure, brown eyes, and beautiful face. *She looks like my mom,* I thought. As I tried to figure out who she was, Hovan began to speak to the crowd in the same mocking tone that he had used during the Trial.

“We have all gathered here because this woman has broken a sacred law of the village!” he screamed. “She has defied the ancient laws made by our founders and has become pregnant by an outsider!”

Hovan smiled at the crowd after finishing his sentence. *This can't be,* I thought. *Can it?* I couldn't take my eyes off the woman next to Hovan. The crowd screamed words of disgust at her for a few minutes until they slowly died down.

"I am sorry to say that the Chief has decided to not banish Amity, even though she has proven that she does not respect the village, or any of us!" Hovan ranted. "She may be free to stay in the village, but do not forget her act of lawlessness!"

At that moment, I realized that she had to be my mother. *Same name, same appearance, but how?* I thought. This wasn't the time to ask questions in my head. I had to ask her myself. I forced myself through the crowd of people to try to reach the platform, but as I did so, Hovan grabbed Amity's arm and pulled her along, and they stepped down off the opposite side of the platform. I wasn't going to reach them. I reached out my hand and screamed my mother's name as loud as I could. She turned and seemed to look directly at me. I waved, but she didn't stop.

"Mom!" I called, but to no reply. Instead, Hovan pulled her harder, and they stepped off the platform and out of view. "No!" I screamed, as it all disappeared.

I opened my eyes as far as they would go, jolting up from what felt like a Sea stone bed I had apparently been lying on. It had been a dream. But before I could continue my thoughts, I heard a voice.

"Whoa," a youthful voice exclaimed softly. I looked across from me at the black-haired boy I had seen earlier, who sat in a brown chair behind a large, bright green table made of sky tree wood. Staring at me, he smiled.

"Are you feeling better?" he asked.

He looked to be around the age of fifteen.

"Yes," I replied. "Who are you?"

The boy's long black hair covered his forehead as it curled slightly inwards at the edges, and his smile seemed to extend from his mouth to his brown eyes. I didn't think I had ever seen him before. He was skinny, but also very pale, an uncommon feature for any villager. Somehow he seemed familiar, though.

"I'm Leon," he said, standing up. He stood a few inches shorter than me and wore thin gray shorts and a black shirt; attached to his neck and lying on his chest was a small black-and-yellow crystal, the Void stone. Which meant that he had also passed the Trial at some point. "I participated in the Trial of Adulthood with you."

"Oh!" I said, feeling stupid. I hadn't taken the time to really notice the other two participants aside from Nicholas and myself. But this kid looked older than thirteen… "I forgot, sorry," I said, trying to sound believable.

“Where are we?” I asked while looking around. The bed I had been lying on was in a corner, and the room's Sea stone walls were painted with a sand-colored substance. Other than the desk, chair, and bed, there wasn't anything else in the room aside from two swords in their sheaths hung up on the wall beside the bed. One hilt was colored bright yellow, while the other was completely black.

“Ah,” Leon said, coming from behind the desk and walking up to the bed as he touched the swords on the wall above it. “My swords.” He then placed his hand on my shoulder. “Come, Zephyr, let’s eat and talk in the kitchen.”

Looking beyond where Leon stood, I saw that at the end of the room was a door. Leon took me by the arm and guided me towards the door. Turning the doorknob, he looked back and smiled as we walked into the room. As we entered, I came to see that Leon had not only a kitchen filled with cooking instruments I had never seen before, but the room also had a large green table and two chairs. On the table were three plates filled with food. On one salad, on another a meat I had never seen before, and on the final a collection of fruits.

“Eat up,” he said, taking a seat.

“I can’t take your food,” I stated while my stomach made a loud noise that seemed to mean it disagreed. “Even though it all looks amazing." Since the Chief paid for most of my things, I always tried to eat as little as I could.

"It took me a while to prepare this, so since I'm the person who has taken care of you for three days, don't you think you should at least honor my request?" he asked, smiling.

"Oh," I said, feeling stupid again. Seemed I was beginning to feel that way a lot lately. I sat down at the table, took my fork and knife, and began to eat.

"Good?" Leon asked.

"Delicious!" I exclaimed. "What kind of meat is this?"

Leon smiled and laughed.

"What's so funny?" I asked.

"You haven't realized it yet," he said and stopped laughing. "That's Barghest meat. More specifically, the Barghest that you fought in your Trial. You've obviously never had it before."

"I hadn't realized I had killed it," I admitted.

"You didn't. Nicholas did after you passed out."

"It's been three days?" I asked, with a mouth full of food.

"Yes," Leon replied. "You missed the final part of the ceremony yesterday."

"WHAT?"

"It's okay," he said as he began to laugh again. "In your

absence, the Council of Elders and the Chief have declared that you passed the Trial."

As Leon mentioned the Council of Elders, I remembered my recent dream. Hovan was part of the council that had tried to banish my mother. I finished all of the food on each plate and looked up at Leon as he gazed at me. We sat there for what seemed minutes as the once strong aroma of food disappeared from the room.

"You have been assigned a mission," he suddenly said, ending the silence.

"A mission?" I interrupted. "What mission?"

"Calm down," he replied as he stood up, taking two plates in hand while balancing the third on his forearm. "It's an S-class mission. The top of the line."

"Why would they give me an S-class mission?" I asked in surprise. "I'm sure you know I've failed the Trial multiple times before this."

Leon brought the plates over to a box on a large counter that spread along a wall in the room. S-Class missions were missions that took place outside of the village and were extremely difficult to complete. Only the top warriors were given them.

"Yes, I know." He walked towards the door leading back

into the bedroom and stopped as he turned the knob. Looking back, he spoke. "The Chief has no power over the missions assigned by the Council of Elders. You know that."

I nodded. It was true. "So?"

"He no longer has the power to protect you. Personally, I think the Council has finally found a way to rid the village of the bastard child who was never supposed to exist by our laws," he bluntly stated with a sad tone.

"You—" I said as I stood up from my chair, but before I could respond, he continued.

"It is not an insult, Zephyr, just my thoughts and a fact," he expressed.

He looked directly into my eyes and put his hand on my chest. I looked down to find that he had his hand wrapped around something that I had not noticed before. Like the one around his neck, I had my own crystal, but unlike his black-and-yellow one, mine was completely clear.

"I have been assigned as your partner for this quest," he informed. "I will leave you with your thoughts. We depart from my house for the village square in an hour. Do what you need to do to be ready."

Leon pushed the door, walked through and closed it behind him. *He's different from the other villagers,* I thought. I had been ridiculed as far back as I could remember, by people my own age, elders, and younger ones. Yet Leon, a younger boy I had never met, mentioned my past like it was nothing. I sat back down in the chair and softly laid my head on the table. His name sounded really familiar, but for some reason I couldn't place it.

Quickly changing subjects, my mind filled with thoughts about the future. *Finally, a mission,* I thought. I didn't care that it was an S-class mission—a mission that was supposedly so hard that most of the time the people sent on them didn't survive. All I cared about was that I now had the chance to find out about the outside world and leave the village that had forced me to feel alone for so long.

I raised my head from the table and started to make a mental list of all the things I had to do within the hour before we went before the Council of Elders. *Finally* was the only thought that seemed to run through my mind at that moment.

Chapter 6:
The Unmei Collection

Leon and I opened the door leading back into the village and walked out. Leon's house was only a few rows from mine in the direction that led to the village, which I had never known until now. In the past hour, I had collected my backpack from my house and packed a bottle of water, a change of clothes, and a small dagger that I strapped on my back, concealing it under my shirt. Leon wore a blood-red shirt and black pants while carrying his yellow-and-black swords on his back, strapped over a backpack. As we began to walk down the path towards the village square, Leon turned his head towards me.

“Did you bring any midas?” he asked.

“Yes. I don't have much, though,” I answered. Midas was how we paid for items and food. They were small golden coins made out of a rock that only the Council had access to.

“Me neither. But I’m sure we can survive,” he said.

“What do you think it will be like?” I asked. “The outside world, I mean?”

“I have no idea, Zephyr,” Leon replied.

“No guesses?”

“Honestly, I have no idea.”

I laughed at how unexcited he seemed. Very few people

had come back from the outside world, and the Council of Elders did not permit those who did to speak about their missions or anything about the world. It was a complete mystery to most of us, and I didn't understand how the village people could be okay with that.

When we arrived in the village square, we gazed upon hundreds of people moving from shop to shop. We began to make our way through the crowd of people until they began to recognize Leon, slowing our pace. They would stop, pat him on the shoulder, and all exclaim, "Great job, Leon!"

Of course, as they passed by him and realized that I stood next to him, they would quickly move away from us and continue on to their next shop. After a few congratulations, Leon seemed to realize that the villagers smiled at him but glanced at me with disgust and disappointment. He looked at me and smiled.

"Come on," he said. "Let's go."

We pushed through the crowd at a much faster pace, Leon ignoring the people who obviously wanted to speak to him. I smiled as we passed the Chief's house a few feet from the village center. *I'll miss the Chief,* I thought.

Beyond the village center was a large Sea stone building that blocked the view of the village sea port. We walked through the village center until we stopped in front of the Council's office. As soon as we opened the door, Hovan greeted us.

"Late! Late! Late!" he exclaimed with a sinister smile. "What fools you are to disrespect the Council so greatly."

"We had to prepare," Leon stated. "We are sorry, Elder Hovan."

I chuckled. I would never call this man Elder, nor respect him at any point in my life.

"And you?" he said as he looked at me.

"Ah," I yawned. "I had just woken up."

"So I've heard," he said, touching his mustache. "Enter."

Hovan moved out of the way as Leon and I stepped into a large room. The room was plain, as the dark blue Sea stone had not been painted, but in the center of the room, a few feet in front of us, were five large chairs facing the entrance. In four of the chairs were four older men. Each one looked similar to the others. They all wore long, dark blue robes that went down to their bare feet, and all had white beards that extended from their chins to their wastes. Hovan, unlike the others, wore a black shirt, pants, and sandals as he sat down in the empty chair located in the center of the Elders.

"Your mission," said Hovan, smiling, "is a relatively simple one." As he finished his statement, the four other Elders all smiled as if they were laughing in their minds.

"What must we do?" asked Leon.

"We, for the village safety, require an artifact of great importance," Hovan stated. It looked like he ran the show, as the other Elders just mimicked whatever emotions he displayed. "Your mission is to bring us the Unmei collection."

"What?" I asked. "What's an Unmei?"

"Fool," Hovan stated. "The accurate question is not what the Unmei is, but what comprises it."

"Shut—" But before I could finish my reply, Leon placed his hand over my mouth, to my surprise.

"It's not worth it," he said, uncovering my mouth. Bringing his gaze back to Hovan, Leon continued, "What is this collection?"

"They—" as Hovan continued to smile while speaking "—are a combination of three artifacts that will grant the village enough power to completely control the demons in Demon's Pool and let peace prosper throughout."

"How is that?" I asked, holding down my temper.

"This is a mission," stated the Elder to Hovan's right. "You do not ask questions that do not pertain to accomplishing your mission."

Before I could come up with a good retort, Leon quickly

spoke. “Where do we search? And what else should we know?” he asked.

Hovan smiled. “Respectful boy. So rare,” he said, and laughed. “You will take an Utsu boat that will transport you to the mainland. You will search the world as far as necessary to find these artifacts and complete this mission as soon as possible.”

“I see,” said Leon.

“Is there anything else?” asked all five Elders in unison. It creeped me out.

“Yes,” Leon replied. “What exactly do the three Unmei artifacts look like?”

“We…do not exactly know,” mumbled Hovan. “This is all part of your mission. Do anything you can to retrieve the Unmei collection from the outside world. You will be rewarded greatly.”

“And what will we get as a reward?” I asked.

“You will find out when you return,” snickered Hovan. “That is, if you can.”

I couldn't help but laugh out loud. They were going to send us on a mission without giving us a description of what we were supposed to be looking for, and they wouldn't even tell us what we would get for completing the mission.

“What is funny?” asked Hovan. Leon turned his head and gave me a look that said, *Don't do anything stupid.*

"Nothing," I replied. I owed Leon at least that for taking care of me while I had been out.

"Good," declared Hovan, standing up. "I will lead you to the port. Do either one of you know how to use an Utsu boat?"

"No—" I replied, but Leon cut in.

"Yes," he expressed, with a slight hint of confidence.

How could Leon know how to use an Utsu boat? We were only taught that they were boats that shot off at a high speed from the village dock and stopped when they reached land—nothing on how to work them.

I gave Leon a baffled look as we followed Hovan, who led us to a door that stood behind where the meeting had just taken place. Walking us through the door and into a tight Sea stone passageway with steps that led downwards, we quickly reached the end of the steps and came into a dark room, lit only by candles on the walls. Beyond where we stood was a bright green pier made of sky tree wood that extended out about ten feet, surrounded by ocean water that extended to the end of the underground cove.

On the left side of the pier was a small wooden boat with two indentations that looked like they were designed for passengers. The boat was also bright green and barely ten feet in length. It was shaped like a pecan, with a few inches of space separating the two indentations and a lever in the middle of the empty space.

"Get in," said Hovan.

Leon walked across the pier until he stood next to the boat and slowly lowered himself in. I did the same, and with each of us sitting in an indented spot, Hovan brought over a large, green, wooden covering shaped exactly like the boat we were on, except that its center area domed a few feet above the rest of it.

"Lie down so I can place the cover on the Utsu boat," Hovan instructed. We each lay down on our stomachs in the two empty spaces. We had enough room to move our arms freely and wiggle our legs.

"Bring us the Unmei collection with speed," ordered Hovan as he placed the cover over us. Everything went completely black, except for two small, faint lights. Leon seemed to read my mind.

"It's my eyes," Leon admitted. "It started happening after I awakened my Void stone."

"Lucky you, that's kinda interesting," I said as I heard him chuckle.

Suddenly, the boat began to shake, the vibrating motion seeming to come from under us.

"It's the Sea stone motor," said Leon.

"How do you know that?" I asked. It felt like we were slowly moving.

"It's a secret," he said while laughing. "Doesn't matter."

The feeling of motion increased, most likely meaning that we were picking up speed. Outside, I could faintly hear the sound of the boat rushing against the sea water.

"How long will we be in this?" I asked. "And how do we get out?"

"We pull the lever when the vibrations from the sea motor stop," he replied. "We're moving at a high speed, so it shouldn't take us long."

"Okay," I said, still confused.

I was a little in awe of Leon. He knew things that normal villagers didn't even speak of for fear of being an outcast. He was two years younger than me, but he seemed to be more mature than his age. He carried two swords, and he didn't look down on me like all of the other villagers. He was different, and he was hiding secrets.

"Why are you so different from the other villagers?" I asked. It felt like I was talking to the dark, even though I could see the faint light from Leon's eyes.

"You mean, why don't I treat you like an alien or an

outcast?"

"Yeah," I unhappily replied.

"Because I—" But before he could finish his sentence, the boat abruptly rocked, and it sounded like explosions were occurring all around us.

"What's that?" I asked.

"I don't know!" answered Leon with a yell, the two faint lights moving around as he maneuvered his head in the dark.

I was getting dizzy. The boat rocked and rocked again as more explosions seemed to occur outside, more frequently and loudly, until one seemed to hit us and I heard a ***CRACK*** sound next to me.

In what seemed like seconds, the feeling of vibrating from the Sea stone under us was replaced by the sound of the boat hitting against something hard. I gathered that the boat continued to move, as the feeling of motion did not disappear nor did the sound of the wood creating friction under us, until we suddenly came to a stop. Leon sighed.

"It's time," stated Leon as I heard the lever next to me being pulled.

As soon as Leon pulled the lever, the cover jolted partly off of the boat, and sunlight seeped through the cracks. Standing up, Leon and I pushed the cover off, and we stood in the boat.

The first thing I saw was a bunch of guys running towards us in the distance. Surrounding us seemed to be sand and nothing else.

"Wow!" I exclaimed. *A bit empty,* I thought, *but at least we've reached the outside world.* As I thought this, the guys, numbering about six, surrounded us while we stepped out of the boat.

Now that they were closer, I could see that each of the guys carried a long sword in the shape of the moon with a gray hilt. All of the guys were tan, with long black hair that went down to their shoulders, and they wore short-sleeve shirts and shorts with something I had never seen that covered their entire feet.

"Who are you?" asked one of the men.

"No, it doesn't matter!" exclaimed another.

"Give us your weapons and bags!" stated one as they slowly began to move in a circle around us.

"Give them up," stated the first man, "or we will kill you."

Leon smiled with a sinister and confident smile I wouldn't have expected to see from him. "No," he said. As he did so, he reached both hands behind his back and pulled his bright yellow-and-black swords from their sheaths. Each sword was about twenty inches long; the yellow one seemed to shine even in the sunlight, while the black one seemed to have a dark aura around it.

“Are you going to help?” asked Leon.

“Of course,” I replied while looking at him. Turning to face the two men in front of us, I unsheathed my dagger from behind my back and held it in my hand. I didn't know how I was going to use my dagger to fight against their long swords, but I would manage—or so I thought, as two of the men raised their swords and charged at us.

Chapter 7:
Exilio

It was exciting. Yeah, I know, not something you would usually say before a fight. Even so, the thought of being in a new land fueled my happiness and excitement. I wanted to explore, learn, and discover as much as I could before having to go back to the village, even if it meant fighting for it.

These enemies had found us almost instantly when the Utsu boat landed, and if I had had time to really think, I would have said that it was strange. But I didn't have that time; instead, Leon and I were surrounded by six guys looking as though they wanted to kill us. Leon looked as though he was happy to be caught in this situation as his smile seemed to widen with every passing second.

I stood back to back with Leon, muscles tensed. Bringing my dagger in front of me in my right hand, I kept my left hand behind my back. In Dentro Village, we had been taught to use a variety of weapons, as well as how to use anything nearby as a weapon in self-defense. After being taught the basics of most common weapons like swords, bows, hammers, knives, and hand-to-hand combat, a student chooses to learn and master a specific weapon; of course, mine was the dagger.

Of the six men that had circled us, the two men in front of

me looked at each other, trying to decide who would attack first. The man on the right with his moon-shaped sword brought his free hand up to his head and scratched it. He looked at the man beside him, then at the other four men surrounding Leon and me, and they all slowly began to move closer to us in unison.

As the men moved in closer and we stood back to back, waiting for them to attack, I couldn't help but laugh.

"Bad luck we have," I said. "It's funny though."

"The fact that you find this funny is funny in itself," Leon chuckled. "But it won't stay that way for long."

Before I could think about what he meant, both men in front of me charged as they brought their swords down. I felt the urge to dodge, but I couldn't, or Leon would be killed.

Instead, I stood my ground. The left man's sword connected with my dagger as I blocked his attack. At the same time, the man who had scratched his head, on the right, brought his sword down, and I used all of my force to push the left man's sword into its path. I succeeded. Both men looked at me in awe.

I'm actually pretty good, I thought. Taking the element of surprise I had gained, I slashed at the scratch man's hand with such force that he released his sword as I brought up a left hook.

I connected with his jaw, and the scratch man fell to the

ground with a ***thud***. Although still in shock, the other man brought his sword up as I tried to turn around. Raising my dagger to try to meet the moon-shaped sword before it cut my arm off, I saw that something had blocked its path and completely stopped the sword. I looked up in surprise.

"Bit slow," said Leon as he brought his black sword, the sword that had saved me, up, forcing the attacker to retract his sword. As Leon brought his left hand up to strike the man with his yellow sword, the man turned around and ran north.

Looking at Leon, I suddenly realized why he was so familiar. People talked about him and his family in the village."What about the other—" I began to ask, then broke off as I started to look around, returning to the task at hand. Around us, the four remaining black-haired men had all been disarmed and were either knocked out or worse. "Wow," was all I could mutter. Leon laughed.

"I'm curious to know how we ended up here," said Leon as he sheathed both of his swords. He smiled as he walked over to me. "You should work more on your fighting skills, Zephyr. Strength is an important key to life."

"Thanks for letting me know," I retorted. I looked up beyond Leon to see that, as he began to open his mouth to reply, the scratch man who I thought I had knocked out was in the motion of bringing his sword down towards Leon's head. "Watch—" I screamed as I threw my dagger, "—out!"

Leon quickly spun around, swords in hand, but as quickly relaxed again as he gazed upon the man who had almost killed him. In the exact spot where I had witnessed the man scratch his head, my dagger was lodged. Leon pulled my blood-covered blade from the man's head and wiped it clean on the dead man's clothes. Walking back over to me, he handed me the dagger.

"Thank you," he said with a slight frown, quickly retreating into a smile. "I really owe you."

I laughed. "I'm glad I had enough skill to help."

"Me too!" Leon said, also laughing.

I took the knife and shook his hand.

"What now?" I asked.

"Let's look for a village before night falls," he replied.

I looked around. A combination of sand and dirt surrounded us. To the south, where the back of the Utsu boat faced, lay the beautiful blue ocean extending into the distance. North of us, barely visible, seemed what looked like hundreds of moving dots and large structures—*a new world village,* I thought.

Leon and I decided to leave the Utsu boat and head towards the village in the north. We walked in silence for a few hours until I could no longer bear to silence my curiosity.

"Leon," I said, walking and looking at him, "how do you know so much about things one may only learn by leaving the village?"

"This is not the time or the place for me to answer that question," he replied, suddenly becoming a little unfriendly.

I frowned. "I know nothing of you, yet you, like every villager, know of me and my family."

"Yes, this is true," he stated. "And you think this is unfair?"

"Yes," I replied. "Why won't you open up a little?"

"Because," Leon began, smiling, "it's unnecessary."

"How so?"

"You'll see soon enough, Zephyr," he answered, pointing ahead of us. "But, for now let's settle ourselves in the village."

I looked in the direction of his pointed finger and couldn't help but frown. The village itself looked similar to Dentro Village—aside from the fact that the ground was hard, and that all of the buildings were lined up to the right and left sides, and were larger, and they seemed to have multiple floors. Each building stood only a few feet from its neighbors, and the rows of houses spread down about a mile. The road between the left buildings and the right buildings was about a hundred feet wide.

As we walked into the village filled with hundreds of bustling people, one thing stood out to me more than anything: all of the people had the same physical features as the men who had just tried to kill us. I reached for my dagger as a middle-aged man with long black hair, tan skin, and shorts but no shirt walked up to us. He was taller than both Leon and me, and he had a very built body.

"Welcome to Exilio," the man said, smiling with crooked teeth, in an accent that sounded as if he was chewing while talking. "I am Adamus, leader of this town."

"Thanks," both Leon and I greeted him.

"My pleasure," Adamus stated. "What brings you to Exilio, outsiders?"

Leon looked at the man as if to decided whether or not to tell him of our mission. "We are from a village far away. We have come in search of sacred items that our village needs to stay protected."

"Hmm," Adamus sighed. "I do not think you will find anything sacred here that could do what you ask. Exilio is a town that was founded by thieves who were exiled from their city long ago." *Wow, a city,* I thought. *I've only heard of such places from the stories that the Chief used to tell me.* "I suggest that you try your luck at the closest city, Rosem."

"How far is it?" I asked.

"Almost a day's walk," Adamus replied. He seemed to be holding back a smile as he gazed at Leon.

"How do we get there?" asked Leon.

"Head straight on north," Adamus said as he turned to face the direction we had been heading, straight through the town. "But before that, why don't you rest here? You've come such a long way. I'm sure you wouldn't mind resting before you set off."

"I don't know," I said, looking at Leon to make a decision. There was something about this guy that I didn't like. Maybe it was just his accent. "I think we should be on our way to Rosem." Leon turned around and looked into my eyes as he spoke.

"We will rest," he said. "Thank you Adamus."

I wondered why Leon didn't think it was weird that the leader of a town we had never been to was offering us, outsiders, a free place to stay and so much information for nothing. But I decided to trust Leon's judgment.

"I guess we'll stay," I said. "If I may ask though, why are you helping us?"

"To help guide others is what a leader must do," Adamus replied with a laugh. "You are safe here." I looked at Adamus with uncertainty. The fact that he was trying to persuade me to want to stay seemed weird, but Leon didn't seem worried, and I was tired.

"Thank you," I said as I walked up and stood next to Leon, facing Adamus.

"Great," Adamus declared. "Let me take you to a place where you can stay."

He led us through people and buildings until we reached our destination. All the buildings were made of something that seemed to be similar to sky tree wood but, rather than bright green, was dark brown. We followed Adamus up three steps that led to a large building; the words "Welcome, INN" were painted on the door.

As we walked through the entrance, we saw a small desk in the front with no one sitting in the chair behind it. Behind the reception desk was another door, which we opened to find a bedroom with a small bathroom connected to it. As I looked inside the bedroom, I noticed that there was only one bed, made of what seemed to be the same substance as the house was made of.

"Only one bed?" I asked.

"Yes, I'm sorry," replied Adamus. "Is this okay?" Before I could reply with a no, Leon answered.

"Yes, it's fine," he said, giving me a quick glance.

"Good, my house is across the road. If you need anything do not hesitate to ask. I will see you off in the morning, young ones," he said, winking at Leon. As he left and closed the door behind him, I lay on the bed and looked up at the ceiling.

"What was that about?" I asked, not expecting a legitimate answer.

"What do you mean?" Leon asked, playing dumb.

"The wink and smiles."

"Oh," he said, facing away from me. "I don't know. Probably some weird custom of this city. You should get some rest, we'll leave early to continue our mission tomorrow."

"Yeah," I replied. "You too."

Within seconds I could no longer keep my eyes open. I didn't know for how long I had been asleep, but when I opened my eyes the sunlight that had illuminated the inn had been replaced by candles someone had lit while I was sleeping. I looked next to me expecting to see Leon, but instead he was not even in the room. *Weird,* I thought, as I heard the door in front of the reception desk open, followed by the sound of footsteps.

Without thinking, I jumped behind the door that led into the room, just as it abruptly opened. Almost instantly, where I had just been lying, a knife quivered as the man who had thrown it slowly walked in with another man behind him. As I looked closely from behind a crack in the door, I saw that the man was the same one who had run away from the fight we had had when we first arrived. With him was Adamus, the so-called friendly chief of Exilio. *Where's Leon? We gotta get out of here,* I thought.

"Where is the boy?" asked Adamus in anger, with no trace of the friendly tone he had had earlier.

"I don't know. Has Leon betrayed us?" the man asked as he took his knife from the bed.

"No. He would be a fool to do so. He must still be around here. Go search for the boy, Ferd. I will talk with Leon about why killing his friend has not gone as planned," replied Adamus.

No, I thought. There's no way Leon had planned to have me killed. Was there? As Ferd and Adamus left the room and the sound of their footsteps disappeared, I moved from behind the door and opened my backpack. Taking my gloves out, I put them on and closed my backpack, then slowly walked outside, making sure that no one was looking in my direction. *First things first,* I thought. Time to find Leon and get the truth.

Chapter 8:
My Will

My white gloves felt good. I always seemed to feel more confident with them on, although I didn't know why. My mother had once told me that they were the only thing my father left for me before he left my mom, but of course she had told me not to tell anyone in the village, or the Council would have made me get rid of them. Directly across from me stood a large building. Through the door, I could just make out Adamus yelling.

I quickly walked over to the door, trying to seem as normal as possible. Luckily, there seemed to be no one around, most likely because it was late. It wasn't dark, though; on every porch, candles burned brightly enough to create light to navigate. Putting my ear against the cold brown door, I listened closely to try to hear what was going on.

"This is foolish!" screamed Adamus. "I was promised, by your so-called Council of Elders, the White Gantias!" I could hear his heavy footsteps as he paced back and forth. "Your Elders are mere cowards! They would not dare cross me. So the only other reason I could think of for the boy not being there is that you tipped him off, Leon."

"I promise," said a voice I recognized as Leon's. "I did not do so. You have my word."

"Your word, boy, the word of a child, is not enough. The fact is he is gone, and we cannot find him. Tell me where he is, and I may be lenient with you yet," said Adamus.

"My mission was to bring him to you safely so you may do what you want to him. I have done so, and I do not know where he has gone," stated Leon.

"You make this harder on yourself, Leon," said Adamus as he stopped pacing. "Lock him in the inn."

All of a sudden I could tell there were a few men aside from Leon and Adamus in the building from the sound of several different footsteps.

"Yes, my leader," said a voice from within.

As I ran to the inn, I thought about what I should do next. Leon had, from the start, intended to betray me. From what I had heard from Adamus, the Council had ordered him to take me to Exilio and bring me to Adamus so he could take…the White Gantias?

I had no idea what that was, but I decided that finding out the truth from Leon and what the Gantias was would be a start before I would do anything else. I quickly slipped into the inn as I heard the door open across the path.

I glanced through the crack in the open inn door to see four men accompanying Leon, two of them holding his hands behind his back, wrapped in chains. Before they spotted me, I ran as quietly as I could into the bedroom where I had narrowly escaped death. I jumped behind the door as Leon was pushed face down onto the bed by the four men.

"We will be back when the leader has decided what to do with you. Stay put," said one of the men as they closed and locked the door behind them. Before I could do anything, Leon spoke.

"So you're here," he said as he turned himself around, still lying on the bed.

"Yeah," I replied as I came out from behind the door, "I am." I sounded more confident then I felt, but I needed to find out the truth from Leon.

"You should have left when you had the chance," said Leon as he gazed at me. "What do you want?"

I laughed. I had wondered why Leon had treated me differently than the other villagers, but it had all be part of his mission. "Why did the Council order you to give me to Adamus?"

Leon frowned. "How do you know so much—" he began to say but abruptly stopped. "I guess it doesn't matter now. Your mother broke the sacred laws of the village, and the only way the Council could get rid of you was to send you on a mission that would get you killed."

Killed? I repeated in my mind. Harsh, but it was the truth, and I didn't doubt Leon's words. I had been taught about the pain of being alone since my mother died, and I had never had a real friend. The villagers had always looked down on me, aside from the Chief, and had never given me a chance. Now that I thought about it, I guess it wasn't that surprising that they wanted to get rid of me.

"It was all an act, then?" I asked. "The mission to get the Unmei collection? Your friendliness towards me?"

Leon looked at the ceiling as he spoke. "No."

"No?"

"The Unmei collection is legend. The mission they gave to us is known to be impossible. No one has ever succeeded," said Leon.

"Then why would they give us that mission?"

"They never expected you to stay alive long enough to try to complete it, since Adamus was suppose to kill you. But they had to give you a real mission so the Chief would not be suspicious."

I began to pace back and forth. "Why would he let them?"

"When the Council of Elders brought their decision to the Chief, he stated 'I believe in him,' and that was it," replied Leon.

I stopped pacing around the bed and looked at him. "Why would you agree to this?"

"They offered me something I could not refuse. I'm sorry," he said, his voice cracking a little. "I didn't want this to happen to you."

"Sure," I said as I turned around to face the wall. "I was never meant to belong in that village." It was true, I felt it with body and soul. The way the village was now, I could never belong, nor did I want to. I thought about how the Council of Elders was power-hungry, the villagers only cared about themselves, and the only one who truly seemed to care for the village and its inhabitants was the Chief.

"It was not an act," said Leon suddenly.

"What?" I asked.

"You're different from the others," he said. "I never truly felt like I fit in with the other kids, but the short time we've been together has been enjoyable and fun. You're a good person, I can tell."

I turned around and laughed. "Don't joke at this point."

"This is no joke," he said, looking into my eyes as if trying to show me he was serious. "I am sorry. I wish I could help you, but I will surely be enslaved or killed by Adamus."

"I will not help you," I said quickly.

"I do not deserve it," he said.

"How were you captured—" I began but noticed his swords were missing. "Where are your swords?"

"In the building across the street," he replied. "You must leave if you wish to escape."

I looked at Leon. His long black hair covered his eyes as he stared at the ground, and his face had lost the cool composure he had when we first met.

"I'm going," I said as I picked the door lock with my dagger. Before I walked out, I turned around and asked one last question. "What's the White Gantias Adamus seeks?" Leon's eyes drifted down from my face until it seemed he was looking at my hands.

"The White Gantias are your gloves," he stated. "I don't know why he seeks them."

"Thank you," I said as I began to walk out of the inn.

"I am sorry, Zephyr," whispered Leon.

I left the inn and stepped into the open path that lead straight through the town of Exilio. Lighted by the candles on the porch of each building, I could see that no one was outside. I looked left towards the north, where the town ended a few hundred feet away. I turned and began to walk as I remembered what Adamus had said.

The city of Rosem was where he had suggested looking for information on the Unmei collection—although my best choice probably would be not to trust someone who was trying to kill me. Having nothing else to go on, I walked a few feet north, but stopped. *I can't leave Leon there to die,* I thought. It just didn't seem right to let someone die when I had the chance to save him, even if he had tried to get me killed before. I turned around and quickly ran towards the building that lay across from the inn.

I slowly walked up to the door and pressed my ear against it as I had done before. Not hearing anything, I turned the knob and opened the door slowly, to not make any noise. Inside the building, on the left was a set of stairs, while a few feet directly in front of me was a large room similar to the Council of Elders' room. Instead of just chairs, it held a large structure that I had never seen before.

Without thinking, I walked up and examined it. The item seemed to be a large chair that stretched a couple of feet so that multiple people could sit on it. It seemed to be made of a soft material. I placed my hand on it, and it felt soft to the touch. Before I could look around any more, the door suddenly opened, and I jumped behind the large chair-like item for cover.

"Whoa!" said one man as two other large, muscular men

entered the house with him.

"The Leader will not be pleased we could not find the boy. I guess we will have to kill the one we have, then!" said one, laughing with the others.

I have to hurry and find Leon's swords, I thought. Watching the three men as they began to walk up the stairs near the door, I recognized two sheaths with one black and one yellow hilt propped up against the side of the stairs. I slowly and quietly walked over to them, grabbed the swords, opened the door, and walked out.

I decided it would be better if I didn't bother with trying to close the door, as it may have made too much noise and attracted attention. I glanced at the path to confirm it was still empty, ran across the path and into the inn, and opened the door to where Leon was located.

As I entered, Leon sat facing away from the door, staring at the wall.

"Have you come to kill me now?" he asked.

"No, at least not yet," I replied. Leon jumped up as best he could while chained and turned around in surprise.

"Why are you still here?" he whispered, his eyes widening as he gazed at his swords. I untied his chain and looked him in the eyes.

"I do not trust you," I said. "You tried to get me killed. But I will change the village, and I will not let the Chief down."

Leon smiled. "Change the village?" he asked in wonder.

"Yes. I will find the Unmei collection and force the village to recognize the Council is corrupt," I stated plainly, surprised at my own little speech.

Leon laughed. As he finished, he looked at me and smiled again. "Oh. You're serious."

"Yes, I am," I said as I handed him his swords and began to walk out the door.

"Wait," Leon said. "I will believe in you, as you came back for me when you had no reason to." Leon got up from the bed, placed his swords on his back, grabbed his bag from the corner of the room, and walked up to me. "I promise to help you."

"I don't need you," I said, trying my best to be confident.

"Then I will accompany you by my own will. I will be your companion," he said as he placed his hand on my shoulder. I brushed it off. It seemed as if Leon was going to follow me whether I wanted him to or not, so I walked out of the inn, and he followed close behind. As I brought my head up to look towards the north to begin our walk towards Rosem, I saw a familiar face.

"Where are you going, outsiders?" asked Adamus as he

walked towards us from the direction we were trying to go. Leon stepped up beside me.

"We are leaving Exilio, Adamus," stated Leon.

"Why?" asked Adamus, laughing. "I had said you would be safe here. And you cannot leave without giving me what I have been promised, Leon."

"My gloves?" I asked. "They were my father's. You can't have them." I faced Adamus with more confidence then I felt I really had. But then again, I wasn't going back on my word to change the village, and this man was standing in my way. "Let us go."

"Foolish boys," said Adamus, coming closer until he was only a few feet away. "I will kill you before I let you leave."

"Yeah," said Leon as he unsheathed both his swords.

"Right," I added as I held my dagger in my right hand. I glared at Adamus.

"So be it," said Adamus. A dark aura seemed to surround him.

All around me, a dark, intense feeling seemed to fill the air. Adamus's muscles seemed to show more through his shirt than before, and his eyes began to glow, though still pitch black. While the black aura around Adamus became stronger and easier to see, something seemed to float up from his chest until it popped out of his shirt.

Taking a closer look, I realized that it was a black–and-yellow crystal—the same crystal that lay around Leon's neck, the Void stone. I looked at Leon and mouthed the word “How?”, but he looked as stunned as I was.

As I turned to face Adamus again, the aura around him suddenly disappeared, and the intense, dark feeling seemed to disappear as well.

Slowly, the necklace around Adamus turned completely black and faded into something like smoke. The cloud left his neck, traveling down to his hands and separating into two clouds, one covering each. Adamus looked at Leon and me and smiled.

As he did so, covered in the smoky substance, he curled his right hand into a fist and punched the ground. As his fist contacted, the smoke enveloped the few plants around it and then faded, remaining only on his hands. As Adamus brought his fist off the ground, all of the plants that had been there moments before had disappeared, leaving a huge black mark in their place.

“I'm sorry to say,” said Adamus as he walked towards us, “your deaths will not be quick.”

Chapter 9:
Sky Pushuu

All five stones—Sea, Ouranos, Void, Balance and Dream—had different, unique powers for each person after their awakening ceremony. The sacred crystals, thought to be found only in our village, had been used since ancient times in Dentro Village.

Together, the crystal's powers could control life, death, nature, time, space, and reality. We were taught all this basic information as children in the village. One of the first things we learned was that only Dentro villagers had access to these sacred stones. So how was it that Adamus, a man from Exilio who also happened to be trying to kill us, had a Void crystal?

Sadly, my thoughts were cut short when Adamus raised his hand. As Leon and I gaped in surprise, Adamus slowly began to make his way towards us.

"Surprised," said Adamus. "To be expected from two weak-looking children."

"How," I muttered, "do you have a crystal?"

"Doesn't matter, boy," replied Adamus. "You are going to die anyway."

Leon chuckled. "Like I said—" He began to walk towards Adamus, "—yeah, right."

Leon and Adamus closed in on each other within seconds. Leon brought his yellow sword in his left hand down in an effort to cut at Adamus's arm. In response, Adamus quickly dodged backwards, then jumped forward, jabbing his clouded right arm at Leon, catching him in the gut. Leon dropped his swords and fell to his knees as he visibly tried to hold back a yell.

"Hurts," said Adamus as he stood over Leon, "doesn't it?" As he finished speaking, Adamus brought his left hand up in an uppercut towards Leon's chin, colliding with so much force that Leon flew from Adamus and dropped at my feet. Adamus laughed. "You are cocky and weak!"

I knelt next to Leon as he lay on the ground, coughing.

"Are you okay?" I asked.

"Yeah—" he said, still coughing, "it's his crystal. It does something to everything he touches." I looked up towards Adamus as he stared at us.

"Maraino, my crystal, grants me the power to wither anything my hands touch," stated Adamus, smiling. "Each punch you take from me drains some of your life force, as Leon has experienced."

It was my turn to try. "Don't underestimate us," I said, standing up.

I had never been one to enjoy or pick a fight, and my confidence wavered a bit as I thought about how easily Leon had been defeated, but I wanted to beat this guy with everything I had. It was less that we were going to die if we lost, but more that this was the first wall in my journey to becoming a person with the power to change the village and force everyone to recognize me. I couldn't let this guy stop me. As the thought of not giving up ran through my mind, my body seemed to warm up, and I felt adrenaline pump through me.

I walked over to Adamus until I stood only a few feet away. For seconds, neither of us made the first move. Adamus smiled.

"Afraid, boy?" he asked, while the clouds around his fists seemed to become denser.

I decided not to let him taunt me, and instead attacked first. I jabbed my dagger at his stomach, but he anticipated my attack and dodged to the left. I jumped back as Adamus swung his fist in a huge arc, barely missing me.

"You're fast," he said, "but not fast enough!" Adamus leaped at where I stood and brought a barrage of punches with him.

Punch after punch I dodged, feeling the air beside me crackle. Stopping for a second, I braced myself for a punch, but instead Adamus dropped to the ground as he brought his legs forward in a sweeping motion, kicking my legs and knocking me off my feet. I floated in midair, unable to react until Adamus brought his right fist down on my stomach. The force of his punch pushed me towards the ground as I seethed in pain, hitting it hard.

Instead of a regular punch, Adamus's punches felt like something was eating at my stomach, while every second brought massive amounts of pain. Taking my unguarded body as an opportunity, Adamus rained down a barrage of punches that felt as if something were ripping my stomach out over and over again.

"AHH!" I yelled in agony as I coughed up blood with Adamus's last punch.

My body felt weak. The warm feeling that had run through me before had disappeared, replaced by pure pain. My vision became blurred. I tried to focus on Adamus as he stood over me, but I couldn't keep my eyes open, and everything went black.

Warmth surrounded me while a warm breeze also blew. It was familiar feeling, like having my whole body covered with soft, warm sand. I looked around the landscape where I stood. Everything was white, the floor, the sky, and everything else as far as I could see. Last time I was here, I had been in the middle of fighting the Barghest creature. This place, my inner world as Sora had called it, was relaxing, even at such a crucial time. *Sora,* I thought. *Where is he?*

"Here," said a voice that flowed like a river. I turned around and jumped back in surprise.

"How did—?" I began to ask.

"I am a reflection of you, your heart of hearts, remember?" he said as he gazed at me with his wide, shiny blue eyes.

He brought his hand over his long, flowing brown hair, using his other hand to move the two strands of hair in front of his face that covered his eyes.

"Oh," I said. "My heart of hearts again. I don't really understand what that means." I sat down. I didn't feel like standing up for some reason.

"You will know in time," he said, sitting with me. "Do you know why you are here again?"

I smiled. "I would say I need your help."

Sora laughed. "Yes, it would seem you are getting beat up pretty badly."

"Well," I said, looking away, "yeah. I guess so. He just got lucky." I smiled. Sora laughed again.

"I am your partner. I am here to help you. So I will tell you something."

"Yeah?" I asked.

"You cannot defeat the man, Adamus."

"What?" I stuttered.

"At least not at your current level. Nor can your friend Leon, as he seems to have been weakened from something dark inside of him," said Sora.

"How do you know all of this?"

"I see everything you see," he answered, laughing. "But we are almost out of time, Zephyr."

"What should I do?"

"The amount of power we can use together as the Ouranos crystal all depends on your energy level, our bond, and your skills. Currently, it seems you have no skill, given the fact that you are forced into coming here when in a dire situation."

"Oh, I see," I said, not truly understanding it all but not wanting to sound stupid.

"I will use your energy to create a force of strong wind energy known as 'Sky Pushuu,' which should be enough to disable Adamus for as long as it should take you to escape onto the road to Rosem. But remember, you will have very little time to run, and it will take a lot of energy to block the pain from your current wounds and to create the Pushuu. You're going to feel that. Understand?" asked Sora.

"Yeah," I replied, "I got it."

"Good," he said, smiling and fading into transparency. "It's time, Zephyr." Just like before, the white world slowly began to disappear, until I could no longer see Sora or anything else.

The first thing I saw as I opened my eyes was Adamus's surprised face looking down upon me. I quickly noticed that the pain from his attacks had disappeared, and the feeling of warmth that circulated through my body and from my gloves felt stronger than ever. I rolled to the left, towards Leon, and quickly stood up. Adamus's smile had left his face.

"How are you still standing?" he asked, dumbstruck.

"I told you," I said while sheathing my dagger and putting both hands, palms open, in front of me facing Adamus, "Don't underestimate us!"

As I finished my sentence, thick crackling seemed to occur rapidly in front of my hands. Something was telling me to hold my hands like this, as I remembered what Sora had told me about sending an attack towards Adamus.

I focused all of my energy on the thought of hitting Adamus, while he just stared in awe. Slowly, all of the warmth that had been running through my body seemed to transfer to my hands, until my gloves started to shine brightly and the space in front of them was filled with a transparent, ball-shaped object.

The object increased in size as all around it the air seemed to crackle and fold in to create the ball, until all movement stopped. Not knowing if I should throw it, I began to panic. *What should I do? How do I use this?* Before I could falter any longer, Sora's soft, flowing voice radiated through my mind:

Just focus on who you want to hit…

Easier said than done, I thought. I looked at Adamus and filled my mind with the intent of hitting him with the ball. As I did so, the ball shot from my hands straight towards Adamus at lightning speed. Adamus seemed to have guessed what was going to happen, so he put his smoke-covered hands into a blocking position; but it did little to help him. As the ball collided with his fingers, the smoky substance disappeared, and Adamus flew straight into a building on the left with such force that he knocked through the wall and fell into the house.

I picked Leon up and began to carry him on my back, walking on the north road leading to Rosem City as my energy rapidly left me and the harsh pain from Adamus's punches returned. My breathing became heavy and labored, and my pace slowed greatly. After walking a few miles away from Exilio,

I couldn't walk on and collapsed to the ground. I didn't care about anything. Despite Leon's weight on top of me, with the overwhelming pain and sleepiness that overcame me, I decided that I would take a short rest. My eyes slowly closed, and my muscles relaxed as my mind drifted off.

Chapter 10:
Delphi the Wise

I looked around in surprise to see that I was in the village square, while from every direction Dentro villagers glared at me with detestation and hate. Their glares seemed so powerful that it felt as if the air around me was becoming thinner. I looked down at the ground in an effort to ignore the villagers and noticed that it seemed closer than usual. I examined my own legs, chest, and arms, realizing that I looked like I had at ten years old.

I wanted to figure out how I had suddenly gone back in time, but all around me the piercing stares of the villagers seemed to get stronger with every passing moment. I began to choke as the air seemed not to exist anymore. I turned to look at the villagers in a plea for help, but they just stared; some pointed, while others laughed as the horrible feeling of suffocation grew stronger.

I tried to scream, but nothing came out as I dropped to my knees in agony. But as I knelt there, suffocating, dying, I felt the pain of something much more powerful. As I could no longer hold myself up, my head began to fall to the ground. The only thing running through my mind, piercing my heart, was the pain of being forsaken even in the very moment of my death.

The first thing I saw was Leon as I jolted up, my head colliding with his chest.

"Whoa, Zephyr!" exclaimed Leon with a surprised face.

I grabbed my throat before realizing that I wasn't suffocating anymore. I looked at my legs and chest as I lay on a bed, seeing that I wasn't a ten-year-old boy and that it had all been a nightmare. Reliving the feeling of my childhood in the village as it had been after my mother's death was horrible. I turned my head to my right as I felt a cold hand on my shoulder.

"Are you okay?" asked Leon. I looked away from him before answering.

"Yeah," I replied. My childhood hadn't been fun, and I had had similar dreams in the past quite often that reminded me of my loneliness, although it had been a while. The villagers had forsaken me and treated me as if I didn't exist since I had been born, but this dream had never been so vivid and realistic. "What happened?" I asked while trying to make sure Leon couldn't see my face in such a weak emotional state.

"First," said Leon as he grabbed my shoulder again, gently turning me, "I have to say thank you. Thank you for saving my life twice. I don't know how you beat Adamus, but it doesn't matter."

I smiled. "I didn't beat him. He was too skillful. I just

bought us enough time to allow us to escape."

"Oh," sighed Leon. "But that is really crazy. I am really indebted to you, Zephyr." He looked away. "I was childish and overconfident about my fighting skills. I'm sorry."

"Why are you sorry?" I asked in shock. I didn't think that Leon was the type to apologize about anything. When I had first met him, he seemed to have such a cool demeanor and mature attitude for a fifteen-year-old.

"Because I wasn't careful, and you ended up fighting and getting hurt when I promised to help you," replied Leon as he punched the bed.

"Leon," I said, "it's okay. Just finish explaining." I didn't feel like dealing with any more problems involving other people at the moment.

"Oh yeah," he began. "We have been at an inn in Rosem City for a little while now." I opened my mouth without saying anything before clearing my thoughts.

"Rosem City," I repeated, taking another glance around me. We were in a room made of a red substance that looked and felt exactly like the sky trees from Dentro Village. In the room were two beds, the one I was lying on and the other that had my bag, my dagger, and Leon's bag and swords on it. Otherwise, the room was empty.

"Yeah," said Leon. "I awoke on top of you after you carried me on your back, and so I gathered all my strength and walked the whole way to Rosem from Exilio with you on my back."

"Thanks," I mumbled, remembering Leon's betrayal like it was yesterday—well, it had been.

"Not needed," stated Leon as he pushed some of his long black hair from in front of his eyes. He looked even paler than he had in the village, I thought. "When we arrived—" Leon began as I interrupted him.

"Are you okay?" I asked. Leon's face changed, his surprised look melting into a huge smile that lit up his eyes. "You're blushing," I laughed. Leon coughed and immediately tried to look more serious.

"Sorry," he said, dropping his voice to a more manly pitch. "Didn't expect you to care about me, especially after what I did to you. No one in the village did, really." I laughed again.

"Yeah, well, I know how you feel, trust me. Come on, tell me the rest of it," I said, laughing and lying back down.

"I got us to Rosem as the sun began to rise, and I found the inn. After renting a room for us, I passed out. That was yesterday, but I've been too tired until a little while ago to do anything."

Leon pointed towards the other bed. A tray of food rested on it. “I got us some food and did some chores to pay off our bill,” he said as he walked over and picked up various fruits and meats. “Somehow they had Karkinos, so I got some.”

The Karkinos, the huge, crab-like monster that Nicholas had faced in his Trial, was a staple seafood in Dentro. After eating, resting for a little longer, and stretching, I grabbed some clean clothes from my bag to change into. As I put on some blue shorts, a white shirt, and my shoes, I noticed Leon looking more depressed with each of my movements. “What?” I asked as Leon looked at me, sitting on the bed.

“I...it’s nothing,” he answered.

“What, Leon?” I pressed, unsure why he was acting strange.

“The bruises from Adamus,” he said, pointing to my chest. I hadn't noticed as I didn’t feel any pain, but I lifted up the front of my shirt to see. All around my abs were brown bruises from Adamus's barrage of punches.

“Oh,” I said as I put down my shirt. “Didn't notice. I heal pretty quickly. We need to find some information on the Unmei collection. So what now?”

“I asked around earlier and heard about a wise man located here who supposedly knows almost everything,” replied

Leon.

I laughed as I thought about how our Council of Elders, the Council that had tried to get me killed, valued themselves as the wisest men in the village.

“So, where is this wise man?” I asked.

“His name seems to be Delphi, but I'm not sure how to find him,” said Leon as he strapped his swords and bag onto his back. After strapping my dagger to my own back and grabbing my bag, I stood up and walked over to the door.

“Let's go,” I said, opening it.

The sun shone so brightly that I had to look at the ground for a few seconds as my eyes adjusted. Leon laughed and walked up next to me.

“I know, it's bright. Took me a while to get used to as well.”

After a few seconds, I felt able to look up. In front of me lay a crimson building with a sign identifying it as the inn. We stood on a road that went off to the left and right, curving as if to make a complete circle. On both sides of the inn were hundreds of red houses and buildings running alongside the road.

The most jaw-dropping thing, though, wasn't the number of houses, their color, or that the buildings were all one floor and completely square, but that behind each house stood another set of houses, identical but on a higher level as the ground sloped upwards. Beyond each level lay another set of houses that went up five more levels, making a total of seven levels. I had never seen a hill so high.

On the seventh level was a small, dark blue hut that didn't fit with the style of the other buildings. It looked as it if came from Dentro. Turning around, I looked at the inn room we had just stayed in, and beyond the inn a huge, deserted marketplace similar to Dentro's village square. A little farther beyond the marketplace stood a huge gate in a wall that encircled the mountain city.

"That is where we entered," said Leon as I took in the sight of Rosem City.

"Wow," was all I could mutter. I mean, the idea of building a huge city on a mountain had never occurred to me, but maybe that was because mountains themselves were talked of as legends in the village. "So, where is Delphi?" I turned around towards Leon to see him looking somewhere. I followed his gaze until I was looking at the top of the mountain and the hut that stood there. "No way!" I exclaimed. "The one up there?"

"Seems so," replied Leon as he began to walk up a set of stairs next to the inn that led up to the second level of the city. Several levels and twenty minutes of climbing later, a thought crossed my mind.

“Where is everyone?” I asked. “I mean, the people?”

“It seems that in Rosem they have a custom to eat lunch at a certain hour within their own homes, every day,” answered Leon. I responded with an “Oh.”

At last, we reached the hut at the top of the mountain. Aside from the stairs leading back down, the hut itself was surrounded by only a few hundred feet of grassy ground, leaving very little room to walk around.

I gazed down. The sight of the city itself and the height we stood at left me amazed. The Chief had told me stories of such intriguing places when I was a child in the village and about how brilliant the outside world truly was, and he was right. Breaking my train of thought, Leon placed his hand on my shoulder.

“Come on,” he said.

We opened the door to the wise man's house, expecting to find an Elder similar to the men on our Council—old, cranky-looking, a long white beard, and tan skin. Instead, we found that the “wise man” eating lunch on a blanket a few feet away from the door was really a wise woman.

“Hello,” she said. Her pronunciation of “hello” sounded more like “h-e-y-a-lo.”

"Delphi?" I asked as Leon and I entered the small, warm house.

"Come, come," she said with a smile. Her accent made it hard to understand her words. "As you can see, I am indeed a woman, and I am called Delphi." She gestured for us to sit down across from her. We did.

"Sorry," I said apologetically. "How did you know we thought you were supposed to be a man?"

"We misheard information," said Leon quickly.

"The citizens tend to do this to outsiders as a joke," stated Delphi as she began to chew on a fruit.

"How do they know we're outsiders?" asked Leon.

"Well," she began while finishing her fruit, "you, Leon—"

"How do you know my name?" Leon interrupted.

"I am an oracle as well as a wise woman. But as I was saying, you could pass as a citizen from looks alone, but your clothes distinguish you. But your friend, Zephyr—" she said as she pointed at me, "his hair is a dead giveaway. No one in our city has such hair. As well as your cloudy gray eyes," she finished, looking at me with interest.

Delphi had long white hair and wrinkly skin, and she spoke in an all-knowing kind of way, even through her thick accent.

"I have foreseen your visit in my visions," she stated as she continued to gaze at me.

"Is there something wrong with my face?" I asked with a little sarcasm.

"No, my child," she chuckled. "Your kind is just so…rare."

"My kind?" I asked.

"Yes, your kind. But are you not here for something?"

"Yes," replied Leon. "We are." Leon looked at me, nodded as if to say *Get to the point*, and looked back at Delphi. "How can we find the Unmei collection?"

The wise woman's eyes widened for a split second as she heard the word Unmei, but she gave no other reaction. After a few seconds, she spoke.

"I can tell you how and where to get the three Artifacts of Destiny, otherwise known as the Unmei collection." Leon and I both smiled.

"How?" we asked in unison.

"I will tell you in exchange for payment," she stated.

"Of course!" I blurted out. "How much?" We were so close, even though we had brought no midas along.

"Far beyond what you can afford," she replied. I stopped smiling instantly.

"Then how?" asked Leon.

Delphi smiled. "Do something for me, and in exchange I shall answer your questions with all of my knowledge."

"What must we do?" I asked impatiently.

"Return my daughter to me," she answered.

"What?"

"My daughter, Autumn, was kidnapped a few days ago by a band of fools from the outcast town of Exilio."

Leon and I looked at each other with pained faces as the memory of Adamus went through our minds.

"Would the leader of this group be Adamus?" I asked, hoping it was not.

"Yes," she replied. "I have seen that you have already encountered him. He has been holding Autumn captive in attempt to force her to wed him. She is only sixteen."

Leon and I frowned. I brought my hand up to my head and rubbed it in an effort to relax.

"We'll do it," I said.

Leon looked at me in surprise. "But Adamus—"

"We only have to find and rescue the girl, correct?" I asked Delphi.

"Yes," she said simply. I looked at Leon.

"Find, rescue, then leave. Simple and easy, as long as we keep away from Adamus," I declared. Leon looked at me with doubtful eyes but then nodded in agreement.

"You must leave soon," commanded Delphi. "The best time to arrive at Exilio would be at night, when Adamus and his gang are busy drinking. The walk will take you a while, and when you arrive it will be dark."

Delphi described her daughter as having long, curly brown hair, brown eyes, and an athletic body, and we left to begin our rescue mission. Leon and I walked up to the gates leading out of the city, looked back at Rosem, and then departed.

I didn't know why, but I felt strongly about saving this girl. She must not only be helpless, held captive by Adamus and his cruel gang, but she would be alone and unable to see those who cared about her.

As we began our journey back to the dreadful town of Exilio, I put aside my thoughts about my nightmare and my doubts about Leon and his true intentions, focusing on figuring out how Leon and I would complete the mission for the wise woman Delphi and come back alive.

Chapter 11:
Autumn's Breath

Amity, my mother, had always repeated one phrase to me as she put me to bed when I was a child: "Cherish all life, not just your own, but others' as well." When I asked her where she got that idea from, she said it was from my father. At that time I had been too young to question her, and she died soon after my fifth birthday, never allowing me the chance to learn more about my father. The Chief never spoke about my family, and so I never asked. I had always thought my father had to be a good person at heart for my mother to love him, but if so, why did he leave us? Why did he allow my mother to die?

My mother, my father, the hateful village, Sora, Leon, our mission, and the outside world. I had so much to figure out, yet it felt as if I had so little time to do so. Since I had fought Adamus, I had not heard the other voice inside my mind that I had learned was Sora, the will of my Ouranos stone. The clear-colored crystal lay as a necklace on my chest, just as most people wore their crystals in the village. As we finished our journey to the town of Exilio from Rosem City, I decided that I would put aside all thoughts other than rescuing Autumn, the daughter of the wise woman of Rosem known as Delphi.

Leon and I arrived at Exilio when the moon seemed be at

its brightest, surrounded by the pure darkness of the night sky. We quickly passed the place where we had encountered Adamus last, marked by the still-damaged building Adamus had smashed into during my attack. We snuck up upon the side of the inn where we had been imprisoned and eventually reached the outskirts of the town without being spotted. Occasionally, one of Adamus's patrol thugs would walk through the center of the road with a candle. When he reached the end of the town, he'd turn around and walk back towards the other side.

"We need to find out where Autumn is located," declared Leon as we stood on the side of the inn.

"And how do we do that?" I looked across the street at Adamus's house, also used as the headquarters for his gang.

"There are only two places they would keep her, I would think," replied Leon in a whisper. "The inn, or that man's home."

I shook my head in agreement, and we decided that checking the inn first would be easiest. We waited for the patrol to pass by us twice as he paced along and began his walk back to the other side of town. We quietly made our way to the inn door, one of us standing on each side of it. Leon nodded, and I opened the door. We waited for a response, my knife in one hand, Leon's swords in both of his. After a few of seconds of silence, we decided that it was safe and entered the inn. We closed the door behind us, and everything grew dark without the light of the candles on the porch outside.

"Stay at the door to make sure no one comes," directed Leon. All I could see of him in the darkness was his glowing eyes. Their normal brown color had disappeared to be replaced by a yellowish color that shone bright enough for me to almost make out his face. "I'll check the room."

"Okay," I replied as Leon walked away to check.

In exchange for bringing back her daughter, Delphi had promised to tell us how we could locate and retrieve the Unmei collection. When we had asked her about it, she had called it by another name: the three Artifacts of Destiny. I still didn't know what they were, nor what they were able to do, but the name sounded intense—and then there was the fact that the Council, who had gone so far out of their way to get me killed, wanted them. The collection couldn't be good thing, even if they said it was. I jumped a little as I felt a hand on my back.

"Nothing here, no good. She has to be in the house," said Leon as I turned to face his glowing eyes.

"We must avoid Adamus at all costs," I said as I remembered what Sora had told me while I had been in the white world the second time... *You cannot beat Adamus.*

"Yes," agreed Leon. "But it'll be different this time, I

promise. That is, if we must meet him."

"How so?" I asked. He had been defeated far too easily when we had fought Adamus before.

"It doesn't matter right now," replied Leon. I was getting a little tired of that particular response.

"Okay," I said, holding back my frustration. "Let's go."

We opened the inn door a crack to make sure that the patrol was not around before quickly leaving the inn, closing the door behind us. After crossing the road and walking up to Adamus's door, we turned around in surprise as we heard a voice.

"Hey!" said a tall, thin, skinny bald man. He wore a sword on his right hip. "Who are you?" he asked as he stopped a few feet in front of us.

"Ahh..." I began as Leon interrupted.

"We come bearing gifts from Rosem for Autumn," said Leon with a smile. *What is he doing?* I thought.

"Oh?" said the man. "Why would Rosem send gift-bearers for a kidnapped girl?" He unsheathed his sword, grabbing Leon's shirt and holding the sword to his neck.

"My friend," said Leon with less confidence, "we are among the few who support her marriage to the Great Adamus of Exilio. Please let us show our support for your master by letting us deliver Autumn her gifts."

The man brought his sword up as if he was about to slash Leon's throat, but instead he sheathed his sword and smiled.

"Good men!" he said as he patted Leon on the back. "I am Jaimei. Come inside. I will take you to Autumn."

Jaimei opened the door to the house and motioned for us to enter. After walking inside, I recognized the large, chair-like structure that I had hidden behind before—this time with four men sitting on it—and the staircase on the left side of the door that led upstairs. The four men on the large structure paid us no attention as they continued to laugh, drink, and talk to each other.

"Don't mind them," said Jaimei. "They're just having a good time. Come upstairs."

We followed Jaimei upstairs, trying to look like we weren't nervous. At the top was a hallway. Down it to the left was a room where Adamus's voice could be heard and to the right a closed door. Jaimei began to walk to the left, while Leon and I looked nervously at each other.

"Jaimei, my friend," I began. He stopped on the way to what seemed likely to be Adamus's room. "Let us bring the gifts to Autumn before we greet your master Adamus?"

"Why would you want to do that?" he asked as Leon began to try to sneak his arm to the sheathed swords on his back. I couldn't think of a way to persuade him to allow us to see Autumn before trying to bring us to Adamus, and it seemed Leon couldn't either. It looked as if Jaimei would turn around and keep walking any second, when a voice resonated through my mind.

"Respect."

I opened my mouth and said the first thing that came to my mind: "Out of respect for the lady." Jaimei laughed.

"It's about time the master's new wife had some respect shown to her. Fine," he said as he began walking toward the door next to the stairs. Taking a key from his pocket, he opened the door and motioned us inside. Leon and I walked in.

The room behind the door was cold and small. The walls were painted pitch black, and in the center was a lone pillow with a girl sitting on it, her back to us

"You have visitors," said Jaimei with a laugh. "They bring you gifts for your wedding." The girl didn't turn around or make a sound. Jaimei looked at us as he spoke. "I will be downstairs grabbing a drink. Let me know when you are ready to see Adamus."

Jaimei walked out and closed the door, leaving it open only a crack, and the girl spoke as Jaimei's steps could be heard walking down the stairs.

"You bear gifts for such a tragedy?" She had the most beautiful voice I had ever heard; it sounded soothing, like a beautiful lullaby. As I opened my mouth and searched for something witty to say, she turned around to look at us, taking my breath. Her long, curly brown hair fell to cover her soft, beautiful, tan face. Pushing the hair back, she revealed her sweet lips and bright, brown, starry eyes, looking as if she could be a goddess. At that moment I couldn't think about anything, and it felt as if I couldn't take my eyes off her.

"Well?" she asked as her smile disappeared.

"Autumn," began Leon. Her name seemed to snap me from my trance. "We were sent by Delphi to bring you back to Rosem." For a second, a glimmer of hope seemed to show on Autumn's face, but it quickly disappeared.

"Is this a trick?" she asked, standing up. She stood only a few inches shorter than Leon and myself.

"No," replied Leon. "I promise." In an instant, the hope reappeared, and Autumn ran over to Leon and embraced him in a hug. I didn't know why, but I felt a little angry at Leon. It was weird for me to get angry over nothing, but I couldn't help myself.

"We've gotta go," I said as I pulled Leon from the hug.

"We're short on time."

"He's right," said Leon to Autumn. She turned to me and smiled, making me feel as if I were going to melt.

"What's your name?" she asked.

"Zephyr," I replied as she walked up to me and put her mouth to my ear.

"Thank you, Zephyr," she whispered. "Such a wonderful name."

I suddenly felt better, but I didn't have time to worry about such small things as I remembered the situation we were in. Leon opened the door slowly, peering down the hall to make sure no one was in sight. He led the way as we began to walk down the stairs, Autumn following behind me. When we reached the bottom of the staircase, we couldn't hear a sound, unlike when we had first entered. Leon smiled as he nodded for us to continue to the door.

I looked at the chair-like object to find that all four of the men who had been drinking before, now with Jaimei, lay there passed out. I couldn't help but smile. We were lucky. Leon quickly opened the door as we followed him out of the house, closing the door behind us. Still afraid to make too much noise, we all waited a few seconds to make sure another patrol wasn't around.

As we walked away from Exilio, Autumn looked up at the sky. Exilio began to look farther and farther away as we continued back to Rosem. Leon's eyes glowed brightly in the night, and Autumn seemed to have a similar but more elegant glow herself.

"You don't understand what you've done for me," said Autumn suddenly. "Thank you so much."

"It's nothing," both Leon and I said.

"I will repay you myself once we return to Rosem," she stated, still staring at the moon.

"Why did you trust us?" I asked, then tripped over a rock. Leon and Autumn both laughed.

"Your friend looked so serious," she said as she turned her eyes towards Leon.

"I'm Leon," he stated.

"And you," she said as she looked at me. "You looked so sincere. Nothing like the men from Exilio."

"Oh," I said. I wasn't too sure what she meant, but I was thankful that we didn't need to fight or encounter Adamus on our way to get her. Delphi had described her daughter simply, but to me she looked as beautiful as a goddess, if they had ever existed.

While Leon led, Autumn and I looked up at the night sky

as we made our way towards Rosem. A few more hours and I would be able to continue my journey with Leon to find the truth about my family and the village, and to prove myself not only to the villagers, but to myself.

Chapter 12:
Tyring

The walk from Exilio to Rosem wasn't as exciting as the rescue mission had been. Leon walked slowly, and Autumn and I trailed behind, barely saying anything most of the way. We explained what happened to us since we had left the village, but after hearing it all Autumn didn't ask about anything else, and we walked on in silence.

We arrived at the gates of Rosem City with the dawn. We quickly entered through the gate into the huge market square area that had been empty when we left. Instead of being clear and easy to navigate, it was now overcrowded, filled with hundreds of moving people. Unlike Dentro Village, where everyone wore a similar style of shorts, t-shirts, and sandals, the people of Rosem's style varied greatly. Some woman wore long dresses, while others wore long pants of different colors. The men wore shorts or long pants, and their shirts were covered by puffy jackets or large over-shirts with hoods.

Each person, whether with family or by themselves, quickly moved around from shop stall to shop stall, buying food, clothes, weapons, and more. Autumn and I continued to follow Leon as we forced ourselves through the mass of people in the market square. Just before we could reach the other side of the square, I lost sight of Leon. I glanced back towards Autumn, but she was nowhere to be seen.

I quickly turned in a full circle to see where Leon and Autumn had gone, but to no avail. All of a sudden, I felt lost in the mass of people. The whirl of bodies was pressing in on me, and it was getting harder and harder to breathe. Suddenly, I turned around as I felt a hand as soft as sand take mine, guiding me through the people. I turned to see Autumn holding my hand and smiling as we stood with Leon next to the Rosem inn.

"I'm guessing you have never been around so many people in such a small space," said Autumn in her angelic voice. I opened her mouth to agree, but nothing came out as all I could do was gaze at her beauty.

"He still has a lot to learn, even though he's older than me," said Leon, smiling. "Come on, Delphi is waiting."

We reached the top level of the mountain city after walking up each level of steps. Delphi's hut hadn't changed—a dark blue color with Sea stone walls modeled like the buildings of Dentro Village. We entered Delphi's house, Leon still leading.

A few feet away from the door, exactly where we had seen Delphi having lunch, stood a large, muscular man who towered over both Leon and me—bald and wearing all black, his muscles clearly bulging through his long pants and t-shirt. He looked at us and smiled.

"Didn't think you would be so scrawny," said the man in a low, soft voice, looking down at Leon and me. Autumn quietly squeezed between us until her gaze fell upon the man. Suddenly, she ran and hugged him as his arms circled around her.

"Brother!" she exclaimed. "You're here!" Tears began to run down her face as Leon and I looked at each other awkwardly.

"Autumn," said her brother, smiling. A wrinkled hand appeared on the man's arm as Delphi made her appearance. Unlike before, when she had seemed sad and tired, it looked as if energy and happiness were flowing through her.

Autumn slowly let go of her brother while Delphi turned her intense gaze on us. "You have done well," she stated. The man walked towards us and grasped each of us by the shoulder.

"Thank you for rescuing my sister from that thief Adamus. I am Endriago, Autumn's older brother. Come sit." He guided us to where we had sat on our recent visit. Autumn and Delphi slowly walked up the stairs as we sat down and Endriago took a seat in front of us.

"We are glad to have returned your sister," said Leon in a serious tone, "but Delphi has promised us something in return."

"I know," stated Endriago. "My mother and sister will be back soon."

"Thanks," I said quickly, trying to brighten the conversation.

While we waited for Delphi to return, we explained how it had been fairly simple to rescue Autumn, since we had been very lucky not to have encountered Adamus. In turn, Endriago explained a little about himself and Autumn.

Apparently, two large and powerful cities, many times larger than Rosem, were at war. One had threatened Rosem that if it did not send fighters to help them wage the war, they would destroy Rosem itself. Rosem's city council had agreed, and Endriago, known to be Rosem's greatest fighter, had been one of the warriors chosen to go.

Endriago also explained that Delphi had seen a vision of his death in the future, and they had thought that he had already been killed. Word around the village had spread, and Adamus had somehow also found out. Taking the chance to kidnap the unprotected Autumn, the beautiful daughter of Rosem's oracle, he took her while Endriago was presumed dead.

He continued his story but explained that Autumn was special not only because of her status and beauty, but because she had the power to speak to non-human creatures, along with other abilities.

"All of the powerful men from different cities seek her hand in marriage as a way to take control of Autumn and her abilities. They wish to control and use her for their own greed, but as her older brother, I would not allow them to do so," finished Endriago with an angry tone.

"Calm down, my son," said Delphi as she walked up behind Endriago. "Go rest and attend to your sister. I must speak alone with these boys."

Endriago smiled at us then gave his mother a kiss on the cheek as his large and bulky figure walked up the stairs. Delphi slowly sat down, and she began to drill into us with her deep gaze.

"You did well, and so I thank you," Delphi said as she smiled. "I shall fulfill our agreement." Leon and I looked at each other, trying to hold back our smiles.

"Thank you," we both finally said.

"What is the Unmei collection?" I asked. Delphi slowly ran her hand through her long white hair as the wrinkles on her forehead seemed to increase in number. "The ancient word Unmei means Destiny."

"The Destiny collection," I thought aloud, and Leon and Delphi looked at me as if I were slow. "Sorry, continue," I said, shrugging it off with a smile.

"The collection is made up of three magical items: the Spear of Destiny, the Valkyrie Shield, and the Tyring Sword. Throughout this world there are many magical and ancient items, but the three that comprise the Unmei collection are the most powerful," said Delphi.

"Three items," repeated Leon slowly, as if taking it in. Delphi waited a moment to allow us to sit with our thoughts, then continued.

"The spear, the shield, and the sword each posses powers beyond any human or crystal—" she glanced at our necklaces, "—could ever have. Or at least any normal human or crystal."

"What powers?" I asked. She made them sound like godly weapons.

"It is said that for each new master of each item, they bestow different powers. Long ago, a master of the Spear of Destiny was said to have been able to manipulate anything he wanted. The same man was the only one to have two of the collection items together, as he also possessed the Valkyrie Shield. He is said to have used it to save his home city from destruction long ago, during an ancient war."

It was hard to really comprehend what Delphi was telling

us, but it began to make sense why the Council would want the Unmei collection. Leon looked at me as if he were thinking the same thing.

"So," I said, "Where and how do we find these items?"

Surprisingly, Delphi's serious expression changed to amusement.

"So young and eager…the foolishness of youth."

I coughed but held back from saying anything, as I wanted her to continue.

"The Spear of Destiny disappeared long ago, and I do not currently know of its whereabouts. And the Valkyrie Shield and the Tyring Sword, although I know where they are, will not be easy to retrieve," said Delphi.

"Wouldn't be fun if they were," said Leon.

"Your cockiness is foolish and ridiculous!" exclaimed Delphi. "But I must keep my agreement. First, you must know that all of the items in the collection will bestow their wielders some amount of power, but only the ones the items choose will be able to use their powers to the fullest extent. Endriago informed you of the two cities that are currently at war, yes?"

"Yes," we both replied.

"The two cities, Cheshria and Sleeves, are the most powerful cities in this region of the world, known as Tyring."

I tried to not look lost or dumbfounded with the terms she was using, but it didn't seem to work too well.

"I know you are not from Tyring, but you must learn about this region quickly if you wish to find the Unmei collection," Delphi declared, looking directly at me.

"We understand," said Leon. "But where are the shield and sword?"

"The sword is in Cheshria and the shield in Sleeves," answered Delphi.

"Should have guessed," I said.

"Cheshria is a dark city run by a council of powerful dictators, and their leader has possession of the Tyring sword. Although the leader of Cheshria has not been chosen by the sword, he is very powerful nonetheless and tricks his people into believing that he has been. Sleeves is powerful, but is also a peaceful city that is trying only to defend itself from Cheshria's attempted takeover," explained Delphi.

"So the Council of Cheshria and their leader seek the Valkyrie Shield, and so they are trying to take over Sleeves?" asked Leon.

"Yes," replied Delphi. "The people of Cheshria are known to be greedy and proud, and their king has told them that they must prove their will and power to the rest of the region by obtaining the shield and destroying Sleeves."

I laughed to myself as Delphi finished.

"I hate people like that," I said, with an angrier tone than I had intended.

"Somewhere along your journey, I am sure by retrieving the two items that you know of you, will find the missing piece of the collection. That is, if you can succeed," said Delphi, with an all-knowing tone and look.

"Thank you," said Leon.

"Wait," I interjected quickly. "One more thing." I took my bag off my back and grabbed my gloves. "Adamus of Exilio wanted these, enough to try to kill me. Why?"

Delphi snatched the gloves from my hands. Her eyes widened as she examined them.

"Who gave these to you, Zephyr?" she asked without taking her eyes off the gloves.

"My father left them to me. Why?" I replied.

"I see," she whispered. "I understand, but it is not my place to tell you. You must find out for yourself about the gift your father left behind for you. It will be a great help to you in the future, I am sure. Remember one thing, though. Those gloves are not for you alone, but also for another with a destiny similar to yours."

After she handed the gloves back, I still had more questions, but I decided that we had gotten what we came for and it was time to get ready to leave. As if reading my mind, Delphi spoke.

"Both Cheshria and Sleeves are located to the north of here, shortly before you come to the mountains known as Devil's Pass."

I laughed again without thinking.

"Devil's Pass?" I mimicked.

"That mountain area is not for the weak. It is the pathway out of Tyring and into the other regions of the world. It is filled with monsters and demons with powers beyond your imagination that boys as weak as yourselves could not handle in the least," said Delphi. That stung, but she was right. We couldn't even defeat one man who had a crystal like ours. "But do not worry. For now, decide which city you wish to travel to first, as you'll reach them before the mountains. I will have transportation ready for you to show my true gratitude for saving my daughter. Now, please leave."

I looked around and waited, hoping Autumn would come and say goodbye as we began to leave, but neither she nor Endriago appeared. Leon and I quickly made our way to the Rosem inn, paid for our room, and made ourselves comfortable where we had stayed the night before.

As the light from the outside slowly faded and disappeared, the room became completely dark. Leon and I lay in our beds. Leon was the first to speak.

"You asleep?" he asked in a whisper. I laughed and looked over towards his bed to see two small, faint yellow lights flicker as he blinked.

"No," I replied.

"What are we gonna do?" he asked.

"What do you mean?" But of course I knew what he was talking about.

"With the Unmei collection, if we are able to get it, I mean," he said, sounding less confident than usual.

I decided on impulse not to let Leon know that I didn't have a plan yet for how to force the village to change for the better or to get rid of the corrupt Council, while also forcing them all to recognize me. So I lied.

"Complete our mission and give the Unmei collection to the Council," I said, thinking to myself that if I ever felt like Leon had gained my trust again, I would confide my plans to him and tell him the truth. It would be nice to have a real friend. *Maybe that's why I went back and saved him from Adamus…* But before I could continue to think, Leon surprised me.

“I'm sorry about how the villagers treated you. They—I mean we—haven't been fair.”

I couldn't help but laugh out loud as Leon's words resonated in my mind. I thought back to all of the days when I was a child and had watched all the other kids play with each other; I would be alone, because their parents would not let me join. I remembered my mother dying, myself calling for help, crying helplessly, and no one but the Chief coming to my aid as my mother died right before my eyes.

“Yeah,” I said as I flipped over to sleep on my stomach, closing my eyes. “Thanks, Leon. Good night.”

“Good night,” Leon replied.

Chapter 13:
Vanishing

Early the next morning, we decided that Cheshria would be our first destination, as the Tyring Sword would be an asset against people like Adamus that we might encounter in the future. We quickly ate the breakfast that we had bought at the market, finishing just in time to hear a knock on the inn room door.

"You there?!" a familiar low, soft voice exclaimed. I walked to the door and opened it to see Endriago standing outside the inn. "Zephyr! Good, you're both up," said Endriago as he peered behind me to look at Leon. "When you're ready to leave, come to the gates of Rosem where you entered. Your transportation awaits. Have you decided where you're headed?"

"Cheshria," I answered. Endriago's expression immediately dimmed.

"That city forces smaller cities like Rosem to fight for them. They are demonic people," said Endriago with a frown. "But you do what you must. I will see you outside the gates."

With that, Endriago's large, muscular figure disappeared, and I closed the door behind him. I already didn't like the sound of Cheshria, but we had to go. Leon and I cleaned up the room, grabbed our things, and left the inn a few minutes after

Endriago's departure. We walked through the city of Rosem, slowly passing through the marketplace. Although it was not as full it had been the day before, there were still many people crowded into the small area. As we reached the gates, I stopped and looked back up at the mountain city one last time.

"Come on," said Leon quickly.

I had no idea what Delphi had meant when she had said she would provide transportation, but as I looked a few feet beyond the gate, I gaped in amazement. In front of us stood a large, square, red wooden object with four circular contraptions on the corners lifting it a few feet off the ground. On the side facing us was a door that looked awkwardly placed so that people could enter, with two windows on each side of the door. Attached to the box were two long, black ropes, and on the other side of the ropes was a large, lizard-like creature with Endriago sitting on its back.

"Finally here, I see," Endriago said as he turned to look at us from his seat on the creature. "This is a Tokage carriage."

"A what?" I asked. The lizard-like creature Endriago sat on was twice as large as the carriage itself, which looked large enough to fit at least four people.

"This Tokage," said Endriago, as he patted the bright red lizard, "is named Priv. He's very fast and smart. Even with his speed, it will still take us a couple of hours to reach the outskirts of Cheshria, so get in the carriage and make yourselves at home. I'll let you know when we arrive."

Leon walked over to the carriage door, opened it, and moved inside. I followed suit, getting in on the other side. Inside the carriage were two cushioned seats that stretched the length of the walls. As I looked above, I noticed four candles, one hanging off each of the corners. Most likely they were needed for nighttime, as right now the sunlight was bright enough.

"Different, but nice," expressed Leon, as the feeling of being in motion that I had experienced riding the Utsu boat began. "Your crystal," said Leon as he looked out at the scenery from the window. "How well can you communicate with it?"

I hadn't really thought about learning to control my crystal. After being called to see the Council, the excitement of awakening it had been put aside in favor of the idea of the mission and having the chance to explore outside the village. Unlike myself, though, most villagers received basic training from teachers after awakening their crystals so they would be able to grow by training in their own free time.

"I don't really know how," I admitted. "It's just seemed to happen, mostly, like a dream, when I've been in trouble."

"That's good. You haven't had any training, yet you have

at least spoken with your crystal's will. But it seems that Dentro isn't the only place that has the ancient crystals, as we have seen from Adamus. I can tell you how to communicate with your crystal, but that's all I can help you with, as we have different crystal types."

"Thanks," I said as I wrapped my hand around my necklace. "So how?"

"It's kind of like meditating," replied Leon as he turned his focus on me. "You relax your mind and body as much as possible and envision your stone in your mind as you close your eyes. While filling your mind with thoughts of your crystal, imagine the place where you feel most relaxed. From there, it'll be easy." Leon sighed. "We still have a long way to go."

"Sounds easy enough," I said.

"Try it now. I'll wake you up when Endriago tells us we're getting close."

I sat back on the seat, leaning against the wall, closing my eyes and trying to relax. I let go of my thoughts about Cheshria, which was easier than I thought it would be, and began to fill my mind with an image of a beach. Slowly it felt as if everything around me were disappearing; the surrounding hot, sticky air was replaced by a warm climate and a cool breeze, the hard seat of the carriage now the soft sand on a beautiful beach, and all of my stress and tension completely released, as if it had never existed.

"Welcome back," said Sora's familiar flowing voice as I opened my eyes.

In front of me was a beach I had never seen before. I sat on the sand, warm ocean water washing up against my feet. I turned around to see that the island I was on was not the village beach I had imagined, but a much more beautiful and calming place. The island seemed to be filled with lush sky trees, but with no buildings or people around aside from Sora and me.

"Where is this?" I asked. "What happened to that empty space? I looked up at Sora as he smiled at me, wiping a few strands of his brown hair from in front of his wide blue eyes as he had done the last time we had met.

"That world from before is called the Empty Plane," replied Sora. His blue eyes shone so brightly with the sun that it was hard to look up at him. "This wonderful place is in the deepest part of your mind, your own creation if you will, known as the Soul Mirror. It is where you can relax the most and we can communicate freely."

"Oh." I gasped as I looked around at how amazing this place was.

It was like a dream resort, a place I would go to relax and

get away. The funny thing was that it was my creation, and I was truly surprised that I had imagined such an amazing place. "To be honest, I don't know what to do now." Leon had only told me how to enter this state, not how to control my powers or get stronger.

"Zephyr," said Sora as he turned around to face the endless ocean. "What have you come here for?"

"I want to get stronger," I answered bluntly.

"Why?" asked Sora as he sat down next to me, still gazing at the ocean, as I had gazed into the sky so often as a child. I had always seemed to be drawn to the clouds.

"I want to be recognized," I admitted. "I don't ever want to be looked down on again, nor do I want anyone else to be." But as I answered Sora's questions, and really my own, my doubts that I had put aside suddenly rose up. Could I really do it? Maybe I really wasn't supposed to have been born...*or maybe I am truly just a failure, like everyone thinks.*

"Zephyr," repeated Sora, this time turning his gaze upon me. "I cannot give you all the answers to your own questions of doubt, but you must understand that to believe in yourself and that you can accomplish anything, even when others don't believe in you, is just as important as having others believe that you can accomplish your goals. Maybe even more important.

When you truly believe in yourself, people who believe in you will find you in time."

As Sora finished, I looked back at him, turned towards the ocean, and laughed. Sora looked like he was going to respond, but instead he began to burst out laughing also.

"Yeah," I said, suddenly shifting back to a serious tone, "I will believe in myself from now on. But I have to make everyone recognize me. I have to become stronger."

"I agree," said Sora. "We are partners. I am your heart of hearts and your crystal. We are tied as one. Together, we will make you a true man of the world."

"I like how that sounds," I said, laughing again. "Last time we met, you said I had no skills and couldn't control my powers."

"Yes," agreed Sora. "When you use our power, the power of the crystal, we must be one not only in soul, but in mind and body also."

"Be one?" I asked, sticking my right hand under the soft sand and feeling its warmth envelop my fingers.

"We are connected and awakened within your soul, which is why you can hear my voice in your mind in times of need. When you hear my voice, the crystal will shine a bright blue color, and you will feel stronger, faster, and more confident. Your mind and thought process will be clearer, and your senses will be enhanced greatly. To summon me, you must do so from your heart of hearts; picture the image you know as me, and call my name with your true intent in mind. That is all," said Sora.

"Sounds simple enough," I stated. "But from there, how do I use my powers? Like that ball of energy I shot at Adamus?"

"That ball of wind energy is called the Sky Pushuu," said Sora flatly. "It is a basic attack that, when done properly, propels the opponent at a high speed, but at your current level it takes a lot of energy. To use the Sky Pushuu, you must place your hands in front of your body, focusing all of your energy into them. After you do so, you must imagine the feeling of warm and cool air combining to form a sphere, like the one you made before. Then, from your mind and using your power, it will form. Try it."

I pulled my hand out of the sand and stood up, facing the ocean.

"Will I get tired?" I asked.

"No," replied Sora quickly. "Here, your energy level does not drop, because we are within your own mind and plane. When you come to this world in a healthy and relaxed state like now, instead of an almost dead one like before, the effects are different. You may stay as long as you wish here, for example. Any training that occurs in this world also produces results in the real world. But understand, your stamina is what it is and does not increase, although it does not decrease. Understand?"

"Yeah," I said. *So whatever I currently have enough energy to do, I can do as many times as I want, but I can't do anything that would require more energy than I currently have.* "Here goes."

I began by placing my hands in front of me, palms facing the ocean, while thinking of the warm and cool air mixing together. As I did so, I started to imagine the two different winds combining into a visible ball; suddenly, all around my hands, air seemed to be moving. Around my left, cool air, and around my right, hot air, accompanied by a crackling sound. Slowly, in front of my hands, a small ball, blue but almost clear, the size of my fist, began to take a shape. Before, I had launched a sphere the size of a person's head at Adamus. This ball looked like a pebble in comparison.

"Why is it so different?" I asked as my thoughts moved away from creating the sphere and onto why it was so small. But as soon as I did so, the sphere and the air rotating around it stopped, and a small shockwave violently pushed me backwards and onto the ground as it slowly dissipated.

"You lost your concentration," said Sora, helping me up from the sand. "It seems that a small Sky Pushuu is all you can currently handle."

I sighed and dropped to the ground, laughing and facing the empty blue sky in defeat.

"How can I make it bigger and stronger?" I asked.

"Practice." Sora dipped his feet in the ocean water. "Just practice, and train. But there is only so much I can teach you without you having a human teacher."

"But if I can only use the energy I have, which seems to only allow me to make this small ball, how will practice help me get stronger and increase the size?" I asked in confusion.

"You have the wrong basic idea, my friend," replied Sora. "Although you are limited to the amount of energy you have when you enter this plane, that does not mean you can automatically control all of that energy. Essentially, although you have not begun to tap into the potential energy you have and you only have a small amount of it now, you cannot completely control even that small amount yet—you can't utilize your energy. Training here will produce immediate effects both here and in the outer world."

After what felt like hours of agony practicing the Sky Pusshu, I was finally able to control the wind energy sphere without too much thought. It increased in size after time, growing to the size of two fists instead of one. After launching the energy ball at the ocean and seeing its small explosion on impact, I lay back down on the soft sand, worn out.

"Sora," I called as he lay down next to me on the sand, looking up at the bright, blue, cloud-filled sky. "What do you think of Leon?"

"He is strong," answered Sora. "But I sense he battles great darkness within himself. And let me tell you now, as we near Cheshria, I sense many powerful and great evils in the city. One of them is a darkness so powerful and demonic, I can feel the crystal's power from here, trying to envelop us in darkness. Leon may not show it, but his aura is that of one who is constantly fighting darkness."

"Wow," was all I could say. Cheshria was looking dimmer and dimmer, along with our hope of getting the Tyring Sword. It seemed Endriago was right about Cheshria being a dark place. The main thing was, though, that I hoped the dark force Sora had mentioned wasn't the leader who Delphi said possessed and controlled the sword.

"You must go," said Sora suddenly. "Leon calls for you to awake."

"Great," I said sarcastically.

"You can come here anytime you wish," stated Sora, standing up. "I will be in your mind, just call. But know you will notice subtle differences as you reenter the real world. Every time you call or come to this world, our connection and powers grow stronger as one."

"Differences?" I asked in wonder.

"Close your eyes, and relax," said Sora, and I followed his directions without much thought. I didn't want to leave the island, but I had to go back; as I reminded myself of reality, I opened my eyes to see Leon's glowing eyes staring at me.

"We're nearly there." Leon motioned for me to look out the window. The landscape was completely covered in dirt, with nothing familiar from our earlier travels. Instead, it was filled with red trees and small green plants everywhere on the ground, no taller than an inch. Looking downward from the window, the circular contraptions attached to the carriage moved along a small dirt road.

"Did he say?" I asked Leon, as I took in the view of a seemingly endless number of red trees.

"No, I just woke you for no reason," said Leon with a sarcastic but joking tone. "Yes, we will arrive shortly, Endriago said. How did your meeting go?"

"Well," I replied, no longer able to hold back a smile from what I would call a success. "I learned a little, and I've become a little stronger in doing so. But there's still much I have to do."

"Yeah," said Leon. "Us both. We've got to devise a plan to retrieve the sword."

I nodded in agreement. But in all honesty, I had no idea how we were going to take a weapon that was probably heavily guarded from a person who was just as heavily guarded, not to mention dangerous, while in a strange city.

"Ideas?" I asked with an empty look.

"We could ask Endriago for—" But before Leon could finish his sentence, the carriage came to an abrupt halt.

Leon and I looked at each other, then stuck our heads out the windows to look towards where Endriago sat on Priv, the large, red lizard. A few feet in front of Endriago stood a large, closed gate with two guards. The guards, after whispering to themselves, slowly began to walk closer to Endriago. Both wore chest armor and leg platelets, and they each held a spear in one hand and a paper and red pencil in the other.

"Name and business in Cheshria?" asked one guard as they stopped on each side of Endriago. In Cheshria? But as I looked beyond the gates, for as far I could see, there seemed to be only more gates and no city.

"I come seeking tools for the great Oracle of Rosem, Delphi. I am Endriago of the Delphi house," stated Endriago, his large figure towering over the guards as he sat on the lizard.

"The Oracle, Delphi, I see," said the guard while taking a glance at the carriage. "And what is inside the Tokage?"

"Servants of Delphi who accompany me," replied Endriago. "May we enter?"

The two guards began to walk towards the carriage, but instead looked at each other, nodded, and turned around. After returning to the gate post, the two guards lifted the lever that opened the gate and motioned us to enter.

"Welcome to Cheshria, Endriago of the house of Delphi," said the guards in unison.

Slowly, the carriage moved towards the gate, while Leon and I kept our heads out the window. But as Endriago and the lizard passed through the gate, something unexpected occurred. First Priv's head, then its red body, and then Endriago's large figure completely disappeared from view.

"What!" I exclaimed.

Leon looked just as surprised as I felt. "Impossible!" The rest of the carriage began to disappear from view, including Leon, the windows as we passed the smiling guards, and then myself. As I looked down, my feet, legs, and chest completely vanished before my eyes, to my despair. As I gazed down at myself, a head without a body, my chin also quickly disappeared. Unable to witness my death, or rather disappearance, I closed my eyes, hoping that this wasn't going to be the end already.

Chapter 14:
Flash Change

It was cold. Not like a breeze that may seem chilly for a few seconds, but it actually, really cold, like the sun itself had died. A few moments ago, I had been afraid that Leon, Endriago, Priv the lizard and I had been disappearing to our deaths. I'm glad to say that was not the case. What was really happening was more interesting; at least, I thought it was.

I opened my eyes, after an intense blast of cold air surrounded me, to find myself still in the carriage. I exhaled, and I could see my breath clearly as it traveled from my mouth into the outside area. This never happened in Dentro, as the climate was warm year-round; as I looked forward towards Leon, I found that he had a similar surprised expression on his face.

"Wow," Leon said as he gasped and exhaled again and again, like a child getting his first toy. Slowly, the feeling of motion from the carriage came back, and I decided that I should look out the window. I was a little afraid that I would find a white space, like the Empty Plane where I had first met Sora, but instead I was pleasantly surprised to find it was something entirely different.

Outside the window stood hundreds and hundreds of buildings, each seemingly larger than the last, towering over the carriage. They were all made of a wood-like material colored either light blue or gray. On top of each building and surrounding them was a white, fluffy-looking substance.

"What's that?" I asked Leon.

"How would I know?" he retorted. "But this is just, I mean, wow."

"Yeah," was all I could say in reply. As the carriage slowly lurched onward, we could see people everywhere on both sides of the carriage. It looked as though we were on a road, but unlike Exilio, which only had one main road, Cheshria seemed to have the large road we were on and also many smaller roads that connected throughout the city.

Filled with the soft white substance and the people, the streets were far from boring. Between each row of houses lay a long street that seemed to stretch as far as I could see. Kids played with each other, jumping in the white fluff (as I named it), and adults everywhere seemed to be rushing away somewhere. Carriages similar to ours passed by on the other side of the road, but instead of being pulled by red lizard creatures, they were pulled by light blue or gray ones.

Unlike Leon and me, in our shorts and t-shirts, all of the people we passed wore long pants, fluffy jackets, and either a hat or hood filled with fur pulled over their heads. After what felt like a long hour of riding through the city, taking rights and lefts on smaller streets and passing large buildings with identifying signs ranging from "Inn" to "Armory," the carriage finally came to a stop. A few seconds later, Endriago knocked on the carriage door as a sign to get out. Leon opened the door and placed his foot on the ground, then suddenly lost his balance and fell.

"It's slippery," said Leon, looking away from me in embarrassment. "You'll see."

Sure enough, by stepping on the same place as Leon without thinking it through, I also slipped and fell on the ground. After a few seconds of relearning how to stand and walk correctly in such a different climate, I decided to focus on where we had stopped. I looked up just in time to see Endriago enter a gray building on the right side of the carriage. The sign on the door read "Tall Tales."

"Sounds like a book," I said as Leon and I entered the building after Endriago.

The inside of the building had two floors. The first was a bar and restaurant occupied by a few people. Leon and I followed Endriago into the bar, sitting down next to him as the bartender smiled at us.

"Endriago, and friends," said the tall, middle-aged bartender, who reminded me of Hovan but without his sinister aura. “What can I get for you?”

“Just water for the three of us,” answered Endriago as the bartender gave him a confused look. “Long trip, don't want to get drunk while having to watch over these two.”

“I see,” said the bartender, laughing and putting three glasses of water in front of us. “What brings you here this time?”

“Times are hard, as you know, Jae. I've come on Oracle business,” replied Endriago, draining his water in one gulp.

“Yes, true for us all,” stated Jae. “And these two?”

“Friends,” answered Endriago while Jae poured him another water. “What’s happening in Cheshria now?”

“The king and his Council have imposed a higher tax on all goods, so I’ve been getting even fewer customers,” replied Jae while cleaning glasses behind the bar. “Sleeves is a strong city, and it does not budge. Although a lot of us want to take control of Sleeves, the king has changed. He’s made life much harder for Cheshrians since the war began.”

“Ah,” sighed Endriago. “Drunk with power, him and that Council of his.”

“It can be the only explanation,” said Jae. “The king has been growing even more powerful and cruel every day since the Tyring Sword chose him; I fear it’s only a matter of time before he turns his back on his people. But I’m just a bartender, what can I do."

For a few moments, Endriago and Jae did not speak as the mood dampened, while Leon and I sat awkwardly next to Endriago. In an effort to lift the mood, I tried to change the subject.

"Sir," I said as respectfully as I could to the bartender, "every person, no matter their status, is valuable. Your king must surely think that."

"So young and innocent," said Jae as he smiled at me. "I thank you for your kind words, but not everyone thinks so simply. What is your name?"

"Zephyr," I answered.

"Where are you from?" he asked.

"Ah," I stuttered trying to think of a place to say, as the laws of the village forbade us from telling outsiders who did not already know of our home.

"It is okay," said Endriago. "He's an ally of Delphi and myself, he won't give away your secrets. You will need his help."

Leon looked at me and shrugged. I decided to trust Endriago's friend.

"We are from Dentro, a village on a small island far out at sea," I said.

"Dentro," repeated Jae. "Can't recall ever hearing of such

a place."

"Leon, Zephyr," said Endriago, "wait outside the bar for just a minute; I need to discuss something of importance with Jae before we continue."

"Okay," said Leon and I while getting up to leave.

"Careful of the snow," said Jae as we opened the exit door.

"The what?" I asked.

"This white stuff everywhere is called snow," said Jae while laughing. "It is easy to slip, be careful."

"Thanks," said Leon as we left and closed the door.

Leon and I stood outside the Tall Tales bar, gazing around at the city that surrounded us. After a few minutes, I turned towards the carriage that we had been in to find that the red lizard, Priv, looked like he was cold. I slowly began to walk over, and Leon noticed where I was going.

"Careful, Zephyr," said Leon as I walked up to the lizard that towered over me, twice as large as the carriage itself.

I stopped a few feet away. The Lizard turned its head towards me with an interested look, as if inviting me to come closer. Priv moved its large head downward so that it looked at me from the same level as I stood, its bright red eyes staring into mine. In the past, I had never had many interactions with creatures of any sort, but the intelligent-looking eyes of the red lizard brought the memory back of when I had fought the Barghest. For one moment, it had gazed into my eyes as if looking into my soul, just as the lizard seemed to be doing now.

Suddenly I felt even colder than I had before and a little confused at the same time. Throughout my mind, like a soft whisper, a snake-like voice resonated as if speaking to me. The voice spoke as if its words were my own thoughts, but at the same time I knew they were not. It continued to speak randomly as I held eye contact with the lizard. Although it sounded like a whisper, I could make out some of its words; *Who is this human boy, Why did master leave me out in this cold, I am thirsty.* I quickly looked away from the lizard as my head began to hurt.

What was that? The lizard's thoughts? No, they couldn't have been. Sora had never said anything about that. I must have been imagining it. As I was thinking of grabbing some water to give to the lizard just in case, the door to the bar opened and Endriago walked out.

"Sorry about that, boys," said Endriago as he walked up to Priv. "Ready?"

Both Leon and I nodded as we walked back over to the carriage.

"What now?" I asked before getting in, trying to hide the

fact that I felt sick.

"We head to the inn," said Endriago, strapping himself onto Priv's back. "Then I'll explain more. It's not safe outside here."

"Okay," I said as Leon and I both entered the carriage, closing the door behind us.

The ride to the inn felt like I was in hell. My head hurt more as time went on, and I felt as though my energy had been stolen from my body. The worst part was, I had no idea why, and did not want to tell Leon the ridiculous notion that I may have heard Priv's thoughts.

When we finally arrived at the inn, Endriago got two rooms, one for himself and one for Leon and me, and told us to meet him in his room in two hours. When I heard that we would have two hours to just relax, it felt as if a little of the pain in my head slowly began to go away.

Leon opened the door to the room, allowing me to rush in and jump on the closer of the two beds. Before I had even landed on the bed, my eyes were closed and all of my muscles relaxed. The pain that still ran through my head as if I had cracked it open slowly began to subside as I continued to relax, listening to Leon moving around the room.

"Are you okay?" he asked. I could tell from the direction

of his voice he was looking at me from the other bed.

"Yeah, just have a headache," I replied very slowly.

"Oh," said Leon. "You know what from?"

"No idea," I answered in an effort to end the conversation; it worked. After hearing Leon jump on his bed and stop making noise, I slowly began to drift off, losing my surroundings.

In the back of my mind, I expected and hoped to find Sora when I opened my eyes. But instead, I found that I was looking from a godly point of view, floating above the outside of Delphi's house. There, in front of the door, screaming, stood Delphi and her beautiful daughter Autumn. Even from a floating point of view, her lush, curly hair and goddess-like tan face made me weak.

"Autumn!" I yelled without thinking. I expected them to turn around and look in amazement at my flying figure, but it seemed as though they had not heard my call. "Autumn! Delphi!" I yelled again, to no avail. Realizing that for some reason they could not hear me, I instead focused on the intense-looking conversation they seemed to be having, as Autumn walked over to the edge of the mountain Delphi's house stood on.

"Mother," said Autumn, "let me go. I can help them."

"No," said Delphi as she focused her gaze on her

daughter. "It is not safe. You were already kidnapped once by such a foolish action, to go to Cheshria or beyond would surely be a wish of enslavement."

"So I have to live confined because of my gifts?" asked Autumn sarcastically.

"That is the fate of an Oracle," replied Delphi after a few seconds.

"I will not accept that, Mother." Autumn turned around and walked up to Delphi. "You may choose to live that way, but I will not. I will help those to whom I owe my life."

"You will not," commanded Delphi. "I will not allow you to put yourself in danger for what is not your destiny. I have rewarded those boys with the information they sought. That is enough. I will not allow you to leave the village. Now come back inside."

I blinked as Delphi finished her sentence, and all of a sudden the scenery changed. I was still floating outside of Delphi's house, but this time the sun was gone, replaced by the night sky and the moon. Hearing the creaking sound of the door opening, I looked down to find Autumn emerging from the house. Instead of the elegant dress she had worn before, she wore tight, dark blue pants, a fitted black shirt, and a mask that covered her face aside from her eyes and a little of her beautiful hair that poked out.

She closed the door, and I watched silently as she turned around, walking towards the steps leading down to the lower level of the mountain town. On her back lay a small black bag, and barely visible under a long black waste band were a sling shot and a small bag most likely filled with poisoned projectiles. Before stepping onto the stairs, Autumn turned around, gazed at her house for a few seconds, and then continued quietly down.

Wow, was all I could think. Autumn was defying her mother's orders and leaving Rosem dressed in the darkest clothing I had ever seen a girl wear. Our village tended to be filled with people who wore light colors as a way of uplifting our spirits, and so dark colors weren't common.

As Autumn walked down the steps, without knowing how, I continued to float behind her. It felt as if I were spying on her, but I still didn't understand how this was possible. So many things were happening so fast that hadn't been explained. It felt as if the world was spinning around me, too fast for me to catch up.

Reaching the lowest level of the mountain city, Autumn looked as if she were gliding as she began to run quickly and silently across the marketplace towards the gates of Rosem. Within seconds, surprisingly fast for anyone, she had crossed the large market area and slipped through the gates undetected. Without a doubt, not only was she amazingly beautiful and intelligent, she was swift and agile.

Pausing a second to take stock of her environment outside the city gates, she stood surrounded by an endless-looking desert. Placing her hands together with the index and middle fingers facing up and the rest of her left-hand fingers on top of her right, she opened her mouth, and under her a gray circle began to appear with lines of unreadable text inside it. But before she could utter a single word, someone else spoke from in front of her.

"The gods have surely shone upon us," said an all-too-familiar voice. Anger began to boil up inside of me just from the sound. "We were just about to come and retrieve you, my beauty," said Adamus as he and five other large men appeared from the darkness of the night.

As soon as he finished his sentence, two of the five men beside Adamus quickly ran up to Autumn and grabbed her arms. Not making a sound or even resisting, Autumn's gaze of pity hit Adamus so strongly that he opened his mouth, closed it, and opened it again before speaking.

"No struggle, my beautiful Autumn?" asked Adamus with a chuckle. "You have made this much easier, but this time we haven't only come for you."

Appearing from behind Adamus's shadow, a familiar tall, bald, skinny man walked up to face Autumn.

"Where are the two boys?" asked Jaimei, the man who had made saving Autumn from Adamus so easy. For some reason, though, he seemed a little different.

"I don't know," replied Autumn.

"Do not lie!" screamed Jaimei. "I have had to bear the weight of incompetence because of them!" This time I looked more closely at Jaimei, noticing that instead of the smooth face like he had when we had first met, he now had a scar that extended from the top of his right eye to the middle of his bald head. "She knows, Master," said Jaimei as he looked back to Adamus.

"Are you sure you will not tell us?" asked Adamus in a tone I think was meant to be sincere.

"Yes," replied Autumn simply.

"Make her tell," said Adamus as he nodded to all five of the men.

The two men holding Autumn slowly took out two swords, held in both their free hands, and placed the blades against her neck. From behind Adamus, the two other men walked up to Autumn, unsheathed their swords, and began to bring them down in a swing toward Autumn.

"No!" I yelled without thinking. "Autumn!"

Chapter 15:
Deadly Beauty

Beauty is a weakness for all. We may say that other attributes come into play when speaking of love, but the idea of liking only certain aspects of someone is illusion. The reality is that all of a person, the things that make them themselves, is what beauty truly is. That is how I once described beauty and love. But for me, at this exact moment, I found that my ideal had come face to face with it's first challenge.

From the first moment I had laid eyes on Autumn, I had been speechless just from the shock of how beautiful she was. Sure, there were many pretty girls in Dentro Village, but none could even begin to compete with Autumn. As I gazed at her, floating a few feet above her and Adamus's gang, only Autumn's beautiful curly hair and eyes were visible while she wore her dark blue, assassin-like suit. Even from this narrow a distance it was hard to see her, because her blue pants and black shirt blended in so well with the night.

Suddenly, I lost sight of Autumn completely as two of Adamus's men brought down their swords towards where she had just been held a few seconds before. I quickly looked around as the men gasped in amazement. Trying to see where she had disappeared to, I had no luck in locating her. It was like she had become invisible.

"Where is she?" yelled Adamus as he walked up with Jaimei to the other four men he had brought along.

"We don't know," answered all four men as they looked around quickly, visibly fearful of Adamus's response.

"I am here," said Autumn. I looked over toward her voice.

She was standing a few feet behind Adamus and Jaimei, her brown eyes almost glowing in the dark like a shining star in the night sky, while the rest of her body seemed to blend in and out of her surroundings.

"How did you do that?" Jaimei asked as he turned around with the rest of the group.

"Adamus," said Autumn as she began to walk towards him. "There is only one reason a group of your caliber was able to capture me. Don't think that you can do so again without the use of foul play."

Adamus and his group laughed so loudly that Autumn began to turn around and walk away, towards what I recognized as the place our journey to Cheshria had started.

"Whoa, missy!" yelled Adamus, causing Autumn to turn around. "Don't get too cocky now. You may be beautiful, but that doesn't mean we will go easy on you forever."

"Don't be more of a fool," said Autumn as she gazed at

Adamus through her mask. “You took me because I let you. Not because you could.”

Adamus and his group immediately burst into laughter once again at Autumn’s words.

“You’re surely joking!” yelled Jaimei. “Who do you think you are? You are just an Oracle’s daughter, and a woman at that! You cannot fight!”

Instantly Autumn’s smirk changed into an intense frown. Noticing this, Adamus spoke to his men while yawning.

“I’m getting tired. Collect her, and we will come back for the boys tomorrow night,” ordered Adamus.

Smirking, Jaimei and the other guards took their time as they encircled Autumn.

“Come on, girly,” said one of the men. “Don’t make this harder for yourself.”

As the man finished his taunt, two of them leaped in an attempt to rip Autumn off the ground and get her off her feet. To my surprise, Autumn elegantly jumped up, like a beautiful bird getting ready to take off, such that the two men completely missed her and collided with each other. Then, seemingly as quickly as she had jumped, Autumn disappeared again from view within the second it took me to blink. It was beyond anything I had ever seen—almost like she was transporting or becoming invisible.

Regaining composure after their collision with each other, the two men who had jumped at Autumn stood back up, unsheathing their moon-shaped swords. All five men scouted the area in search of Autumn, but with no success.

"Come out, come out!" screamed Jaimei with excitement. "Little girls shouldn't play—" But before Jaimei could finish his sentence, he dropped to the ground with a stunned expression. The other four quickly glanced at each other in surprise and confusion, circling around Jaimei with curiosity. As soon as the men lowered their swords and brought their faces towards Jaimei to examine him, one by one, within seconds, each fell to the ground with a THUD.

Floating over the men, I gazed in surprise as small bruises began to appear on the center of each of the men's heads, encircled by a grey color that seemed to seep through their natural hair color. The color itself reminded me of one of the ancient stones of power, specifically the Dream stone—the same stone that Nicholas of Dentro had been chosen by, allowing him to have the power known as projection. Was it possible that Autumn also had a stone?

Before I could finish my thoughts, Autumn's voice resonated from a few feet behind Adamus.

"I told you, men of your caliber won't be sufficient."

"Girl!" yelled Adamus as he quickly turned around to face Autumn in anger. "I cannot hold back after this, even for you." With those last words, the veins on Adamus enraged face grew bigger and more defined as he visibly flexed his muscles through his clothes. From under his shirt shone a black-and-yellow light, which Leon and I had found out earlier was his Void stone. Around Adamus's hands spread the black, smoky substance that had the ability to wither anything Adamus touched, allowing him to destroy pieces of a human's life force.

"It does not matter what you can do, baby Oracle. You cannot defeat me and my crystal Maraino. I will rip your soul from your body for your ignorance," yelled Adamus as he began to charge towards Autumn's sleek figure.

"I warned you," whispered Autumn as she disappeared into the darkness, causing Adamus to stop his charge.

Before Adamus even had the chance to look around, Autumn appeared from the darkness behind him. Running towards him, Autumn jumped forward, using her foot as it landed on his back to propel herself upward, then extending her left foot into a kick as it connected with Adamus's neck. She slowly began to drop back towards the ground after her amazing attack, and Adamus quickly brought his hand up from his side to grab Autumn, holding her up by her foot.

"I am not so easy!" yelled Adamus as he began to laugh.

Held by her foot so that her body floated a few inches off the ground, Autumn brought her free leg around in a wide, sweeping motion to hit Adamus's neck again, forcing him to drop her to place his hand on his neck. Adamus backed a few feet away.

"You're more energetic than I thought," said Adamus, sticking his black cloud-covered hands in front of his chest. "I am sorry it has come to this. Maraino!"

After he yelled his Void stone's name, something unexpected occurred. From Adamus's hands, the smoky substance that caused anything and everything to wither and die spread and grew to make a large cloud, as large as Adamus himself, forming right in front of him. Within seconds, the cloud began to move towards Autumn as she stood in awe.

"Interesting," stated Autumn as the cloud closed in on her.

"This will turn you to dust," said Adamus.

Throughout this unbelievable and intense battle, Autumn had been disappearing and reappearing almost instantly from the darkness, making me wonder why she didn't just do so now, as the cloud approached her, instead of silently standing in wait.

My thoughts changed as the cloud hovered, inches from devouring Autumn, and I watched as she placed her hand between herself and the cloud. A gray aura appeared around her body, like a mist. It became so thick that, for a second, I could not see her. The mist suddenly disappeared from around Autumn, while a gray, glass-like wall the size of the cloud itself formed between Autumn's hand and Adamus's cloud.

"What is that?!" screamed Adamus as his cloud stopped in place, unable to force its way through Autumn's gray shield.

For the next few moments, Adamus moved his hands in a throwing motion in an effort to control his cloud and force it through Autumn's creation, but to no avail.

"You cannot kill me," stated Autumn as Adamus pulled the cloud back towards himself. Within seconds, the large cloud reverted to the smaller black substance and covered Adamus's hands.

Slowly, Autumn's shield-like creation began to fall to pieces and disappear. As it vanished completely, Autumn placed both of her hands in front of her to face Adamus. All around Adamus, the gray shield that had stopped his withering cloud appeared, enclosing him in a solid, clear box. With only inches to move, Adamus quickly began to punch the wall, which seemed to have no effect.

"Your air will soon run out," said Autumn as she walked by the confined Adamus towards Cheshria. "Give—" But before I could hear the rest of Autumn's words, the scenery changed as I opened my eyes to a pale hand shaking me.

"Wake up, Zephyr!" yelled Leon as he shook me.

"I'm awake," I squealed in sudden anger.

It had all been a dream. Autumn, Adamus, Delphi, and the ridiculous fight. Taking a second to look around and remember where I was, I shook off the dream as nothing more than a desire to see Autumn again.

"You wouldn't wake up," said Leon as he sat on his bed in our room. "Are you okay?"

"Yeah, I'm fine." I actually meant it. When I had first lain down, I had felt sick and had been trying to get rid of a headache, and now it was gone, along with my sleepiness. "What's going on?"

"Endriago will be here soon to meet with us," said Leon.

"Oh," I replied.

I decided to not tell Leon or Endriago about my earlier encounter with his lizard, Priv, or my last dream about his sister Autumn, as Endriago opened the door and entered our room. He sat on my bed with a sigh. I walked over and sat beside Leon as Endriago gazed at both of us.

"How are you feeling?" asked Endriago with a smile.

"Pretty good," we both replied.

"Good, good. Now my friend, Jae, will be at your service in case anything goes wrong while you are here. We have also found someone who can guide you through the king's palace and city so that you can reach your goal. Of course, you are to let the guide think that you are visiting Cheshria from Rosem on business and are taking some time off to sightsee," said Endriago. "The Tyring Sword will not be easy to retrieve, and although the king of Cheshria only wears his sword when he is going to battle, it is guarded by two of his strongest warriors when it's here. You will have to either defeat them or find a way to distract them so you can retrieve the sword."

"Hmm," I mumbled while taking in Endriago's plan. "Where will you be?"

"I will be departing after I drop you off at the palace gates," replied Endriago.

"I see," said Leon. "And if we cannot retrieve the sword?"

"Any attempt at stealing the sword will cause the palace to go into an uproar, and as such they will try to find and either kill or imprison you both. If you cannot retrieve the sword, flee the palace, and head towards the Tall Tales bar we were at earlier. My old friend Jae will see to your safety from there.

Understand?" asked Endriago.

"Yes," both Leon and I replied. "Thank you."

"There is no need," stated Endriago. "I am indebted to you both for saving my sister. Also, even though I have little doubt in your combat skills, I urge you not to fight the two guarding the sword. They are revered as some of the strongest in all of Cheshria, known together as Cheshria's Teeth. They're very powerful."

"Thanks for the suggestion," said Leon as he looked away from Endriago.

"Now, are you both ready?" asked Endriago.

"Yes," we replied with excitement.

Standing up, Endriago beckoned for us to follow him out the door. We stopped to pick up our stuff: Leon's yellow and black swords, my dagger, and our bags. Although Endriago left in a rush while we were busy getting our things, Leon and I took our time to make sure we were ready for the journey ahead.

"Let's go," said Leon to me as we walked out the door into the cold and onto the slippery white substance known as snow.

As we began to walk towards Endriago, who stood petting Priv, a large man stepped into our path.

"Excuse me," said the man in a low voice as he turned

around to see whom he had cut off. The tall man stood at least seven feet, with a large black beard, pale skin, and fluffy, light blue clothes with an unfamiliar emblem on his shirt. In one hand was a whistle and in the other a large scythe.

"What do we have here?" asked the man as he swung his scythe around, looking at us.

Chapter 16:
Bad Tourists

I had been familiar with many weapons from as far back as I could remember. Swords, spears, scythes, arrows, and anything else you can think of. But to be honest, scythes were the only ones that really freaked me out. After my mother had passed away, I had been forced to witness the trial of a thief in Dentro Village.

The thief was found guilty, and everyone in my class at the village academy, about twenty kids total in my year, witnessed his death. After the decision had been made, they brought the thief up to the village center and publicly decapitated him with a black scythe. At that time, the Council of Elders had decided that each academy student at the age of ten would see what would come of their actions if they defied the village rules.

The seven-foot-tall, pale, bearded man who stood in front of Leon and me held the weapon that reminded me of that horrible event from my childhood. Although this man's scythe was blue and a bit shorter than the black scythe from the execution in my memory, it still brought chills to my body as the man swung it around so casually in his right hand.

"Let me ask this again," he said gruffly as he looked down at us. "What do we have here?"

The man wore clothes similar to what we had seen many others wear, except that on his jacket was an interesting emblem. A small, circular patch that sat on the left side of his jacket, it depicted a fierce blue dragon holding a sword while standing on a mountain covered in snow.

"We're visiting," replied Leon.

"For business," I added quickly.

"Young boys such as yourselves?" said the man as he stopped swinging his scythe around. "What business exactly?"

"Oracle business," said Endriago as his large figure appeared next to Leon and me.

"Really, now," said the man as he looked Endriago up and down. "Which oracle might that be?"

"The great Oracle Delphi of Rosem," stated Endriago as he looked into the man's eyes. "These boys were captured from Sleeves. We bought them recently. May we pass now?"

"I see," said the man as he moved out of our way. "Good passage to you."

After walking back to Endriago's carriage and waiting for the man to walk out of ear's reach, we all sighed in relief.

"That was close," said Endriago. "He was a palace guard. Those fools patrol at every hour. Now I'll bring you to the palace gates, where your guide will meet you both."

Leaving the carriage behind with Priv, Endriago led us for what felt like miles of walking. It wasn't the walking itself that made it harsh but the intense wind mixed with snow, and the cold that came with it. After turning onto many different streets, I began to notice that each new street would be wider than the last, with fewer houses on each side. While the number of houses would decrease, their size would do the opposite, until the blue houses on each side of the streets looked large enough to hold over twenty people. Finally no longer able to take walking through the snow and wind blowing against my face, I stopped to rest for a second.

"What's wrong?" asked Endriago as Leon took the time to also rest.

"How much farther is the palace?" asked Leon.

"It is too cold here," I stated while shivering.

"Look up," said Endriago as he pointed to the end of the street we had just entered.

As Leon and I brought our heads up to look in the direction of Endriago's finger, we both gasped in surprise. At the end of the street, a large golden gate, towering over fifteen feet high, separated what lay beyond it from more than ten streets that connected to the gate. Behind the shining golden gate stood the largest structure I had ever seen.

The palace itself looked large enough to fit a small city inside, and the building exterior was a mixture of white and blue colors. All over the palace walls, which extended farther than I could see, were large drawings that resembled the picture I had seen on the palace guard's emblem from before.

"This is amazing," I said aloud without thinking.

"Yeah," agreed Leon.

"Yes," said Endriago as he chuckled. "Yes, it is."

Looking more closely at the palace gates, I could see a distant figure with long blond hair. "I'm sorry to say I must leave you here, my friends," said Endriago as he closed in on us, arms widespread.

Pulling Leon and me together, Endriago brought us in for a big hug. Surprised, Leon and I stood awkwardly as seconds went by before Endriago let us go.

"Good luck to you, Leon and Zephyr," he said as he walked behind us. "Remember, you will always be welcome at our home in Rosem."

Waving goodbye and thanks, Leon and I slowly made our way to the golden gate entrance. As we moved closer and closer, I could clearly make out the distant figure's features. A boy, around the same age as us, stood a few inches shorter than Leon and me. He wore a large coat with a hood covering his back, while his hair covered his forehead.

"Zephlaya and Reon, I presume?" asked the boy.

"Zephyr and Leon," we corrected.

"Sorry, Zephlar and Rayon?" said the boy again.

"Zeph-yr and Le-on!" we repeated with annoyance.

"Sorry 'bout that," said the boy as he bowed his head in apology. "Name's Kolt. I'll be your guide today."

"It's okay," I replied. Kolt smiled.

"Let's get going then, shall we?" asked Kolt as he beckoned us through the palace gates.

"Are these usually unguarded?" asked Leon.

"Yes," replied Kolt as we followed him onto a large field covered in snow. "There are so many guards inside the palace that the king and his Council don't see a need for them outside. They're confident no one will attack the palace."

"I see," stated Leon.

"I have been wondering about the entrance to Cheshria," I admitted as we continued walking towards the large palace entrance.

"Yes?" asked Kolt.

"How is it that we seemed to disappear when we entered Cheshria? We had been surrounded by large red trees and short grass, and then the landscape completely changed as we entered into Cheshria to find snow and freezing weather."

"The answers to those questions are only known by a select few, and sadly I'm not one of them. All I can say is that a very powerful, ancient spell hides Cheshria from the outside world," replied Kolt.

"Interesting," muttered Leon.

Shortly after finishing our conversation, we entered through the palace gates to experience another disappearance and environment change. As I walked through the gates, just like before, my hands, followed by the rest of my body, disappeared in front of me. Unlike the cold snow and air that lay outside the palace entrance, the palace itself was filled with warm, soothing air and a sweet scent.

"Wow," both Leon and I exclaimed as we set eyes on the inside of the palace.

Immediately in front of us were four large hallways, each leading in different directions as they stretched on. At the entrance to each hallway stood separate signs with four names from left to right: Market, King's Rule, Council's Rule, and Mass.

"Now, as your guide, I will show you anywhere we are able to go," began Kolt. "The market, the king's quarters, the Council's residency, or where everyone else from slaves to guards live. Which?"

Leon and I looked at each other, our thoughts clear.

"The king's house," we both replied.

"Sure," said Kolt as we began our walk onto the pathway labeled "King's Rule." "It's late, so the king is most likely drinking with the Council. He himself does not like outsiders, so this is a perfect time."

After walking in silence through the dim hallway for over ten minutes, passing nothing but fire-lit lamps, we finally came to a halt as we reached the entrance to the king's area. Blocking the entrance and looking at us with interest were two guards dressed exactly like the man we had seen before with the blue dragon emblem. Holding scythes at their sides, they glared at us before speaking.

"Business?" asked the guard on the left.

"Just a tour for two tourists from Rosem," replied Kolt, grinning. "Gotta make a living."

"You know the rules while the king is not here. You and your guests will be punished for any mischief," stated the guards as they slowly moved aside from blocking the entrance.

"Yes," said Kolt quickly, beckoning us to follow him as he rushed past the guards.

The first room itself was filled with many different types of paintings, sculptures, and people—most likely slaves—cleaning said items. Two rooms, accessible through the two entrances on the left and right sides of the first room, were unguarded and open.

"Those guys always send shivers down my spine," said Kolt in a whisper as we followed him through the entrance to the right. "They've got too much power, I think."

"What's that patch they wear?" asked Leon. I had been thinking of asking the same thing.

"It's important history for us," said Kolt as we walked through another room filled with statues of naked people, other sculptures, and more paintings.

After walking through two rooms, both looking exactly like the first, Kolt came to a halt at the entrance to the next room.

"The king's bedroom and kitchen are the two rooms beyond the next, but I ask that as we pass through this coming room, please do not make any movements to enter farther into it," said Kolt, turning around to look at us.

"Why?" I asked.

"The king's most prized possessions are located there, guarded by the two cruel killers we call Cheshria's Teeth. If you walk past a certain point, they'll take it as a threat and kill you. I'll also get thrown in jail." Kolt frowned. "Just don't, ok?"

"Yeah, of course," we replied.

Turning around, Kolt slowly began to walk through the entrance leading to this dangerous room. Before following, Leon and I looked at each other, silently preparing to follow the plan we had made earlier, before meeting Kolt.

Quickly entering the darkened room and catching up to Kolt, we looked to our left to find that about fifty feet away lay another, smaller room, enclosed by a golden gate. In front of the gate, staring straight as us as we walked through, stood two muscular men. The man on the left, tall and fierce-looking, had long black hair, with one strand colored blue like the houses of Cheshria. Looking at us with a smile, he slowly swung around a large, dark blue scythe.

The man on the right, although much shorter, looked just as intimidating as the first. Barely half our height, the man also had long black hair with one blue strand, and huge muscles that rippled through his shirt. Instead of holding a scythe, he stood leaning with one hand on top of a large blue hammer.

"Finally," said Kolt as we walked into the next room, "that's over with."

But before Kolt could turn around to look at us, both Leon and I quickly jumped beside him, colliding our hands with his neck—softly, but fiercely enough to knock him out, and he slowly began to drop to the ground. Grabbing him, Leon placed his body up against the wall beside the entrance leading back into the previous room, so that no one could see him through the door.

"It's time," said Leon as he looked up at me.

"Let's go." We slowly walked through the entrance leading back to the two deadly men.

Chapter 17:
True Fear

To be honest, I felt bad leaving Kolt unconscious, as he had been nice to us. Not being used to kindness myself, it made me feel worse the more I thought about it, so I decided to stop as we walked into the room with the two men known as "Cheshria's Teeth."

For a second, both of the men looked surprised as we began walking towards them instead of straight back to the other entrance, but their expressions quickly changed to smiles.

"We knew," said the tall, muscular man in a low voice, holding the blue scythe. "You were up to something."

"Yes," mimicked the shorter but even more muscular man. "We knew."

"What are you talking about?" asked Leon sarcastically.

"This is good for us, though," said the tall man, continuing on. "We have been bored, just standing guard."

"Where is the sword?" I interrupted.

"It does not matter what you want, but what you seek is behind these gates. Kill us, and you may retrieve your prize," declared the tall man.

"Allow us some fun, don't die too quickly!" yelled the short man before covering his own mouth.

"Careful, Dolo. You don't want to alert the guards and end our fun too quickly," said the tall man as he looked at the shorter one.

"Yes, Fonos," replied Dolo. "Can I kill them now?"

"Greedy there, aren't you, brother," said Fonos, visibly tightening his grip on his scythe. "To the quickest go the spoils!"

With his last word, both men launched from where they stood straight towards us. Covering almost fifty feet in seconds, the first to reach us was the taller man as he swung his scythe at our feet. Jumping back in response, both Leon and I unsheathed our weapons. Pulling out his yellow and black swords, Leon launched himself at the taller man, only to be forced to jump back as the short man's hammer embedded itself in the floor where Leon had just been standing.

"Fast," said Dolo, picking up his hammer from the ground. "More fun for me!"

"He is immensely strong," said Leon as he backed up next to me. "I'll take him, while you take the taller guy. He has a longer reach, but it'll be faster if I can eliminate the short guy so we can double-team the taller. Can you handle him?"

My dagger in hand, I realized that I would be pushing it to fight someone with such a large advantage in reach. But I didn't want to seem weak.

“I'll do it,” I said with just enough confidence for Leon to believe me and go.

“What,” yelled Dolo as he smashed his hammer onto the ground in front of us, “are you doing?”

Deciding to attack before they did, Leon and I launched ourselves at our respective opponents. Tucking my dagger close to my chest, blade facing the man, I quickly ducked as Fonos brought his large scythe blade slashing through the air inches above my head. Before I could even bring my head back up, I jumped to the side as the tip of Fonos's scythe impaled the ground where I had just been.

“This might be fun after all,” said Fonos as he pulled his scythe from the ground.

Despite the crazy screams of enjoyment from Dolo a few feet away from my own fight, I wasn't able to look towards Leon, because I knew I would be killed instantly. Swinging his blade in circles behind his back and passing it from his left to his right side, Fonos launched himself off the ground straight towards me.

He was closing in on me faster than I had anticipated. Fonos slashed his scythe through the air, missing my face, but still making a small cut on my cheek.

“How?” I questioned, as his scythe had not touched me.

Taking my distraction as a chance to attack me more relentlessly, Fonos began swinging his scythe continuously, vertically, horizontally, left, right, barely allowing time for me to recover from each slash. But even though I would dodge each slash, feeling the scythe cut through the air, small cuts began to appear on my cheeks, neck, face, and arms.

"You don't understand," stated Fonos, finally stopping his onslaught. "Do you?"

"Understand what?" I asked, trying to sound tough.

"Why you are getting cut, even though you have dodged my blade," replied Fonos.

"Then explain what I'm missing!" I exclaimed in annoyance, really at myself for not knowing the truth.

"When you fight someone and your weapons touch, both souls react. But when you have great fear in a fight against an opponent with a much greater power, and you're too cowardly to even touch blades, you allow that person's aura pressure to overpower your own," stated Fonos.

"Aura pressure?" I asked, unknowingly changing the mood.

"I thought this would be fun, but it seems like you are both just child's play. You do not even know the basics of combat. Go home to your family, little boy," taunted Fonos.

Suddenly and unexpectedly, my anger began to rise at Fonos's words.

"Stop," I muttered.

"What, little boy?" asked Fonos while slowly making his way towards me. "I can't believe children like you imagined you could get your hands on the Tyring Sword. Weaklings like you shouldn't be allowed to live."

Everything he said just pissed me off. It was more than the fact that he was just insulting me. In reality, the tall muscular man reminded me of the villagers in Dentro. Not physically, but mentally, as he tried to degrade my existence. I had been called weak, stupid, traitor, and many more things that I always tried to ignore before. But for some reason, this time, I couldn't.

Thinking I could catch him off guard, I quickly launched myself off the ground, dagger pointed at Fonos's chest. A momentary surprise on his face, Fonos abruptly jumped to the side to evade my stab.

"Oh, the child has some fight in him after all," taunted Fonos.

Deciding to just go for it, I launched myself again at Fonos, getting to within a few inches of his chest, but suddenly I felt a huge amount of pain and fell backward on the ground, landing hard. Fonos had done what I had not expected; instead of using only his scythe to attack me, he evaded my dagger while simultaneously punching me in the gut. It was simple, but took more skill than I realized.

Forcing myself to stand up and face my seemingly unbeatable opponent, I smiled, trying to look like I still had something up my sleeve.

"That is a good look," said Fonos, bringing his scythe up, "to die with."

The idea of death had always hit me hard. Throughout this battle, I had wondered where Leon was, as he was supposed to finish the other guy and come help me. But I decided that this was something I had to do on my own. I had to fight this guy and beat him. Otherwise, I would need Leon to come to my rescue. All my life, I had been looked down on as weak and a disappointment by almost every single villager in Dentro. This time, I would try my hardest to prove them wrong.

Taking my focus off of Fonos and his scythe for a second, I sent one name resonating through my mind: *Sora.* Almost instantly, from under my shirt, a bright white light began to shine. Although somewhat tired and still aching from this fight, I slowly began to feel stronger, faster, and calmer. After the light slowly began to die down from my crystal, Sora's voice rang in my head.

He is very strong. I don't know if we can beat him.

We have to try, I thought in response.

I felt really good, stronger and more powerful than when I had last fought Adamus, but something still felt wrong. Although the glow of my crystal should have been a surprise, Fonos was smiling.

"Better," he said. "But still not good enough. Your aura is stronger, but it cannot compete with mine."

He is correct, said Sora in my mind. *His aura is overwhelmingly powerful. We must run or he will kill us.*

No, I replied to Sora's advice. *Leon is depending on us. And we have to get the sword.*

But before I could hear Sora's response, Fonos laughed aloud.

"You look like you have potential, just like your friend," said Fonos as he turned his head to the right.

A few feet away, Leon, battling Dolo, was obviously being overpowered by the latter's brute strength. Smashing his hammer around in an effort to pound Leon, Dolo would eventually catch him off-balance and smash his hammer against Leon's swords. Each time the weapons would collide, Leon would be brought to his knees from the sheer force of Dolo's attack. Wildly laughing and continuing his onslaught, Dolo looked as if he were getting closer and closer to beating Leon.

"He will die soon," said Fonos as he turned back to face me.

Knowing that I was still no match for Fonos with my dagger, I decided on the only other plan of attack I had. Bringing my hands in front of me, palms facing Fonos, I focused on the idea of hot and cool air visibly mixing together. Suddenly, all around my hands air seemed to be moving; around my left hand, cool air, and around my right, hot air accompanied by a crackling sound. Slowly, in front of my hands, a small ball, blue but almost clear, the size of my two fists, began to take shape. Just like in my dream-like state before entering Cheshria, where I had practiced on a beach, the Sky Pushuu formed in front of my hands.

Not giving Fonos enough time to react, I launched the Sky Pushuu through the air, straight for Fonos. Momentarily surprised, Fonos brought his scythe up, spinning it at an amazing speed as he did so. Placing the scythe between him and the Sky Pushuu, they met with a bang.

Instead of propelling Fonos through the air like I had thought, the Sky Pushuu floated in place, its momentum stopped by the scythe's rotation. Slowly but surely, Fonos's scythe began to deplete the wind energy ball, the cold and warm air dissipating, leaving nothing behind.

"Unbelievable," I stated in awe. He truly was too powerful for me to defeat by myself.

"That's it?" yelled Fonos, bringing his scythe to a halt. "I expected more."

"Why?" I asked. "How?"

"If I were to connect with my own crystal, this would be even less fun. And besides that, you have lost this battle," replied Fonos, pointing towards Leon.

Leon's swords lay a few feet from him as he faced Dolo. One arm was badly hurt, to the point where he had to keep pressure on it with his other, and his body was covered in blood. I did the only thing I could think of as Fonos and Dolo began to walk towards both of us, weapons in hand, ready for the kill.

"Run!" I yelled, picking up my dagger from the ground, making my way back towards the door leading to the palace exit. Looking back to make sure Leon was following, I found that he had already caught up to me, swords in hand.

"We must escape if we want to live," he exclaimed, gasping.

Not taking the time to look back again to see if Fonos and Dolo were in pursuit, we ran as fast as we could, reaching the pathway connecting the four areas of the palace. Far off, we heard a guard scream "Close all gates!" Deciding that we should escape from the palace altogether, Leon and I made our way towards the end of the palace gates, exiting through the golden gates that had looked so beautiful before.

After what seemed hours of treading through the cold and snow, Leon bleeding heavily, we finally reached the bar Adamus had told us to head to if we got into trouble. As we entered Tall Tales, the bartender, Jae, looked at us with surprise. Taking no time to ask questions, he ushered us in, bringing us to a secret room behind the bar as two guards entered behind us. Bringing his hand to cover his mouth to tell us to stay quiet, he quickly closed the door behind the bar as the two palace guards rushed in.

"Where are they!?" screamed the guards as they faced Jae, scythes at the ready.

Chapter 18:
Cryns Lake

For me, the world had honestly been a very disappointing place. Despite all the world has to offer, life is full of disappointments. My life had always seemed like one big failure; from the death of my mother, leaving me alone, to failing the ancient ceremony of my village multiple times and never being the best at anything, it all seemed sad. And at that moment, even so more than all the others, I felt even more disappointed at having to run away from a fight.

Fonos had been much more powerful than I had expected. It seemed Leon had been in the same situation with Fonos's brother, Dolo, when they had fought. Fonos's fighting skills and experience far outmatched my own, along with what he called his aura, a term I had never heard before. Even after using my crystal and the move I had thought would defeat anyone, the Sky Pushuu, Fonos had completely overpowered me to the point where he could kill me anytime he wanted. As even more questions began to circulate through my mind about how he was so powerful and what an aura was, my concentration refocused on the situation at hand in the Tall Tales bar.

"Where are they?" asked the two palace guards as we

hid in the secret room behind the bar.

"Who?" replied Jae, wiping a dish in his hand as we watched through a small slit in the hidden door.

"Don't toy with us, bartender," said one of the guards, slamming his scythe on the bar floor.

"I don't know what you're talking about," said Jae with a confident tone. "How about sitting down and buying a drink or two?"

"We will search—" started one guard before stopping to listen as noise came floating in from outside the bar. After popping their heads out the bar door, both guards quickly returned to talk to Jae. "All guards have been ordered to search the outskirts of Cheshria and surroundings. We will be back," finished one of the guards as both walked out of the bar.

Clearly waiting to make sure the guards had actually left, Jae eventually came back into the secret room behind the bar.

"You two," said Jae as he brought back bandages and a bottle of liquid I had never seen before. "What happened?"

"We lost," I quickly stated without much thought. It was the truth, no matter how disappointing and sad it was.

"I was hoping you wouldn't say that," said Jae, opening the bottle.

Leon's body, although more muscular than mine, looked

frail as he lay down with a defeated look on his face. Both of his arms and shoulders were coated in blood, while the rest of his body seemed to be covered in bleeding cuts.

"I'm okay," whispered Leon.

"No," said Jae, pouring small doses of liquid all over Leon's cuts, "but this will help."

As drop after drop of liquid reached Leon's open wounds, a weak sizzling sound could be heard, like something cooking in a pot over a fire. Leon closed his eyes, not letting any noise out of his mouth, his expression pained.

"What is that?" he asked, barely understandable.

"It's a medicine called curar," replied Jae. "It speeds up the healing process, but it can be very painful, depending on the severity of the wound."

"Thanks," said Leon after Jae had finished spreading the liquid.

"And you?" Jae looked towards me.

"I'm okay," I said with a certainty that persuaded Jae not to pursue trying to heal me.

Although I was tired, I was not badly wounded like Leon, nor did I want to act like a wounded dog that needed someone else to lick its wounds. Instead, I felt angry. Energy coursed through my body, allowing me to think only of becoming stronger and defeating Fonos. Leon and I had come face to face with our first true obstacle, and we had lost.

I was beyond simply being tired of losing. Just thinking of it brought me dread. I wanted to win. I wanted to become the strongest so I could return to the village a different person. And personally, I wanted to become stronger than Leon, so I would not have to continue to depend on his strength.

"You two must leave Cheshria for a while," declared Jae slowly.

"No!" I yelled, feeling stupid for my sudden outburst. "I mean, there's something we've got to get."

"I know," admitted Jae. "But the guards will not be ordered to stop looking for you both for a few weeks. And, as you just said, you lost to the ones that stood in your path. How would it be different this time if you tried again?"

"It will!" I exclaimed, knowing it wasn't true. "I just don't want to give up."

"I never said," Jae smiled, "to give up. I am just suggesting that you leave Cheshria for a while before you try again. Use that time to become strong enough to achieve your goal."

"I agree," said Leon unexpectedly. "We don't stand a chance at our current levels. And if we try again, I won't run away from a battle. Not again."

Looking at Leon, then turning back to face Jae, I realized that my argument had been a lost cause.

"Fine," I croaked. "Where should we go?"

"To Sleeves," said Jae. "One of the few places the Cheshrian guards won't be able to bother you."

"Sleeves," I repeated. "Are you sure?" I still wasn't happy with leaving, even if it was the better choice.

"Yes," declared Jae while handing us both glasses of water. "I am confident that you will be able to find everything you need to become stronger. Sleeves is very different from Cheshria. I went a few years ago, before the war. It will take some effort, but you should be able to find someone there who can train you both."

"We should go," advised Leon. It looked as though it took all of his strength to speak.

"Okay," I groaned. "How will we be able to leave Cheshria and get there?"

"I'll handle that," said Jae with a small smile. "You two will be able to rest so that when you reach Sleeves, you will have regained your strength."

"Really?" I said in surprise. "But why are you doing this for us?"

"Because I am deeply indebted to Endriago. He's my friend, and he has saved my life countless times. But that story is for another time. I'll be right back," finished Jae, closing the secret door behind him.

Leon and I didn't speak, even after Jae had left, for more than a few minutes. I guessed that he was too tired to speak and it would be better for him to rest, but there were still things I wanted to talk about with him. A few minutes later, Jae returned with two large, puffy jackets like those we had seen the citizens of Cheshria wear.

"The ride to Sleeves will take a few days, and it will be very cold for half of it. These are for you." Jae handed us the jackets.

After putting mine on, I felt as if my upper body was wrapped in pillows that had been in the sun for a day.

"Thanks," I said, feeling a little better at the sudden warmth.

"Thank you," muttered Leon, dropping his chin down onto his neck while he did so. Closing his eyes, he looked as though he had fallen asleep.

"The path you seek is not easy, my friend," Jae said. "Before I let you go, what is your deepest desire, the true reason that you seek power?"

"I've been alone for so long," I expressed with sadness as I looked Jae straight in the eyes. "Originally, it was to prove something, both to myself and to the people who had tormented me my whole life. But recently…now that I have a friend…and after meeting Delphi and Autumn and Endriago…it's not so much that I want power or strength, but that I know I need it to protect the people who have shown me light when I thought there was only darkness. I want the power to protect."

"I can feel so much pain from you, but at the same time I see that you have never given up hope or your belief in people. Just remember that the true power to protect, the power you seek, is harder to obtain than the power to destroy in many ways. But I can tell you'll come to understand where true strength comes from soon enough."

"Is that a good thing?" I asked, trying to take in Jae's words.

"It is, but let's get you both out of here." Jae picked Leon up and put him on his shoulder. "There's a carriage waiting for you behind the bar."

I followed Jae and Leon out of the secret room and towards the back of the bar, and we walked out of a big black door and into the cold air of Cheshria once again. Directly in front of us, exactly like Endriago's, was a big Tokage carriage. In front of it stood a large, yellow lizard covered by three blankets which were attached together by a large grey chain, covering the entirety of the lizard except its head.

"Come, come," whispered Jae urgently as he stood next to the carriage door.

Having placed Leon into the right seat inside the carriage, Jae looked at me with a sorrowful expression as it visibly took all of my energy just to lift my foot off the ground high enough to get inside the Tokage carriage.

"Don't worry," said Jae, holding the door open. "You can just rest, I assure you. Above your seat is food for the journey that will last you until you reach Sleeves. Your driver is a trusted friend of mine, from Sleeves, and he will make sure you arrive there safely."

"Thank you," I said with as much feeling as I could; I felt more tired than I had realized, and I was beginning to fall asleep.

"When you return," said Jae with a smile, "you will always have shelter here. Good luck."

Checking one last time to make sure we were in good enough condition to be left alone, Jae closed the carriage door and gave us a final wave as the familiar feeling of motion began. I forced my eyes to stay open as long as I could so I could make sure Leon was okay, then I lay back down in my seat and took one last glance out the window at the falling white snow before closing my eyes.

I looked around as I found myself floating above the guard post at the entrance to Cheshria. The two guards who had greeted us before sat in their seats, watching over the mystical gateway. The moon, although shining brightly, barely lit the pathway towards the post; from within the shadows moved an elegant but deadly-looking figure. Quickly recognizing the barely visible figure to be Autumn, I smiled. She moved through the shadows with such grace and elegance that the guards didn't even notice her passing through the gate. It was an amazing sight.

The scenery around me suddenly changed, replaced by the Tall Tales bar. Facing Jae, Autumn smiled as he handed her a glass of water.

"What brings you here alone?" Jae asked Autumn from behind the bar.

"I'm looking for two boys," replied Autumn as she sat down across from Jae.

"Oh, that kind of trip?" asked Jae with a smile. "I thought you were still a bit too young."

"Funny," said Autumn, laughing. "But this is serious. I owe them for showing me something important."

"Endriago told you he brought them here?" asked Jae.

"No," replied Autumn. "I just guessed they would have been here since my brother brought them."

"Smart. Yes, they were here. But you just missed them."

"Missed them?"

"They left about four days ago."

"Why would they leave?" asked Autumn. "Unless they were able to—"

"No," Jae quickly interrupted. "They weren't strong enough to retrieve the sword from the palace. I sent them to Sleeves to train."

"Oh," sighed Autumn. "I should leave, then."

"Stay for a day or two," said Jae with a smile. "Rest before you leave. They'll be in Sleeves for a few weeks at least, I'm sure."

"I guess," muttered Autumn. "For a few days. But then I need to leave so I can help them."

"Good," stated Jae as he handed Autumn another glass of water. "Now fill me in on how you've been!"

Waking up to the force of being thrown across the inside of a carriage was not a good feeling. Honestly, it makes you want to act like it's everyone else's fault you woke up.

"What?" I yelled as I opened my eyes to find myself on

top of Leon.

"Get off, please," mumbled Leon from under me.

"Sorry," I said, moving back over to my side of the carriage. "What was that?"

"I am glad our crystals grant us the ability to rest for extended periods of time without food. Plus, it seems they even allow us to heal faster," replied Leon as he pointed at the window. "But, to answer your question, I think we've arrived."

Instead of what I had expected—mainly snow—I found that we were surrounded by the same trees that grew in Dentro Village. After slowly realizing that the carriage wasn't in motion, I opened the door and jumped out. I took a few steps away from the carriage and couldn't help but smile as the warm, familiar feeling of sand began to surround my feet. Looking up from the sand, I found that I stood before a large, shiny blue lake. Beyond the lake stood huge gates and, beyond them, what I assumed to be Sleeves extended as far I as could see.

"Welcome," said a pale, muscular, red-haired man, "to Cyrns Lake."

"The Lake of Cryns," repeated Leon as he stepped out of the carriage.

"Legend has it," said the man as he gazed into the lake, "at the bottom of this lake is the entrance to the cave of the ancient Fire Dragon of Sleeves. No one dares to go below a certain depth, as they may unwittingly enter the path."

"Can't you just leave once you find it?" asked Leon sarcastically.

"It is said that you cannot until you face the dragon, or die trying," replied the red-haired man.

"Okay," I said, wanting to continue on towards Sleeves. "How do we get across, then?"

The man chuckled. "You swim, of course."

"Swim?" I stuttered. "Didn't you just say—"

"Yes," interrupted the man. "But for people who have never entered Sleeves before, this is a must. It is common practice for new entrees to swim across the lake."

"Are you sure?" I asked.

"Yes," answered the man, laughing again. "Do not be afraid."

"We aren't," stated Leon as he placed one foot into the lake.

Speak for yourself, I thought. But whether I was afraid or not didn't matter. We had to do this to continue on our journey.

"The city is beyond the gates," said the man. "Let's get started."

Running with more speed than I thought possible, the red

haired man dived into the lake, quickly surfacing and making his way across.

"It should take us about five minutes of swimming," stated Leon. "Let's go."

"Okay," I said. Leon and I entered the lake. At least it was warm. "Here we go," I said before thrusting my head into the water.

Chapter 19:
Punishment of Sleeves

As I slowly moved through the lake, swimming with precise movements, the warm water reminded me of when I had played in the ocean that surrounded Dentro Village as a child. Unlike the water that filled Cryns Lake, the shiny blue water around Dentro was so clear that the villagers of Dentro were able to see through it into the depths of the ocean.

Like all of the other children, I would go down to the beach and play in the sand any chance I could get. Although none of the other kids' parents allowed them to play with me, my mother would go swimming and play in the sand with me, making sandcastles and other shapes, until I fell asleep on the warm sand and my mother would carry me home. After she grew too weak to leave her bed, I wasn't allowed to go down to the beach without an adult to watch over me. As such, my warm and enjoyable experiences swimming as a child had ended early.

Despite the fact that it had been a while until I was old enough to go to the beach by myself, I never allowed myself to lose the swimming technique my mother had taught me. Thanks to her lessons and my hard practice after her death, I was able to keep pace with Leon as we swam through the lake's waters towards Sleeves. It was only after we had been swimming for about five minutes that I realized there could have been other creatures living in the lake.

"Leon," I said, tapping his back to bring him to a halt. "Sea monsters."

"What?" he asked with a confused look.

"That man never told us whether or not there are creatures in this lake," I stated as we both treaded in place.

"Yeah, he just mentioned the dragon cave legend," said Leon. "But let's not waste time finding out. We should head to the city before anything else."

"Yeah," I agreed as we continued swimming towards the city.

Leon and I picked up our pace until we finally reached the city of Sleeves's beach. Stepping out from the warm water and onto the even warmer sand, I waited for Leon to follow as the man who had brought us from Cheshria greeted us once again.

"You made it," announced the red-haired, muscular man. "That wasn't too bad, now was it?"

"Yeah," Leon and I agreed in a snort.

A few feet beyond where the man stood were beautifully built red gates joining two large red walls; the walls seemed to spread around the whole city, which itself was so large that when facing the outskirts, the was barely visible.

"Whoa," I uttered in amazement.

"Amazing, I know," said the red-haired man. "The walls of Sleeves were built long ago to protect the city from intruders. Good thing, too, as they have helped us fight off Cheshria's forces. Let's head into the city, shall we?"

"Wait," said Leon as the man began to walk towards the bright city gate. "You never told us your name."

"You never asked," joked the man. "I am Jordan of Red."

"Of Red?" I asked. I had read in our textbooks that some other cultures used last names, but I didn't recognize his.

"Yes," said the man, chuckling. "My family is known as the house of Red. But there will be time for this later; we should get inside before the afternoon ends."

"Why?" I asked.

"The lake creatures only come out in the morning and evening. They rest during the afternoon," replied Jordan.

"Interesting," noted Leon.

"Let's go," commanded Jordan as we all began walking off the sandy beach towards the bright red gates.

After standing idle in front of the gates for a few minutes, Jordan stopped looking beyond the gates and glanced upward. Interested in why the gates weren't opening, why there weren't any guards, and why Jordan had directed his gaze towards the sky, I copied his movement.

On each side of the gate, placed on top of the large columns that framed it, stood two hut-like posts. From afar, they looked as though someone had recently left them in a hurry—papers and telescopes were scattered around in a mess.

"This isn't right," said Jordan with a confused look. "The guards are always here."

"Seems like they aren't now," said Leon, stating the obvious. "You think something happened?"

"Obviously," I said. "What should we do?"

"We are going to enter the city without the gate guards, my friends," replied Jordan.

"What?" both Leon and I asked in confusion; the gate entrance stood at least twenty feet tall, and it provided nothing to hang on to while climbing.

"I assume you both can aura walk, correct?" asked Jordan while turning his gaze towards Leon and me.

"Aura walk?" we both repeated.

"Oh," sighed Jordan. "I guess I expected too much of you, although this explains why you have come here to seek masters."

"Teach us, then," I muttered quickly.

"It's not my place to teach you, so we will have to figure out a different way," said Jordan, slowly walking up to the gates.

Up close, we could see that the gate was formed of many red rods. Jordan placed his hand on one of them, then slowly backed up while still facing the gate entrance.

"I will open the gates from the other side," stated Jordan, then quickly pushed off the ground with incredible speed towards the gate.

Inches from colliding with the gate, Jordan quickly jumped onto it, feet landing on two of the gate rods.

"Wow!" Leon and I exclaimed as Jordan stood sideways on the gate without falling.

"This," said Jordan, taking a few steps upwards on the gate rods, "is called aura walking. When I open the gate, it will only be open for a few seconds. Get through as fast as possible, understand?"

"Yeah," we answered, still in awe.

Within seconds, Jordan had run upwards almost twenty feet and onto the top of the gate. After reaching the top, Jordan quickly jumped onto the other side of the rods and made his way down towards the ground. After a few minutes of waiting, we heard a loud screeching sound from the direction of the gates. They opened.

"Let's go," said Leon as we ran through.

The gate was closing with unbelievable speed, and we barely made it. The screeching died behind us.

"Good," said Jordan as he walked up next to us. "Let's find out what's happened before we find you masters."

As we turned to face the city, I felt the coolness of a breeze and salty air, a feeling so relaxing I closed my eyes to just enjoy it.

"What are you doing?" asked Jordan, chuckling.

"It's common where we come from," replied Leon in my place. "A relaxing and cool breeze in warm weather such as this is seen as good luck. Although our air is not as salty as here."

"I see," replied Jordan. "Sorry to rush you, but the fact is that I have somewhere we need to be in a little while."

"Sorry," I said, opening my eyes.

Sleeves was, unlike Cheshria, a magnificent sight. Its warm climate made me feel at home, but the layout of the city itself was unlike anything I had ever imagined. Everywhere on the ground were miniature versions of green sky trees, barely three inches high, thinner and softer than sky trees themselves. They city looked as though it were made of huge sections of little towns put together. Each town area comprised twenty to thirty light-green houses built next to each other, with stores set up all through each section. Directly in front of us stood a long road that branched in four different directions; the only path that did not lead to another town-like area, the north path, seemed to lead towards a large, red-painted building, not unlike the chief of Dentro's office.

The lone office, although architecturally similar, surpassed the size of the Chief's office by at least five times. After following Jordan further down the path, finally coming to a stop a few feet away from the office building, the sound of clapping began to ring out from it.

"This is the chief of Sleeves's office, also known as the House of Judgment," said Jordan.

"House of Judgment?" I asked in interest.

"Yes," Jordan went on as he turned his gaze towards one of the windows, the view blocked from the inside by a mass of people. "Here, any major crime is looked upon, and a punishment is decided for the public to see. No wonder the guards weren't on their posts. It must be a big one today."

"Cruel," uttered Leon.

"Cruel?" Jordan turned to face him. "Cruel you say, my friend? I do not disagree with you on that. But to be in that position, you must do something—or be framed for something—that cannot be forgiven."

"Like?" I asked. Jordan turned to look at me.

"Murder, extensive theft, repeated crimes, or treason," he replied. "There has to be a penalty for those who don't follow the laws, or this city wouldn't survive. We are not like Exilio, a lawless town of exiles and thieves. Here, there are normal men, women, and children."

"I see," said Leon.

"Let's find out what's going on." Jordan motioned to use to follow, and we all went through the door into the building.

The inside was almost unremarkable. There were two floors. The first floor, where it looked and felt like hundreds of people were standing, held the main attraction, and everyone stood facing a large platform in front of a set of stairs leading to the second floor. On the black platform stood four men, on whom it seemed everyone's attention was focused. Two of the four men, both wearing masks, looked larger and more muscular than even Adamus. They stood next to a smaller, older man, who sat in a chair facing the large crowd.

Behind the grey-haired, tired-looking old man in the chair stood an overweight, cruel-looking, short, blond-haired man.

"That man," whispered Jordan, pointing at him, "is Vice Chief Greer of Sleeves. He's in charge now, because our chief is often ill."

Greer slowly gave a wide, cruel, devilish smile as he walked around the platform, circling the man in the chair as the crowd erupted in cheers. He reminded me of the second in command of Dentro, Hovan. But unlike Hovan, who just radiated an unpleasant feeling, this man seemed to have evil written all over his face.

"My dear people!" exclaimed Greer, stopping in front of the crowd. "You have been called here today to witness the punishment of a true criminal. You know him as Karlir, the military leader who not only supposedly saved Sleeves from an attack by over ten thousand men with only three hundred soldiers, but also befriended the great Fire Dragon of myth, receiving the Valkyrie Shield as a gift over fifty years ago from the dragon himself. But if this is true, why would he try to steal the shield back after willingly giving it to our beloved chief?"

"Traitor!" screamed a section of the crowd. "Liar, fake!" screamed even more.

"Yes, yes, my dear people. Since his supposed great deeds, Karlir has done nothing to help us but grow old, while no proof has ever been shown. Our council has decided…" Greer paused to listen to the crowd's applause. "…that this man be condemned to death for treason, cheating, and lying to his people and our chief, as well as grand theft. In three months, we shall bring this man back to this exact spot, to meet his deserved end!"

The room filled with the sound of applause from the crowd. The two muscular men wearing black masks grabbed the elderly man, Karlir, by the arm, forcing him to stand up. Although tired and old, Karlir looked as though he wasn't just another old man, even in that moment.

"Why would they do that to him?" I asked into Jordan's ear so he could hear me over the deafening sound of applause. "After all he has done for the city?"

"Our Vice Chief Greer said that Karlir had tried to steal the Valkyrie Shield, our city's prized possession, but I don't believe he would do so. And if he had truly wanted to, he would have easily been able to, as very few of us would stand a chance against him."

"The old man sentenced to death?" I asked in disbelief. "In a fight?"

"Yes, that old man. His name is Karlir of KaRyu, and he," said Jordan, looking stunned and displeased, "was supposed to be your future master."

Chapter 20:
Three Month Discipline

"Karlir of KaRyu," said Leon as we all took in the mess we had stumbled upon. "Was he supposed to be my master also?"

"I'm not sure," replied Jordan as the large crowd of people we were in began to force past us to make their way out of the House of Judgment. "All Jae asked me to do was deliver you to Karlir, and so I will."

"Looks like that plan is messed up," I stated sarcastically, considering my future master was going to be killed soon.

I had been opposed to coming in the first place, but now that we were here, all I wanted to do was find a master and get stronger.

"What now?" asked Leon.

"Let's get out of here," said Jordan as he directed us to the exit through the crowd of rowdy people.

Taking a second to look back at the old man known as Karlir, I gazed beyond the platform to find that the two guards were pushing him up the stairs to the second floor of the building. After following Jordan outside and stopping a few feet away from the entrance, Leon and I came to a halt as Jordan turned around to face the red building once more.

"We'll go talk to him and find out what happened," declared Jordan. "Our fool of a vice chief is truly taking advantage of the chief being ill."

"How are we going to do that?" I asked. "Won't he be locked up?"

"Luckily, no," said Jordan with a smile. "Since he's been given the death penalty and it will be carried out in three months, he can be free until then within Sleeves. Even so, he does have to follow certain restrictions, like not being able to leave Sleeves or to leave his family grounds without an escort."

"So we're going to see him at his home, then?" asked Leon. "Where we're from, when a felon is given the death penalty, he's locked up until his sentence is carried out."

"I see," said Jordan. "Karlir lives in the district next to this one."

As he finished, Jordan directed us to follow him onto the eastern path from the House of Judgment, leading to the next district, where Karlir lived. Making our way through the hundreds of people who had just came from witnessing the declaration of punishment, we eventually arrived in the eastern district. As we stepped off the path and into the district, a tall sign stood in front of us with the words "East Section A."

"This is one of the oldest sections in the city," said Jordan as our gaze followed his.

The area itself looked exactly like the one we had just come from, but without the large red building in the center of the district. On both sides of the roads that led through the center of the area lay houses and other buildings, while in the center was a merchant area with different stores. In the middle of the merchant area, the road that went straight through the district split into two new directions, both leading towards other districts that lay what looked like another couple of minutes away. The only thing that looked different from the other area's layout was a lone large, green house right to the north of the merchant center—the only direction the main road did not branch in.

"I see you have found Karlir's home," said Jordan as Leon and I looked at the large house. "Looks like we aren't the only ones who have business with him, though."

Right in front of the house's large yard stood about twenty people of various ages; they circled around the front of the yard. We took our time walking through the district and looking around, walked past the market, and arrived in front of the house's yard where the people stood. Soon it was apparent we weren't just looking at the house, as we began to walk on to the yard, and one of the people stood in front of Jordan to block our way.

"Do you realize whose home this is?" asked the man, who looked around the age of thirty.

"Yes," replied Jordan impatiently. "Please move, my friend."

"Do not associate with this traitor!" yelled the man as he moved out of our way. "I'm warning you! Nothing good will come of it!"

"How much of a fool can you be these days?" muttered Jordan as we walked by him.

Jordan's expression looked different. Before, he had had only a happy smile on his face, but now he looked tired and displeased with every new person he met or saw. We walked towards the house across the front yard, which was at least fifty feet long, with the miniature green sky trees covering the ground.

"What are these called?" I asked, pointing towards the plants in the yard.

"You don't know?" asked Jordan, chuckling. "That's grass. But you'll have time for questions later; we should hurry and speak with Karlir."

"Okay," I said in agreement as we continued our walk across the yard until we reached the front door of the house.

The building itself stood two stories tall, with two large

front doors, windows next to them, and windows on the second floor. The roof, colored red, was large enough to hide us from the sunlight as we stood in front of the double doors. Jordan knocked on the door three times before turning around to face us.

"You heard what he had accomplished from the Vice Chief," said Jordan. "Even if you do not believe, act like you do while we are here. Understood?"

"Yes," agreed Leon and I as the sound of the door opening quieted us.

"Who are you?" asked Karlir in a low, knowledgeable voice as he answered. He stood about six feet tall, an uncommon trait for most of the people of Sleeves I had seen so far. He looked around the age of seventy-five, had grey hair, pale skin, and black eyes.

"I am Jordan of Red," replied Jordan as he turned to face Karlir, standing a few inches taller than the elder.

"Ah," breathed the old man. "You must be the grandchild of the family, yes?"

"I am," stated Jordan with a laugh.

"So, what are you here for, my boy?" asked Karlir with a pleasant smile, something I wouldn't have expected from someone on death row.

"I was sent by Jae to bring these two boys—" said Jordan, waving his hand at us, "—to meet you. Jae has asked for you to become their master."

"Master, you say?" repeated Karlir with a chuckle. "To be a student is not free. How will they pay for this, if I do accept?"

"Jae said you would say such, and so he said that by teaching them, you can pay off your bar tab."

"That bartender," sighed Karlir. "Come in, come in."

Karlir gazed at us with an expressionless look. Walking into the house, I noticed it had the largest rooms I had ever seen. The living room, which we walked into first, had a long sky tree table that glimmered as if it was polished every day. From what I could tell, the house had so many rooms that it would take days to explore them all. After sitting down in chairs that faced each other in the middle of the living room, I looked around to see paintings of dragons, warriors, mountains, and more placed all over the walls. In particular, between two paintings of a large red dragon and a young boy with blond hair, a silver whistle hung on the wall.

"So, Jordan, who are these two boys?" asked Karlir as he looked at us, sizing us up.

"I'm Leon," declared Leon without hesitation.

"And I Zephyr," I stated. He looked at me sharply. For a

moment, he seemed younger, stronger. I could see the warrior in him—

"We come from a distant village," said Leon. The old man looked back at him, and the moment passed.

"I see," said Karlir, as if he instantly knew we were hiding something. "And why do you want to be trained?"

"To be stronger," said Leon.

"So we can achieve our goals, and make our dreams a reality," I answered in turn.

"Your dreams, you say?" repeated Karlir with a smile. "And if you find that you cannot achieve your goals and dreams?"

"That's not an option," said Leon while glancing at me.

"No?" repeated Karlir in interest.

"People have called me a failure my whole life," I said without thinking. It wasn't like me to just tell others about my past, but the old man's eyes seemed to have a warm look. "We will never find that our goals are unachievable, because that would kill our dreams and our spirits."

"And even more, it would kill the dreams of those who will follow behind us in the future. As such, we will never give up," finished Leon.

I turned to face Leon, and we both smiled with

determination in our eyes. And it was at that point that I knew I could trust Leon not to betray me again.

"You are both truly young," said Karlir, laughing. "But I like what you stand for."

"Thank you," we both said in response.

"Jordan," said Karlir, turning his attention away from us. "I will accept Jae's proposal. I am sorry to say that I will only be able to train them for three months, given my sentence."

"Thank you," said Jordan. "Respectfully, Karlir of KaRyu, why are you letting them do this to you? I don't believe you would betray Sleeves, or the Chief."

"I appreciate the thought," Karlir remarked. "It seems that past deeds cannot keep you safe from present cruelty, as the Vice Chief has taught me. I was sleeping when they broke in and charged me with trying to steal the gift I had given to the city and the Chief so long ago. But I am old and tired. My time is long gone, and I have nothing to truly live for. So I do not see a reason to fight against that man."

"Even so!" yelled Jordan. "You are a hero! My parents used to tell me stories when I was a child about your heroic feats. They should not be disrespecting you like this!"

"You are too kind, Jordan of Red." Karlir put his hand on Jordan's shoulder. "It seems my hope in the new generation may be renewed yet. I will train these two boys, and in three months they will be more powerful than they could ever imagine."

Leon and I couldn't help but smile at each other after hearing Karlir's words.

"But," said Karlir as he noticed our smiles, "it will not be easy. It will be the toughest three months of your life—I promise this. Are you prepared?"

"Yes!" Leon and I exclaimed.

"Good." Karlir smiled. "Come back in three months, Jordan of Red. They will be ready then. Is this acceptable?"

"Of course," replied Jordan. "Well then, I should be off."

Standing up from his seat, with Karlir following suit, Jordan smiled as he shook all of our hands. Stepping out the front door, Jordan looked back at us one last time.

"Take care," he said, then closed the door.

"Zephyr and Leon," said Karlir as he gazed at us. "You are from Dentro Village, are you not?"

Both Leon and I looked at each other in confusion. No one was supposed to know about the village, as one of the main laws of missions was to tell no one about our village, particularly its whereabouts.

"How did you know that?" I asked.

"We are from different times, and I have seen many

things over the years," replied Karlir. "I once fought alongside a man named Zephyr, about seventeen years ago. He looked far different from any other person I have ever met, much like you—Zephyr. He had hair like yours, as well as those cloudy gray eyes."

Could he be talking about my father? The man who had abandoned me and mother, leaving us to be looked down on by the villagers while having to make our own ends meet? The cruel man that never come back to check on us, or even to my mother's funeral?

"He always talked about Dentro. He even brought me there once," finished Karlir. "Did you know of him?"

"No!" I yelled, then realized my mistake. "Sorry, he doesn't have a very good reputation with my family."

"I see," stated Karlir with a frown. "I am sorry to hear that. But let us begin with your training as soon as possible. I have only one rule: while you are here, you will always do exactly what I say. Understood?"

"Yes, we will," we replied.

"Good, now follow me," said Karlir. He took us through one of the many doorways out of the living room.

After walking through a long, narrow hall, we reached a large, empty white room with no windows. On the right wall hung hundreds of different weapons, some that I had never seen before, some familiar. On the left wall hung shields, different types of armor, and a long, green pole that stuck out from the wall.

"This is one of my training rooms, now also yours," declared Karlir. "For me to teach you, I must see your abilities and determine the level you are each at currently. Both of you, stand in the center of the room."

We put our bags down next to the door and walked over to the center of the white training room with just our weapons and training clothes on. Leon and I waited for Karlir's instruction.

"Now," said Karlir as he closed the door to the room and walked a few feet closer to us, "begin your fight to the death!"

Chapter 21:
Friendly Rivals

Although I knew Leon was stronger than me, I still felt excitement knowing I could actually compare our fighting skill. When I had first witnessed him fighting those Exilio thugs, all I could think was *beautiful* as I gazed on the sight of Leon defeating the men. As he used both his yellow and black swords, it looked as though they were truly an extension of himself. With one swipe of his yellow sword, a ray of light seemed to flash by; with a swipe from his black sword, enveloping darkness cut with powerful force.

"To the death?" we asked Karlir in unison.

"Yes," answered Karlir as he stood in front of the door leading to the exit. "Do not hold back. Begin!"

Without another word, both Leon and I jumped a few feet away from each other, stopping to size each other up. Leon unsheathed his two blades, yellow in his right hand, black in his left, and smiled. At the same time, I unsheathed my dagger from my left leg pocket while tapping my right pocket to make sure I still had my gloves.

"Sure you're ready?" asked Leon with that familiar cocky smile.

Instead of taking the time to reply, I decided to use the

opening Leon had given me, and so I lunged. Covering the space between us fairly quickly, I brought my left hand, clasping my dagger, into a thrust towards Leon. Realizing that he would not be able to parry, as my attack had almost reached his stomach, I halted.

"What are you doing?!" yelled Karlir in question as he walked up to us.

Holding my dagger still, the blade barely an inch from impaling Leon, I looked up to see Leon's stunned expression.

"I hadn't expected you to be so fast and aggressive," stated Leon, the stunned look fading.

"That wound would have been fatal," said Karlir as he guided my hand away from Leon. "Begin again, but this time I hope you will be serious. I do not want you to stop if he is truly this weak."

"I won't hold back," said Leon as our new master took a few steps back.

"I didn't ask you to," I retorted, sounding angrier than I had intended.

For seconds we stood, weapons held a few feet from each other in dead silence. At that moment, the world did not matter. Everything revolved around this fight, a combat between partners, a challenge between friends.

This time, Leon struck first. Launching across the empty space that split us, he brought the yellow sword in his right hand down in an effort to slash. Jumping backwards, dodging the slash, I quickly ducked as Leon side-slashed with his left sword, barely missing my head. Taking the opening Leon had left, I pushed off the ground with all of my strength, forcing my right fist into Leon's stomach in the area he had left open by swinging both swords. Toppling backward, Leon quickly recovered and jumped away, swords crossed in front of him.

"You really aren't as weak as I thought," said Leon, but without a smile.

Suddenly, Leon launched himself faster than before, this time bringing down a rain of slashes. Each slash was executed so quickly that it was all I could do to dodge, let alone counterattack. I felt pressured. With each slash, I was forced a step backward, until finally I saw Leon's barrage slow enough that I could jump back and escape his reach.

"Tired?" I taunted. It wasn't something I usually did, but I was still angry about how cocky Leon was.

"That a joke?" asked Leon.

But as he finished his sarcastic reply, Leon did something I hadn't expected. He disappeared from my sight. One moment he was standing a few feet in front of me, and now he had suddenly disappeared without a trace. I quickly glanced at Karlir before realizing that he had to still be here, as the master's expression hadn't changed. I realized that letting my guard down in awe had been a mistake as out of the corner of my left eye I spotted the yellow ray of light that was actually Leon's sword as he swung.

Unable to dodge in time, I jumped back, bringing my left hand up in an effort to block Leon's attack. Pain shot through my arm as I looked at the source of it. A large, red mark had appeared on my arm, as if I had been burned by Leon's slash. The most surprising thing, though, was that the force of Leon's slash had been so powerful it had forced my dagger out of my hand.

"I told you," said Leon, as I looked up to see him smiling a few feet in front of me again, "I'm not going to hold back."

"How did you disappear?" I asked, feeling weak and stupid.

"Sorry, Zephyr," replied Leon as he took a step forward. "When you get to my level, then you'll know."

Leon vanished again as he took another step forward. Realizing that my chances of winning were low as I had to fight fist against sword—not to mention the fact that Leon seemed to be able to disappear—I quickly took my white gloves out of my right pocket and curled my hands into fists. The only option I had was to call Sora, and so I closed my eyes. Yeah, I know, not the smartest thing to do while in the middle of a fight, but it was the only thing I could think of. Clearly visualizing Sora's light tan skin, wide blue eyes and long brown hair that went down to his eyebrows, I felt his presence like a warm breeze surround me.

"Thought you had forgotten about me," said a familiar, comforting voice.

"No way," I said as I found myself sitting on the beautiful beach I had imagined once before. Sitting next to me sat Sora, smiling as the ocean water softly crashed onto our feet.

"Your friend," began Sora as he turned his head up to gaze upon the never-ending ocean, "is very strong."

"Tell me something I don't know," I said jokingly. "How can I compete with someone who can disappear?"

"You can't," replied Sora before turning back to face me. "So it's a good thing he isn't actually disappearing."

"What do you mean?" I asked in confusion. "I saw him do it before my eyes."

"To be correct, you didn't see, is what you should be saying," Sora laughed.

"What?" I asked in frustration. "I don't understand."

"Leon is doing something similar to what that man,

Jordan, did when he walked up that gate," said Sora.

"Aura walking?" I asked.

"More like aura running. He is using his aura, in combination with his crystal, to allow himself to move at a much higher speed than he normally could. Although it takes a lot of energy, he is using it because at your current level, your eyes and body can't keep up," answered Sora.

"So why didn't he use it when we were at the gates?" I asked aloud, really thinking the idea to myself.

"I would think that he didn't know he could use the technique in that specific way, as he looked as stunned as you when Jordan showed us," explained Sora.

"So could I also use my aura?" I asked, hoping the answer would be a yes.

"No," replied Sora, to my displeasure. "I have told you as much as I know about auras, as I know only a limited extension of your own current knowledge. As such, because you do not truly understand auras yet, I do not know how to utilize ours. All I can do for us is to allow us to see Leon's aura. The gloves themselves have their own aura, although they don't completely match our own."

"The gloves?" I asked.

"The white gloves, or Gantias as Adamus called them,

are special. But that is all I can sense," said Sora.

"I still don't know how to win, then," I declared with little hope.

"Neither do I, I am sorry to say. But we are out of time. As I told you before, when you are healthy and relaxed, time does not flow the same way as it does in the real world, and as such you can stay as long as you like. But now, you're stressed and pressured, in the middle of a fight. Our time is up, but we will do our best together. Agreed?" asked Sora as he held out his hand.

"Of course," I said as I shook his hand.

Sadly, the beautiful beach that lay in the deepest part of my mind was gone. Eyes open, senses alert, I moved my gloved left fist a few inches from my face and my right beside my chin, elbow tucked against my ribcage. I quickly turned my head right, left, and upward, then gave a quick backward glance. Leon could come from any direction, at any moment. Then, it came again.

Like a shadow of darkness, from the corner of my right eye, came Leon's sword. It was quick, but not as fast as he himself seemed to be able to move. Jumping back, I dodged his black blade as it whizzed by me. Thinking that I was safe from this attack and Leon was going to disappear again, I found that I was badly mistaken.

Unlike with Leon's last one-slash attack, he used the force of his downward left slash to flip forward in midair, bringing his yellow sword forward with him as he finished the flip. Still being in midair myself from my earlier dodge, I did the only thing I could to block his attack. Bringing both my fists up into a collision with Leon's sword, I expected the gloves to be slashed and ripped apart. Instead, the blade and the outer side of my fists held each other in place as they collided.

Leon pulled his yellow blade away, this time bringing his black blade down onto my gloves, and the force of the collision propelled me backwards. I fell to the ground, hard. Although the impact hurt, having landed on my back, I forced myself up and ignored the pain. But man, did it hurt. I had half expected Leon to ask me about my gloves, even though I didn't know much about them myself, but it seemed the time for conversation had ended. Leon was visibly drained—apparently, using his aura took a toll. We both wanted this to end.

Coming to the conclusion that I couldn't take another hit from his sword, as the pain was already making it hard to keep standing, I decided to gamble on my last attack. I stretched my arms in front of me, both palms facing Leon.

"I'm going to end it with this," I said in the most confident voice I could muster through my pain.

"Go ahead and try," said Leon as he crossed both swords in front of him, covering most of his upper body.

I turned my focus to the idea of cool and warm air mixing together, imagining the two as blue and red mist. The blue and red rays of energy slowly began to appear in front of my hands. As I mixed the two into the form of a blue crystal ball, pulling the rays of the two energies from all around me, the loud crackling sounds began. A crystal ball the size of two fists materialized in front of my palms.

I had been hoping Leon had not witnessed my attack during our previous battle against the two fighters in Cheshria—the lost fight against the two brothers Dolo and Fonos. It looked like my gamble had been well placed, as Leon was stunned by the sight of my materialization. Knowing that I could not hold out any more, I sent a surge of energy through my body to launch the ball at Leon, and it worked. The ball itself was so fast that it covered the few feet of distance between Leon and me in seconds, giving him no time to dodge.

The sound made by the Sky Pushuu as it came in contact with both of Leon's blades was deafening. It sounded like the repeated slamming of a door, but ten times louder. Even so, I couldn't help but stare in awe and anger as Leon held his ground, slowly being pushed back. Was my attack so weak that anyone could block it? It had failed twice now, and it had been my last hope of winning. Although Leon seemed to be holding his own against my attack as it rotated into his swords, the expression on his face looked pained.

Just as it looked like Leon was going to lose to the force of the Sky Pushuu, he quickly jumped backward, bringing both swords outwards to his sides. The ball, although slower, continued to move toward him as Leon held his swords in midair.

Instantly, all around Leon, yellow and black rays of energy began to appear. His eyes, which had been brown, turned a swirling mixture of black and yellow, while his black hair now had two yellow tips on the front of his bangs. Almost as fast as they had appeared, the rays of black and yellow moved from around Leon and seemed to attach themselves onto both of his swords, black with black, yellow with yellow.

Both blades now illuminated by a powerful, bright glow, Leon brought both of his swords into downward slashes a few feet from my energy ball. Not understanding why Leon would slash at the empty space, I realized my stupidity. He wouldn't waste his energy swinging for no reason, and I was right.

As soon as Leon swung his swords in the direction of my Sky Pushuu, a yellow-and-black wave in the shape of the blades flew from both his slashes. In less than a second, the waves

connected with the ball, and an explosion of smoke erupted.
Boom!

As I fell to the ground, totally drained of energy, I blinked to find empty space where my energy ball had just been and both of Leon's blade tips pricking my throat.

"Enough," said a voice I had forgotten existed. "Well fought, both of you."

"You lose," exclaimed Leon with a smile as he fell backwards to the ground, both his blades following him.

Looking at Leon passed out on the ground made me feel better about losing, but it still didn't change the fact that I had lost. As I gladly lay my head on the soft ground, I closed my eyes in an effort to ignore the pain shooting through my body.

Chapter 22:
Devil's Pass

I opened my eyes to find myself staring through a window, the beautiful night sky visible like a painting. Alone in the center of the sky, hung the moon. Although surrounded by little shinning lights, the beautiful moon, separated from the rest of the stars, seemed to have its own bright aura. As I continued to gaze at it, I felt more relaxed than I had been for weeks.

Sitting up, I found that I was in a small but cozy-looking room. Forcing myself to get out of the bed, I walked over to a mirror next to the door. Looking back at the small bed, I saw that my dagger, gloves, and travel bag had been placed next to it.

Hungry, I decided that I should go and talk to Karlir. As I grabbed the door handle to open the door, a slight pain, strong enough for me to flinch, ran through my left arm. Looking at it, I found that the red mark that had been made during my fight with Leon was still there. Opening the door, this time with my right hand, I almost walked into a wall before realizing I was in one of the thin hallways that made up Karlir's home.

"You're awake," said Karlir with his cold but oddly welcoming voice from down the hall. "Come."

Taking my time, I turned right down the hall, eventually walking into the fire-lit living room we had spoken in earlier.

Karlir, sitting in one of the four chairs in the center of the room, smiled as I sat down across from him.

"How did you sleep?" He handed me a plate of meat and vegetables.

"Thank you," I replied as I took the plate. "Okay."

"Good, good. I am glad you're awake. I have wanted to speak to you alone, Zephyr," stated Karlir. "Leon awoke earlier, but I sent him to rest a bit longer."

"Have I done something wrong?" I asked while stuffing my mouth. I couldn't help it. The food was beyond good; it was amazing.

"No. You did well yesterday. But as I witnessed, you and Leon are very different. Between your powers, level of skill, and experience, it looks as though your training will have to be very different from each other in order for you both to become stronger in three months. To make this work, you will have to be trained daily by different masters, as I cannot watch over you both. So I have decided that I will train you and my younger brother will train Leon. Are you okay with this?"

"Of course," I replied as I finished the last piece of meat on my plate. "I'll do anything to become stronger. If I don't, I won't be able to make my dreams a reality."

"You sound just like me," Karlir mused, "when I was

young."

At that moment, we both smiled and laughed. Although at first I had thought of Karlir as a cold-looking man, I was slowly beginning to think that he wasn't at all what the people of Sleeves were making him out to be.

"When will we start my training?" I asked with excitement.

"As soon as you are ready," replied Karlir. "We will leave after you have completely healed from your battle."

"Leave?" I asked in confusion.

"Yes," answered Karlir. "This place is not suitable for the training I will give you. We will travel to the mountains known as the Devil's Pass."

"Devil's Pass," I repeated. I remembered that Delphi had mentioned something similar while describing where Cheshria and Sleeves were located. If I remembered correctly, she had stated that the pass was the pathway out of this region and into the other regions of the world. Not only that, but it was home to many monsters and demons with unbelievable power.

"There I will spend the last three months of my life, training you. You better make it count," said Karlir as he looked at me with determination in his eyes. "It won't be easy."

"Let's go," I blurted out. "I'm ready now."

"Are you sure?" he asked.

"Yes," I replied.

"Get your stuff and meet me at the front door in five minutes," Karlir declared as he grabbed my plate and headed off into another part of the house.

Standing up from the chair and making sure not to use my left arm, I walked back towards the hall and into the room I had been sleeping in before. After walking over to the bed, grabbing my bag and dagger, and putting my gloves in my pocket, I moved towards the window to look up at the beautiful night sky once again.

"The darkness of the night is truly a sight, isn't it?" asked Leon's familiar voice.

"Yeah," I agreed. "But it's not completely dark with the moon's light."

"That's true. So I'm guessing you're off?" Leon asked as I turned around to see him leaning on the door.

"Yeah," I said, walking up to him. He smiled in his black shorts and white t-shirt. "And you?"

"I begin my training tomorrow morning. Karlir's younger brother, Kuchi, will bring me to our training ground. That's all I know. You better get stronger if you are heading to those mountains," he said with a smile.

"I will. You better too, 'cause if you don't, I will beat you next time," I said with a serious look.

"I believe it. You surprised me before. See you in three months," said Leon as I walked past him and into the hall.

I stopped. "Leon," I called. "Are we friends?"

"Of course!" said Leon as he popped his head into the hall. "You were there for me when I had lost my way. You're a good friend—a best friend."

"Best friend?" I repeated, momentarily surprised. "Then don't worry."

"Don't worry?"

"As your best friend, if you ever lose your way again, I promise I will do everything I can to bring you back. But you have to promise the same."

"Of course," Leon promised. "Good luck, Zephyr."

"Thanks," I said, looking back. "You too."

As I walked through the living room and up to the front door, Karlir brought his heavy gaze down on me again.

"You better be ready," he said, opening the door.

"Now I am," I replied.

The night sky and cool breeze were refreshing. Following Karlir through his yard, this time empty of protestors, we made our way through the town fairly quickly. Karlir moved at a much faster pace than one would think he could, and within minutes we were out of his district and back at the main path next to the House of Judgment. Instead of heading south, towards where we had entered the city, we walked north beyond the house. After passing through three districts laid out just like Karlir's, we reached a set of red gates, identical to the gates we had entered through before.

"Sleeves is positioned on the outskirts of the Tyring region. The south gate leads towards the rest of Tyring, while the north gate leads towards Devil's Pass Mountains," stated Karlir as we walked up to one of the gate guards.

After talking to the guards, Karlir and I walked through the open gates. It looked as if an agreement had been made regarding Karlir leaving the city. Hearing the loud screeching sound of the gates closing, Karlir and I stood on a mixture of sand and grass. Seeing me look at the ground with a puzzled expression, Karlir spoke.

"The ground will change to a rocky surface as we enter the mountain region."

"Oh I," was all I could come up with in reply. As I was still getting used to the idea of mountains, everything about it fascinated me. But I decided it was better to wait and experience it for myself than to slow us down by asking questions. I wanted to begin my training as soon as possible.

Karlir had stated that our training would begin with the trip there. Instead of walking, we would run for as long as possible, with small intervals of rest for me. In all honesty, it surprised me that an elder like Karlir, no matter how great he had been in the past, could run at such a fast speed with such consistency.

We ran for almost forty-five minutes without stopping, until I asked for a break. From then on, we ran for about half an hour at a time, until I needed to rest for a short five minutes. Each time, Karlir jogged in place as he waited for me to recover.

"We are almost there," said Karlir as the large mountains became more visible with every passing minute.

After two more hours of running alternating with rest, we finally reached the mountains as the night sky had slowly begun to change into dawn. Devil's Pass was actually a range of hundreds of majestic mountains. In between each mountain lay rocky pathways, large enough for around five people to fit through with a few feet in between. Although there seemed to be no specific way through the mountains, one path, starting at the first mountain we came upon, had a sign placed at its opening that read "Devil's Pass." Karlir walked up to the sign and tapped it on the side.

"This sign is over fifty years old," exclaimed Karlir. "The man I mentioned before, the one with your name, made this with me."

In truth, I had always wondered about my father. I had so many questions that no one seemed to be able to answer—or want to answer—back in the village. Even the Chief knew almost nothing of my father. My mother, before her death, never spoke of him until she lay on her deathbed. The only thing she said in regards to him was, "Do not blame your father, for he has more to deal with than you can imagine, and he truly does love us."

From what Karlir had said about the man who looked similar to me with the same name, it sounded all too likely that this man was my father. The only thing that anyone in the village seemed to know about him was that my mother had gone away to the outside world on a mission and completed it, but not without bringing two outsiders with her when she returned. If that was true, those two men must have been Karlir and my father. My first priority was to get stronger, and so with that thought I decided that if I had time, I would ask about my father after doing so. I could not allow myself to get distracted.

"How far are we from where we will train?" I asked to try to change the subject.

"We are fairly close," replied Karlir as he pointed towards

a snow-covered mountain a few mountains deeper into the range. "That is where we will begin your training. As you get stronger and times goes on, we will move farther into Devil's Pass."

Walking through the pass was interesting to say the least. Surrounded by huge mountains on both sides, some capped with snow, I gazed at the rocky surfaces with caves everywhere. It seemed the farther up the mountain I looked, the more frequently caves appeared.

"Those caves," I murmured in a questioning tone.

"Those caves are home to many different monsters and demons," stated Karlir as we continued to walk on the path. "We will make one of the caves our own, if we must, when we arrive at that mountain."

"So we're going to kill the demon or demons that live there?" I asked. I wasn't used to killing demons at all.

"If we must." Karlir suddenly stopped walking, forcing me to halt a few steps behind him. "Here we are."

I looked up to where Karlir faced. In front of us lay a combination of grass and rocks. Bringing my head up to look at the rest of the mountain, I saw that about a hundred feet up, the ground changed from grassy to snow-covered. As we walked up the mountain and passed into the cold, snowy climate, I couldn't help but begin to shiver.

"Shorts and a t-shirt are perfect for this," said Karlir in a joking tone. "Don't worry; once we get into the cave, you won't be so cold."

Too busy trying to keep myself warm to answer, I nodded in response. After a few more feet of walking, I turned backwards to see how far we had climbed up the mountain. Although every mountain was as large and visible as they had been earlier, everything else, including the path, looked as small as a dot. And, as I realized when I turned my head to look up at the top of the mountain, we were only halfway up.

"It's hard to breathe," I said, as I had to consciously think about inhaling with more force.

"That's what happens when you go farther up towards the sky," stated Karlir. He pointed to a cave entrance. "Here is where we will make camp."

Entering the cave, which was as large as most houses in Dentro, Karlir took out a candle and lit it by swiping his hand over the tip. Placing the candle on the ground, he picked up a fist-size rock and placed it on the tip of his left hand's index finger. Facing the darker, unexplored part of the cave, Karlir flicked the rock with his right hand, sending it spinning towards the other side of the cave. Amazed at how fast the rock flew from Karlir's finger, I watched as the rock hit the ground and a loud, familiar growling sound could be heard. Within seconds, a large, black, dog-like creature appeared just feet away from us.

The Barghest, covered in gray hairs, with its large, monkey-like face and sky-pointed ears, slowly began to move towards Karlir. Although it was twice the size of both Karlir and me, Karlir did not flinch as the Barghest, on all fours, began to charge towards us. Suddenly, as the Barghest got within five feet of Karlir, red, ray-like beams began to surround him.

Similar to the black-and-yellow rays that had appeared around Leon during our past fight, the red rays surrounding Karlir circled him blindingly and with great speed. Although Leon's display of surrounding rays had been surprising, the pressure that seemed to accompany Karlir's was crushing. It felt as though I was being pushed downward from all directions. I had to force myself to stay standing.

Like me, it looked like the Barghest had trouble handling the invisible pressure. Whimpering with an expression I had never seen on a demon—one of fear—the Barghest ran past us and out of the cave. As it left, the crushing and suffocating pressure disappeared, along with the red rays surrounding Karlir.

It took me some time to recover from the surprise and

from being crushed, and so Karlir set up camp as I did so. In all of the four corners of the cave, he placed candles, and after lighting up the entirety of the cave, he left and came back with sky tree wood to build a fireplace.

"Are you okay?" he asked as he clapped his hands together near the wood, effortlessly creating a strong enough spark to light it.

"You are truly amazing," I blurted out without thinking. "What did you do back there?"

"What I used was called presión," replied Karlir as he unpacked various weapons, foods, and items. "Do you know what your aura is?"

"I have heard the term," I answered, annoyed at my own ignorance. "But I don't know what it is."

"Your aura is the physical manifestation of your soul and will energies combined. Your soul is where all of your potential energy is stored and created, your crystal is a separate entity from yourself, and your will is your mind's power," stated Karlir. "When you gain the ability to use your aura, you will be able to see the auras of others and use your own to enhance any abilities granted by your crystal, and any natural ones as well."

"Enhance my abilities," I repeated. "Like aura walking and presión?"

"Yes. By focusing your aura energy underneath your feet, it is possible to do things like walk on water, move at incredibly fast speeds, and strengthen your own legs. Although these are not easy to learn and take intense training to completely master, there are many other things aura energy is useful for," stated Karlir while holding a long, black-sheathed blade in his hands. "Aura presión is a fairly advanced ability where you use your fighting spirit, killing intent, or ambition to overpower the will of others. Although everyone can obtain this ability through training, not everyone has the ambition to have powerful presión. Understand?"

"Yes," I said, sitting and listening as intently as I possibly could.

"But you can also use your aura on weapons for multiple purposes," Karlir announced, standing up and unsheathing a beautiful, silver blade.

While holding the blade in his right hand, the sheath in his left, Karlir nodded towards the entrance of the cave where a large boulder sat. Within seconds, red rays began to appear around Karlir again, but this time with less shine and pressure. Although not crushing like before, I could still feel the pressure around me, and I had to work a little to keep myself from lying down.

"This," said Karlir as he disappeared from where he just stood, reappearing next to the boulder, "is called aura stepping. And this," he said, bringing his sword, now faintly glowing red, down on the rock, "is using your aura with a weapon." With just one slash, he marked the boulder with a large line running down it. In what seemed less than a second, Karlir appeared across the fire, facing me and sitting back down.

"Amazing," was all I could mutter.

"It is," agreed Karlir with a smile. "You will truly understand once you are able to use your own aura. I demonstrated the uses of it to help you realize what you will be training for."

"Thank you." I placed my hand on my forehead. Why had I never heard of auras in Dentro, but Leon seemed to have? Although I had taught myself how to fight after my mother died, I had never heard of the concept of an aura before my fight with Fonos in Cheshria. "How can I unlock my own aura?"

"Through training," declared Karlir with a smile. "Harsh training is the key. And because we don't have a lot of time, your training will be even harder than usual. I want you to begin by placing these weights on your body."

Karlir handed me a weighted chest vest, leg weights, black weighted shoes, and a whistle. After putting on the weights, I took the whistle and placed it on my neck.

"How much does all of this weigh?" I asked, using all of my energy to keep myself from falling down.

"The vest is one hundred pounds, the leg weights are each twenty, and the shoes are five. When I was your age, I trained with twice this weight. And so, every two weeks, we will add weight according to your training progress," said Karlir.

"And the whistle?" I asked.

"If while we are here you get in any trouble that you cannot handle, blow that whistle, and I will be able to locate you. Use it for emergencies only, understand?" he asked with a stern look.

"I understand," I stated. "Now what?"

"First, I want you to move that rock I just slashed from the entrance of the cave to the other side of the cave," commanded Karlir.

"What!" I exclaimed. "That's over a hundred feet!"

"So?" He sat down next to the fire, holding a paper.

"I can't move this at all," I grumbled as I tried to force the stone to move. Even pushing all of my weight against the stone, which stood as tall as I, it wouldn't budge.

"You will have to do that before we move on to the next part of your training," dictated Karlir. "Looks like you have some work to do."

And so, trying to push an unmovable rock, my training that would allow me to change everything began.

Chapter 23:
Bloody Past

"Leon," called Kuchi's deep and all-knowing voice from one of the four rooms that made up the small but cozy hut we were in. "We resume training in five."

"Alright!" I exclaimed loud enough for Kuchi to hear me over the rain pounding on the roof and through the walls of the hut. I loved the rain, and even more so the gloom and darkness it brought.

It had been a week since Zephyr and I had split up to begin our training. For the entire length of it, Kuchi had trained me intensively. Even though he looked around seventy, was the same height as I, and had gray hair, he had demonstrated his mastery of fighting on the first day. He told me to attack him with everything I had, and I did so, but I couldn't land even one hit on him. Although there were many great fighters in the village, none of the ones willing to train with me in the past were even close to Kuchi.

In Dentro Village, I had always been the prodigy of my age group. My parents were both the heads of construction, which comprised mostly family, and were known as two of the most powerful fighters the village had ever produced. My parents were named the Dentro Due, and soon after, they had two children.

The firstborn, my older brother, was recognized as a prodigy at the age of five after defeating a gang of armed thieves in the village. At the age of seven, the Council decided he was strong enough, and he took and passed the Trial of Adulthood, receiving the Void stone. At the age of ten, when I had just been born, he completed a series of outside, high-ranked missions that earned him the title of genius. And finally, when I turned seven, he did something that would forever change my life for the worse. My older brother, Blane, murdered my parents and the entire construction force before fleeing the village.

I picked up both of my swords in preparation to continue training. Memories of that fateful night still haunted me every time I picked up a weapon. Earlier that day, my parents had passed down the family heirlooms: one yellow-and-black sword for the eldest child, and one yellow and one black sword for the younger. My brother had just completed a mission where he had driven off over twenty Barghests from invading the village by himself. Thus my parents saw fit to show how proud they were. In return, later that night, after I had gone out delivering a letter from Blane to the village Elders, I came back to find that my parents and the construction force (made up of most of the rest of my family and close friends) had been murdered.

Crying in agony at the sight of my parents' lifeless and cold bodies, I saw from a distance a hooded figure with a sword on its back running behind another, larger figure. Deciding to get revenge, I chased after the figure until we reached the outskirts of the village. Seeing an Utsu boat on the village dock, I realized that I wouldn't be able to catch the person before they escaped.

"Stop!" I screamed, almost choking on my own tears. "Please!"

And with that, the hooded figure turned around as I gasped in the horror of the nightmare I was trapped in. Blane stopped in his tracks, beginning to unsheathe his sword. After walking a few steps closer and realizing that it was me who had called him, he sheathed his sword before running up to me and pulling me into a hug. I didn't know what to do, or what to believe. My kind, caring, and amazingly strong brother had killed our family? It seemed like an impossible turn of events.

"I'm sorry, Leon," whispered Blane in an apologetic tone with his low, now shaky voice. "I'm sorry."

After holding me and crying in front of me for the first time, his tears dripping on my neck, he let go of me before bringing his hand down towards my neck. Everything turned black.

After that, everything went downhill for me. Although not

as powerful or skillful as my brother, I had a similar aptitude for learning and had also always been referred to as a prodigy. My skills far surpassed those of my same age, and I had been looked upon with great promise, my name known throughout the village.

After Blane murdered our family and left, I became known as "that kid," and was treated with pity, ultimately left alone by all. Although some had come to help me, there was no one left in the village who understood me or who really cared for me.

It was at that time that I changed from a happy, easy-going person to a cocky, arrogant, and vengeful person. I forced myself beyond my natural genius-like abilities and grew stronger with every passing day. I also distanced myself from the villagers, as I decided that trusting no one was better than placing trust in anyone but myself. I had always been separated from others because they saw me as too good, and I soon lost almost all communication with the villagers. Vengeance was the only thing that filled my mind and fueled me to keep getting stronger.

Because of my family's incident, I was not allowed to take the Trial of Adulthood early like my brother—in fact, the Council was so nervous about me that they made me take it two years late. Even so, the village Elders would allow me to secretly complete outside missions for them. Each mission involved traveling to Exilio for trade or business deals with the bandits. When I finally turned fifteen this past year, I took and passed the Trial easily. After receiving the Void crystal, which everyone in my family had received, I was offered a proposal by the village elders. In exchange for delivering Zephyr to Adamus, the head of Exilio, they would tell me the whereabouts of Blane.

Zephyr had surprised me in Exilio. I had accepted and almost completed the mission when I handed him over to the Exilio bandits, which would have led either to his death or his enslavement. Though I had almost gotten him killed, he had risked his life to save me, and for that I would always be indebted to him. It was there that, for the first time since my brother had betrayed me and my family, I had felt like I could confide in someone.

I had decided that after we retrieved the Tyring Sword, I would tell Zephyr about my true reasons for wanting to grow stronger. But after being defeated so easily by the man from Cheshria, Dolo, I realized that I had been straying from my true goal. I needed to do anything and everything I could to become strong enough to kill Blane, even if it meant forsaking a comrade.

Pulling my mind back to the present, I walked out of the small four-room hut and into the open grass field that surrounded us. Standing a few feet away, soaked by the rain, Kuchi turned his all-knowing gaze towards me.

"You truly are a fast learner," he said.

Kuchi had decided that we would conduct our training at what was known as the "elite training ground of Sleeves." Isolated from the rest of the city, it consisted of the four-room hut surrounded by four grassy fields, each the size of a Sleeves district. After demonstrating his abilities and mastery of skill, Kuchi explained what auras were. Although everyone had the ability to use them, only a select few actually learned how to control them.

Kuchi explained that although I had been using my aura without knowing what it truly was, I was already fairly advanced by being able to move at high speeds, known as aura stepping. After explaining the uses of the aura, Kuchi made me complete two types of training every day. For the first part of the day, I would use all of my strength to try to land a hit on Kuchi, and for the second part of the day, I would meditate. Sitting in silence in the middle of one of the grassy fields, I would relax my mind and deepen the connection to my Void crystal.

"Today," said Kuchi as he motioned for me to come

closer to the center of the field where he stood, "We will focus on using your crystal."

"Are you sure?" I asked. "I already—"

"I am the master, am I not?" interrupted Kuchi.

"Yes, but—"

"Enough," declared Kuchi. "Every day I must deal with such disrespect. While still so weak, do you truly question my teachings?"

That stung.

"No," I replied, barely audible. "I will do what you instruct. I will get stronger."

"I will trust you to make the right choices in what you do with your power. But remember, murder and vengeance never solve any problems; they only create an endless cycle of bloodshed," said Kuchi. "Now, with your crystal, have you discovered the nature of your power?"

"Yes," I answered. "When I'm connected with my crystal, Kurai and Hikari, the two spirit manifestations of my crystal, join with me in my mind."

"Two manifestations, you say?" asked Kuchi with an interested look. "I have never heard of this. And what is the nature of your power?"

"It seems that I have the ability to control light and dark

energy," I replied. "Not that I truly understand what that is."

"I see. It's as if you have two abilities in one. But, as I have witnessed in your training, your control over your power is very limited."

"Yes," I agreed, even though I didn't like to. "Using both of my swords, I can manipulate the dark and light energies into a copy of my two blades, and I can propel them by slashing downward."

"Interesting," concluded Kuchi. "Although you have learned to increase your stamina when aura stepping, walk horizontally up surfaces and on water, and increase your control over your aura presión, learning to master your abilities with your crystal will not be so easy—even for a quick learner like you."

"It doesn't matter," I exclaimed. With just the thought of my brother, rage filled my body. "I will get stronger."

"I like your spirit," chuckled Kuchi. "If you weren't so weak, I would like to test that spirit myself. But this is not the time for that. For the next few hours, I want you to harness your dark and light energy around your body, and shoot it in the form of small spheres until you can do so consecutively for five minutes."

"Okay," I said, gripping both of my swords tightly.

"Oh," said Kuchi while walking back towards the hut, "you are to do all training without your swords until I say otherwise. I want you to be able to shoot the energy from your index finger."

"Fine." I sheathed both swords. Taking both sheaths off of my back and placing them on the ground, I walked a few feet into the center of the field, standing up straight. Bringing my hands up, with both index fingers pointing out towards the empty grass fields, I began to focus all my energy into my hands.

"Call me when you are done so we can begin your real training!" exclaimed Kuchi before disappearing into the hut.

With every moment, I needed to get stronger. Although I was focusing all of my attention on harnessing my aura and controlling my Void crystal energy, somewhere in the back of my mind two thoughts continued to float around: How was Zephyr doing? And more importantly, when would I be able to kill that man?

Chapter 24:
Demonic Misconceptions

To be honest, I had never been troubled by an inanimate object so much as by this one large rock. I mean, it was a rock. Seriously, why did it have to be so difficult? Anyone watching me would probably be thinking, "Oh come on, Zephyr, take it like a man," but I'd like to see them try to move a rock their own height and twice their width. It had been two weeks since I had finally moved that rock, making it three since I had begun my training with Karlir.

For the first few days of my training, I had the mindset that I was only allowed to move it using my hands. But realizing that this was impossible for anyone, I decided one day to work together with my crystal. On the fourth day of training, I used the Sky Pushuu, propelling it into the center of the rock. Small lines, about five inches tall, slowly began to appear the center of the stone, which was oval-shaped. Created from the speed of the rotation fueling the sphere's offensive attack, it took four of these attacks over a period of two hours to force the rock to budge from its spot.

In seven days, using too many of my Sky Pushuu to count, I finally managed to move the rock a little over a hundred feet, by accident of course. Smiling, Karlir walked over and patted me on the head as I sat down, still amazed at the amount of energy and time it had taken to move the rock.

After giving me a day to rest, Karlir pointed out a few ways I had changed during my efforts to move the rock. Through realizing my own limitations, I had figured out a way to move around them. Also, even though I hadn't realized until he pointed it out, by using my own attack over and over, not only had I strengthened the link between my crystal and me, but I had increased my overall stamina in three ways.

I could now manifest and perform the Sky Pushuu more than twenty times before feeling the effects of energy loss, and I could control the size of the attack from the size of a fist to the size of an average human head. Apparently, to Karlir's eyes, my aura presión and total amount of energy had increased and become more stable because of the strengthened link between my crystal and me. And finally, the overall time Sora's presence could remain active in my mind had also increased to as long as I wished him there.

From then on, Karlir implemented four different types of training throughout the day. The first session, which began as soon as the sun rose, was combat sparring. Karlir decided that although I was fairly proficient at using a dagger, my true strength was in hand-to-hand combat. He decided that I should stop using the dagger, and so I left it in my bag for safekeeping.

Thus, every morning, Karlir would instruct me on hand-to-hand techniques, which he referred to as tai-jut-su. Apparently, within tai-jut-su, there were many different fighting styles which only masters knew, but because I did not have enough time to learn any of the styles, I would train extensively in the basic form.

In the afternoons, Karlir would instruct me on focusing my energy and gaining control of my aura. Although it took me at least a full week, I finally managed to gain the ability to use my aura and manifest it as physical energy. The process was similar to when I focused on making the Sky Pushuu, and eventually I learned how to separate the many uses of my aura energy. From walking up cave walls to aura stepping and aura jumping as high as eight feet, to even enhancing overall strength, my proficiency in using my aura greatly increased.

Third, in the early evenings, Karlir would make me sit down and meditate outside. At first I was resistant to the idea because of the snow and freezing weather, but Karlir hinted to another way of using my aura. By focusing it and covering myself with an outside layer of constant energy, I would be able to keep myself warm.

Although it took some time to get used to, I soon

mastered the art of controlling my temperature by surrounding myself with a thin aura coating, barely visible as a faint glow on my skin. After I had learned this useful technique, Karlir instructed me to meditate outside while connecting with my crystal.

Over time, focusing and connecting with Sora became easier and easier as I visited the depths of my soul in the form of a beautiful island beach, on an endless sea, called my Soul Mirror. As the flow of time in the real world did not match that of the one in my Soul Mirror, I spent what seemed around a week there each day before Karlir would rouse me from my concentration.

At first, Sora and I used the free time to explore the island, sit on the beach talking and laughing, and other leisurely things. But after three days of meditating each evening, equating to three weeks in my Soul Mirror, Karlir asked me about what I had been doing. Thinking that it sounded foolish when I looked back on it, as I was supposed to be training, Karlir corrected my misconceptions.

"Your Soul Mirror is a reflection of your soul, just as your crystal's manifestation within your mind is the reflection of your crystal's will," he said. "If relaxing is what you wish to do, then that is what you must do. But remember to focus on your ultimate goal."

The next day, after meditating and arriving on the beautiful, soft sand, I walked over to Sora and we smiled at each other.

"Are you sure you don't want to stay relaxed?" asked Sora.

"Yeah," I said laughing, "I'm sure. Let's begin training."

"I've been waiting for you to say that," said Sora, smiling.

From then on, Sora advised me on learning how to use more of my Ouranos crystal's powers. My stone still hung as a necklace under my white t-shirt. I learned that my aura and crystal energy were very different. After Karlir explained that everyone, even people without powers from crystals, had auras, he added that the powers my crystal provided me fed off my own aura, as an aura was replenished over time, with rest. In turn, after Karlir's explanation, Sora revealed the nature of my own power to some extent, as he did not truly know all of it himself.

He explained it as "the ability to manipulate, generate, and absorb air or wind."

When I had learned the basis of my crystal's power, Karlir implemented the fourth and final training method. Every evening, before passing out, I would be instructed on using the Ouranos crystal abilities I learned with Sora in real combat. By sparring with Karlir, this time not permitted to move from my beginning position and only able to use my wind manipulation, I advanced quickly. Within my Soul Mirror, Sora enlightened me on how to use my ability. Simply by focusing my thoughts on one strong will, such as blowing a gust of wind from my hand, I could do so as long as I had enough aura or physical stamina left.

Now, two weeks after moving the large rock and being pounded with tai-jut-su, wind manipulation, and aura skills, I felt like every bone in my body was going to break. Even though I had obviously gotten stronger, I felt weaker than before. As I lay against the hard, rocky wall of the cave, Karlir snored a few feet away. Forcing myself to get up with all of my might, I slowly made my way over to the entrance of the cave and looked outside to see the empty darkness of the night mixed with beautiful, white snowflakes.

Covering myself in aura energy automatically after doing it so often during training, I walked about a hundred feet down the mountain from the cave, sitting down next to a small, blue sky tree covered in snow. I lifted my hand in the air to feel the cool touch of the snow, but it instantly vaporized when it came in contact with my finger tip. I remembered that I needed to uncover my aura cloak.

Only releasing the cover of energy from the tip of my

hand, I smiled as I felt the soft flake of snow touch my skin, slowly melt, and drip as water. The outside world was truly amazing, I thought to myself, as I stood up to return to the cave before Karlir woke.

Turning around towards the cave, I looked up to find two gray-haired Barghests growling a few feet away. Both of them were taller than I, one of them at least double my own height. Not wanting any unnecessary confrontation, I tried to make my way around the Barghests by slowly walking to their right.

Apparently they were hungry for Zephyr-meat, and it seemed my plan to avoid them was fruitless. Growling and glaring at me with their angry red eyes, both of the Barghests slowly began to crawl closer to me. Deciding that the fastest thing to do would be to try to scare them away, I opened my eyes a little wider and glared at the smaller of the two.

After I had gained the ability to use my aura, Karlir had mentioned that I would be able to sense the aura presión of others when it was being used. As I gazed at the smaller Barghest, I tried to sense its aura. But, unlike when Karlir used his around me, I couldn't feel any crushing or physical force from the Barghest. The only thing I could feel was its piercing stare and its basic killing intent. And somewhere even deeper, I sensed another, less obvious emotion.

Suddenly, the small Barghest began to charge across the space separating us. Still keeping my eyes on it, I increased my own aura presión by strengthening one emotion within my mind: my killing intent. Feeling my own aura presión grow stronger as I strengthened my determination and will power, the small Barghest abruptly stopped in its tracks, only a few feet away.

"GO!" I commanded as loudly as I could through the howling of the snow-filled wind.

Instantly, with a look of fear in its eyes, the Barghest yelped and took off down the mountain. Turning my vision towards the larger Barghest, I repeated the same action of forcing my presión upon it. The Barghest was visibly afraid and looked like it was fighting against an invisible force pushing down against it, but unlike the other demon, this one did not run.

Its eyes were also different from the other animal; in spite of the fact that I could see pain and its killing intent within its eyes, I could also sense kindness within it. Taught in Dentro that demons could not have feelings or emotions, I settled upon the idea that I was imagining things. While now growling even louder than before, it scratched its claws against the snow-covered ground.

Zephyr, called Sora's river-like voice in my mind, each word flowing together like a poem, *what now?*

It looks like I haven't completely mastered using my aura presión, I thought back. *I don't want to kill for no reason, as we still have food left over from hunting earlier.*

Very true. So?

Sora's voice resonating in my mind had become a common phenomenon over the past two weeks. Providing me with advice and help in any situation if I asked for it or he saw fit, he had become a valuable asset.

I won't kill it, I decided. *I'll just force it to leave.*

Swiftly crossing the snowy space separating us, the Barghest launched itself through the air, claws outstretched to slash at my face and neck. Deciding that the fastest way to end this would be to make it realize it was outmatched, I quickly pushed off the ground.

In the past second I had been a few inches in front of the Barghest, while now I had almost instantly moved a few feet behind it. Growling and yelping in frustration, the Barghest moved its head in search of where I had gone. Not wanting to waste any more time, I clapped my hands together to alert it to my presence.

Jumping around to face me, howling and pointing its dog-like nose towards the sky, it kept its eyes on me as it brought its nose back down. After clapping my hands together, I realized that I had left my gloves in the cave, and so I decided that using tai-jut-su would not be the best idea. Pointing my right hand out, palm facing the demon, I imagined wind blowing from my hand. Instantly, a strong gust of continuous wind began to blow from my palms towards the dog, accompanied by a *PSHHHH* sound.

The wind hit the stunned Barghest before it could react, propelling it into the air and dropping it a few feet behind the where it had just stood. After a few seconds, the demon slowly picked itself up.

A little more powerful than you had intended? asked Sora with an audible frown. *We need to train more.*

A little, I said, frowning as well.

Need a lot more training, declared Sora with a joking tone, but I knew he was serious.

Admiring its courage for not accepting defeat, I decided that I would end it with one more gust of wind. As the Barghest sprinted across the field in an effort to attack again first, I placed the image of a less-powerful wind blowing from my hand within my mind. But as I began to release it, the sight of the Barghest's sharp claws changed my thoughts from a soft attack into the image of a claw. And so, as I released the attack from the palm of my hand, I yelled in displeasure at the result.

Hitting the Barghest directly, the large diagonal slash of

compressed air that had been shot from my palm dissipated. The Barghest, now on the ground, squealed in pain as I looked down upon the large beast to find a deep wound stretching from under its right eye to the end of its stomach.

Good job, said Sora with sarcasm. *What now? Are we going to leave it there to die?*

I frowned again. *You know I wouldn't do that.*

I waited five minutes for the Barghest to finally fall unconscious. It closed its eyes, and its aura presión grew steadily weaker as its killing intent disappeared from my senses. Focusing a large amount of my aura energy into my arms, I picked up the Barghest under its stomach, lifting it and placing it onto my back. The creature was at least twice height and width and three times my weight, but the large killer dog's gray fur was soft as it rubbed against the back of my neck.

Slowly entering the cave so as to not wake either the Barghest or Karlir, I placed the Barghest on the far right of the cave, far enough away from the back that Karlir or I would have time to react if it were to wake. But it seemed that I had either taken too long or been too loud during my encounter, as Karlir's voice resonated throughout the cave, to my surprise.

"And what have you brought here?" asked Karlir as he appeared behind me, kneeling next to the Barghest's face. "A

Barghest!"

"Yes," I admitted. "I didn't want to kill it, since there was no need to."

"You aren't in full control of your powers yet," stated Karlir. "Do not worry yourself. I will handle this. Get some rest, morning will come soon."

"Are you sure?" I asked, feeling guilty. I didn't want to leave my master fixing my problem.

"Yes, yes," he declared. "Now go rest!"

Walking over to the back of the cave where I had been sleeping the past three weeks, I lay down on one of the soft cots Karlir had brought along for us. I couldn't help but think one thing—*I didn't want it to die*. I didn't know if it was just me being selfish, or whether it was because I may have seen something I had been taught didn't exist in demons, but I just didn't want to end its life.

"Don't kill it," I pleaded, sitting up from my bed.

"As a master-student pair," stated Karlir, turning his warm gaze towards me, "we must have the same ideals. And don't worry, we mostly do. Trust in me. Get some rest, Zephyr."

Good, I thought to myself. For the second time in a long time, I would trust someone. "Good night, Master," I said as I closed my eyes, the world disappearing around me as I felt myself falling asleep.

Chapter 25:
That Hated Smile

It had now been almost three months since I had begun my training with Kuchi. Every day of training had brought something different, and with it, a new experience to help me grow stronger and move towards achieving my one true goal. Over the past two months, I had increased my physical strength by doing hundreds of pushups and sit ups a day and sparring even when it felt like I couldn't move anymore.

Through working with Hikari and Kurai, my crystal's two manifestations within my mind, I had learned to overcome my own weakness and control more of my abilities. Hikari, a blond-haired, white-eyed, short teenage boy, trained me in manipulating my light powers. Kurai, a black-haired, black-eyed, tall, skinny teenage boy, trained me in the use of my dark powers.

Unlike before, when I could only shoot energy in a shape copied from something else, I could now manipulate dark and light energy with ease. From covering my swords in dark and light energy to increase their power, to encasing someone in complete darkness, it felt as if I could do almost anything.

Aside from my overall control over my crystal's abilities, I had also learned to use my aura in conjunction with my natural skills. My aura-stepping speed had increased from ten times the speed of a normal person to a pace that couldn't be seen at all by the untrained eye. Also, I had honed my aura presión to such a great extent that I sensed I could do almost anything. It all felt truly magnificent.

The only thing that had been a continuous problem throughout my training was something neither Kuchi nor I understood. It first occurred when I had been walking through a district in Sleeves and a woman had screamed "Thief!"

She was pointing at a man who had just run by me. I turned around, only to be reminded of that murderer I called my brother and when he had run away from his crimes.

It was at that instant I felt Hikari's presence, the crystal manifestation of my light powers, almost disappear from my mind. Hikari had always been the voice in my mind telling me to do the "right" thing, while Kurai, the dark manifestation of my powers, had always been the one telling me to give in to my desires. From within, it felt as if Kurai had taken over my mind, and suddenly everything went black as I stared at the fleeing thief.

When I opened my eyes, I found that I had my leg placed on his stomach, both my swords impaling his chest. As I looked down at the pitiful face of the dead man I had just seen running away, I smiled. Although I could not remember killing him, I felt no sorrow for a man who would run away and not face his crime.

After killing that man, it seemed that whenever something reminded me of my past, I would black out, waking up in a different place. But with every blackout, I found that the things I had always wanted to do, like take the life of those who didn't deserve to live, such as unlawful people, had been done for me.

But I also realized that if I could not control this power, I would not be strong enough to take revenge on my brother, Blane. And so today, the day before Zephyr was supposed to be back from his training, I decided to ask Kuchi what I should do.

"I knew that something was different about you," stated Kuchi. "Especially after that one day of sparring a few weeks ago. I had not planned to tell you about it yet."

"What?" I asked. I didn't remember anything unusual.

"After you told me about how you wanted to kill your brother, I used it to taunt you into releasing all your power," admitted Kuchi.

"Yeah," I said. "So?"

"You stood completely still, and suddenly your aura presión filled with true killing intent," replied Kuchi.

"Isn't it good for my killing intent to be strong?" I asked.

"It increases the strength of my own aura presión, right?"

"Yes, usually," replied Kuchi. "But it was like you were a different person. Your eyes turned black, and dark energy began to shoot out from your body in massive waves. All around you, the flowers wilted, and the energy from your body began to scorch the ground itself, turning the field black. It was at this point that you looked at me, and repeated the same phrase over and over again."

"What phrase?" I asked, although I suspected I already knew the answer.

"Kill Blane," answered Kuchi.

"I," I began with a stutter, "don't remember this."

"Your movement changed, and you attacked me with such ferocity that I had to truly defend myself. It was not a game, but a life and death battle. In all honesty, it took everything I had to knock you out without killing you," said Kuchi.

"No!" I exclaimed. "If I can't even control my own powers, I will never be able to match up to Blane."

"When you use your powers, your eye color changes from brown to a combination of yellow and black because of how you control the balance between both light and dark energy. When you went berserk that day, your eyes were only black, and the only emotion I could sense from you was hatred—and a feeling close to insanity.

"I think this phenomenon occurs when you try to release more of your crystal's power than you can handle. Because you are powered by the sole idea of vengeance, the two sides of your power aren't equal, and so the stronger one takes over."

"Which part of me is stronger?" I asked.

"Without question, the raw power of your dark form overtakes your controlled powers. But because you cannot control it, you really should not use it," answered Kuchi.

Blane had been a genius at the age of seven and had mastered all of his powers by the age of ten, while I, at fifteen, was still having problems with my own. If I could not control them, I would just have to learn to use them to my advantage. If I wasn't strong enough to defeat Blane at my current level, I would have to find a way to go into this dark form, as Kuchi called it.

"You must truly find the path you are going to walk," began Kuchi, "or your life will be filled with loneliness and pain."

"My path was chosen for me," I declared as I looked Kuchi in the eyes. "I am an avenger. Pain is my strength. Those who do not recognize or choose to try to block my way—I will kill them without hesitation."

"Does Zephyr know this?" asked Kuchi with a grim look.

"For now," I started as I looked out one of the windows in the hut, "Zephyr is a friend. We have a common goal, and being with him has helped make me stronger. But if he tries to stand in my way, or I see that I can become stronger by killing him or leaving him, I won't hesitate to do so."

"This is truly saddening," said Kuchi as he stood up from where we sat in the hut. "Although I do not agree with your methods, I believe that you will someday change for the better. Life is a gift, do not forget that. Get some sleep. Tomorrow, we will meet Zephyr and Karlir."

"Okay." I walked over to my bed and climbed in.

While trying to force myself to sleep, two voices suddenly echoed through my mind.

Leon, called Kurai's low, malicious voice, *we must find Blane.*

No, stated Hikari, his voice soft but mature. *Thinking of Blane will only cause pain. Remember the debt you owe Zephyr for saving your life. Live in the present, not the past.*

Kurai is right, I thought. *Finding and killing that man takes all precedence.*

Yes, yes, yes! exclaimed Kurai.

You truly have fallen, stated Hikari, and his presence seemed to vanish.

That weakling is gone, said Kurai. *Although only for now. It's for the better that you look towards the darkness for true strength.*

I'm going to sleep, I thought in response. I was tired and wanted to be well-rested for tomorrow.

Remember, began Kurai as his dark presence began to dissipate, *I can win you your desires. I am your true power.*

After both presences had disappeared from my mind, my only thought as I drifted off to sleep was the image of killing my brother.

With morning, Kuchi and I left the hut and made our way back to Karlir's estate within twenty minutes. Feeling rested, I was truly interested in seeing how powerful Zephyr had become. I had decided to myself as I awoke that if he could not keep up with me, I would have to leave him and continue on my own.

As we walked up to the door, we found a tall, muscular, red-headed man smiling at us.

"Leon!" he exclaimed. "You look different."

"Different?" I mimicked with a sigh.

"In a good way," stated Jordan, the man who had brought us to Sleeves. "'Stronger' would be a better word."

"A true understatement," I declared.

"Hey," said Kuchi as he patted me on the shoulder.

Allowing myself to shrug him off, I looked upward towards Jordan with a frown.

"Enough play, where's Zephyr?" I was tired of waiting, as I had really finished my training within the first two months. The last month had just been to hone my skills and rest.

"He's—"Jordan was interrupted by a familiar and lively voice.

"I'm here," declared Zephyr.

As I turned around to find Zephyr and Karlir standing a few feet away, smiling, I couldn't help but be amazed at how different Zephyr looked. Wearing dark blue shorts, a white t-shirt, and open-toed sandals, his gray-and–black spiky hair, which had barely covered his forehead, was now long enough to shield his cloudy gray eyes.

His arms, which had had almost no definition before, now had visible muscle even without him flexing. Although he had been taller than I when we had first met, I had grown taller, but he still stood at least a few inches taller than I. His skin, which had been a fairly dark tan, was now a much lighter tan, as if he hadn't been in the sun for a while.

But as I waved two fingers at him in greeting, it wasn't his physical appearance that really got me. It was more of the look of confidence that he now had, something he hadn't had before.

And although I could sense a small amount of aura from Kuchi and Jordan, I realized that it felt as if there was nothing being emitted from either Karlir or Zephyr. Had he only grown physically stronger? And not ability-wise?

"Zephyr," I said as he stepped up to me, a foot away and still smiling.

"Leon!" responded Zephyr. He always looked so lively, something I had come to dislike. "How have you been?"

"Have you gotten stronger?" I asked, intentionally ignoring his question.

Zephyr laughed as Karlir smiled and hugged his brother.

"Of course," he said. "I wouldn't waste my master's last three months for nothing."

I had forgotten that Karlir was supposed to have the death penalty carried out three months after his ruling by the Vice Chief of Sleeves, Greer. I looked at the elderly man with disappointment. Why would such a powerful man choose to allow himself to be killed? But he wasn't my master, nor was he my concern.

"Zephyr!" exclaimed Jordan as he and Zephyr shook hands. "You look so much stronger and more mature, just like Leon."

"Thanks," said Zephyr, bringing his hand up towards the

back of his head and smiling. "It's all thanks to Karlir."

"He's modest," stated Karlir, walking up next to Zephyr and patting him on the back. Unlike me, Zephyr only smiled as his master praised him.

"Leon," called Karlir as he turned around to look at me. "I can sense from your stable aura presión that you have truly improved. Am I right?"

"Yes," I boasted in response.

"Good," he commented. "Then this would be a good time to test each other's improvement out, I would say."

"Ours?" asked Zephyr with a confused look. "You want Leon and me to fight again?"

"Yeah," I muttered. "Even after what happened last time?"

"I thought you would have learned," stated Kuchi with a frown. "The past is the past, and you have both trained extensively."

"I agree with my brother, Kuchi," stated Karlir.

"Our levels were so different," I said, shrugging. "I don't want it to be unfair."

"If you think so," said a voice I hadn't expected to respond, "then let's spar. Would be good to test out our training somewhat."

It looked as though Zephyr's self-confidence really had risen, as he would never have spoken up against my own taunts in such an assured tone before.

"Fine," I grunted.

"Good," repeated Karlir. "As I am sure this will be a very different fight than before, you can both begin on my outside training ground. I think it will be large enough for a quick test of abilities."

Next to the path leading up to Karlir's home was a field sixty yards in length, large enough for me to fight without having to hold back. I walked over to the center of the field with Zephyr. Standing at the edge of the field, with Karlir and Kuchi, Jordan mouthed *Good luck!* to both of us.

Gazing at Zephyr again, I realized that he no longer had a dagger sheath on his back, and his white gloves hung on his right side attached by a clip. Lying on his chest, on top of his white t-shirt, was his clear, oval-shaped Ouranos stone. Still not being able to sense anything from him, I couldn't help but chuckle.

"Let's have fun," exclaimed Zephyr. He patted me on shoulder before backing up a few steps.

Like me, Zephyr was familiar with pain, hatred, and loneliness. When I had first met him after the Trial in Dentro, he had reminded me of someone I had met long ago.

One time, when I was younger, I had stopped to take a quick dip in the ocean at the beach on my way home from the Academy. After swimming around for a few minutes and realizing that my parents would get angry if I were to take any longer, I rushed out of the water, then stopped in front of a boy around my age sitting with his head against his thighs, crying.

Still standing in the shallow water on the shore, I called out to the boy.

"Hey!" The boy instantly wiped the tears from his face, only to have more flow down as he looked up at me with his gray eyes. "What's wrong?"

"My mother is dying," he said softly through his tears. His voiced sounded so innocent and scared.

"I'm sorry," I said. I couldn't leave him there like that. "Hey, do you love your mom?"

"Of course!" he yelled, tears rushing down his face at a faster pace.

"Does your mom love you?" I asked again in the kindest voice I could make.

"Yes," he replied before burying his head in his lap again. "Why?"

"My older brother once told me that love is so strong,

even death can't stop it," I stated.

"So?" asked the boy, still crying.

"I don't know how bad it is to die," I said as I kneeled down in the water, "But I know that if you love your mom enough, she will never truly leave you."

"Really?" asked the boy as his tears slowed. "Is that true? I won't be alone?"

"Of course!" I sat up and splashed the boy with salty, warm ocean water. "And you know, just 'cause I'm gonna be nice, I'll be your friend so you won't ever be alone. So don't be sad, okay?"

Slowing standing up and rubbing the last few tears off his face with his shirt, the boy looked up at me and smiled. "Okay."

"Good!" I yelled in response as he jumped in the water, playfully tackling me.

"Hey, what's your name?" he asked as we resurfaced.

"Leon," I answered. "What's yours?"

"I'm—" But before he could answer, I turned around to the sound of my name.

"Leon!" yelled my mother as she walked up to us, grabbing me by the hand and pulling me away from the beach. "You shouldn't be playing with that boy."

"But why?" I asked in anger as tears began to roll down

my face. "He's my friend!"

Although that day was long ago, I had never forgotten what it felt like to have something taken away from me, even by my parents. Before we separated for training, it had been obvious that Zephyr still harbored dark feelings of resentment towards the villagers along with knowing what it felt like to be separated from others, to be different, and so I took a liking to him. But now it looked as though he had forgotten what it had been like for him, and so, with this battle, I would remind him.

"I will remind you—" I pointed my index finger towards his neck, "—of the difference in our skill."

Chapter 26:
Growth

Facing Leon as he looked at me, ready to start our sparring match, I couldn't help but smile. In the past three months, Karlir had taught me more than I would've ever learned by staying in Dentro, and for that I was grateful to him. He had taught me not only how to use my powers and become stronger, but also a new way of looking at the world.

Before, I had believed that I would never be strong or good enough, and that I would always fail to fulfill my goals, no matter how hard I tried. Even when I put on my toughest face, there had always been a seed of doubt I could never get rid of. But looking back on my training, Karlir had changed my way of thinking for the better.

During one of our last few weeks together, Karlir and I had traveled from the snow-covered mountain we had been on to a warm, grass-covered one. Although it was deeper into Devil's Pass, with stronger monsters lurking around, Karlir brought me up to the top of the mountain, overlooking most of Devil's Pass. It was made of hundreds of mountains, from grass- to snow-covered, and I gazed down in amazement as Karlir and I sat next to each other.

"What do you think of when you look down?" Karlir had

asked.

"I don't know," I replied. "I guess a bunch of caves and mountains?"

Karlir chuckled. "It is that."

"What about you, Master?" I asked.

"I see more than I could ever understand," he declared as he pointed at a snow-covered mountain. "Snow is such a beautiful creation. It's soft and never falls from the sky with the same shape. Each flake is different."

"Yeah," I agreed.

"But look over there," motioned Karlir as he pointed at a warm-looking, grass-covered mountain. "Although that's a very different climate, the warmth and grass that grows in it makes it a truly relaxing place to be."

I laughed. "Yeah, I guess so."

"Although our time together has been short, I haven't had as much fun as this in a long time. And to be honest, although I don't have any family left aside from my brother, if I did have a son or grandson, I would want him to be like you."

For some reason, I couldn't help but smile as he said those words. It had been a long three months. And since my mother died, I hadn't spent this much time with anyone until now, as the villagers wouldn't even come near me if they could avoid it.

"What do you mean?" I asked as Karlir turned to look at me.

"Zephyr," he said, holding up two fingers, "there are two kinds of aura presión, when you get to a certain level of control. One, killing presión, is powerful enough to kill. The other, known as worldly presión, is limited to knocking others out, but it has many other uses as well."

"Oh," I sighed. "Which one is better to have?"

"What you have is dependent on what you believe in and the nature of your personality. For one like myself, who has trained for years, I can use both. But as I do not believe in killing needlessly, I do not use my killing presión. Worldly presión, although it may not seem as powerful, can be used to win a fight or for minor healing purposes."

"Healing?"

"Yes. By sharing your own aura as energy, you can speed up the healing process for yourself and others, and even help heal mortal wounds to some extent."

"That's amazing!"

"Yes, it truly is a wonderful gift. But as I was saying before, your worldly presión is unlike any I have ever felt. When you first came here, before I taught you how to suppress your aura presión, you were essentially leaking worldly aura presión from your body, and a large amount at that."

"Wow," I exclaimed. I didn't really know how to respond.

"As I have gotten to know you, I have seen that you are one who cares for all, not just your friends, your family, or yourself. You love nature and everything it comprises, even the so-called demonic creatures of our world. You truly are a kind person. That is also why I split you and Leon up for your training."

"Yeah," I replied. "I was wondering about that. Why did you?"

"Unlike you, Leon emits killing aura presión. But like you, he was emitting a large amount of it subconsciously. Since a person is always born with a natural type of aura, killing or worldly, you master that far more quickly, as it comes naturally. I was born with a worldly aura, and my brother was born with killing. Although most but not all who possess killing tend to have a more cruel way of looking at the world and are easily pulled into darkness, my brother is not one of those. But from what I sense from Leon, he is."

"Leon." I frowned. "So you split us up because of our aura types. But from what you're saying, he's being pulled into the darkness?"

"Yes," answered Karlir. "From when we first met, his aura presión gave the feeling of loneliness, hate, and rage. I was hoping that you would know why I may be sensing such feelings from him."

Although I had always known of what happened to Leon's family, as did everyone in the village, I had never really thought about it, as I had been drowning in my own self-pity. Even after Leon's family was murdered, he had still become so strong. He was confident, powerful, and smart. He was what I had always wanted to be.

After explaining the massacre of Leon's family by his brother, I watched as Karlir sat in silence for a few minutes before speaking again.

"That truly is painful and saddening news," he said. "I do not blame him for turning to the darkness. Are you friends?"

"Yes," I replied with a shrug and a smile. "He almost got me killed, and I saved his life at one point. But after that, I never looked back and just tried to be friendly with him. I've never had a true friend. I think he's the closest I've ever had."

"You truly are caring," said Karlir with a smile. "I know you have many plans and goals for after you finish your training, but I will tell you now—I think you are the only one who can drag Leon from the darkness."

"I don't know," I stated. "I don't think I'm strong enough. You saw our last fight. And all of his skills were greater than mine."

"Yes, at that time he was more powerful and advanced than you. But you must never give up so easily," responded Karlir as he gazed at me. "You are more powerful than you can imagine; you have so much hidden potential. Just look at how powerful you have become in such a short time. It would have taken most people years of training."

"So how do I bring him back into the light?" I asked in frustration. "Please tell me, Master."

"In truth," said Karlir as he looked down at the mountains, "I don't know."

"You don't know?" I exclaimed. "How am I supposed to know something that not even the man who befriended and trained with a dragon knows? The man who defeated ten thousand men with only three hundred at his command? How can I, someone looked down on as a failure, even do something like that?"

"Because—" began Karlir as I interrupted him.

"I'm a failure, I'm not smart, I'm not a great fighter and I—"

"I know you will find a way," declared Karlir as he placed

both his hands on my shoulder.

"Wha—" I muttered in surprise, I only to stop as Karlir smiled at me.

"I believe in you," he said, still smiling.

"You believe in me?"

"Of course. Even if you cannot defeat your opponent with strength, use everything you have, including your love of life and kindness. That is your true power."

I smiled. For the first time, it felt like I had father.

"Would you mind," I asked as I stood up, gazing at the mountains below, "if I called you my grandfather?"

"Grandfather?" he chuckled, also standing up. "I'm not that old!"

We both laughed as hard as we could.

"Well," I yelled as I started making my way down the mountain, "how about Gramps, old man?"

"What?" exclaimed Karlir as he started running after me. "I told you, I am not old!"

And so, as I listened to Leon boasting that he would remind me of the difference in our skill, I didn't let myself get angry at his degrading words. Karlir's statement echoed through my mind. *I believe in you. And remember, even if you cannot defeat your opponent with strength, use everything you have, including your love of life and kindness.*

It might sound lame, weak, or unrealistic to others, but I had decided that I would not let the old man's belief go to waste.

"I'm ready," I stated as I looked at Leon. Although we had both grown taller, he was still shorter than I. Almost as skinny as I was before, he now had at least three times the muscle mass, and he must have had intense training to tone and shape his muscle into a slim fighter's build. He was still pale, and his long, black hair covered his eyes.

"Where's your dagger?" he asked.

"I don't use it anymore," I replied.

"Are you sure that's a good choice?" he asked in amusement. "You might think twice after we begin."

"Then let's start," I declared.

"Begin!" yelled Karlir from the end of the field near his house.

Instantly, I could feel both our aura presións push against each other, like light and dark. And as Karlir had pointed out, his aura had a large concentration of pure killing intent. As our auras pushed against each other, equally matched, Leon looked a little stunned.

"Wow," he stated. "It looks like you didn't train for nothing."

"Yeah," I replied, deciding it was time to start.

Releasing my white gloves from their holder at my side, I slowly slid them on, not losing concentration on our aura presión battle.

Unsheathing his familiar black and yellow swords, Leon began walking towards me. After taking a few steps, he smiled and disappeared from where he had just stood, like in our previous fight. This time, though, I was ready.

Through the corner of my eye, I saw Leon's yellow blade coming at me, slashing towards my neck. I ducked, only to find his black blade in the process of slashing down at me as I looked up to find him maneuvering in midair. Deciding that dodging wouldn't work, I smiled, then used my own aura step to seemingly disappear and move a few feet away from where I had just stood.

"So," said Leon as he landed on the ground, "looks like I'm not the only one who can aura step now. This might be more challenging than I thought. But there's still so much more, Zephyr!"

As he finished, Leon aura stepped in front of me, covering ten feet in less than a second. As he brought his yellow blade in a horizontal slash aimed at my shoulder, I jumped back, only to find him behind me, slashing with his black blade. I aura stepped a few feet away again, and we continued our attack-and-dodge game for what seemed like minutes.

"See," he said, taking a break from his onslaught. "You can't counterattack against me without a weapon."

"Just fight," I insisted while looking at him. His eyes truly looked as if they were filled with hatred. Even though I had only been dodging his attacks and not attacking him, it didn't mean that he had been correct in his assumption.

This time aura stepping and appearing directly in front of me, Leon brought both of his blades down on me from midair. Surprised that he would challenge me head-on, I moved both my hands up towards his blade, focusing my aura energy into my hands. I collided with Leon's blades and closed my hands around them. A stunned expression on his face, his feet landed on the ground, blades still caught by my hands, and I looked him in the eyes.

"Don't," I said as I let go of his blades, pulling my right hand back and forming a fist, focusing my aura energy into my hands to increase my strength and bringing my fist forcefully into his stomach, "keep underestimating me!"

As I pushed my fist into his stomach, I could feel his abs and muscles fight against the impact. Even so, I knew it had to hurt as he flew back a few feet before hitting the ground.

"No way," he said, getting up and slashing the air with his swords. "When did you become so strong?"

Tired of talking and hearing his boasts and taunts, I ignored his question. Taking it as a hint to get on with our fight, Leon lifted up both of his blades, pointing their tips straight into the air. Suddenly, just like in our previous fight, dark and light energy began to swirl all around him. Unlike before, though, when he had had what looked like an equal amount of yellow and black energies around him, barely any yellow energy seemed to be there.

Within seconds, the energy around him completely disappeared, forming into yellow and black balls. They floated on the tips of his swords, the smaller, yellow ball on top of his yellow sword and the large, black ball on the black sword's tip. Leon pointed the tips of his blades towards me.

"Let's see you stop this," he murmured as blasts of yellow and black energy suddenly erupted towards me from the energy balls.

Realizing that if I decided to dodge his attack, Karlir's house would be hit by its full force, most likely destroying the whole residence, I stretched my arm in front of me, palm open.

What are you going to do? echoed Sora's voice within my mind.

It's okay, I thought pleasantly. *Let me handle this one alone.*

Okay, said Sora as his presence within my mind weakened a little to allow me full concentration.

Thinking that the only way to stop Leon's attack from destroying anything it touched would be to counter with a similar attack, I imagined a huge, swirling gust of wind, large enough to match and take over Leon's oncoming blasts.

Instantly, a tornado-like wind swirled from my hand into a large wave of wind energy, rushed from my palm, and collided with Leon's black-and-yellow blast. ***BOOM!***

All around us, dust from the explosion slowly settled as I looked at Leon to find him gazing back to me. We truly were different people than we had been when we had parted three months ago. Not allowing him an opening, I concentrated on the thought of aura energy below my feet, propelling myself with an aura step towards Leon.

It looked as Leon had the same idea, though, as we suddenly reappeared halfway between where we had stood, now barely three feet apart. He brought his swords down in vertical slashes, and I brought my right fist in an uppercut towards his chin. Leon and I suddenly stopped in place as an unexpected figure appeared in the middle of our attack.

"WHAT ARE YOU DOING?!" yelled Autumn, one hand held in front of Leon and the other in front me.

Chapter 27:
A New Chapter

"What's going on?!" screamed Autumn as she turned her head back and forth, looking from me to Leon. "I leave your side for five minutes, and you two have become enemies!?"

As I looked at Autumn's confused and stunned expression, I couldn't help but gaze upon how beautiful she was. In all the cities and towns I had visited on my journey, I had seen no one as amazing as her. It wasn't something as simple as her physical appearance that got to me, but rather the combination of everything about her.

"Zephyr!" she yelled as she stood up straight to face me. "I wouldn't expect this from you. What happened?"

Taking a second to take off my gloves, I looked at her and couldn't help but place my hand behind my head and start laughing.

"What's funny?" she asked angrily.

"We were sparring," said Leon suddenly as he placed his swords into the sheaths on his back. "You ruined it."

"Hey," I said to Leon as he turned and began walking towards Karlir, Kuchi, and Jordan.

"Oh!" exclaimed Autumn, blushing. "I'm sorry for intruding." Quickly turning around, she began to walk away towards the others.

"Hey!" I exclaimed softly as I put my hand on her shoulder, guiding her to turn and face me. "I'm glad to see you."

She smiled and placed her arms under mine to give me a hug.

"Sorry to interrupt," said Karlir as he walked up to us, followed by Jordan, Kuchi, Leon, and an unknown man holding a long, silver sword. "I would like to say I have more time to have fun, but it looks like my time is up. For good."

"What!?" I yelled, pulling away from Autumn's hug. "No, does it have to be so soon?"

"Yes, I'm afraid," declared Karlir as he looked at the man next to him. "This man was sent by the Sleeves Council to take me where my punishment will be carried out."

"But you aren't guilty!" I yelled again. This wasn't fair.

"You knew this would happen when we came back," stated Karlir as he placed his hand on my head. "Just remember, although I may no longer be in this world physically, as long as you carry my legacy through your own actions as my one and only student, I will always be there to guide you."

This is foolish, said Sora within my mind. *How could he let them do this to him?*

"Even my crystal doesn't agree with this," I said

unhappily. “This isn’t right.”

“It may not be,” said Karlir as he turned around, following the man with the sword. “But life isn’t fair.”

“Master,” I called as he looked back at each of us one last time.

“Take care, Zephyr, Leon, and my brother.”

It was the hardest thing I had ever done, not being able to do anything at all. The Vice Chief of Sleeves was charging my master, Karlir, with treason for a crime I knew he did not commit. The only thing I truly didn’t understand was why Karlir would let them. He was more powerful by far than anyone in Dentro, and most likely in Sleeves, so he could escape if he wanted to. But that wasn’t like my master. I knew he wasn’t a coward.

“Jordan,” I called as we continued walking towards the Sleeves House of Judgment to witness Karlir’s execution in front of a mass of people. “How will they kill him?”

“Beheading,” replied Jordan, barely audible.

“The law is the law,” said Leon.

It had been a few hours since Karlir had left, and Autumn, Leon, Jordan, and I had decided that being there for Karlir would be better than letting him die friendless in front of hundreds of people. Kuchi did not want to witness his own brother’s death, and so he had decided to leave Sleeves and head towards Devil's Pass to travel outside of the Tyring region.

"The law is the law?" I exclaimed, stopping in my tracks to face Leon. Although I knew Karlir had told me that keeping my composure was better than being guided by anger, I couldn't control myself. "He didn't do it!"

"It doesn't matter," replied Leon expressionlessly. "This is nothing compared to what else is out there, so get used to it."

"Leon!" I walked up to him, grabbed him by his shirt, and looked him in the eyes. "Do you care so little for others' lives?"

"Nothing matters," stated Leon as he slapped my hand from the collar of his shirt, "except ending the life of one man."

It was no use—Karlir was right, but far more so than I had thought. Leon seemed not only to have changed physically, but personality-wise also. Aside from his cruel and dark aura, he seemed meaner, selfish, and apathetic towards anything or anyone that wouldn't help him achieve his goal. Folding my hand into a fist, I almost decided to punch Leon in the face, but I realized that I didn't want Autumn to see me like this.

"Fine," I said as I turned around and began to walk towards the gates of Sleeves.

"Zephyr," called Jordan, "where are you going?"

"I'll meet you there," I said as I began to focus my aura underneath my feet. "Go ahead."

After aura stepping towards the gates of Sleeves, I looked up at the large, red gate and wall towards the two guard huts on top. Checking to see if there were any guards inside, I realized that the huts would be empty, just like when we had first come to Sleeves, as a punishment was to be carried out. Molding aura energy underneath my feet once again, I quickly began to run vertically up the red wall until I reached the top. Standing, looking out towards Cryns Lake, I didn't really know what to do.

As it was in the middle of the afternoon, the lake creatures weren't currently out. The lake itself, a clear, shining blue, was a truly magnificent sight. Ever since my master had told me that nature was part of us and we were part of nature, I couldn't help but appreciate the beauty of it all. The lake waves brushing up against the sandy end of Sleeves beyond the gates, the small ripples created from little movements within the lake, and the sunlight reflecting off the surface of the water created a view that was nothing short of amazing.

As I continued to gaze at the lake, I found myself looking at a small school of fish. Karlir had told me that the reason the weaker creatures, such as the fish, no longer came to the surface while the sun shone at its highest was because at one point the people of Sleeves had hunted and almost brought them to extinction. The school, moving slowly through the water, began to change their direction to go down deeper into the lake.

Although all of the fish followed a large one, one of the smaller fish seemed to decide to go up towards the surface, making the rest of the fish stop in response. Looking back at the one lone fish, they seemed to decide that following and retrieving it was not worth their own lives, and they continued on like nothing was wrong.

After looking at that school of fish, something registered in my mind, allowing me to see what I needed to do. Turning around to face the direction of the House of Judgment, I jumped off the top of the gate wall. Suspended in midair, I decided that it would be faster to travel in the air rather than on the ground, as there would be less chance of me being spotted at this height. I quickly focused aura energy beneath my feet once again. This time, though, instead of using it to propel me off the ground, I quickly released the energy from under my feet, creating a small blast of energy to propel myself through the air.

After aura stepping all the way to the House of Judgment, I landed on the roof of the building as quietly as I could, apparently undetected. Even from outside and above the room, I could hear Greer, the overweight, short Vice Chief of Sleeves, speaking.

"You have all waited long enough!" he announced as the crowd began to applaud. "But no longer shall you wait for this traitor to be given the proper punishment. Death shall come to those who deserve it! Bring the scythe!"

By opening my body and mind to the aura presión of others, I allowed myself to be able to sense the whereabouts of the individuals within the building. Most of the people inside had very weak and unstable aura presións that would pose barely any threat, but I sensed some, aside from Leon's, Jordan's, and Autumn's, that seemed strong enough to be formidable. Suddenly, Leon's aura presión disappeared from the mixture of people below, to my surprise.

"Zephyr," called Leon, standing a few feet away from me on the roof. "What are you planning to do?"

"I don't know," I lied. I had the feeling that Leon would try to stop me if I were planning to interrupt the execution. But as I sensed the killing presión of the person standing near Karlir's aura increase—most likely the executioner—I realized that I was running out of time.

"Leon," I said as I held my hand up towards the sky, quickly forming a head-sized Sky Pushuu energy ball in my hand.

"What—" he began, stopping in mid-sentence as I

brought the ball smashing down against the roof.

Having completely obliterated everything that made up at least half of the roof with my attack, I looked down to see hundreds of people looking up at me in surprise, including the Vice Chief. Luckily, my intrusion had stopped the executioner in mid-slice, inches from Karlir's head as he lay, face planted against the ground, neck outstretched. Using the moment of surprise to my advantage, I quickly jumped down from the roof, landing next to Karlir and using my aura energy to cushion my fall.

"Who are you?" asked the muscular executioner, dressed in all black and holding the scythe.

"Zephyr," I replied as I realized that Karlir had been drugged. Pulling one of Karlir's arms over my shoulders, I looked towards Greer, the Vice Chief. "You are a cruel man, to frame one who has done so much for his home."

"Do not play with us, boy! What do you think you are doing?" screamed Greer as his three chins shook with his whole body.

"I'm not letting you kill my master," I declared. "He is innocent."

"Get him!" commanded Greer.

Not wasting any time, the executioner charged at me,

scythe ready to slice. Deciding that fighting would be a waste of time and energy, I concentrated on escaping from the building. Pushing off the ground by aura stepping, I left the house of punishment through the open space in the roof. Not looking back, and keeping a tight grip on Karlir, I could hear the screams and shouts as the people within the building tried to chase after me. Within seconds, I was beyond the gates and on the beach of Sleeves, overlooking Cryns Lake.

"Zephyr," yelled Jordan and Autumn as they appeared next to me. I hadn't realized until now that Autumn could also aura step.

"Are you here to try to stop me?" I asked, backing up towards the lake so I would be able to escape rather than fight them.

"Of course not!" yelled Jordan. "I was hoping someone would do it, because I was about to."

"Me too," declared Autumn, with her beautiful voice. "You saved my life before, remember? We're here to help you."

"You guys," I said, laughing. "Thanks."

This was the first time I had ever been offered help, other than by my mother and the chief of Dentro. Although I had never wanted to depend on someone else for anything, it felt good to think that I could.

"So," I said, feeling dumb, "what should I do now?" And with that, we all laughed again, even in the face of a mob chasing after us.

"Our best bet is to head across the lake. That'll give us too big a head start for them to catch up," said Jordan.

"What about Leon?" I asked, even though he had almost succeeded in trying to stop me.

"He's over there," said Autumn as she pointed across the lake to a distant figure.

"He would be," I murmured. I would deal with him later.

After aura stepping, which thankfully was a lot faster than swimming, we reached the other side of the huge lake in less than two minutes.

"I didn't want anything to do with this," stated Leon, glaring at me as we landed on the beach across from Sleeves. "But you got me involved."

"Yeah," I said, still angry with him trying for stop me. "That's your fault."

I was already tired of his dark, cruel remarks and actions, and I didn't have time for them. Jordan was already walking away, and I followed him. Karlir finally seemed to regain his senses as he removed his arm from on top of my shoulder.

"What's this?" he asked, a little confused. "Don't tell me

you all—"

"Yes," I interrupted, turning around and kneeling down as a sign of apology. "I know you asked me not to, but I couldn't let you be killed."

"Why?" he asked, expressionless.

"I won't be the one to leave someone I care about to die, not while I am alive," I replied while looking towards the ground, expecting an angry response. "You mean too much to me, Gramps."

"Zephyr," he said, motioning for me to stand. "Thank you."

I was surprised, and that was the honest truth. Throughout my training, Karlir had always told me never to disobey his orders, but I couldn't obey him this time. After seeing the school of fish leave their comrade alone, I had decided that I would never be the one to do that. I smiled.

"There is no point in looking back at the past," said Karlir to us all. "From now on, none of us will be allowed back in Sleeves. They will have a city warrant for us, a bounty, and pictures of us everywhere. It is unheard of to defy the law, and so they will take the strongest action they can to try to capture us. We have set a bad example."

"Yes," agreed Jordan, "we must be more careful from

here on out. All of us."

"I'm sorry," I said as I faced Jordan. "You won't be able to return home."

"It's worth it," replied Jordan with a smile.

"Ugh," sighed Leon in disgust, turning around to gaze up at the clouds.

"From now on, you must decide for yourself what you are going to do. It is time for us, student and master, to split, at least for now," said Karlir as he directed his attention towards me.

"Why?" I asked in confusion. "You aren't coming with us?"

"No," replied Karlir. "My brother told me he would leave Tyring after my execution, and so I feel it is my duty to follow him. He is my younger brother, of course. And you must also travel your own path."

"But—" I said, only to be interrupted.

"Zephyr," Karlir said, smiling. "You have become strong. Even if you still aren't strong enough to achieve your goals, you have the will and determination to make up for it. Not to mention you now have comrades to help you. I know you will be able to do it."

Without realizing it, I had formed a friendship and a powerful bond with my master.

"Okay," I said as Karlir walked away. "I'll try my hardest."

"Good!" he yelled. "You have my trust!"

And with that, he disappeared, traveling at such a high speed that I could barely keep track of his movements.

"I must also leave you," declared Jordan.

"You too?" I asked. "Why?"

"Because even though Karlir did not steal the Valkyrie Shield, someone did, and I'm going to find out who. I want to help you in your quest. Kuchi told me about your goal of collecting the Unmei collection so that you can change the world for the better. I'm putting my trust in you, just like Karlir. When I find out who stole the shield, I will meet you in Rosem City—you have to pass through there after retrieving the Tyring Sword from Cheshria."

"Thanks," was all I could say to Jordan. He was truly a kind and helpful person. "We won't let you down."

"I'll be off, then," stated Jordan as he disappeared into the wind, like Karlir had moments before but at a slower pace.

"What about you, Autumn?" I asked, smiling at her. To me, she seemed to shine even brighter than the sun.

"I owe you both my life," she declared, smiling back at me. "I'm going to stay with you and help as much as I can."

"You ready?" I asked Leon as he turned around to face

Autumn and me.

"You both better not drag me down," said Leon with a serious look. Although I didn't like his attitude, he was strong, and I needed his strength. I could not do this all alone.

"Okay, let's go," I said, as we all began to release our aura presión in preparation for aura stepping. "To Cheshria."

Chapter 28:
Red Snow

It took about three days of aura stepping to reach Cheshria. Autumn, Leon, and I had stopped each night at a traveling inn on the way. Even though I was anxious to get to Cheshria, I had decided to try to use the traveling time to get to know Autumn better.

Each night, while at an inn, all three of us would sit outside and gaze up at the stars. Leon had been silent since Jordan and Karlir left us. He would stare up at the stars, almost with a look of hate. After talking with Autumn and asking her how and why she had followed us, I had learned that my dreams from before hadn't been just dreams.

As she described what had occurred after she disobeyed her mother and left Rosem, fighting Adamus and his gang and meeting with Jae the bartender, I didn't really know how to react. For the time being, I decided not to bring up the topic of how I had been what could be seen as spying on her in my dreams, as she might not take it well.

Autumn also explained to me how she had defeated Adamus and his ability to wither anything he touched and drain its life force. She said that aside from her more advanced tai-jut-su skills, or hand-to-hand combat, her own crystal's ability had allowed her to overpower him. By communicating with her crystal and merging their consciousnesses, just like Sora and me, she was able to manipulate light energy to a certain extent and create a wall or shield-like object, known as an energy shield.

When she surrounded Adamus with a box-shaped energy shield and cut him off from oxygen, he passed out from lack of air. Deciding that he was not worth killing, Autumn left him and his men unconscious, telling one who woke up that if they ever tried to attack Rosem again, she would hunt them down without mercy.

I couldn't help but admire Autumn's courage and strength. When I asked her why she had come after us and waited three months to see us, she stated that it was the least she could do for us having risked our lives for hers. In all honesty, her kindness made me smile and laugh at myself for how selfish my own goals seemed. Autumn was here, for us, while we never thought of how our goals affected the people trying to help us. But on the final night before we reached Cheshria, as we sat and gazed up at the glowing night sky, I couldn't help but feel bad.

"Autumn," I said, and she turned to face me, sitting a few inches away. "I'm really thankful for you trying to help us, but you don't have to come with us. You will only be in unnecessary danger."

She smiled. "You don't realize it," she said as she looked at me, "but you have another power, aside from your fighting skills."

"What do you mean?" I asked, a little confused.

"You have the ability to understand people's emotions and relate to them."

"I don't really understand," I admitted. "I mean, don't most people try to understand and relate to each other?"

"Yes," she replied. "That's how people form bonds. But you're different. With just the past three nights, we have learned a lot about each other. You told me how everyone where you came from treats you. But even so, look how strong you have become, even continuing to try to understand others despite being shown such cruelty by so many for so long."

"Oh," I sighed.

"You are truly an amazing person," Autumn said as she looked back up towards the sky. "When you described how your life was in your village, you never said that you hated those who treated you that way, or that they were bad people. I only say what I just said because unlike you, I can see the cruelty in their actions. Even though your parents may have done something shameful in your village's view, it wasn't your fault, and you never did anything to deserve to be treated that way by your whole village."

"Thanks," I whispered. I was speechless. No one had ever told me that I was not in the wrong, and that I should not have been treated that way. And with her last words, I had no will left to try to stop her from coming along with us.

"You're the best," I said as she moved closer to me.

I felt stupid but really warm as Autumn's skin rubbed against mine. I had been jealous when we first met, as she had seemed to like Leon more, but maybe I had been wrong. Maybe I really could be like normal people and have friends, relationships, and all the things I had never truly had, especially after my mother had died. She laid her head on my chest, and I could feel the heat from her body as it combined with mine.

"Zephyr," she said with a smile as she brought her head up from my chest, looking into my eyes.

As she gazed at me, I did something that I had only dreamed of, almost like my body was moving on its own. My right hand softly held the back of her head and touched her beautiful long hair, and I used my left hand to stroke her cheek, bringing my nose so close to hers that I could feel the warmth of her breath brushing my bottom lip.

Staring into her starry eyes, I tilted her head backwards, closed my eyes, and slowly and softly pressed my lips against hers. It felt as if time around us had stopped, leaving us with not a care in the world. Her lips and mine seemed to mold together perfectly, as if made for each other. Slowly, her tongue rubbed against my lower lip, and we immediately granted entrance into each other's mouths.

It was like a playful fight as our tongues wrestled for dominance; eventually giving up, though not seeming to mind, she let me take over. In that second, she moaned into my mouth, and I into hers. I didn't want it to end, but it wasn't my choice as we separated to breathe.

Looking into her eyes, I couldn't stop myself from smiling, and we both laughed. That was my first kiss, and most likely the best I would ever have.

"You two done?" said Leon, speaking for the first time in three days. "If so, we should all probably get some sleep for tomorrow, unless you would rather be making out than achieving your goals, Zephyr."

I frowned. Leon was a downer, but he was right.

"Yeah," I replied to him as we all got up to head back into the village.

The next morning, we arrived at Cheshria within a few

hours. The empty desert wasn't a welcoming sight compared to the beautiful Sleeves or Dentro. Although none of us had spoken on the way there, I couldn't help but smile, and it seemed Autumn couldn't either. Looking indifferent, Leon glanced at us both as we stood a few feet away from the two huts where the city guards were located.

"You both need to forget about last night," stated Leon with a serious tone. "It's going to drag you down, like all unnecessary things. If you don't, I'm going to leave you behind."

"Just worry about yourself," I retorted as we began walking towards the huts.

I couldn't help but think how it all looked exactly the same as when Endriago, Autumn's older brother, had brought us. This time, unlike before, the two huts were empty.

"This can't be good," declared Autumn. "The Cheshria guards are known for never leaving their positions, unlike in Sleeves."

"Something must have happened," I guessed as we walked past the posts and into what looked like an empty desert.

As we continued to walk, each part of our bodies slowly began to disappear, from toes to neck, and I watched my body vanish before my eyes once again. And, like before, after my eyes followed the rest of my body, Leon, Autumn, and I suddenly found ourselves at the entrance to the snow-covered city of Cheshria. When I had last been here, all of the snow had been white. Looking around now, I felt sick. The snow was red.

"What?" yelled Autumn in surprise as our mouths dropped at the sight before us.

Like before, Cheshria was still cold, and the snow and wind surrounded us to make it even worse. After focusing my aura energy around me like a cloak to keep me warm, I couldn't help but feel sad as I looked upon the once very white city to see blood stains all over the snow.

All around us lay what seemed like an endless amount of unmoving bodies. Most of them looked like adults, while some seemed to be around the same age as us. It was like they had been at war.

“You,” called a voice so weak that I barely heard it.

Rushing over to where it came from, I found a blond–haired, tan boy, around the same age as I.

“Did you come here to help us?” he asked, stuttering.

“We—” I began, only to be interrupted by his weak whisper.

“No, it doesn't matter,” he declared. “I am going to die anyway.”

“Don't say that,” cried Autumn as she came over and

placed both of her hands on the boy's stomach, where a large gush of blood seemed to be emerging.

Immediately, I sensed Autumn's aura energy as she focused it onto her hands in an effort to convert her energy into stamina for the boy, trying to heal his wounds. It was something that Karlir, my master, had said only a few people could do.

"What happened?" asked Leon. "Tell us."

"Don't talk if it's painful," I said to the boy.

"It's okay," he replied. "We tried to overthrow the king and the Council."

"What?" I exclaimed.

"Our leader, Kolt, began to organize it three months ago," he said.

I felt a tinge of recognition at the name, but couldn't quite place it.

"So?" asked Leon.

"We gathered as many as we could to help fight. It was easy—many felt the same way as us." He coughed and brought up blood.

"Are you alright?" I asked, a stupid question as I could feel his aura presión weakening, even with Autumn pouring her medical aura into him.

"Yes," he replied.

"Tell us your goal," ordered Leon as he looked down at the boy.

"Our goal," he said with a smile, "was the treasure of Cheshria."

"The Tyring Sword?" I asked.

"Yes," admitted the boy. "And for a while, it looked like we could do it. But the king sent his greatest warriors against us—untrained commoners and working class. It was a massacre."

"And your leader?" asked Leon.

"He's probably still alive. He's different from us. Somehow, he has power, and he would never tell us how he got it. But he's headed to the king's chamber to get the sword before the king does," answered the boy.

"No!" yelled Leon. "We need that sword!"

"Why are you telling us this?" I asked. "We're just strangers."

"Because," he said, his aura presión almost completely faded away, "I at least want someone to remember me."

"What's your name?" I asked as the boy's eyes began to close.

"It's—" he whispered, then took his last breath.

"Hey!" I yelled as I shook him softly. "Hey!"

Slowly turning around as I felt Autumn's soft hand on my

shoulder, I couldn't help but yell.

"He's dead," said Leon, stating the painfully obvious.

I always hated seeing someone die at such a young age, which happened often in the trial of adulthood, but I had never witnessed or participated in a war like this one. But with his last wish, all he asked was to be remembered and acknowledged. It was painful, mainly because I had had nightmares as a child in which I ended up like him.

"Let's go," I commanded as I lay the blond-haired boy's lifeless body on the snow.

The city, comprising hundreds of roads, was filled with gray and light-blue buildings. On some roads lay dead bodies, while on others people could be seen fighting each other. Some of the people looked like commoners, dressed in long pants and fluffy jackets and holding knives and other common weapons, while the others were the palace guards we had encountered before, wearing fluffy light-blue clothes and wielding large black scythes.

"I'm going to see if anything happened to Jae," said Autumn as we began walking down one of the streets leading towards the palace. "You both head to the palace to get the sword. I'll warn you though, if you come in contact with the king of Cheshria, or any of the younger-looking Council members, don't fight them. Just run."

"Why?" asked Leon and I together, to my displeasure.

"The king is king for a reason. He's the strongest in the city, and some of the Council members are also very powerful. They're on a similar level to Karlir," answered Autumn before waving and running off towards Jae's bar.

"Interesting," muttered Leon. "Come on."

Aura stepping to the palace had its benefits. Not only did we have to see few dead bodies as we traveled at a very high speed, but the smell of them was limited. Having reached the gates of the palace, we entered as silently as we could, moving past the hundreds of fighting people in the palace yard. Although it seemed like a few people did notice us, they were too busy fighting to confront us. We were lucky in that regard.

Immediately in front of us were the four large hallways leading in different directions. The signs were unchanged: Market, King's Rule, Council's Rule, and Mass. Even though there seemed to be guards at each of the signs, they were all busy fighting with the rebels.

After running in silence through the dimly lit hallway leading towards the king's residence, we reached the entrance. Throughout the hall lay dead bodies of the rebels, while in front of us stood two large guards, both holding scythes, with the patch depicting the blue ice dragon on their shoulders.

"More fools, huh?" asked one of the guards.

"We don't have time for you," stated Leon as he pointed his index fingers at the guards.

Before I could stop him, Leon unleashed two large black balls from the tips of his fingers, which hit the two men and propelled them into the room beyond us. Walking up to them and checking their pulses, I found that both men were dead.

"You killed them," I stated.

"Yes," admitted Leon. "They were in the way, and they were trash. Let's go."

Leon truly had changed and become even crueler. When we had first left the village and fought together for the first time, he hadn't killed the men that attacked us but instead just knocked them out.

I sighed, but continued on behind Leon as we turned right into the next room filled with paintings and furniture. Moving through each room, I realized that nothing had been touched or moved out of place. Those two guards truly had not let anyone through, meaning they had been responsible for all of those dead people piled in the hallway—truly an unsightly scene.

After walking through the two rooms that looked identical to the first, just as we had on our failed infiltration three months ago, we stopped at the entrance leading into the next room. Located here, supposedly, was the sword, guarded by the two most powerful fighters in Cheshria aside from the king himself.

Launching ourselves into the next room, prepared for a battle, we found that the two men known as Cheshria's Teeth were no longer guarding the room fifty feet beyond us or its golden gate. In truth, I was itching to fight that tall man, Fonos, again, and I saw the same look of disappointment upon Leon's face. We both walked up to the golden gate, observing it. Increasing my own natural physical strength by focusing my aura onto my hands and arms, I ripped the gate off its hinges, throwing it a few feet behind us.

As we walked into the empty looking room, I spotted a small figure running towards what seemed to be a casket.

"Is that—?" I asked we rushed after the figure.

We caught up to what turned out to be a boy with long blond hair that covered his forehead, standing a few inches shorter than Leon. He turned around to face us, inches away from the coffin.

"You guys!" he yelled, first in surprise, his expression slowly becoming angry.

"You," muttered Leon, making me feel dumber for not remembering who this kid was.

"I didn't think I would see you again after you tricked me and left me to get arrested when you tried to steal this here—" he said as he patted the coffin.

Instantly, I remembered who he was.

"Kolt!" I remembered the tour guide whom we had knocked out in order to try to take the Tyring Sword. "I'm sorry."

"It's too late, Zephlar and Rayon!" he screamed as he pulled open the casket. "Because of you, I went through true hell. I'll be able to return the favor, using this power!"

I can't believe he still can't say our names right, I thought to myself. *But I guess we're equal, since I didn't recognize him.* Opening the casket, Kolt pulled out a long, shining, silver sword. In the center of its hilt was a black jewel.

"Wait!" I yelled as Kolt held up the sword, laughing.

"No!" he screamed in response. "I have waited so long for true power. The power to hurt those who hurt me! I finally have it!"

But as he finished his sentence, within seconds, a large dark cloud of mist began to surround him. Screaming but still clinging to the sword, as if not able to release it, Kolt disappeared within the dark mist as it completely enveloped him. **BOOM!**

I glanced to the right, about fifty feet away, where a large hole had been made through the wall, leading outside. A wind began to blow snow into the room, and three figures stepped through the wall and inside as well.

The figure standing a few feet in front of the other two was at least six foot five, and his long, flowing black hair, round face, and muscular, pale body showed greatly through his long white pants, white shirt, and crown.

Standing on the larger man's left side, one of the men also wore white pants and a white shirt, although his hat was dark blue. He stood at least six feet tall, had medium black hair similar to Leon's, and had fairly large muscles on both his arms and legs but still looked thin enough to be agile. His eyes looked as though they were pitch black, darker than an empty night sky. On the man's back lay a black-and-yellow sheath, the hilt sticking out of it—a stunning combination of yellow and black.

The man to the right of the king, a short, plump, familiar-looking man, held a large hammer. It was Dolo, one of Cheshria's Teeth.

"Where is my sword?!" yelled the man in the middle angrily, eyebrows raised as he looked around frantically. "I'll kill you all!"

Chapter 29:
Hate Among Brothers

As I examined the situation at hand, I thought about what would be the best action to take. Looking at the three men, I remembered how Autumn had warned us not to confront them. Apparently their powers rivaled those of my master, Karlir, against whom I had no chance.

Across from them, completely engulfed in black mist after taking the Tyring Sword from its coffin, was Kolt, or what was left of him, if anything.

"Who pulled my sword from its resting place?" yelled the man standing in the center of the three, wearing the crown.

All three the men walked closer to us and the black mist, then stopped a few feet away.

"Who are you?" asked the king as he looked at us with an angry expression.

"Zephyr," I said in response, waiting for Leon to respond with a cocky answer from behind me. When I didn't hear him reply, I answered for him. "And this is Leon."

Instantly, as I finished saying Leon's name, the man standing to the left of the king, wearing white pants, a white shirt, and a dark blue hat covering most of his face, took a step forward in front of the other two men as if to get a better look at us.

I sensed Leon's presence disappear, and I looked back to see him not standing behind me anymore. Feeling his aura presión appear near the man who had taken a step forward, I realized that Leon had already gone on the offensive.

Leon unsheathed both his swords, while in the same motion slashing downward, ripping the man's hat into three pieces as it landed on the ground.

He was breathing heavily, with the angriest expression I had ever seen Leon have. I got a better look at the man as his hat fell off. He looked almost exactly like Leon—medium black hair, cold black eyes, and pale skin with an empty expression on his face. Prompting Leon to jump a few feet back towards me and lift his right hand, the man spoke.

"It's been a while," said the man, his voice cold and emotionless, giving off a deadly aura. "Leon."

Looking up with the angriest face I had ever seen, Leon brought both his yellow and black swords to his sides.

"Blane," said Leon, grinding his teeth together. "Brother."

Wait, I thought to myself. *Leon's older brother, the one who murdered their whole family, brilliant like Leon but with even greater potential, was named Blane.* This man was a true genius, and he was way beyond our level.

"Oh," said Dolo. "His swords are the same colors as yours, and he looks very similar to you. I fought him before, but he was weak. Who is he?"

"My little brother," replied Blane as he gazed into Leon's eyes.

"I thought you told us you had killed everyone in your family," said the king suddenly in a calmer tone.

I knew it, I thought to myself. This man was the infamous traitor who had run away from the village after killing his family and leaving only Leon alive. This was the man who dominated Leon's life, his thoughts, and his ambitions.

"Blane!" screamed Leon, interrupting my train of thought. "I will kill you!"

"Oh," said Dolo, laughing.

"Just like you wanted," said Leon as I felt his aura presión increase so greatly it would have brought a normal person to his knees, "I hated you. I loathed you. And just to kill you, I've thrown away my friends, my happiness. I've lived and survived!"

As I listened to Leon yelling in anger at his brother, I realized that the power of a bond wasn't necessarily good. Yes, bonds and friendship may make life worth living, but not always in the ideal way for everyone. For someone like me, who never had friends or a real bond while growing up, I never realized the damage a bond could do.

For someone like Leon, who must've idolized his brother at one point, to have had that bond and all of his others ripped apart by this one man…he must have lived for the sole reason of avenging those bonds, those people, and those friends.

"Leon!" I yelled as he brought his black sword up, pointing towards the sky.

Instantly, a huge wave of black energy surrounded his sword, taking on its shape.

"Dark power?" Blane mumbled with a surprised look.

Bringing his sword down in a slashing motion, Leon released the wave of energy, propelling it through the air in the shape of a crescent moon straight towards Blane.

"Die!" screamed Leon.

As it approached Blane, the two men behind him slowly began to smile. Bringing his arm in front of him, Blane opened his hand to catch the huge wave of dark energy, completely stopping its movement.

"What!?" Leon and I stammered. Leon had put enough energy and force into that attack to completely obliterate several large buildings.

Blane closed his hand, crushing the wave and releasing

an explosion of dark energy and a cloud of smoke. I had to cover my face from the dust and wind, and when I looked back towards the cloud where Blane had stood, his figure was no longer there.

Turning my attention to Leon, a few feet away from the huge cloud of smoke, I found myself looking at Blane as he appeared in front of Leon. He whispered something in Leon's before bringing his fist upwards in an uppercut, connecting with Leon's jaw.

"Foolish little brother," said Blane as he looked down at Leon. "I have no interest in you right now."

Landing directly in front of me after being propelled by Blane's single punch, Leon wiped away the blood dripping down his chin as I walked over to him.

"Are you alright?" I asked.

I saw the same look of hatred on his face as I had seen when he had first realized that Blane was here. This time, though, as I looked into his eyes, I could tell something was different.

"Don't interfere!" he screamed, knocking my hand away as I tried to put it on his shoulder.

Suddenly, a huge amount of aura presión began to push down upon us, and we both had to drop to one knee to keep ourselves from falling.

Looking towards the three men, I felt that the aura presión wasn't coming from them. In fact, they looked fine, even with this huge force pushing us down. Remembering Kolt, I looked north towards where, seconds ago, he had been engulfed by a dark mist. Kolt was standing once again, holding the Tyring Sword.

Unlike before, when he had been a short, blond-haired, blue-eyed, scrawny-looking kid, Kolt now wore a silver suit. The suit, made of what looked like a thin armor, seemed to glow, while a dark aura seemed to constantly flow from him. A silver helmet covered the back and sides of his head, leaving space open for his face. Gazing at us all with a new look in his blue eyes, he began laughing hysterically.

"You dare laugh in my presence?!" yelled the king, towering over all of us, flexing his muscles underneath his shirt while taking a step in front of Blane to face Kolt.

"You don't recognize me," said Kolt in the lowest and darkest voice I had ever heard, far different from his original voice. "Do you, father?"

"Father?" repeated the king. "Do you know who I am, boy? I am King Luis of Cheshria. Everyone knows I killed my son when he was born. He was born physically weak, too weak to even have a chance at upholding my regime."

Kolt was the son of the king of Cheshria? That didn't make sense, I thought to myself. Why would the son of the most powerful person in the city be doing something as low as leading tours?

"Did you really think my mother, Malia, would let you kill her son?" laughed Kolt. "You are a fool."

"That woman?" mumbled the king. "I banished her to a far-off island; she should be dead by now."

"No!" yelled Kolt as I tried my hardest to stand up.

A continuous amount of killing presión seemed to be coming from Kolt, most likely from the power of the Tyring Sword. It looked as if, when Kolt got angry, the power of his aura presión increased, as did the glow surrounding him, his suit, and his sword.

"What is it you want, trash?" asked Luis as he took a step towards Kolt. "Do you want to kill me for trying to kill you and banishing your mother?"

Kolt laughed, again with an insane look.

"Killing you and destroying what you aspire to have will come later," said Kolt as the black mist from earlier began to appear around his legs, making its way up towards the rest of his body. "First, I'm going to find Malia."

"I won't—" began Luis as he lifted his arm, aura stepping towards Kolt, bringing his fist down where Kolt stood.

BOOM! It was as if lightening had struck the room. I looked up to find the ground crumbling underneath Luis as he stood where Kolt had just been, his hand stuck in the ground after his punch had created such a powerful shockwave. Floating above Luis, in the form of a cloud of black mist, Kolt's new, lower voice spoke.

"I want her to witness the destruction of those who have hurt us!"

And with those last words, the cloud began to move towards the huge hole in the wall leading outside. Dolo, preparing to jump to attack the cloud before it reached the hole, stopped in place as the king spoke.

"Let it go," he commanded, appearing between Blane and Dolo as the cloud moved through the hole and into the sunset sky.

"But he took the Tyring Sword!" Dolo protested.

"Do not worry. I know where he is headed," the king assured him.

"Where?" Dolo asked as the presión around Leon and me disappeared, allowing us to stand up again.

"To the island where his mother is," replied Luis.

"To Dentro," added Blane, emotionless.

"I should have killed them both," declared the king, making fists.

"I've never heard of Dentro," admitted Dolo.

"It's a village that's fairly off the map," explained Luis as he looked at Dolo and Blane, ignoring us. "And it is where our strongest Council member came from."

"Oh!" exclaimed Dolo, patting Blane on the back. "Looks like you get to go home."

Blane sighed in response, paying no attention to Leon. Regaining his composure, Leon glared at the three men. Walking forward a few feet, he picked up both of the swords that he had dropped after being punched by Blane.

"We need to head to that island," Luis was saying. "I should have invaded Dentro years ago and taken the villagers as slaves, and my son's surprise attack did more damage than I would have thought. Dolo!"

Dolo stood straight up at attention with his large hammer held at his side. "Yes, Your Majesty?"

"I want you to take word to your brother, Fonos, and let him know of the events here. Tell him to finish off the enemy, and as soon as he is done, get the troops ready to mobilize. We will be invading Dentro as soon as we finish up here," stated the king.

"Yes, sir!" exclaimed Dolo.

"Blane," Luis called next. "I want you to gather the other Council members and inform them of the plan. Form a plan of attack, decide who will stay behind, and let me know when everything is ready. Understood?"

"Yes," replied Blane.

"And what about you, Your Majesty?" asked Dolo, swinging his large hammer around with ease.

"There is something I must prepare if we are to defeat my son. Although he is weak by himself, that village won't be so easy to invade. We should have the upper hand in numbers, but they have many powerful warriors. And now that my son has the sword, his power is formidable. He will do anything to stop us. I must prepare myself for our attack," he said.

"How long do we have?" asked Blane.

"One week," declared the king. "We will leave to attack then."

"What about them?" asked Dolo, pointing towards us.

"I will let Blane decide, as one of them is his little brother. I must make preparations," said the king as he launched himself off the ground and through the hole leading outside, disappearing into the distance.

"What should we do?" asked Dolo, beginning to drool. "Can I kill them?"

Expecting a fight, I started to retrieve my gloves from my short pocket, only to stop after Blane's response.

"Leave them," he ordered. "They aren't a threat. Let's go."

Leon, hearing those last words, exploded in anger. Launching himself off the ground, he lunged at both of the men, only to slash at the air as they disappeared from sight.

"Foolish little brother," restated Blane as he stood right outside the hole in the wall, alone. "You are ***weak***, because you don't have enough ***hate***."

And with those last words, he aura stepped with such speed that I could not keep track, only realizing he was gone as Leon dropped to the ground, smashing his fists into it repeatedly. Aura stepping next to him, I grabbed both of his hands, stopping him from hitting the ground as his blood dripped onto my arm. Although we had failed to get the sword, we didn't have time to waste stewing. This time, our village was at stake.

"Zephyr, Leon!" called a familiar beautiful voice. "There you are!"

Letting go of Leon's hands as they dropped to the ground, I looked up to see Autumn standing outside the hole in the wall.

"Autumn!" I exclaimed, happy to see a friend. "We need to get out of here."

"Yes," she agreed, aura stepping to Leon and me. "We should go back to Rosem. My mother and brother should be able to help us."

Nodding my head in agreement, I turned my attention back towards Leon to find him lying on the ground, unconscious. He seemed to have passed out from the shock of seeing Blane. Picking him up and placing his arm over my shoulder, I nodded towards Autumn, taking off and aura stepping out of the building. It was time to prepare to head back to Dentro.

Chapter 30:
Homecoming

I explained what had happened between Leon, his brother, Kolt, and the king of Cheshria to Autumn on the way back to Rosem, and we arrived within a few hours' time. Without any questions, Delphi greeted us with a smile before rushing us in to start healing the unconscious Leon. She used the same type of aura energy as Autumn, and she seemed to be even more proficient, as it only took her a few minutes to completely heal Leon. Endriago was there, too, looking on.

After Delphi finished tending to his wounds, Autumn came forward to her mother to apologize for disobeying her orders. Without letting her speak, Delphi smacked her daughter, surprising both Endriago and me.

Then Delphi wrapped her arms around Autumn, hugging her. Over the next few hours, we relayed all of the events from when we had first left Rosem until our return. Surprised at how we were able to study with two of the known strongest masters in Tyring, she expressed happiness at the fact that we had both become more powerful. While Leon was sleeping, I used the time to inform Delphi of Leon's past and the confrontation that had occurred with his brother a few hours earlier.

Saddened by his story, Delphi admitted that she had

sensed sadness and hate within the depths of Leon's aura and soul when we had first met. But because it didn't seem to have arisen in his personality, she had decided that it would be better not to inform us of the sleeping darkness within him. Reminding her that we were short on time, I decided that both Leon and I would return to Dentro as soon as he awoke and bring Autumn along with us if she wished—leaving out the fact that bringing an outsider back to the village, just as my mother had once done, was forbidden. But for the sake of the village, I needed Autumn's help.

Seeing me falling asleep multiple times while waiting for Leon to awake, Delphi suggested that even though we were short on time, with only a week until Cheshria would attack Dentro, I should stay the night and be well rested for the day ahead. She pointed out that I would need to be at my best to succeed, and I eventually agreed and passed out within seconds.

Awaking in the morning, I looked towards one of the windows to see the sun slowly rising. Standing directly outside of Delphi's house and staring out across the view from the highest point on the mountain city was Leon.

"How are you doing?" I asked him as I walked outside, followed by a yawning Autumn.

"When they attack the village," said Leon as he turned around to face us, "I will kill Blane myself. Don't get in my way."

Deciding that being confrontational was not a good start to the day, I smiled.

"I'll leave him to you, then," I replied, then turned to face Autumn. "Ready?"

"I was ready yesterday," she responded with a smile. "Sleepyhead!"

"Alright!" I declared, pumped up. "We have only six days until they attack. Let's go!"

Unlike before, when we had to walk from Rosem to Exilio, the trip was much speedier, and we ran into no problems this time. Aura stepping, we reached Exilio within two hours, whereas before it had taken us from sunup to sundown to arrive.

As we walked into the bandit town, the thought of running into Adamus crossed my mind. Reminding myself that Autumn had defeated him already, I ignored any lingering thoughts about Exilio, and we quickly made our way through the one-road town. Within another two hours, we had travelled through the desert that separated Exilio from the sea, reaching the ocean shore.

"Any ideas on how we should get to the island?" I asked, looking at Leon and Autumn as we stood on the sandy beach. "Swim?"

"Sky step?" suggested Autumn.

"Takes too much stamina," I stated. If we sky stepped, essentially gliding by blasting invisible aura energy from underneath our feet that allowed us to momentarily float, we would have very little energy once we arrived at Dentro, if any.

"I could bring—" I began to say, stopping myself in mid-sentence. Training with Karlir, I had learned many techniques that I had not shown Leon yet, and I meant to keep it that way for as long as possible.

"How about we skate?" I suggested. During my training, Karlir had taught me the basics of manipulating aura energy to my advantage. Skills such as climbing buildings and trees, water walking, super jumping, and surface launching were basics.

As I had progressed further into my training, I discovered and was taught how to enhance those basic abilities. Like aura stepping, which strengthened our legs to allow us to reach much higher speeds than normal, these other abilities allowed me to achieve feats I had only dreamt of when younger. From super jumping and launching off surfaces to sky stepping and from water walking or running to water skating (constantly keeping aura under my feet while also blasting just enough to allow me to move through the water as if skating) were just some.

"Let's just go!" commanded Leon suddenly. "We're

wasting time."

Realizing that he was right, Autumn and I nodded, and all three of us began dashing towards the water. As I placed my foot down onto its surface, instead of sinking in, I continued to run on the water as if I were on land. Increasing our running speed until we left the shallow part of the beach, I changed the form of my aura energy from just releasing it under my feet to blasting energy into the water to allow me to push off of it at a high speed.

Although it took more aura energy than just running on water, aura skating was more efficient than sky stepping, and it would help conserve our energy for when we would finally arrive.

It took almost two hours, and within that time we were able to see many things I had only dreamed of seeing before, such as dolphins, small uninhabited islands, and the beautiful open sea.

Slowing our pace as Dentro Island came into view, we decided to land at Demon's Pool, so as not to alert the villagers to our presence nor to the abilities we had learned. Dentro Island, while fairly large, was only accessible at Demon's Pool and the village's sea port. The village itself, located on the higher section of the island surrounded by trees, was blocked by cliffs from any entrance other than Demon's Pool and the sea port.

Knowing that Demon's Pool was called that for a reason, I realized that what I had feared in the past seemed like almost nothing now. The demons and creatures in Demon's Pool could not compare to the horrific ones that lurked in the large mountains of Devil's Pass.

We reached the island without being spotted. I placed my feet on the soft, sandy beach and suddenly remembered how much I missed the island itself. Even though I had always been treated cruelly and looked down upon by the villagers, I had always loved the nature of the island—the beach and sand, the lush, green sky trees, and even the creatures that had surrounded the village.

"This place is beautiful!" exclaimed Autumn with a smile as she dipped her small, soft hands in the sand.

"Yeah," I agreed, returning the smile. "Yeah, it is." *But not as beautiful as her,* I thought to myself.

As we made our way through Demon's Pool and onto the path that led to the village, I noticed something had changed. About a hundred feet away from us was a small guard hut post, similar to the ones that stood on top of the gates of Sleeves. Inside were two middle-aged men, armed with sheathed swords.

"That's strange," I stated as I brought all of us to a stop

on the path. "We never needed guards before."

"Really?" Autumn asked. "How were you able to see any monsters or attacks coming?"

"We never had to," I said. "Many of our village's buildings are made of a special stone called Sea stone. It's supposed to be able to keep those creatures away, as well as speed up the natural healing process if you sleep in a bed made of it. Something must have happened."

"What should I do?" asked Autumn.

"I didn't want to make you worry, but there is a special law about outsiders in our village," I admitted. "We aren't supposed to tell anyone of our village or bring any outsider back."

"Why not?" she asked with a frown. "I only want to help."

"There have been two instances in the past when an outsider was welcomed into the village. The first happened long ago when the second leader of the village, the chief, brought a wife back from the outside lands. After living here for a short while and seeing the riches we had, she left on a trip to her home. When she returned, she brought with her a band of thieves that proceeded to destroy the village, kill the people, and steal the resources we had acquired and labored for over time," I explained.

"Wow," exclaimed Autumn grimly.

"Although I just found this out recently, the second instance happened seventeen years ago," I declared as I looked up at the sky. "My mom brought my father here. While he was here, he gained many of the villagers' trust, until the day my mom realized she was pregnant. The next day, my father left the island without a word."

"How cruel!" commented Autumn.

"It's all in the past, those things don't matter," I said, lying.

"That's not true," interrupted Leon suddenly. "My goal does not lie in the present, or the future. It lies in the importance of the past."

"Leon," I said, walking up to him and putting my hand on the back of his shoulder, "Blane—"

"I don't owe you an explanation," declared Leon as he shrugged off my hand. "Let's go."

"Fine," I murmured. "Autumn, we will act as if you belong to the village. Can you do that?"

"No problem!" she exclaimed with another beautiful, shining smile. "I won't say anything until I'm needed."

"Sounds like a plan," I said as we all began walking up the path to the guard hut post.

"Are you—" asked one of the middle-aged men, stepping out of the hut to take a closer look at us, "—Leon and Zephyr?"

"Yeah," I replied, putting my hand on the back of my head and laughing. I wasn't used to being called by my name here so casually.

"Leon!" exclaimed the guard. "You look so different. Stronger and more mature, I must say."

Leon nodded in response. The man looked a little confused, like he was used to Leon's friendly nature from before he left the village.

"And you..." said the man with obvious dislike as he looked at me. "I almost didn't recognize you. We had thought we wouldn't be seeing the likes of you here again."

"Yeah," I said, grinning, remembering all the times I had been called *you, that kid, devil* and more, "well, looks like I ruined your hopes. Sorry about that. Let's go."

Surprised at my response, as I had been known for taking all of the villagers' taunts and insults, he moved out of our way as we continued on the path. Mouth wide open, he even forgot to ask who the third person behind us was.

"So," said Autumn, "people are like that to you because of what happened with your parents?"

"Yeah," I replied. It wasn't a subject I liked to talk about, even with her it seemed. "I never knew before I left the island why they were like that to me. Everyone except our chief, of course."

"I'm sorry," she said in response.

"It's okay. Not your fault. Let's head over to the Council of Elders to report that we have returned," I advised.

"Council of Elders? Like the Cheshria Council?" asked Autumn.

"Yeah, they are a bunch of cruel old men that dictate everything we can and can't do. The only one who has the power to overrule or combat them is the Chief," I answered as we began passing village houses.

"Won't it be suspicious if I'm with you when you talk to them?" asked Autumn.

"Don't worry about it," I replied, stopping and giving her a hug. "I'm glad you're here. Let me handle the rest."

"Okay," she whispered as we parted, Leon now a few more feet ahead of us.

As we continued walking, nearing the village square, we passed the village houses that were stacked side by side, as well as the large, green sky trees on our left that went as high as the eye could see. We soon arrived at the village square.

Looking towards the square, it seemed just as busy as

usual, like it had been before we had left a few months ago. We began to make our way towards the village center.

Surprised at our stronger, more mature-looking physical appearances, the villagers soon got over it and returned to their normal looks of displeasure and dislike as I walked through the crowd behind Leon and in front of Autumn. Passing the Chief's two-story house, we reached the village center where the Council of Elders' office stood, blocking the view and the path to the village sea port.

Walking up to the building, we found ourselves making our way through what seemed to be half of the village's population, a crowd of a few hundred people in front of the Council building.

"What's going on?" I asked a random man standing in the crowd.

Opening his mouth to answer me, he stopped and closed it as he realized who I was. Giving me a frown, the man moved a few feet away from me before turning his attention towards the building again.

"I should smack him!" exclaimed Autumn, making me smile. "These people are so ignorant to how you feel!"

"Thanks," I said.

"Come on," said Leon as he pushed people out of his

way to make a path towards the building entrance.

"Hey!" screamed one person in the crowd as all three of us reached the door entrance. "It's Leon! The son of the Dentro Duo and brother of—"

But before another person could say a word, Leon turned around, increasing his aura presión to where it would cause a normal person to fall unconscious, which it did. Slowly, a few people in the crowd, including the one who had been yelling, dropped to the floor.

"Leon!" I yelled, causing him to lower his aura presión. "What are you doing?"

But before Leon could respond, the doors of the Council building opened with a loud creak. A round, pale face, black beady eyes, and mustache gazed at us with a sinister look.

"Late once again!" exclaimed Hovan, the Vice Chief, with a surprised look until he quickly transitioned into his familiar sinister expression. "What fools you are to disrespect the Council so greatly, and twice at that."

Expecting Leon to apologize like he had when we had come to find out our mission details, I was pleasantly surprised when he did not.

"Let us in," Leon directed, ignoring the Vice Chief's statement.

"My my," murmured Hovan. "Looks like your body shape wasn't the only thing that changed during your long mission. Come in!"

Hovan moved out of the way as Leon and I stepped into the large room, followed by Autumn. The room was just as I remembered, complete with the four elderly Council members seated in the center.

Hovan, unlike the others, wore an all-black shirt, pants, and sandals as he sat down in the empty chair located in the center of the Elders.

"And who is this?" asked Hovan, pointing at Autumn with an interested look as we walked in front of the Elders.

"She was lost on a mission long ago," I stated, lying off the top of my head.

"Long ago, you say?" asked one of the Council Elders. "Her name?"

"Autumn," I replied, afraid that they were going to figure it all out.

"You did well in leading her back home," stated another of the Elders.

"Yes," they all agreed. "Looks like you aren't a total failure."

I frowned, holding myself back from their insult.

"What about your mission?" asked Hovan. "I did not expect you to come back so soon."

I laughed at their blatant lie.

"Or not at all, you mean?" I asked half-jokingly, remembering how they had assigned Leon the mission of selling me to Adamus in Exilio to get rid of me.

"You knew?" sputtered one of the Elders in surprise.

"That doesn't matter," stated Hovan. "I'm sure no one would have missed you, aside from our chief. But since you're here, what about your mission?"

"The Unmei collection?" I asked in a sarcastic tone.

"Yes!" mimicked Hovan and the Elders, "The Unmei collection! Do you have it?"

"No," I announced.

"Excuse me?" asked Hovan, his sinister smile wiped off his face.

"We don't have it, or at least not yet," I replied.

"And you dared to come back here!?" yelled Hovan as the Council began murmuring in anger. "How could you fail us?"

"It's a work in progress," I said, trying to explain.

"You!" yelled Hovan while walking up to Leon and grabbing him by his shirt with his bony fingers. "You failed twice, and you dare show your face here again with this abomination?"

Leon kept his eyes directed at the ceiling.

"Leon!" yelled Hovan in anger. "Not only did you not get rid of this devil and unlawful child, you couldn't even retrieve the Unmei collection! I thought you were supposed to be a prodigy! It's too bad your brother left."

But like before with the crowd, I felt Leon's aura presión increase dangerously fast as he lowered his eyes towards Hovan. Sensing something was off, Hovan dropped his hand from Leon's shirt, taking a few steps back before patting his chest and gathering himself.

"Two failures," he said. "Two fools. I'll lock you in jail!"

"Did you forget that you tried to have me sold as a slave?" I asked, interrupting.

"That doesn't matter," he said with his evil smile. "No one is going to believe the village outcast."

Although I didn't want to accept it, he was right. No one would believe me, nor would they even care. But I was forgetting the more important reason for us being here.

"The village is going to be attacked," I declared with a serious tone while looking at Hovan and the Council Elders.

"What do you mean?" they asked in response.

"As I'm sure you know, one of the cities in the outland is called Cheshria. The king, although I don't know how, has decided to make Dentro and the villagers his slaves. He will be sending a large force to take us over in six days," I explained.

"And why should we trust you?" asked one of the Elders. "You, who should hate and despise us."

"This is still my home, even if most of the people here aren't worth my consideration. I don't want this beautiful island to be made into a wasteland, nor do I want to see innocent people get hurt," I stated.

"Trying to sound so righteous," stated Hovan. "We need proof before we can believe such ridiculous statements. The village has only been attacked once since its founding, nearly four hundred years ago."

"The son of the king of Cheshria stole one of the Unmei artifacts, the Tyring Sword, from his father. It has granted him massive and unbelievable strength. And he is headed here," I stated.

"Why would he be?" asked an Elder.

"Because, seventeen years ago, a woman was banished from Cheshria to this island. At whatever time, she snuck in, and integrated herself into our village without being given away until now. The boy believes that the woman, the wife of the Cheshrian king, is still here. The boy, Kolt, is on his way here to retrieve his mother and rescue her from her banishment," I answered.

"When will he be here?" asked Hovan.

"He already is," I replied. When I had first arrived on the island, I had sensed his presence and the presence of the Tyring Sword. He was in a very old and forbidden part of the island, resting, from what I could tell with my aura sense.

From what I gathered, it seemed that in order for him to be able to utilize the powers of the Tyring Sword well enough to defeat not only the village, but his father also, he would need to rest until he fully merged with the sword's powers. The problem was I didn't know how long that would be.

"Where?" asked Hovan, a hint of fear in his voice.

"He is deep within the western forest of Demon's Pool," I replied, also explaining why he had not attacked the village.

"Is there anything else we should know?" asked Hovan as he walked over to a door on the far side of the room.

"For now, I can't think of anything," I declared.

"Good," said Hovan as he knocked twice on the door.

Moving out of the doorway, Hovan stepped aside as two people walked into the room.

"Put them in jail," said Hovan with a smile, "until we figure out what to do with these failures, including the girl."

"Okay!" yelled one of the guys, who looked familiar. "Remember me, kid?"

Looking at the guy who had spoken, he stood tall, over six feet, with short, black hair, tan skin, and a lanky figure with fairly large muscles. Hanging around his neck was a gray Dream stone necklace like the one Autumn had.

“It’s me, Nicholas,” he said with an overconfident laugh. “The one who defeated the Karkinos within seconds, and the one who saved you after you failed to finish off that Barghest but somehow passed the test anyway.”

“Yeah,” I replied as I looked up at him in annoyance. I disliked his cocky tone and the fact that he had called me *kid*. “So what?”

“Come to jail quietly,” he said with a smile, materializing a large axe from thin air into his hand. “Or I’ll have to force you.”

Chapter 31:
Farewell

It had been four days since Leon, Autumn, and I were put in jail. In all honesty, I should have expected something as low and ridiculous as this from Hovan. But even though we were wasting time locked up, we didn't want to cause an uproar in the village by breaking out. From what I could tell through my aura sense, Kolt was still resting in the western forest of Demon's Pool, an area crawling with fairly powerful creatures.

With only two days left, all three of us were beginning to get anxious. But from what I could tell, Hovan had at least heeded my warning and begun preparing the village forces, although our population could not compare to that of Cheshria. From what I could tell about the foot soldiers that had been fighting when I had been in Cheshria, most of them were regular people without powers. Unlike them, everyone in Dentro had a crystal and knew some fighting techniques for defense. The only problem was, even though we had a fair amount of power for such a small village, Cheshria's forces would most likely outnumber us by too much.

The jailhouse, a building with large cages stacked next to each other, smelled like rotten meat. We were locked in chains and sitting a few feet away from each other, Leon in his corner of the cage with his eyes closed, meditating, while Autumn and I discussed our plans too quietly for the guard standing outside the jailhouse to notice.

We decided that the best course of action was to wait for the attack to begin, as the village would be organized in their defense strategy by then. After escaping the jailhouse, we would split up and help the villagers protecting the village, trying our best to combat the strongest member's of the Cheshria force, the king and his Council.

The next day, the day before the village was supposed to be attacked, I could suddenly hear yelling from every direction. It was obvious that we were under attack, but I didn't hear any screams of fear, as I had expected.

Instead, all I could hear was the steps of our soldiers moving in combat sandals towards one area. Realizing that even our guard had headed in that direction, Leon, Autumn, and I increased our aura presións and broke free of the chains that had held us for five days.

Departing from the jailhouse as quickly as we could, all three of us jumped onto the roof of the building to get a better look over the village. Located next to the Council of Elders' building, we didn't have to search far; we spotted what we were looking for a few hundred feet away in the village square.

Surrounded by hundreds of villagers wrapped in light green sky tree armor, holding weapons of all sorts, were five people.

Standing on top of a guard hut that had been erected in the center of the village square, the king of Cheshria, Blane, Fonos, Dolo, and an unknown woman looked down at the villagers. All of them except for Blane looked excited to be surrounded by so many enemies.

"Villagers of Dentro," announced Luis. "I am the king of a far-away city called Cheshria. Although to most of the outside world, Dentro has been a myth, I have known about its existence for quite some time, more recently from the stories provided to me by my Council member, Blane. I am pleased to finally be here myself."

"Blane!" murmured the crowd of village soldiers in fear and surprise.

"As of now, you have two options," stated Luis with a smile, towering over everyone, his muscles seeming to bulge out of his clothes. "You can surrender without a fight and become a slave state of Cheshria, or you can face my wrath and my thousands of soldiers that are heading here now to eradicate you all. It is your choice. Make the right one."

Instantly, whispers of doubt began to spread around the crowd of soldiers. Some murmured "Don't give in," while others murmured "It's no use."

As the majority of the soldiers began to lean towards giving up, whispering about it being impossible to defeat an army of that size, a figure appeared on the opposite side of the village square.

"My dear people!" yelled the Chief of Dentro, walking toward the king of Cheshria. "Don't lose hope. As we have inherited the will of our ancestors, we cannot allow it to be broken in the face of danger."

"Who are you?" asked Luis.

"I am the Chief of Dentro, Roman. Will you not leave our island peacefully?" asked the Chief.

"I am sorry to say, old man, we won't," replied Luis with a laugh.

"That's a shame," stated the Chief, with the first frown I had ever seen him have.

"If you are the chief," began Luis, "then you must be the strongest in the village, correct?"

"I was," replied the Chief, "at one time."

Without another word, the king of Cheshria aura stepped in front Roman, and to everyone's amazement and displeasure, struck the Chief full-force in the chest. In shock, I watched as Luis pulled his hand from the inside of the Chief's chest. Blood followed, spilling on the ground.

"Chief!" screamed the crowd.

Without hesitating, I focused my own aura energy underneath my feet, appearing behind the Chief. Surprised by my sudden appearance, Luis looked at me with recognition.

"You," he said with a surprised tone.

Having caught him off guard, I lifted up the frail body of our chief as carefully as I could and aura stepped as far away from the village as possible without hurting the Chief.

Having reached the beach of Demon's Pool, I placed the Chief on the soft sand as he smiled up at me. Kneeling down next to him, I hung my head.

"Chief, I'm so sorry!" I said, barely holding back my tears. "I was in shock, I couldn't move. I'm so stupid!"

"It's ok, Zephyr," whispered the Chief.

I could tell it was taking all of his concentration and energy just to speak.

"I have lived so long already. I am thankful for that. Listen, Zephyr," he commanded in a whisper. "I am beyond sorry for what we have all made you go through. How it must have felt…so much hatred and hostility…to be treated with an animosity so intense as to be annihilating…to have around you so many who would deny you even the right to exist in our village..."

From after my mother's death to before I had left the village, the only person to ever acknowledge me and my existence had been the Chief. He had been the closest thing I had ever had to family. He would take me out to eat, protect me from bullies, and even act as my parent when other kids brought theirs to social events. As a child, I had fallen asleep in his office so many times that he had built me my own room. After one night of talking about traveling, the Chief confided in me the regret he harbored about his late wife.

A few years after marrying and becoming the chief, Roman and his wife went on a mission one final time. In battle, while he was distracted, the Chief's wife sacrificed herself for him, taking the blade of an enemy that had been meant for him. Although he was the chief, and had always been the happy, smiling face that the villagers loved, he had felt isolated from the rest of the village after his wife's death. It wasn't until my mother entrusted me to him that his isolation had ended.

"Chief!" I screamed as tears rolled down my cheek. "I don't care about any of that! Just don't die! Don't leave me!"

"When people reject someone's very existence and then look at that person, their eyes become cold, as cold as an ice storm in the deepest winter," whispered the Chief as he lifted his hand onto my shoulder, smiling. "I know I can pass my will on to you. You have true strength, not just the power of our techniques, but with your ability to understand others. I believe you will be able to change the village for the better, something that in my lifetime, I could not accomplish."

"Chief!" I screamed again as his eyes began to slowly close. "No! No!"

"I'm sorry, Zephyr..." whispered the Chief, with his last breath. "I didn't get to see you fulfill your goals, but I'm glad I have gotten a glimpse of the man you are becoming..."

As his eyes closed for the final time, with a peaceful smile upon his face, one of the greatest people I had ever known passed from this world. At first, nothing went through my mind. I didn't know what to do or how to respond, and so I continued to kneel next to the Chief's lifeless body.

No one was here. No one had tried to save him. After everything he had done for the village, for those selfish villagers, not even one had tried to protect him! The only thought running through my head—*Why? Why?!* Why did the old man have to die? As my tears steadily dropped on his cheeks, I couldn't help but yell "WHY?!" This pain, the death of someone I cared about...I didn't know if I could bear it again.

Gazing at the old man's lifeless face and his smile, I

couldn't help but feel angry, but at myself. The Chief had used his last few breaths to apologize to me. For me, it was something that he alone in the village had never had to do.

In my eyes, he was my hero. He had saved me from being alone, even teaching me the strength of a bond. Looking back, I had never taken the time to tell him how I truly felt. Instead, I never tried to take his feelings into account, his life. I was a selfish kid. But as I looked at the old man's peaceful smile, remembering all the good times we had, I realized that if I gave up now, his sacrifice would be in vain.

Remembering his last words, *I believe you will be able to change the village for the better,* I understood that although he had passed away, he had left all of us, including myself, with something very important. Something that I would later have to pass on to others as well.

Looking up at the sky, I watched as the clouds that had been covering the sun moved away, allowing light to shine down. After finding Sea stones from around the beach and placing them around the Chief's body, so that when I came to get him after the battle demons would not have been able to touch him, I looked down at him one more time.

“Old man,” I said with a smile, wiping my last tear away, “thank you.”

After aura stepping back to the village square, I realized that the battle had begun. Standing on the debris that had been the guard hut a short time ago, I looked over to find our forces combating the five enemies that had appeared. Although each of them was surrounded by village warriors, all five of the enemies were effortlessly defeating each warrior in seconds. Blane, Dolo, Fonos, the unknown woman and the king of Cheshria, Luis, were all destroying parts of the village as they slaughtered the village forces.

"Is this all you have?" yelled the king of Cheshria, a few feet away, defeating villagers and destroying buildings with flicks of his finger.

"What happened with the Chief?" asked Leon as both he and Autumn aura stepped next to me.

Surprised that Leon had not charged at Blane yet, I answered him. "He is dead," I stated numbly. "But we don't have time to falter."

Clenching my hand and forming it into a tight fist, I turned around to face Leon and Autumn.

"I won't get in the way of your revenge, Leon. Just don't lose," I said as I looked at him.

"Naturally," he replied with a serious but smug tone.

"I'll handle the woman on the Council, Katjul," declared

Autumn.

"Katjul?" I repeated.

"She's very powerful, but you'll need to take care of the others. My powers are best suited for fighting her," said Autumn with a confident smile. If you are to fight the king, what will we do about Fonos and Dolo?"

"The king," I repeated as I looked at him from afar. I could sense that he was fiercely powerful, even though he hadn't been using his true power. "I don't know—"

"We will handle them," said a familiar cocky voice. Turning around to see the speaker, I was surprised. "That alright?" asked Nicholas as he looked down on us.

"You?" asked Leon with a quick look.

"Yeah," replied Nicholas. "That a problem?"

"No," I said, interrupting. We needed all the help we could get. "You aren't going to try to throw us back in the jailhouse?"

"Right now?" he said with a chuckle. "I'm not at as foolish as you think. I know your powers have evolved since you left. The Chief warned the stronger fighters in the village that we would have to trust you if we wanted to win. Just don't make me regret following his orders."

"Thanks," I said as looked him in the eyes. "I won't forget

this."

"Don't get cocky, devil boy," Nicholas stated with a blank expression. "This doesn't make us friends."

"Of course," I agreed. "Now that Fonos and Dolo are covered, we must go."

"I'm going," declared Leon as he looked back at us, anger in his eyes.

"Good luck," I said to Autumn as we both aura stepped towards our respective opponents.

Deciding to trust Nicholas in keeping the Cheshria brothers busy, I appeared a few feet in front of Luis, blocking the villagers from attacking him.

"Hey!" screamed some of them. "It's that boy!"

"Stand back," I commanded. I turned my head towards the village warriors as they tried to get by me. "He is too strong an enemy."

"And you think you can beat him?" asked a random person in the crowd of warriors. "A village failure, someone as weak as you?"

"Oh good!" yelled the king with a yawn as he glared at me. "I was getting tired of these weak animals."

"Sorry to make you wait," I said as I glared back at him.

Seemingly shocked at the fact that I was brave enough

to confront the king of Cheshria, the man who had killed our chief with one blow, the crowd backed up to allow us space.

"You killed the old man!" I stated in anger.

"I don't like weak old animals," he chuckled. "They are worthless and don't deserve to live anymore."

I was done talking. This man was the embodiment of cruelty. I was going to kill him myself. Instantly, as I glared at the king's eyes, I could feel our aura presións push against each other. Luis's enormous aura presión, a bundle of pure killing intent even darker than Leon's, was eating away at my own aura. This wasn't going to be easy, and even worse, the chances of me coming out victorious looked slim.

Chapter 32:
Explosion! King of Cheshria

"You are all so weak!" yelled the king of Cheshria, laughing hysterically.

"Leave them out of this!" I yelled in response, as the memory of our late chief ran through my mind.

Not waiting a second more, I took the moment to attack. I aura stepped in front of Luis, swinging my right fist towards his face. Although surprised, he easily moved back far enough for my fist to completely miss.

Using the momentum from swinging my fist, I turned in midair, bringing the right side of my body around so that I was facing the sky, allowing me to bring my right leg smashing towards the right side of his face.

Expecting to land a hit, I realized I had underestimated him as he brought his hand up in a guard position, blocking my kick with ease. Grabbing my foot before I could retract it from his blocking hand, he used his free hand to lift me up, propelling me a few feet across the ground.

Being thrown through the air wasn't really on my list of favorite things, but it helped me understand how strong the king was physically. With one hand, he had been able to throw me with relative ease, without the use of his aura. His punches or kicks weren't hits I could take multiple times and survive.

Landing on two feet, I looked up towards the king.

"Wow!" yelled someone in the crowd of villagers. "Maybe that boy can do something."

"Come now, Zephyr," Luis taunted. "Aren't you angry? Don't you want to hurt me? This is your chance! Your chance to avenge that old man you called Chief."

A few hundred feet away, I caught a glimpse of Autumn engaging Katjul and Leon glaring at Blane with a hateful expression. It didn't look like either of them would be able to come to my aid, so I was truly on my own. This was my time, he was right. I couldn't just let him go after what he had done.

Aura stepping in front of him again, I thrust my fist at his gut. He dodged as quickly and easily as before, taking a step back as my fist rolled through the air. I had left my back open, and he took the opportunity to bring his elbow down against it. I stumbled forward in agony. It hurt. He was just playing with me.

"Come on, Zephyr," he taunted again. "Try harder. Put some anger into it."

Before I could recover from stumbling, he aura stepped in front of me, bringing his fist up into my chin, making me catch my lip with my tooth. I tasted blood. He really was on another level, just like Autumn had said.

"I can tell," said Luis as he looked at me.

"What?" I asked, in pain.

"The reason you are all so weak," he answered as he closed his fists, "is because you fight for others! Now, forget about those weaklings and fight for only yourself! Give in to what you truly want!"

"I won't let you trample on our chief's dreams," I stated in reply, standing up straight to face him.

"Dreams? Your chief's dreams?" he repeated with disgust. "You weakling! I fight only for myself, that is why I am strong and you are trash!"

Instantly, all around the king of Cheshria, a cloak of fire covered the outside of his body. The orange flame completely encased him, causing heat waves to emit from where he stood. Turning the palms of his hands toward me, he smiled.

"I call these fire bombs!" he yelled.

Within seconds, small balls of fire around the size of pebbles began shooting from his palms. Surprised, I didn't react in time and allowed the oncoming projectiles of fire to hit me. Each one hurt, but not enough for me to stop standing.

"I'll play with you for a while before I kill you," he stated, laughing.

"Look!" yelled the crowd of villagers that surrounded us.

"He really is too weak. He always has been! That child, the child of those outlaws. It really was impossible for him to try!"

Sighing as he stopped firing his fire bombs, I looked at my tan shorts and white shirt. Little holes had been made from the small balls of fire, and the combined force of the attack had actually hurt. Before I had time to react again, he sent another barrage of fire bombs, and another, and another, until I fell to me knees. I forced myself to stand up.

But as he hit me and continued to attack, I couldn't help but feel something inside me grow stronger and stronger. *What is this feeling?* I thought.

"Ahh!" I yelled as another onslaught of fire bombs branded itself onto my skin. I didn't know why, but I understood that I couldn't lose to this guy. I didn't know if it was because of the Chief, my pride, or the village, but I didn't want to lose, even if it killed me.

Standing up straight and taking my white gloves out of my shorts pocket, I looked Luis in the eyes as I put them on. *I don't know how far I'll get,* I thought to myself, *but I'll do the best I can.*

"It's useless!" he screamed as I finished putting my gloves on.

As he launched another barrage of fire bombs at me, I

aura stepped ten feet to the right of where he had aimed his attack. Seeing that I had moved, he turned his hands towards me, pointing the attack at where I stood. Not giving him a chance to hit me, I aura stepped back to my previous spot, and then back again, until he stopped his attack altogether in an effort to predict where I would go. Aura stepping again, I took his unguarded moment to appear behind him, thrusting my fist towards the back of his neck.

When my fist was inches from it, he aura stepped a foot in front of me and turned around in the same motion, allowing his palms to face directly at me. Laughing hysterically as he had me trapped, I made an expression of fear as his fire-bomb technique came closer to hitting me once again. This time, though, I smiled.

Bringing my fists up in front of me while placing my left leg a few inches in front of my right, I stood in my basic tai-jut-su position. Focusing my aura presión into my fists, arms, and eyes, I increased my vision so that I could see each individual fireball as it propelled through the air towards me.

I pulled my right fist back in preparation, then began throwing punches with one fist after the other, meeting each of the flaming projectiles and destroying them as my punches connected.

I could see the king's surprise, giving me an opening. I took it, aura stepping in front of him while bringing my right fist upwards in an uppercut, connecting with his chin, hard. The blow launched him a few feet off the ground and away from me, but he turned around in midair, faced his palms towards me, and sent another barrage of fire bombs, which this time I could not dodge.

"He did all that," said someone in the crowd, "but he still only managed one hit!"

Although I had been hit again by his technique, I was glad I had been able to at least hit him—meaning it wasn't impossible after all.

"Hey, boy!" called Luis as he stood up and laughed. "Looks like I underestimated you a little."

"I once thought people like you were strong," I admitted as I faced him, already recovered from his counterattack. "I thought that because you fought selfishly for yourself, you were strong. And so, as someone who was alone, I thought I could be that way also. But that's not why I wanted to be strong. I have come to understand you can't be truly strong if you fight only for yourself."

"What are you saying, you fool?!" laughed the king.

"Someone once said to me," I recalled as I thought of the

Chief, "a person is only truly able to be and become strong when they wish to protect someone they share a bond with and care for."

"I may have underestimated you, boy," said the king as he closed both of his fists and brought them up in front of him, "but don't get cocky!"

Like before, a large cloak of fire began to encircle Luis, but this time the flame seemed different. Similar to before, heat waves could be felt from his physical body, but this time the air around him seemed to burn as it made a continuous crackling sound. He was finally serious.

"Demon!" murmured the crowd.

"Then," I said as I began to focus my mind and body, "I will get serious, too."

He's strong, declared Sora from within my mind.

I know, haven't you been watching? I said playfully. *This will take everything we have.*

Yes, agreed Sora. *It will. Let's go all out.*

I could feel my aura presión and power course through my body. Before, I had been holding back my presión so that it would not affect those with a weak consciousness, but I could no longer afford to do so; and so, all around us within the crowd of villagers, people began to fall unconscious. But even after I had unleashed my full power and aura presión, the king of Cheshria's presión still seemed to be overpowering mine.

He aura stepped in front of me at a much faster speed than before, and it took everything I had to block his punch. But I was smart enough to know he would punch again, and I stepped backwards to dodge. Aura stepping and disappearing from in front of me, he reappeared in the same place instantly as if to confuse me, launching a punch with his opposite hand. But I was ready for it. I dodged out of the way again by taking a step back, allowing his punch to ***whizz*** by me as he had done to me earlier. It was his next attack that I wasn't ready for.

Luis aura stepped again, this time appearing behind me, but as I turned to face him, he disappeared and reappeared on my left side. And with that, I made my first mistake. By turning to try to block his attack, I let him get through my defenses, allowing him to jab at me underhanded, catching me in the gut again. ***Oof!*** It hurt, but I could still go on, at least for now. But it was only a matter of time until his monstrous strength depleted my stamina.

The crowd of villagers didn't matter to me anymore. They were almost like the wind, on the edge of my mind.

“You can't survive forever,” chuckled Luis. “Eventually I'm going to kill you, just like I killed your chief.”

He was taunting me. I understood that he wanted me to attack blindly so that I would be open, but I wasn't that naïve.

"Don't worry, I'll make sure to have some fun with your little girlfriend over there before I kill her, too."

I lost it. I ran at him in anger, this time not even aura stepping. He took a simple step back, and another, dodging all of my swings. Bringing my right arm as far back as I could, I swung with all my strength, missing and almost falling over in the process.

I could hear the villagers laughing and murmuring again, but I didn't pay any more attention. I had to prove them wrong and not give up so easily.

"You finally have it," said Luis with a cruel smile. "Anger, pain, all for the sake of fighting for yourself, is better!"

He brought his knee up into my stomach, causing an intense pain to run through my body, but I was in a calmer mindset again. I had to be in control, as the only way I could win against someone who outclassed me would be to outsmart him. So I smiled back as I recovered from his knee attack.

"You are smiling," he declared. "Why?"

"Yeah," I replied, continuing to smile. "You aren't really as much as you're made out to be."

He obviously hadn't expected that, as he jabbed a few

times at me, causing me to aura step a few feet away from him.

"Yeah, you're strong." I brought my hand up to my head and pointed at it. "But you're lacking in other ways."

He appeared in front of me so quickly that all I could do was duck as he brought his left hand swinging across from side to left. It had barely missed me—I had felt the breeze of its passage rustle my hair. If he had hit, my head would have been on fire and my neck may have been broken. Not wanting him to attack again, but realizing that I was making him lose his control, I aura stepped a few feet farther away from him again.

"You can't even control your own son!" I exclaimed. "You tried to kill him because you were too weak to take care of him and his mother. What kind of leader are you?"

Luis staggered for a second, completely taken aback. I was getting to him, through those large muscles, I could see it in his eyes. He was done playing around; it was time for the kill.

With a loud roar, Luis ran straight at me, muscles bulging, never mind aura stepping. As I brought my arm up to defend myself, Luis dropped to one knee and kicked up at me with his foot, hitting me right in the solar plexus, knocking the air out of my lungs.

As I doubled over, he stood, bringing his knee up to collide against my forehead. Although I was fast enough to bring both my hands in between his attack and my head, the impact of his knee and the amount of aura presión he was emitting made me see green and yellow spots. My ears rang louder than they ever had before.

I recognized from the sounds of the crowd that they were no longer laughing at me, but I could barely hear anything, let alone them. I tried to get some space between us by aura stepping backwards, but as I brought my foot down on the ground, I felt a flash hit me on the lower part of my chin, which must have been Luis's fist. I spun around so fast that everything around me blurred and I could no longer focus. As I dropped to my knees, I gazed upwards in time to see Luis's large fist, covered in orange flame, heading straight for my face.

Remembering the Chief's last words, I brought my hand in front of my face in an effort not to give up. Catching the full brunt of the blow with my hand, I didn't feel any pain. But at this point, it was more that I couldn't feel the pain after having been beaten up so badly. My nerves could no longer handle it. Although I had blocked the blow to my face, the sheer force of it had propelled me onto my back.

As I lay, Luis leaped on top of me, launching a barrage of fire-covered punches at my chest and stomach. Not only did it burn with each punch, but I knew he had to be breaking bones, even as I reinforced my natural strength with my aura presión.

As the barrage began to slow down, eventually stopping, Luis got right in my face.

"I will kill you," he hissed. "This is what your future and the future of your village holds. I will end your existence!"

Chapter 33:
The Chaos Demon

Not yet, I thought to myself. I knew that at my current level I would be finished here, unless I did something that Karlir had forbidden me to do. During my training, I had achieved a state of immeasurable power. It happened one day while Karlir and I had been sparring, going all out on each other. Drained of most of my energy after fighting with Karlir for over an hour, I gazed at him to see that he had not even begun to sweat. It was at that point that I was reminded of my past failures competing with the other villagers. I felt like I wasn’t getting anywhere.

But that time, as I reflected on my failures and letdowns, I realized I couldn't afford to lose anymore. In the past, after my mother had died, I had lived and fought only for myself. I had learned from my many mistakes and thought nothing of losing, as it felt like no one cared. I took the Chief's kindness for granted and started to make up a list of reasons the villagers hated me.

Was it my appearance, because I was an orphan, because I hadn't met my father, or because I was weak? I could never figure it out. As a kid, I spent half of my time training endlessly to gain the skills that seemed to come easily for others, and the other half I spent forcing myself not to tear up every night.

As I had looked at Karlir standing in front of me, waiting for me to get up and continue, I understood that I had changed. I had people like Karlir, Autumn, the Chief, my mother, and even Leon that cared about me and depended on me. It was at that moment that within my mind, I felt Sora's presence grow stronger until it seemed as if we were one.

All of Sora's knowledge, strategic way of thinking, and influence began to combine with my own, as if we were mixing two fruits together in an effort to make a new substance. My vision, energy, and reaction time increased, and I quickly jabbed at the air.

Amazed, Karlir looked up at me and smiled.

“I knew you had great potential,” he said, laughing, “but to think you had this as a trump card!”

“What's happened?” I asked, unsure as to why I could feel the wind blowing from every direction.

Even with Sora's combined knowledge, it looked as though he did not know what had just occurred, aside from the fact that our strength, speed, and stamina had increased by at least twenty times, maybe more.

“I don't know,” replied Karlir as my vision suddenly blurred. “Whoa there, boy,” he muttered as I dropped to the ground.

I placed both hands on the ground, breathing hard. I wasn't sure what had just happened. The power boost I had achieved was replaced by my normal state.

That form, said Sora's voice within my mind, *drained all our remaining energy too quickly. It's dangerous.*

"I have only seen something of a similar nature happen twice in my life," stated Karlir as he helped me up, placing my arm around his shoulder and directing us back to our cave training home. "The first was when I got in a fight with the other man called Zephyr, whom I once mentioned to you before we began your training."

"Yeah," I mumbled in response to the mention of the man who could have been the father who had abandoned my mother and me.

"Zephyr had arrived in Sleeves shortly after I had won the Valkyrie Shield as a gift from the ancient Dragon of Sleeves for surviving a battle against him. I had just been named a hero. I was young, cocky, and angry, as I had lost all of my men in the battle. Zephyr had been accused of stealing, and so I was asked by the vice chief to get rid of him.

"Overconfident, I ignored his pleas to stop as I confronted him outside of the city. Launching off the ground to attack him, I stopped in my tracks as I found that the sheer pressure of his aura brought me to my knees. In disbelief and denial, I unleashed my full power on him, sending a tsunami of flames large enough to destroy half of Sleeves at him."

"What?" I exclaimed with a chuckle. "You were young once?"

"Shut up," he said jokingly, using his free hand to pat me on the head. "Seconds before the flames reached him, Zephyr was suddenly covered in silver waves of energy, and his eyes were almost completely clear, shining as bright as the sun. All around his body was a white glow, almost godly. Confused and in awe of this mysterious man, I gazed from afar as he placed his hand in front of him, palm facing towards the wave of flames. Within seconds, the wave of flame was extinguished and a huge blast of air collided with my body. If I had not had aura energy underneath my feet, I would have been blown hundreds of feet into the sky. Zephyr had used just the wind to obliterate my tsunami of flames."

"Wait," I interrupted. "Were you stronger then, or now?"

"I was at my prime," he said with a sad look on his face. "Zephyr instantly appeared in front of me at an untraceable speed, bringing his finger towards the center of my head. Realizing that I had utterly lost and that he would kill me, I waited for death to come, closing my eyes. But when it didn't, I opened them to see Zephyr tap my head with his finger, smiling."

"No," I expressed in disbelief, waiting for him to continue.

"Yes," said Karlir as we entered the cave and sat down across from each other. "The second time was not long after that fight. Zephyr had asked me to accompany him to the homeland of a woman he had fallen in love with, and so we traveled with her until we reached Dentro Island. What we didn't know was that she had broken a sacred law of the village by bringing us there. A few hours after we arrived, the villagers wanted to throw us in jail, but to everyone's surprise, a demon attacked."

"A demon?" I repeated. "A demon attacking should have been nothing for the village."

"Ordinarily, it seemed so. But this demon was like no other," explained Karlir. "Apparently, the demon had been asleep for hundreds of years, since the first chief of your village fought it. The demon took the form of a dragon, but even so, it was clearly not one. It looked as if it were made of smoke; its body was completely black, except for its yellow eyes that seemed to glow in the dark. As large as half the island, the beast emitted an aura that was the darkest and cruelest thing I had ever felt."

"What was the demon called?" I asked, a little angry that I had never heard this story, even from the Chief.

"They referred to it as the Chaos Dragon," replied Karlir with a sigh. "The demon destroyed almost half of the village, taking out hundreds of soldiers in the process. The chief at that time, although fairly old, was powerful enough to keep the demon from attacking the village by himself after directing its attention away. Even so, it looked as if it was only a matter of time before the demon destroyed the whole village. Reluctant at first to help the people who had tried to throw us in jail, I followed Zephyr as we made our way over towards the woman we had travelled with. Zephyr kissed her one last time, and he and I left to fight in the incredible battle between the chief and the Chaos Dragon."

"What made you decide to help?" I asked.

"I'm not sure myself. Maybe I was just following Zephyr, or maybe I didn't want innocent people to get involved; I will never know," he admitted. "Zephyr asked for five minutes to concentrate his power, which would allow him to destroy the beast. Those five minutes were the hardest of my life. It took everything the chief and I had to keep the demon at bay. In the end, Zephyr went into that powerful state again, effortlessly creating a huge tornado. Engulfed by the storm, the demon cried out as it disappeared. As the storm subsided, all around where the demon had stood were black flames."

"Black flames," I repeated.

"Warning us not to touch them, Zephyr floated higher and higher into the air above us, still covered by the silver waves of energy. His eyes glowing even brighter than before, Zephyr held out his hand right hand, palm facing upwards to the sky. Seemingly from nothing, three weapons, which I recognized as the ancient weapons known as the Unmei collection—including my Valkyrie Shield—lay on his palm. He levitated the weapons away from himself and directly above the debris from the battle, and all three weapons began to shine as the black flames surrounded them. They were shining so brightly I could no longer bear to gaze at the light, but the brightness slowly died down. As I observed the once-beautiful area, I realized that all of the flames had disappeared. With the sword, spear, and shield nowhere to be seen, Zephyr dropped to the ground, no longer in his god-like form."

"So he saved the day," I said sarcastically. "Why have I never heard of you guys being in Dentro?"

"So impatient," he pointed out with a chuckle. "We were thanked for our help, and the villagers agreed to make an exception to the sacred law, just once, for us both. Appreciative of their decision, we thanked them, as we had already stayed longer than I had planned. I had business to attend to in

Sleeves, because at that time it looked as though war was stirring."

"With Cheshria?" I asked.

"Yes," Karlir revealed. "Before we left, the vice chief, named Hovan as I recall, directed us to Zephyr's female companion's abode."

"Hovan," I mumbled. "That devil."

"Indeed," agreed Karlir. "While we all discussed the future inside her home, we were all too focused on each other to realize that Hovan was eavesdropping. Zephyr's companion was angry that he was no longer going to stay with her. As he made his way towards the door with an apologetic look, the woman used her last resort, stating she was pregnant with his child. Surprised, Zephyr and the woman came to an understanding; I didn't understand it myself. But when we began to make our way towards the door, all of us realized that we had made a great mistake in letting our guard down, as we heard footsteps near the door. Yanking it open, we realized that it was too late, and the woman's secret was out."

"So he told everyone," I stated. "Why didn't you just catch Hovan before he could say anything?"

"I wanted to," admitted Karlir with a frown. "But Zephyr advised against it. He said that it was time for us to depart, and so we left without another word."

"Wait," I interrupted again. "My father left before I was born. Hovan soon put my mother on trial in front of the whole village, and she was ridiculed for the rest of her life for bearing an outsider's baby. The end of that story sounded exactly like what happened to my...parents..."

That's when it all hit me. Sure, I had been connecting the pieces over time, but after hearing this story I was sure. I had to come to terms with the fact that my father was the man Karlir referred to as Zephyr. He looked like me, and we had similar powers. I began breathing hard.

"Zephyr!" yelled Karlir as he ran over to me, kneeling down. "What's wrong? You're hyperventilating!"

I passed out. I guess learning what had happened between my father and the village was too big of a shock for me to handle. And maybe, because I had always imagined my father as a cruel person for leaving his son, the fact that he was the savior of the village was too much as well.

Later, I had explained to Karlir my connection with those events. Karlir had given me a few days to come to terms with the information, and then he had begun to train me to master the form he had referred to as god-like.

As I forced myself back to the present, I could feel every

muscle in my body aching. A few feet away, walking in circles around me, was Luis, talking to the crowd of villagers that surrounded us.

"What now?" he said, still laughing hysterically. "Will none of you help this boy? No one will stop me from destroying this village!"

Focusing on getting up, I forced myself off of my back and onto my knees. Placing my right hand on my right knee, I pushed myself up.

"Still alive?" asked Luis in a mocking tone. "You're weak. This is it for you, boy."

Standing upright, I felt sick. I no longer had enough energy to use basic aura skills like enhancing my strength, but that didn't matter. I wasn't going to give up my dream.

As he walked straight towards me with a devilish smile, just like before, a large cloak of fire began to encircle Luis; I could feel heat waves from his body, as the air around him seemed to be burning, crackling like before.

"Die—" began Luis.

"No!" I interrupted, the crowd of villagers in total silence. "I have always been called outcast, monster, and devil. People ignored me. You killed the first man to acknowledge my existence. But this time, I'll make everyone recognize me!"

"How can someone like you do that?" he yelled, holding out his hand, palm facing towards me.

Materializing in front of his palm, a ball of fire the size of a village house formed.

"Die!" he shouted again as the ball made its way towards me.

It's now or never! I heard Sora say.

Feet away from being burnt to a crisp, I relaxed myself, opening myself to nature. Slowly, within my mind, I could feel Sora's presence resonating with my own until we were completely one again. This time, though, I felt different than during my training. Silver waves of energy surrounded me as my body began to shine with a white light.

Deciding to follow my instincts, I looked at the huge mass of fire heading straight for me. Kicking off the ground with more force than I had intended, I launched myself through the air and across the ground to meet the gigantic fireball head on.

Chapter 34:
A Predicted Future

Everything had led up to this battle. As the village erupted with screams and explosions, I was only focused on one thing.

"Little brother," said Blane as we stood about twenty feet apart. "What do you plan on doing here?"

All around us, I could feel smaller auras disappear. A few hundred feet away, I could tell Zephyr had started his fight with the Cheshrian king. Dressed in a short-sleeve black shirt, with long white pants and black shoes, Blane calmly looked at me.

"Blane, what do I plan on doing, you ask?" I said, forcing myself to stay calm, "I plan on killing you."

"Killing me?" responded Blane. "Well, let's see you try to do it."

As Blane finished, I felt the slightest disruption in the air, and I turned to find Blane standing next to me. Smiling, I brought my fist up against his as we turned in unison, facing each other, fists locked against each other. In the same motion, almost instantly, Blane drew his black-and-yellow sword from his back and out of his sheath with his free hand, guiding the blade's tip towards my right eye while changing the fist that had been against mine into a grip to hold my right hand in place.

Unable to use my right hand, I bent down, bringing my left hand behind my back, unsheathing my black sword, and moving it in front of my eye. Seeing the sparks fly from the blades' collision, Blane released his grip on my hand, sheathing his sword and using his free arm to bind mine again.

Jumping slightly off the ground and rotating himself towards me, Blane brought his right leg upwards towards my face. As I quickly brought my sword down to block his kick, Blane brought the same foot onto the other side of my sword, kicking off it while using his left leg to swipe through the open space between us. His foot connected with my face.

Surprised at his skillful acrobatics but at the same time knowing he hadn't been called a genius for nothing, I forced myself back upwards after being hit in the face by Blane's kick.

Catching him seemingly off guard in midair, I regained my footing while unsheathing my yellow sword, slashing upwards towards Blane. Already ahead of me, Blane grabbed my blue shirt, pulling himself around me and dodging my blade, still in midair. As he slashed upward and pulled on my shirt, Blane used my own momentum to lift me off the ground and throw me back down.

Backflipping off the ground and back onto my feet, I focused my light and dark energy into both my swords, launching off the ground towards Blane. As I slashed downwards, two waves, yellow and black, shot from my swords straight at Blane.

Aware of my double wave shot from our previous encounter in Cheshria, Blane easily jumped up, completely dodging my attack. Having predicted his movements, I aura stepped behind him, thrusting both my swords into Blane's stomach.

My swords effortlessly pierced through my brother's body, and I cursed my stupidity as I realized I had been fooled. Instead of blood coming out of Blane's wound, yellow-and-black energy slowly leaked from it. Pulling my swords out, I jumped a few feet backwards as the fake body made of light and dark energy exploded like fireworks. When the bright lights had died down, I turned my gaze to the right a few feet away to where my brother stood.

"You are stronger than I thought," admitted Blane. My blades were up against his neck. After realizing that the body I had stabbed was made of energy, I had aura stepped behind Blane in an effort to surprise him.

"You know," I said as I moved my blades closer to his throat, "there is something I want to know before I kill you."

"What is it, little brother?" he asked without a hint of

emotion.

"Before you knocked me out that night, you said something to me," I said as I recalled that nightmare. "You said that it was all to protect me! Protect me how?"

"Why would you want to know that now?" he asked.

"Even though you were a prodigy, there's no way you were able to kill both our parents and the rest of the construction force," I claimed.

"So you figured it out," said Blane. "It was to protect you from our village Elders, Hovan, and King Luis of Cheshria."

"What?!" I exclaimed as I pressed my blades close enough to his throat to prick the skin. "Why would you need to protect me from that fool and our own village? Don't lie to me!"

"That is the truth," he assured. "Whether you believe me or not is your choice."

"Don't lie to me!" I screamed again.

There was no way that I had needed to be protected from the village, especially at the expense of our own family's life.

"The truth, or what everyone sees as reality, is defined by what you want it to be. Is it right to kill someone because they believe in something that you believe is sinful? Should we stop someone who enjoys pain from cutting themselves? What makes us right and them wrong? Reality is a mirage that we create to keep ourselves from going insane, and so is the 'right thing' to do," explained Blane.

"So?"

"Your truth relies on your assumption that you are a part of the village and no one would ever harm you," answered Blane. "Anyone's and everyone's truth can turn out to be a mirage."

"I wanted to believe you!" I yelled. "When I was younger, I wanted to think you had a reason, or even maybe that you were framed. But things are different now."

He aura stepped away from where I stood to ten feet behind me. I slashed at the air, my swords barely whizzing by Blane as he moved.

"I am stronger. I can kill you," I stated as we glared at each other. "I will kill you. I will avenge our family."

"Looks like you have finally gotten strong enough to carry our name," acknowledged Blane with a chuckle.

"Does that mean you're ready to stop this game of running?"

"I can tell you were close with that boy, Zephyr," admitted Blane. "I thought that you would realize hate was the only way to gain the power necessary to combat me. Yet you still wish to fight me, with such a weak state of mind and heart?"

"I have no friends. My only goal has been to kill you. Let's see if I really have such a weak heart, brother."

"You have become a truly cocky little man," he said mockingly.

He slowly walked closer and closer toward me, then stopped when we stood within sword's length.

"Our powers are unique from most others'," he stated. "From the time you awaken them, you are forced to lean towards one side of energy more than the other. Those who lean towards the light help others without hesitation. Those who lean towards the dark without controlling themselves go berserk with power. Their anger takes them over, and their dark powers slowly begin to eat away at their souls. Most eventually learn to balance their energies, allowing them to unlock their true potential. But there is another essential part of our powers."

"What is it?" I asked rudely.

"Long ago, right before the founding of our village, the most powerful and evil person in our family lived. He was a cruel man who led others using hate and fear. He was the child of a god and a human, something no one in the village knows but our family, the deceased chief, and the family of a villager named Amity," answered Blane.

"The son of a god?!" I repeated. "How is that possible?"

"Oh, it was possible," replied Blane with a smile. "Years ago, the gods of our universe lived among us, even mating with us. The ancient legend was that half of the gods' human children decided that humanity was unfit to govern itself, and that they would do it instead. They used their powers to connect with each other, and some of the gods who sided with the dark children built weapons for them, creating portals to connect the different worlds throughout the universe. To combat them, the other half of the gods' children came together in an effort to protect the different worlds from the dark children's reign."

"And?" I asked. "What does that have to do with us?"

"Our ancestor was one of the four dark children, also one of the most powerful, their leader. Within our direct line, his blood resonates the strongest. What's ironic is that, just like yours, his childhood best friend was the leader of the four children of the light," stated Blane.

"What do you mean?" I asked. "Just like mine?"

"Although unlike us, your friend Zephyr is also the direct result of a light god mating with a human. His mother was the villager called Amity. Our deceased chief, Amity's father and Zephyr's grandfather, also knew of our families' ties to the dark children, although Zephyr was never informed of the truth. For a long time, our family had been conspiring to revive the dark children's goals. Their first plan was to destroy the village," said Blane with a smile.

"No..." I muttered in disbelief.

"Yes. Although I am currently stronger than you, our family intended for you to continue the plan. The village Elders knew this, and so they did things to stop you from progressing, like holding you back two years from taking the Trial of Adulthood," explained Blane.

"How did you know that?!" I yelled, still shocked and in disbelief.

"With my current abilities, I have been able to come back frequently and check up on you in the village," answered Blane. "The village Elders discovered our family's plans to revive our dark ancestors and achieve their goals, and so they organized a secret mission: to kill everyone in the construction force, especially the Dentro Duo and their direct line. Since I was serving directly under the village Elders as an elite fighter, I learned of their plans and pleaded with them to spare us. Unable to change their minds, I offered that I would lead the mission if my younger brother would be spared."

"NO!" I screamed at him in anger. "You're lying!"

"They agreed," continued Blane as if I had said nothing.

"I led the mission, along with King Luis of Cheshria, who was somehow forced to join—I don't know how. With our combined strengths, we were able to kill all of our family members, except you."

I coughed. I wasn't sure if I should believe him, but it wasn't something he would joke about before a fight to the death. Or maybe it was, as I had believed Blane to be the perfect older brother, caring, fun, and always there for me, helping me grow stronger.

"Our family died for you, little brother. I sacrificed my life, my title, and our family for ***y-o-u***." He muttered the last three letters of his sentence. "Seventeen years ago, two years before you were born, a demon made of dark energy attacked the village. Our ancestor, before his death, left a portion of his dark energy in the form of a black dragon to defend his descendants from the wrath of a light god or one of their children. At that time, one of the light gods had entered the village, and so it awoke and attacked."

I stepped back to create more space between us.

"You are too weak to continue with our plans. I have been trying to protect you and force you to become strong, but you still haven't unlocked your true potential," stated Blane as he put one foot in front of the other, slowly making his way towards me with an emotionless expression. "I am the only one left who will be able to achieve the goals of our family and ancestor!"

I knew I could attack; I knew I could run. I knew I could do more than take slow steps backwards, and yet I couldn't. I had never been afraid. I had used hate and anger to allow me to move forward and grow stronger. Why wasn't it working for me now?!

"LEON!" yelled Blane as he walked forward, his eyes and face changing from expressionless to a wild, almost insane look. "You are the beginning of my journey! By killing you and taking your swords and crystal, I will fuse our powers together—did you know you can do that within direct bloodlines? Did your great master teach you that? From the moment we learned this, long ago, our ancestors have killed their own family members, taking their crystals and weapons and fusing their powers together to make themselves stronger! But because the village forced us to control ourselves, this custom stopped. But no more! We are the last! But I can't do it alone…I won't be able to kill the light children with my current power."

"No," I whispered as Blane made his way to me. "No, no, no!"

"***NOW, COME, FIGHT ME, LITTLE BROTHER! LET ME KILL YOU AND BE FREE FROM THIS WRETCHED LAND!***" he yelled with cruel passion.

As my brother walked towards me, yelling about our family's destiny and past, I realized that I didn't care. I understood his intentions. It wasn't for our family, our past, but his desires that he did it all. Remembering the cold, soft, pale, lifeless bodies of our parents and family after witnessing my brother run away from the scene, I stopped backing up.

"So it has all been for this," I said with all the confidence I could muster. "It has finally come. The time to achieve my goal."

"So you finally get it." Blane stopped walking, unsheathing his black sword as it shone in the burning sunlight. "You said that you were going to kill me, but you can't beat me as you are now."

"You can boast about your power all you want," I replied as I unsheathed my yellow sword from my back. "But using the pain you have caused me and my hate, I will kill you."

"Oh?" he mumbled as he pointed the tip of his black sword at me.

"This time," I said as I unsheathed my black sword, holding both in my hands while pointing them at Blane, "you die. You won't be able to run away this time."

I slashed downward with my blades and held them to my sides. Blane and I launched off the ground at each other, finally serious.

Chapter 35:
A Brother's Final Gift

Everything was at a speed faster than the untrained eye could follow. Constantly aura stepping around the small battlefield we had created, Blane and I jabbed our swords at each other in an effort to land a hit. This battle was beyond anything I had experienced before. Blane was a master. He was a genius, powerful, swift, smart, and deadly.

With every thrust of my black and yellow blades, Blane countered by thrusting his black tip straight towards mine. As our tips collided, I could feel the sheer force of our attacks creating shockwaves that vibrated the air around us.

For what seemed like forever, we continued to play the game of block and thrust. Within the split second that it took to launch into the air or to aura step, we would exchange blows, the tips of our swords connecting while we repeated the same motion over and over. All the while, I kept my eyes open, searching.

By what seemed like luck, Blane aura stepped away from our repeated blows, landing on a stick that caused him to lose his focus. Spotting an opening, I launched myself at him, aura stepping to appear in front of him and bringing my yellow sword in an upward slash. Caught off guard, Blane blocked my slash with his sword, the power of my attack forcing it to fly out of his hand and land a few feet away.

Without hesitation, I tried to bring my black sword slashing up towards his neck, only to be stopped midway by Blane's movements. He had grabbed both my left and right hands, essentially holding me in place, so all our hands were restricted—or so I thought.

As I glared at him with as much killing intent as I could, we looked into each other's eyes. I could feel my body shaking with anger and energy as I struggled to break free from his grasp. Almost instantly, to my horror, another Blane appeared above us, thrusting his sword downward towards me.

I spent a large amount of aura in the form of a shockwave to force Blane into releasing me, and I let go of my swords and aura stepped a few feet away. Although reluctantly, I realized I had been outclassed again.

As the fake Blane that had been gripping me began to dissipate into dark and light energy, the real Blane walked in front of it, glaring at me intently while dropping my swords behind him.

Even though it was weird to fight without my swords, I wasn't going to quit. Leaning downwards and swiping the ground with my hand, I jumped backwards a few feet while flicking the two pebbles I had picked up. By increasing my own physical strength and pouring my aura energy around the pebbles like a cloak, I increased their destructive force until they could rip straight through the human body and continue on for miles.

Jumping upwards to dodge the pebbles, Blane looked at me in surprise. A shroud of black energy surrounded my hands then headed straight for him as I directed my hands towards his position. But I knew that wasn't why he had a look of surprise on his cold face. Surrounding him, from every direction except directly in front of him, were the fallen pebbles I had picked up from the ground a second earlier. He was trapped in midair and unable to aura step. I looked on in delight as he had no choice but to take one of my attacks to escape.

Shrouded in a cloud of dust, I gazed toward the space Blane had previously been located in, only to find that a large, black square made of dark energy now occupied it instead.

It reached about five feet in each direction. I smiled at my creation. I had trapped him in the black box, where he would eventually run out of air before being able to break out.

I took a step forward, then stopped and opened my eyes in shock as Blane appeared in front of me, his eyes gazing straight into mine. He quickly directed his fist towards my stomach.

"Aaahhh..." I groaned. Disappearing from in front of me and appearing behind me, he kicked my back, launching me off the ground and several feet across the battlefield.

As pain erupted through my back, spreading through all of my muscles, I lay on the ground and opened my eyes. The black box I had created, although still above me, had been a mistake. I should have known. As I looked up at the back side of the box, which had been outside my field of vision, it was clear that Blane would have broken out of it with his level of power. The back was completely obliterated, and the rest of the box followed as the dark energy began to dissipate and lose form.

I forced myself up and off the ground. I hadn't noticed the black wall of energy behind me, towering over ten feet.

As I brought my hands up to focus my dark energy into them, Blane appeared in front of me again, punching me in the stomach while locking my left hand against the energy wall with his right. As he completely sealed off my movements by stepping on my foot and gripping my arm against the dark wall, I couldn't do anything but breathe.

He brought his free hand towards my neck and wrapped his fingers around the necklace that held my crystal. It felt like I had to scratch an itch all over my body. Once our mind and souls fused with our crystals' after we were chosen by them, it pained us constantly to be separated from them or for them to be in the control of someone else.

I remembered stories of people who had been left alive but had their crystals taken. They slowly began to lose their minds. As Blane began to pull, forcing the necklace chain to press up against the back of my neck, I yelled in agony.

"AHHH!" It felt like he was ripping off a limb.

"I'm sorry, Leon," he said as he pulled harder, straining the chain. "This is our *truth*."

"No," I said, screeching through the pain. "*This* is the truth."

Instantly, before he could pull my crystal off, dark energy with a cloudlike form completely enveloped my body. Underneath my feet, the ground slowly began to disappear as if it were being eaten. Realizing the danger, Blane released my necklace and jumped a few feet back. Standing up, I released the technique to save for later, as I knew I would need it.

Without giving me a chance to recover, a wave of dark energy erupted through the air from Blane's hands, straight towards me. I tried to use my leg to push off the ground and away from the wall, but an intense pain blasted through my legs. I wouldn't be able to dodge the energy in time. Just like a second ago, dark, cloudlike energy began to surround me until it covered me completely, aside from my eyes and mouth, as the wave hit me.

Enveloped in dust from the explosion, I had completely countered his attack with my own special move.

In response, as the dust began to clear, I released my dark form and blasted my own wave of dark energy toward Blane. But as I looked up, I found that he had launched the same attack again, and our energies collided.

After a few seconds of our waves fighting against each other, mine slowly began to push his backward. Surprised, I smiled, only to look on in horror as Blane did something I had not expected.

Shining all around his hands, large amounts of light energy began to form. Launching the yellow energy from his hands, it reached the back of his previous black wave, only to change color. To my amazement and horror, Blane's light and dark waves slowly combined, as they combated the momentum of my own dark wave. Quickly destroying my wave completely and continuing its movement towards me, now a mixture of yellow and black like Blane's sword, the wave dissipated inches before reaching me.

Although shocked, I realized that Blane had meant to use this to show the extent of his power. He had destroyed my energy with more energy. Because I leaned towards the dark side, I did not have complete harmony between my light and dark powers, unlike Blane. But with twice the output, a fused cloud took even more energy to maintain.

Having regained a little of my strength, I launched myself off the ground, aura stepping. I was only able to cover a few feet with my aura stepping, as I needed to maintain my own energy. Blane began blasting yellow-and-black colored beams. A mixture of both energies, they were far more powerful than my own normal attacks.

At first, I dodged them completely, but Blane seemed to be getting better at reading my movements. His attacks neared where I was landing with each step. As one of the beams barely missed me, passing within inches of my face, the force of the attack launched me off the ground and dropped me a few feet away. Realizing that the only way I would be able to beat him was by surprise, I lay on the ground and acted as if I were unconscious.

“Finished already?” he mumbled as he made his way towards me, reaching down to grab my crystal. But to his surprise, as his eyes widened, my body slowly began to almost evaporate in front of him, just like the technique he had used on me previously. Like him, I could create a fake copy of myself made of dark energy, but unlike him, I could only afford enough energy to do it once. Taking this as my chance, I had created the fake and used it to cover a hole in the ground underneath, where I had created a black box made of energy to protect me while I released my power.

Deciding that this would be my final attempt, as I was beginning to run low on stamina and energy, I put my hands together and focused on synchronizing all of my aura energy with my dark energy. Just like before, dark energy with a cloudlike form completely enveloped my body aside from my eyes.

The technique, which I had planned as my trump card, I referred to as my dark form. Using my dark energy to cover my body like a cloak, anything I touched would be reduced to pieces too small for the naked eye to see. But, in cases where I did want the floor underneath my feet, I had to consciously keep the energy surrounding me from obliterating everything.

Sensing Blane falter above me as he dropped to his knees in exhaustion, I placed my hands on the underside of the black box's roof. Releasing as much energy as I could at once, I felt the ground around me shake as huge blasts of black energy erupted through it. For almost half a minute, large blasts of dark energy shot around the battlefield Blane and I had created, until all of the energy I had released had been blasted into the sky.

Drained of most of my energy, I let the black box around me evaporate as I jumped aboveground, landing a few feet away from Blane. As my dark form also dissipated, leaving me in my normal state, I glared at him.

Visibly exhausted and breathing with intensity, he bled from the shoulder of his right arm. A hole in the front of his shirt was covered in streaks of blood that leaked from his mouth. Although I hadn't been able to kill him, I had injured him badly.

"Looks like all those fused attacks of yours, combined with dealing with my own attack, drained you," I stated as I dropped to my knees, exhausted.

"Don't act all tough," he responded. "You're almost out of energy, too."

I laughed.

"Do you think I spent my whole life trying to become strong enough to kill you and didn't come prepared when I finally had the chance?" I asked. "My final attack will be unrivaled in power, just like your fused energy."

"What?" he murmured, his expression showing his doubt.

Lifting my hand, I pointed my finger towards the sky.

"No..." he muttered as he looked up.

Unlike before, when the sun had been shining brightly,

the area covering the island was now completely black, as if it were night.

"This attack," I said as I faced the palms of my hands towards the sky, "gives you a glimpse of the depths of hell. You can't evade it, and its destructive force would be able to kill everyone on this island if I wished."

I had taken a gamble that Blane would have been too busy evading the dark blasts rising from the ground to realize the sudden changed in sunshine, and I had released all of my energy into the sky. Although I had no energy left to add, I could manipulate the dark energy by will. I would focus on attacking Blane, and the energy would track him, making it unavoidable.

"Brother," I began as the energy slowly began rotating like a tornado, "let the gates of darkness drag you to your death!"

The blast was almost instant. The huge black tornado surrounded him, blowing everything in its path away. As I closed my fists, the tornado constricted. ***BOOM!***

"Finally," I said as I dropped to my knees, the aftermath of my attack leaving debris and Blane lying face-down on the ground. "It's over. It's over!"

My body shaking and my energy completely drained, I glanced towards where Blane lay. To my horror and dismay, yellow-and–black, flame-like energy was beginning to build up all around him as Blane slowly picked himself up off the ground. With his white pants and black shirt covered in holes and dirt, the flame-like substances surrounded Blane, the energy creating shockwaves and pushing my hair upwards constantly.

Like me in my own dark form, Blane was now completely covered in energy, but unlike my own, his was shaped like flames and a mixture of yellow and black.

“Without this,” he said as he stood up, coughing blood, “I would have been dead. You truly have become stronger, Leon. Enough even to challenge those on the level of chief. But like you, I was still holding back my own power. This form is called Totus.”

“Totus?” I repeated.

“My mixed-energy attacks and this form require the use of both dark and light energy in harmony,” stated Blane. “Leon, if you are holding back, stop. This fight is not over yet.”

Judging from the energy output of his form, even if I had had enough energy to achieve my own dark form, I would still be outmatched.

“What's wrong?” he asked as the force of the shockwaves increased until I had keep myself from moving backward. “Are you too worn down, and completely helpless?”

"What?!" I yelled as I tried to force my dark form.

But as I tried, fully aware that I had no energy left, every part of my body began to ache.

Leon... called a dark, gloomy voice in my mind.

Kurai? I asked, knowing that it was one of the two manifestations of my crystal.

I can help you. The voice grew stronger within my mind. *I can help you get your revenge! You need my help Leon...Just let go. Let me do it.*

"AHHH!" I screamed as all around me a massive amount of dark energy enveloped my body.

The pain was staggeringly intense, almost as if someone was lighting my skin on fire. Although I looked like I was in my dark form, covered in black, cloud like flames, the amount of energy surrounding me was on a different level than what I could normally produce or control. As I tried to move my limbs, I realized that my body was moving on its own, walking towards Blane. I was no longer in control of my body.

"So," muttered Blane as he stood in place, a few feet away, "you must be the dark side of Leon's crystal."

As my mouth opened to answer, I thought that even though I was no longer in control of my body, it would still be my voice that would come out. To my surprise, that didn't seem to be the case.

"YOU!!!" screamed a dark but childlike voice, full of energy. "I have waited for this moment! Thanks to you, Leon's energy is so low that he's lost control over me. Now I am free! ***FREE***!"

Remembering what Blane had said about our powers, I understood why I was no longer in control of movements. Since the moment I had awakened my powers, I had leaned towards the dark side, or Kurai, rather than the light side, Hikari. Although they had both always been within my mind, manifesting themselves, Hikari had slowly begun to show up less until during my training when I decided to throw away all of my bonds and focus only on vengeance.

Because I didn't have the energy required to control my powers, and I had tried to pull out more, Kurai was able to take control, putting me into a state the villagers call berserk mode.

When this had happened in the past to others, they would go on rampages, killing anyone and anything. Eventually, after someone defeated their dark manifestation in battle, leaving it weak, the person would regain control of their dark energy. If they weren't able to, their soul was eventually overtaken and eaten by their own crystal.

Slowly, my mouth opened as Kurai roared. The ground

shook, and the clouds in the sky dissipated, leaving it empty as the sun shone downward.

But as my mouth closed and my gaze turned towards where Blane stood, I felt Kurai's surprise—Blane had disappeared. Inches below me, he reappeared. Bringing his fist in an uppercut, he smashed his fist against my black-energy-covered chin. Expecting not to feel any pain, as my normal dark form negated most attacks, I was launched off the ground and straight into the sky.

Although I myself could not feel the pain, I could feel Kurai in distress and pain from Blane's attack. I was high enough to see a clear view of the whole island when Blane appeared above and brought his foot down, kicking my stomach.

Hitting the ground hard enough to make a small crater, I felt Kurai's presence slowly diminish until I could barely sense it. The dark energy around me disappeared. I could control my body again.

Amazed at the fact that I could still move at all, I stood up, leaning on my right leg and placing my right hand on my left shoulder. Coughing up blood, I looked at Blane as he stood a few feet away.

"This—" he said as he began walking towards me, step by step, "—is it, Leon. Now, your power is mine."

But as he took his next step, he yelled in pain and brought his energy-covered hands up towards his mouth. Evaporating as it touched the energy, Blane coughed up blood as his body visibly shook and the yellow-and-black flames began to lose energy they had been putting out previously.

Stepping backward, I almost tripped over something, and I looked down to see what it was. Lying a few inches from me were my swords. Picking up my black sword first, then my yellow one, I ran across the few feet between Blane and myself and jumped into the air, slashing downward at him as he stood, coughing.

I was expecting to land a hit, but the energy around Blane instantly rose again, and my swords flew in two different directions. Launched a few feet across the ground, I backed up into a boulder as my brother began making his way towards me again, this time outstretching his hand in the direction of my crystal.

As he reached his hand towards my chest, my legs shaking in fear, all I wanted to do was scream. But seconds before his hand would have reached my crystal, the color of the energy surrounding him changed from a mixture of yellow and black to yellow alone. Putting his arm around me, he pulled me into a hug. He brought his face in front of mine.

"I'm sorry," he whispered as he placed his hand onto my head, as if petting an animal, "little brother."

Dropping his hand, he smiled and placed something in my own hand. All of the yellow energy surrounding him disappeared, and Blane slowly fell to the ground, landing face up.

Breathing heavily, I looked down in fear and shock at my brother's body. With his eyes still open, covered in wounds, blood dripping down his mouth, he had died.

Too tired to even stand, I couldn't support myself, and I began falling face-first towards the ground, until something interrupted my fall. Landing on what seemed to be someone's shoulder, I looked up with the last of my will to try to catch a glimpse. Only being able to see long blond hair, I heard a voice before my eyes closed and the world around me disappeared.

"Reon, right?"

Chapter 36: The Day That Came Too Slow

Most people would hesitate before launching themselves through the air towards a fireball the size of a house. I mean, it's a fireball. But as I rolled my hand into a fist, directing my punch towards the mass of flames, I felt nothing. Instead of my white gloves burning or pain from the oncoming attack, the fireball combusted in front of me.

"What?!" yelled Luis in shock, a few feet away.

Eager to test out my new power, I jumped off the ground without releasing aura underneath my feet. Like when I had fought the Barghest so many months ago, I was floating in midair, but this time it was all according to my will. Although trained people could move through the air with aura sky steps, no one could float in one place.

Laughing out loud at the fact that I could now fly, I looked up at the sky above Luis as I landed softly on the ground. Surprised and a little worried that the sky had turned almost completely black, I wouldn't be able to do anything about it until I had defeated Luis.

"So, the little boy was hiding something, eh?" he said with a smile. "You surprised me for a second there. But that doesn't mean you have time to daydream just because the color of the sky has changed. I'll make sure to leave your lifeless body face up so you can stare at the sky as much as you want after I have killed you."

"You are an empty person," I stated as I glared at him. "You don't deserve to be king, and you know it."

"Really?" he asked in response. "Why not? I am the strongest. I have been the strongest. No one can stand against me and live. The kingship is a symbol of power, and I am the embodiment of power. A foolish child like you could not understand."

I knew he was a lost cause, but I also knew I had to try.

"This is the last time," I said with confidence. "Stop your attack. Go back to your people and help them. Be a better person, be a better leader. A king isn't what you say it is. Yeah, they are powerful, but they also care about the wellbeing of their citizens. Our chief was that. You're lucky our chief was old and the village is filled with cowards. But that doesn't matter. Please, stop your attack."

"You are a fool, Zephyr," he said as the air around him changed. "I won't stop till these villagers are my slaves."

"Fine," I said as brought my hands upwards into a boxing position. "Then I won't hold back."

Almost effortlessly, I pushed myself off the ground and

into the air as Luis directed a barrage of fireballs at me. Easily dodging the gigantic masses of fire by moving through the air, I backflipped as Luis's fist flew by me, barely missing.

Everything felt easy, as if I were dancing, and each movement through the air came naturally. Appearing in front of me, his body covered in raging red flames, Luis continuously punched at me as I quickly dodged each jab. Ducking, stepping backwards and sideways, making sure not to let his flames touch me for good measure, I decided that I had been on defense for too long.

Catching his left fist with my right hand and his right fist in my left hand, making him stop his assault in surprise, I brought my right knee upward, colliding with his stomach. Feeling my knee connect, I dropped it and brought my left knee flying towards his stomach.

Repeating the process, I launched my first real attack on Luis since the start of our fight. After bringing my right knee down for the tenth time, I let go of his fists and flipped forwards, kicking the top of his head with my heel.

Landing on all fours, Luis looked upwards from the ground as a stream of blood ran down from the corner of his forehead. Without smiling anymore, Luis directed another assault of fireballs towards where I had been floating in the sky.

Predicting his movements, I continued to dodge his attacks as I slowly made my way down towards him. When I was only a few feet away, I launched my own assault of Sky Pushuu, the size of a fist. Rapidly propelling it from my hands, I moved my hands towards Luis as he aura stepped in an effort to dodge.

Instead of continuing my Sky Pushuu attack, I pushed and willed myself through the air towards Luis as he moved to dodge my last Sky Pushuu. Appearing inches from his face, I swung my right fist, feeling his muscles tighten as my hand collided with his face. Propelled through the air, Luis landed a few hundred feet away on the ground and rolled until he came to a stop, coughing up blood.

"How did you suddenly become so strong?" he asked in a whisper.

"I won't let you destroy this village," I stated.

He forced himself up, and the flames around him increased until they were as strong as they had been before I launched my attack. His stamina and strength were ridiculous.

Deciding that staying on the attack would be better, I punched the air with my right fist. As my arm extended, a silver-colored blast of compressed air, the size of my fist, launched straight for Luis. Although surprised at my new technique, Luis aura stepped a few feet away, and the blast of air whizzed by him.

Appearing in front of me as I retracted my arm, Luis brought his flame-covered right foot up towards my head. Ducking to dodge his kick, I pushed off the ground and flew backwards, away from the Cheshrian king. Still in midair, I extended my right arm, then my left arm, and repeated the process as I created a barrage of small compressed-air blasts strong enough to destroy a village home easily.

As Luis aura stepped, dodging my barrage of compressed-air punches, I launched myself through the air as fast as I could toward the place I had predicted Luis would appear next. Just as I thought, Luis aura stepped to a few feet in front of a green sky tree, allowing me to catch him off guard.

Grabbing his left wrist with my left hand, I pulled him forward and into my elbow. Retracting my elbow from his stomach as he lurched forward in pain, I brought my right fist up in an uppercut, connecting with his jaw, allowing me to feel his teeth grinding against each other. Realizing that with his amount of stamina he would still get back up, I released his wrist from my grip and brought both of my hands to my sides.

Focusing my wind energy on my palms, I began to form a Sky Pushuu in each of my hands. As I looked at Luis in anger, the king still incapacitated from my earlier assault, I changed the shape of my Sky Pushuu and focused even more energy than I had originally intended. Although I saw him blast flames towards the ground, I ignored him and continued bringing both of my attacks up towards Luis's chest. Both Sky Pushuus, in the shape of stars the size of two children, collided against him.

Rotating, the Sky Pushuus completely erased any trace of flames covering Luis's chest, ending with a large explosion as my attack passed through Luis's fire coating.

The dust around him dissipated, and I looked in surprise as he was nowhere to be seen.

"Over—" coughed Luis from a few hundred feet behind me, "—here, kid."

Turning around, I looked up to find a huge wave of flames the size of half the island heading straight for the center of Dentro Village through the sky and across the land. But as I tried to move my legs, it felt as if I were stuck to the ground. Looking down at my feet, I realized Luis's plan.

Since he could no longer beat me, he had decided to put all of his energy into destroying the thing I was fighting for. Underneath the layer of rock Luis had melted right before I had blasted him with my attack, my feet were stuck and wouldn't budge. There was no way I would make it in time to stop the village from being destroyed.

"No!" I screamed as I blasted the rock apart with a Sky Pushuu.

Dropping to my knees as the flames reached their destination, I screamed in agony at the thought of all the innocent villagers whose lives were about to be ripped from them. But as I looked up one last time towards the village in the distance, I caught a glimpse of three distant figures standing before the flames as they collided with the village land. Instantly, a huge explosion appeared, followed by an enveloping, thick black fog.

Behind me, I heard hysterical laughter. I turned towards Luis to find him lying on his back, coughing up blood.

"This is what you all deserve," he said as he laughed. "Weak, pitiful creatures who cannot defend themselves should be eradicated from this world. It is for the better!"

Having been focused on the fact the village was going to be destroyed, I hadn't bothered to sense the auras of the three figures. As I recognized who had stood in the way of the flames, I calmed down and realized that I had nothing to worry about. I chuckled at how long it had taken them to come back, and I thought of how indebted I was to Karlir, Kuchi, and Jordan for how much they had helped me.

Walking over to Luis and looking down at his blood-soaked body, I smiled as he looked up at me.

"What are you smiling at?!" he screamed in a scratchy version of his original sinister voice.

"Our village has its problems, just like every other. But we are strong, not because of our hate, or the number of individual warriors we have, but because we stand together to protect the place we call home. You have failed," I stated as I looked at him.

"That was everything I had, and you defeated it. I was once like you, kid," he admitted as I felt his life force begin to dissipate completely.

"What happened, then?" I asked, no longer caring that he was our enemy. He wasn't a threat anymore.

"I tasted power," he whispered, no longer sounding like the cruel man from before. "I grew tired of being among the weak, and so I drowned myself with power, sacrificing the love of my life, my friends, and even my son."

"Why would you do that to yourself and your family?"

"You do not understand the effect power has on people. Those who have it either control it or are controlled by it. Those who don't, fear it and wish to seek it for themselves."

"I do understand," I said truthfully. "My village has feared and detested me my whole life, forgetting the fact that the power

I was born from saved them. They are selfish fools, and some may say they don't deserve my protection. But if I let them die when I could save them, just because they are ignorant, then that would make me no better."

Luis chuckled. "You are a weird boy," he said, coughing up blood. "It is too late for me to change back, nor do I want to. But I admire your determination as one who holds power beyond many others. You have done what I could not—you control it instead of letting it control you. I am dying, but I should at least die with honor and give you a reward for beating me. Kneel down."

I knew I couldn't and would never forgive Luis. He was a cruel man who had killed the Chief and many innocent people, abandoned his family, and tried to enslave and destroy my village. But as I looked down at him, coughing up blood and barely holding onto life, I kneeled down. His body slowly began to turn to flames.

"It's okay," he said as I began to move away. "I am converting my life force into energy so that I can deliver your reward personally, kid."

Slowly turning into fire, his body began to emit heat. Surprised that I could feel the intensity of the heat but it no longer hurt like during our fight, Luis spoke one last time as he looked me in the eyes.

"Don't lose to it," he whispered.

"I won't," I promised as he completely erupted in flames, his body no longer visible.

I jumped back as the flames began to make an empty circle, floating in the air. A yellow light erupted from the center of the flame circle, and it died down after a few minutes. I picked up a long white spear, barely taller than me but covered in a blue glow, the tip a clear crystal.

"Zephyr," said a familiar voice. "You did it."

Turning around, barely holding myself up, I dropped to my knees in exhaustion as Karlir aura stepped beside me, holding me steady.

"Just lean on me," he said with a smile as I lay my chin on his shoulder. He lifted me on his back.

"Thanks, old man," I said, smiling. "Looks like I'm out of energy."

"Seems so," agreed Karlir with a chuckle. "I am proud of you, Zephyr. Not only did you defeat the king of Cheshria, you found one of the three Unmei artifacts, the Spear of Destiny. You have grown and made me proud to be your master."

"No way..." I said in awe.

"I saw from afar what happened as the Cheshrian king

used the remainder of his energy to open a portal to another land," said Karlir as we began making our way back to the village.

"A portal to another land?"

"Zephyr, there are many places that you have not been to, and not just on our own world. And I fear your destiny lies beyond this world. At some point, the Cheshrian king had travelled to a far land within this world, beyond Tyring. Having found the Spear of Destiny there, he covered it with his most powerful flames, an ancient and uncommon technique. Using some of his life force to boost his own power, the technique granted him the ability to create portals. As he died, he created a portal and brought the spear here, for you," explained Karlir. "But enough for now. I know you are exhausted."

"Wait," I said as I remembered that the whole village had been at war. "What about the others? And the Council members?"

"We arrived shortly after Autumn defeated the Council member Katjul. Along with a boy named Nicholas, we took on and defeated the small invasion force that had arrived with Luis. The village is safe," answered Karlir.

"I didn't have time to think about it before, but earlier, the sky covering the island turned black. What happened?" I asked.

"It was Leon," stated Karlir.

"Leon?" I asked. "What happened to him?"

"All we know is that he killed his brother, Blane. We found Blane's body, but we could not locate Leon," replied Karlir as we reached the end of the forest that stood before the village outskirts. "Don't worry, Zephyr. We will find him," Karlir assured me as we reached the village outskirts.

But as we walked closer and closer, our voices were drowned out by what sounded like cheers.

"What…" I asked in awe. It looked like the whole village was standing in front of us.

"ZEPHYR! ZEPHYR! ZEPHYR! ZEPHYR!" yelled the villagers as we stopped a few feet away.

"They have all been waiting for you to return," said Karlir. "I think they all have something to say to you."

As I slowly stepping slipped off Karlir's back and onto the ground, kids from all over the village ran up to me, smiling, pulling on my shirt, and even calling my name. "Zephyr! Welcome home! Zephyr!"

"Nicholas and I let the villagers know what occurred while you were fighting," said Kuchi as I felt his presence appear next to Karlir.

As I looked up from the kids, I found that all of the

villagers were bowing towards me.

"Zephyr!" they all yelled in unison. "We are sorry! We are sorry! We are sorry!"

Walking forward towards the villagers, I smiled, wiping a tear from my cheek as it rolled down my face. I couldn't believe what was happening.

"Everyone!" I yelled as loud as I could, causing them all to stand straight. "Thank you."

"ZEPHYR! ZEPHYR! ZEPHYR! ZEPHYR!" cheered the audience over and over again.

My energy still low, I tripped over my own feet, unable to stop my body from falling forward.

"Clumsy as ever," joked Autumn as she held me up by the shoulders and kissed me.

Our lips parted, and I couldn't help smiling as tears rolled down my face. I embraced Autumn as the villagers continued to cheer my name.

"Good job, Zephyr," said Nicholas as he walked by, patting me on the back. "You really outclassed us all. I was wrong about you. Thank you."

One by one, the front row of villagers made their way towards me as the cheering died down.

"Zephyr," said a middle-aged woman with tan skin and

dark hair, "We were all scared of you and your power, and so we detested you and shunned you. We had no idea what you would choose to do in the future."

"But," said a man a few rows back, "you sure are amazing. Thank you not only for saving us, but for never giving up on us."

"You never gave up on us," said another villager with a smile. "So let us return the worry, hope, and sacrifice you have given for us! We will work hard so that we can help protect you next time!"

I had always heard that being able to understand other people's emotions was a gift beyond comprehension, even though I had never understood how that could be. But now, I realized that I had only made it this far because of that same gift. As Autumn and I found ourselves surrounded by the cheers of the whole village, I looked up and smiled. I had never thought this day would come.

Chapter 37:
Over and Out

It had been a week since we had saved the village. I sat on the steps of the late chief's house, looking out at the busy village center filled with hundreds of people shopping, and I thought back to how, not so long ago, my only wish had been to be accepted by the villagers. They had hated and ignored me, and so whenever I got the chance, I would always act pleasantly towards them, purposefully making it awkward when they were forced to interact with me in some way.

I had trained beyond what any kid should, and I had kept my determination by holding my memories of my mother close. Although she had been physically weak after bearing me until she passed away, she had always encouraged me to pursue my goals. My mother once said to me, during her last days, "Become a hero like your father. Be true to who you are, and never lose sight of that. Never give up, and remember, I will always watch over you."

"Hey, Mister Hero!" yelled Autumn as she jumped from the sand and onto me, hugging me tightly. "The new Council was looking for you earlier. You missed the meeting!"

"I know," I said, smiling as I held her in my arms, bringing her closer toward me as our lips touched, slowly releasing her after a few seconds. “I'm not really good with meetings. It's better if I trust them with the politics.”

“Zephyr…” she said playfully as we sat on the steps together, Autumn's head resting on my chest, both of us looking toward the village center.

“It's okay,” I said, trying to ease her mind. “I’m trusting Nicholas to lead the Council well, unlike Hovan. I am glad he’s in jail.”

“Something else is bothering you, isn't it?” asked Autumn as she looked up at me with her beautiful, bright brown, starry eyes.

“Yeah,” I answered. “Any word on Leon?”

“I'm sorry,” she said as she brought her head down, resting on my chest once again. “We’ve searched everywhere. And as you know, neither Karlir or Kuchi nor myself could sense his aura, just like you.”

“I guessed not.”

“What do you mean?”

“After I fully recovered, three days after I defeated Luis, I sensed a slight presence on a small island not far from here. It’s not Leon's, but the son of the Cheshrian king, Kolt’s,” I replied. “He was originally after his mother. When I interrogated Hovan, I found out she had unexpectedly died a few years ago.

Somehow she got caught in the crossfire during the execution of Leon's family, which Luis helped Blane complete."

"I'm sorry to hear that," said Autumn as she squeezed my hand.

"Death is always sad. But I fear he has another plan in motion." I softly rested my chin atop her head.

"Another plan? Should we call for Karlir and Kuchi to return from their trip across the land?"

"No," I said quickly. "I'll handle this alone. They've done more than enough for me and this village."

"What's the plan, then?"

"I am sure Leon is with Kolt," I stated. "Kolt has the Tyring Sword, and I'm sure he's using his new powers to hide their presences."

"That's possible?" asked Autumn in awe.

"With the sword in his possession, it seems so. But it also seems that the sword can't mask its own presence completely," I replied. "That must be what I can sense, as my powers have been enhanced since my fight with Luis."

"Why would he be hiding Leon?" Autumn asked as we got up from the stairs, holding hands and walking through the village center.

It was too busy and loud for me to converse with Autumn,

so we walked through the village center without speaking, waving back at everyone that smiled and waved at us.

"Zephyr! Good to see you!" said one elderly villager as we walked by.

"Hero! Hero!" said a person behind a food stand. "Discounted food for our hero!"

"They love you now," said Autumn as we left the village, making our way towards the beach.

"I'm sure he plans on using Leon," I said, picking up where we had left off. "Leon is clever and a very powerful asset. But his past has left a hole in his heart, so he has been corrupted and seeks more power, just like the king of Cheshria did once. I'm not sure what's going to happen, but I have a feeling it's going to happen today. That's why I asked you to meet me at the Chief's stairs."

"We can always defeat them if they attack the village, right?" asked Autumn with a smile.

"I don't wanna make your beautiful smile disappear, but I'm not so sure that we could," I admitted.

"But you may be even stronger than Karlir and Kuchi now!" expressed Autumn as we sat down on the wet sand, the waves washing against our feet and the sun shining down on us.

"Stronger? Maybe with my inherited powers. But Karlir

and Kuchi possess skills far beyond my level, even now. But with the Tyring Sword, Kolt may be even stronger than Karlir. With Leon backing him up, I'm not sure if we could win alone," I indicated with a frown.

"So what can we do?" asked Autumn in dismay.

"I don't think Kolt is going to attack the village, at least not directly," I said. "But if he does, I will protect you and the village with everything I have."

"It's because of this that the villagers wanted to elect you chief," whispered Autumn as she hugged me again, holding tightly.

I laughed. "Me? Chief?" I said. "Never thought I would hear that. Following in the Chief's footsteps doesn't sound too bad—he was my hero—but I don't really know if I'm truly ready for that."

"Zephyr, you can do anything," she assured as she kissed me. "Do what you feel is right. I will always support you. Now we should head back to the village so we can discuss the next chief with the new Council—" But before Autumn could finish her speech, a loud sound erupted around us. **BOOM!**

"What's that?" asked Autumn as we turned toward the village center, where the explosion seemed to have come from.

"I have no idea," I said quickly as I grabbed her hand.

"Let's go."

Aura stepping until we landed a few feet from where the explosion had occurred, we walked out of the crowd of people that surrounded the site.

"What?!" murmured Autumn as we walked up towards the explosion site.

In the dead center of the village stood a large, black orb the size of a village hut. Next to it stood two familiar figures.

"Zephyr," called Leon as he stood between us and the orb. Kolt walked up next to him.

Leon had changed. Although his long, black hair still covered his forehead, his eyes reflected only darkness, and his aura seemed even more intense and dark than before.

Next to him, smiling, stood the blond-haired, blue-eyed Kolt. Taller than Leon and around my height, Kolt looked even more muscular than Leon and me combined. The sword's effects were truly frightening.

"Ah yes," said Kolt in a different tone than I had last heard him use in Cheshria, when he stole the sword. "Zephyr, one of the light's chosen four."

"What?" I asked. "What are you doing here? What is that black orb?"

"So many questions, Zephyr," commented Leon with a

sinister smile. "I thought you knew everything after your training."

"Leon," I said. "What happened? You just disappeared."

He looked towards Kolt, as if for the okay to answer my question. Kolt nodded.

"Be swift, Leon," said Kolt as he made his way towards the black orb, stopping in front of it. "It will be ready soon."

"What will be ready?" I asked in frustration as Autumn moved closer to me.

"The portal," answered Leon, to my surprise.

"Portal?"

"We have always been enemies, Zephyr—not only us, but our families, too," Leon said.

"What do you mean?" I asked.

"You truly know nothing," mocked Leon with a smile. "There's a war going on involving much more than just our little world. Our world, Tye, is nothing compared to all the others in the universe."

"Tye is a beautiful planet, and it's our home. You plan on abandoning it?" I asked.

"Oh no, Zephyr," said Leon, looking upwards before returning his gaze to me. "I will be back. And when I do come back, I will be strong enough to completely annihilate this world and you."

"Nooo…" murmured Autumn. "Why would you do that?"

"Zephyr is not the only one descended from the gods. You just happen to be from the light side instead of the dark, like me. Originally, I was supposed to destroy just Dentro Village. But I plan on doing so much more than that," stated Leon.

"Leon!" called Kolt as he took one step into the orb, his right leg disappearing. "I'm going on ahead."

"You must have realized it by now," said Leon as Kolt completely disappeared from behind him and into the portal. "Our destiny, I mean."

"Our destiny?" I repeated as Leon began stepping into the portal. "Wait, Leon!"

"Our destiny has always been to fight each other," declared Leon, turning his head and glancing at us as his body began to disappear. "One of us will die. But I am sure you don't have the guts to face death. Stay here. I'll destroy as many villages, people, and worlds as I need to until I gain the power to kill you and destroy Tye. Goodbye, Zephyr."

I jumped to grab Leon's hand before it disappeared, but I just grazed it, as he was no longer on our planet.

The crowd, silent before, now began to erupt in murmurs as I looked at the black orb.

"Zephyr," said Nicholas as he walked through the crowd,

standing next to me. "You know what you should do."

"Do what you must," insisted Autumn.

"Are you sure?" I asked, looking down at her.

"I said I would support you with whatever you chose to do," she answered with a reassuring smile.

Turning around to face the larger portion of the crowd, I breathed in as much air as I could before opening my mouth.

"Villagers!" I yelled, surprisingly creating a silence throughout the crowd. "I want to thank you all for accepting me. It has meant a lot, and I hope I have helped changed the village for the better. I was honored to have been offered the position of village chief, but I'm sorry to say I won't be able to fulfill it."

"What?!" murmured the crowd in response.

"I don't know for how long, but I am leaving the village. I can't sit by and willingly let someone hurt innocent people," I stated. "And I can't give up on a friend."

"What people?!" asked voices from the crowd.

"The portal seems to be shrinking," whispered Autumn from behind me.

Turning back toward the portal, I saw that it had already shrunk to half its original size.

"Villagers!" I yelled again. "I ask you to trust me, and know that I will be back, however long it takes. Dentro is my home, and it will always mean a lot to me. But while I am gone, I ask you to entrust yourselves to someone I trust absolutely."

"Who?" asked the villagers in surprise.

Stepping directly in front of the portal and placing my right hand in the air, the Spear of Destiny materialized in my palm. Even if I could create my own portal with the spear, I had no idea how to do so or where Leon and Kolt had travelled to. So instead, I decided that my best course of action was to take the portal before it disappeared.

"As you all know, this is the Spear of Destiny," I said to the villagers. "It has great power, and so I am entrusting it to the person I think should be the chief in my absence, until I return, if your offer still stands."

Turning towards Nicholas, I whispered into his ear.

"Thank you for everything you have done," I said. "I ask only one more thing of you; please counsel your new chief and make sure she stays safe."

"I will," Nicholas whispered back, "hero."

The portal had shrunk to around my height now. I rushed over to Autumn, embracing her with as much of my strength as I could without hurting her.

"I love you," I whispered into her ear, breaking our embrace to kiss her soft lips. After a few brief seconds, I pulled away, aura stepping back to the portal and placing my right foot inside it as it shrank below my head.

"Cheers to the new chief!" I yelled. I gently threw the spear into the air as the crowd "ahhed" in unison at the recipient.

Looking back one last time, I glanced up at the beautiful sky before dropping my head and gazing at all of the people around me. Nicholas, the villagers, and the new chief, Autumn, were not only the people I cared about, but the people who actually treasured the precious bonds we had developed over time.

Satisfied, I ducked, as the portal had shrunk below my neck, and placed my other foot into the orb. With my friends in my heart, I stepped into the darkness, with the hope that one day I would be able to return.

ABOUT THE AUTHOR

Eighteen year old R.J. Tolson lives in Arlington, VA (United States) a metropolitan area of Washington, D.C. He was born to a dentist father and a lawyer/professional tennis player mother, who instilled in him the importance of passion in one's life. Throughout his childhood, R.J. wrote endlessly, often into the late hours of the night.

Fantasy and fiction novels have always been R.J.'s biggest loves. Some of R.J.'s biggest influences have been the works of D. J. MacHale, Jonathan Stroud, J. R. R. Tolkien, Jenny Nimmo, Christopher Paolini, C. S. Lewis, Eoin Colfer, Stephen King, Cinda Williams, and J. K. Rowling.

R.J. attended and graduated from a private boarding high school, Cheshire Academy, and studies at Whittier College in California. Along with his writing skills, R.J. speaks Spanish, Chinese, Korean, Japanese, and Greek. He also works on composing classical and jazz music from time to time, as well as the production of pop and hip-hop music.

Although fairly young, he prides himself on how he tries to take every day as a learning experience and to grow from each and every aspect of his life and the events that occur around him.

Sports have always been a big part of R.J.'s life. He played soccer in high school and on multiple club teams, along with tennis, swimming and more. He also trained in karate for seven years, nin-jit-su for six, and the art of senjutsu (sage in comparison to a monk) for four. He has a black belt in each.

He is the CEO of multidivisional international company RJTIO LLC and it's divisions, including but not limited to Forever Trust Charity, RJTINC, RL Infinity International, and BurstOut. He is also a President of Sages of Essence. He studies and teaches metaphysics and is involved in economics and the stock exchange.

When R.J. isn't writing, he enjoys hanging out with his friends, playing soccer and tennis, going to soccer games, listening to and composing music, and reading. R.J. loves to work out, eat delicious food, and broaden his horizons.

Visit

www.rjtolson.com

Follow on:

Twitter, Facebook, Youtube, Goodreads & More

#RJTolson #BeLimitless #ChaosChronicles

Made in the USA
Middletown, DE
05 March 2015